MW01503705

THE SECRETS OF HAVENWOOD

AN INEVITABLE
MAGICK

LEX KELLY

To the young girl I once was, the one who dreamed of being a published author, I'm sorry I let self-doubt get in our way for so long. But thank you for holding onto that dream. After all these years, we're finally making it come true—together.

CONTENT WARNING

An Inevitable Magick is an Adult contemporary fantasy romance. This book contains mature themes, including:

- Profanity
- Explicit sexual content
- Brief references to substance abuse. (remembered)
- References to blood and fatal wounds in the context of a crime scene. (discussed after the fact)

From Earth we're born,
To Earth we're bound.
In her depths our power found.
When at last to ash, we burn,
To Earth our ashes, we return.
In cycles of life our power refined,
And thus our endless journeys entwined.

CHAPTER ONE

$\mathcal{T}$he effervescent tingle of magick coursed through Liv Terrabella as she padded across the damp earth on bare feet.

With each footfall into the loose soil, she grounded herself in the small wonder that connected her to the source of her magick. Welcoming it as it flowed through her and back into the earth, feeding and withdrawing from her in the same cyclical rhythm all flora and fauna had with nature—taking in life and giving back in death.

A heavy early morning fog blanketed the woods surrounding her, cocooning Liv in the perception of total privacy as she wandered through the small garden behind the secluded cabin she shared with her sister. The cabin itself wasn't much to take comfort in, but the woods...they were the closest to home she'd found in years.

Surveying her earthen sanctuary, her eyes caught on something white protruding from the top of a rosebud. Her breath caught on an expectant inhale; a slight smile lifted her lips.

"It's back," she breathed, dashing to the rose.

The piece of parchment was twisted into the center of a deep red flower in the early stages of blooming as if it were being pushed out of the bud as it opened.

The flower unfurled into its full bloom under her gentle touch, allowing Liv to withdraw the small scroll of parchment.

It took only a moment for the light sensation of hope floating through her body to evaporate into something heavier. The magick wasn't right.

She unrolled the parchment to find one word scrawled across it in deeply saturated black ink.

Condolences,

Her breath caught in her throat, her chest tight and rigid as she read the word. Like black smoke on the wind, the note suddenly wisped into nothing, disappearing from within her grasp, leaving her with only a remnant of the magick the note had carried warm on her fingertips.

Liv took a quick step back, her mouth falling open in surprise as her mind raced through rationalizations too quickly for her to grasp onto one.

What the hell just happened?

She wracked her brain…who could have sent it? She stilled then, at an even more alarming thought—what if the sender was somewhere nearby, watching her right now?

No! She forced her thoughts into submission. This was just her overthinking again.

Liv backpedaled from her momentary dissension into paranoia, reminding herself that it may have taken a while, but news of her mother's passing would have found its way back to their hometown by now. Someone there must have felt obliged and would no doubt have the ability to find a way to send her the simple note. That was all. It was thoughtful, she supposed, though she did wish they'd have done so in a slightly less unsettling way.

No one was after them. That had been her mother's paranoia, and she wouldn't adopt it like she had her nightmares.

The rationalization assuaged her fear, allowing her breathing to ease back into a natural rhythm, but the disappointment lingered.

Her eyes drifted over to a patch of Calendula where she'd once unearthed a very different parchment in a very similar way, and she couldn't help but wonder where the relic from her past was now.

Frustration wove through her tensing muscles, at that damned bit of magick-infused parchment for planting that toxic seed of hope in her in the first place, but more so with herself for being so quick to dismiss it. Even now, months later, her body still reacted viscerally to the idea that it had finally come back to her again.

And that was exactly why hope was such a dangerous little seedling to allow to take root.

Despite her frustration, her mind couldn't help but follow that tiny bit of hope back to the wonder of six months before—of finding the deed for the first time.

She'd walked through the front door of their cabin, instinctually feeling for her sister's presence, the same way she did every night. But the responding energy she'd found hadn't belonged to Ivy.

Wary but unable to resist the call of magick she'd never felt outside of her hometown, she'd followed the essence from the dim entryway, through the outdated kitchen, and over to the small table wedged in the corner.

There, in the center of the wooden surface, she'd found a single piece of parchment—no envelope, postage, or explanation for how it had gotten there. And even though she knew magick and logic rarely intersected, it was still a shock to find the sudden connection to her past just…sitting there.

She'd tentatively taken the old document into her hands. Though discolored from age and—judging by the single jagged edge—having been torn from a book, it was otherwise perfectly preserved.

Three words penned in looping script across the top of the page had given her all the information she needed about what it was and where it had come from.

Deed of Land

She still wasn't sure if it had been an invitation or a demand, but either way, the essence of magick emanating from the page had felt comforting and familiar in a distant way, like a half-remembered dream. It had guided her into long-buried memories…memories that always seemed to lead back to *him*. To bright blue eyes that glittered with flecks of gold in the warm Southern California sunshine.

To going home.

Liv had indulged the memory for a few moments, allowing it to cast its warmth and light over the shadowy places within her.

It wasn't like she hadn't thought about going back before that moment —for the first several years after they'd left it had been all she could think about. The people she'd left behind, the home, the land, and the source of her magick.

Knowing the magick that flowed through the deed as she did now, she couldn't help but suspect that the timing of its appearance, less than a month after her mother's death, had been a calculated move. As if the magick within knew who'd been the driving force behind them leaving.

But as easily as the fond memories had come on, reality had followed, crashing over her like an icy wave, washing away any warmth she'd gained.

She'd winced, remembering the *way* they'd left so quickly—cloaked in the darkness of night, without a word as to where they were headed, without explanation, without a single goodbye to the people who'd meant so much to her. So much less than they'd deserved, than *he'd* deserved. Less than the home they'd left behind deserved.

And at the end of the day, it had been her choice. One she knew those she'd left behind couldn't understand.

So, rather than being taunted by what she couldn't have, she'd pushed the memories aside and taken the old deed to her room, buried it beneath some books in her bedside table, and naively believed that would be the end of it.

Three days later she'd been abruptly pulled from sleep by a sudden shift in the air around her. Instinctually, she'd reached over and switched her bedside lamp on.

Through the haze of sleep and the sudden onslaught of light, it had taken her a moment to process what she was looking at. The deed that should have been deep in a drawer was resting instead on the edge of her nightstand, offering her a chance to reconsider.

Butterflies flitted inside her at the sight, before she remembered to counter that all too dangerous hope by reminding herself that she didn't have a home to go back to...just a house. There was no one waiting for her there. Not with how she'd left them all high and dry. Not with how she'd abandoned him and all their plans.

And then she'd added on what a pure delight the tantrum her sister would no doubt throw if she suggested moving. Again.

"Find someone else," she'd whispered to the deed before she let it fall from her hand into their compost bin.

A week later it had been waiting for her on the seat of her car when she'd left for work. There'd been no sign of the coffee grounds she'd known Ivy had dumped on top of it.

A mile down the road she'd rolled her window down and freed the deed to the wind, refusing to check the rearview to watch it drift away on the breeze.

The next day it appeared in the shower.

She'd stuffed it down the drain.

About a week after the shower incident, she'd found it dangling from the roots of that Calendula when she'd harvested it.

That time she'd simply left it there in the mud.

Over and over, week after week she'd remained locked in a battle against a piece of parchment as it found increasingly creative ways to sneak up on her, something she suspected the magick fueling it got great enjoyment from.

It never came in predictable intervals, and even though she'd wielded her stubbornness like a sword against it, that pesky seed of hope it had deposited in her had refused to be ignored. From the seed of hope, a bone-deep *want* had grown, to return home. To be wrong. A list of reasons it would be worth it to try—one she'd mentally dubbed her "What if?" list.

Most of the items on that list revolved around the practical: she'd made a promise to her mother to keep Ivy safe, and though she knew it wasn't what her mom had meant, wouldn't Ivy be safer in a town where she wouldn't have to explain away her magick? Where she would have the space to harness it? Plus, there were the wards on the town that acted as a magickal security system—was there a better way to uphold her promise than that?

And then there were the reasons that were just for her, things she kept hidden in her heart so she wouldn't have to endure the longing. Her home, her friends, and always *him*. The idea that she was wrong, and those same reasons to stay away were suddenly reasons to go back.

Yeah, hope had done a good enough job at coming up with arguments in favor of returning home that slowly what had felt impossible almost began to feel obtainable.

But even six months after the deed had first shown up, even with that hope threading through her like a vine, it was hard to imagine a world in which the warm welcome she craved would be waiting for her back home.

For Liv, wishful thinking and reality intersected about as often as logic and magick. So, she needed to stop.

The mud that stuck to her knees and shins as she knelt in the dirt was a welcoming balm. Sometimes she felt so disconnected from her roots that she considered burying herself naked in it.

That separation too, was keeping the temptation to return, and her "What if?" list alive.

As she reached into the patch of *Aconitum napellus*, known to most as Aconite or Wolfsbane, a little grin lifted one side of her mouth.

She had little doubt what the people in her hometown would think of her growing such a plant. She could all but hear the whispers, wondering what the Terrabella women "really" used their plant magic for. All the while admiring the Azaleas she always grew alongside the Wolfsbane, and all the while oblivious to the true nature of the nectar that dwelled within the Azaleas themselves. Too quick to judge what they didn't understand.

But really, she thought, the point was moot.

For over three months, the longest the deed had ever stayed away before reappearing had been ten days.

But nearly three months had passed since the last time it had gotten the jump on her, appearing in the leftovers she'd brought to work for lunch. Somehow the damn thing had been completely unmarred by food or the bite she'd taken out of it.

She couldn't really say which of the many emotions the deed brought with it had driven her to do what she'd done next, but whatever it was propelled her to take the most extreme action against it yet. She'd made a beeline from the break room to her desk and, without pausing to consider, fed the deed through a shredder, then simply returned to her lunch.

She'd grown so accustomed to the deed reappearing no matter how she'd disposed of it that it had taken her nearly a month to accept that she'd gone too far.

Her pro-con lists were irrelevant—her invitation was rescinded.

Liv dismissed the pang of regret as simply missing the small connection to her roots and returned to the task at hand, creating a stronger sleep tincture.

Her sister had come outside, and now she could feel Ivy's eyes following her around the garden from the back porch a few feet away. It was generally the closest she got to the garden.

"Did you have another nightmare last night?" Ivy asked after a few moments.

"No, I think it was just a one-time thing," Liv lied. The truth was she'd been having them most nights since their mom's death. But it wasn't something she wanted her sister worrying about. She wouldn't have even told her about the nightmares, but Ivy had heard her that first night, and there hadn't been a point denying it then. A single nightmare was easier to dismiss than the alternative.

"Oh, good. I was starting to worry." Liv looked up at her sister, a little surprised by the relief in her voice. She hadn't realized Ivy had been that concerned for her.

Her sister sipped her coffee before continuing, "I was starting to worry that shit was hereditary. The last thing I need is for my only inheritance to be chronic nightmares and paranoia."

Liv swallowed the scoff that nearly broke free. "Rest assured, your beauty sleep is safe."

A sudden pinprick of awareness drew Liv's eyes toward the distant tree line. Through the low fog, Liv wasn't sure if the dark figure she saw was real or the product of a lack of sleep. But she was spared considering her sister's words about hereditary paranoia when Ivy hopped off the edge of the porch and came to stand next to her.

"What is that?" Ivy asked, taking a typical step toward the danger rather than away.

When the feel of strange magick drifted to her through the earth, Liv decided to take the risk and released the smallest tendrils of her own magick into the ground beneath her, willing the earth to warm and thus the fog to thin.

The magick began to work immediately, slowly revealing a dark form amongst the Maple and Birch trees.

Even as the last tendrils of fog disappeared, the figure never became anything clearer than the shadowy shape of a motionless man.

"Ivy, no!" Liv felt the raw edge of Ivy's magick too late to stop her. A sparking shot of power propelled haphazardly in the general direction of the stranger, falling short and scattering across the tall grasses near the forest line. It took less than a heartbeat for the drying grasses to catch fire.

Ivy lifted her hands again, but this time Liv was quick enough to stop her, "It's not worth—"

"What the hell?" Ivy cut her off, looking toward the trees.

Liv turned back to the stranger, her stomach toppling through her feet as she watched the figure step through the flames and toward them.

"He's a witch. He has to be."

Liv ignored Ivy's deadly curiosity. "Get inside." She shoved Ivy behind her toward the house, while keeping her eyes fixed on the figure. It continued to advance toward them at a leisurely pace, remaining shrouded the entire way.

Liv took a few backward steps, and nearly tripped over her sister, Ivy of course choosing that moment to argue with her. "What if they need help? Why do you always jump to the worst-case scenario so quickly."

Liv turned to Ivy and grabbed her by the arm. "You're the one who threw fire at them. Go. Now." She all but dragged Ivy around the side of the cabin, through the front door, out of sight of the stranger and away from the growing fire.

Once inside it took Liv less than a minute to run through the small cabin to ensure everything was locked and as secure as it could be without magick.

Then she joined her sister next to a small window that looked out toward the forest, searching for any sign of who or what had been out there. But the only indication that it hadn't all been an illusion was the scorch marks in the field left behind by Ivy's fire.

Whoever it had been had enough magick to extinguish Ivy's flames and had at least chosen to put it out instead of letting the forest, and their house, catch fire. But they'd also remained shrouded, hiding their identity—and that was troubling. Her mother's fears and rants about someone being "after them" whispered from the back of her mind.

Just as her heartbeat started to return to normal, a familiar magick snapped within the house, and a piece of parchment cut through the air so fast Liv barely had time to react, snatching it before it could slap her in the face.

"Whoa! What's that?" Ivy asked, trying to peek around her hands.

This time Liv didn't ignore it. She didn't throw it away or shred it. This time the message was received.

Despite everything she'd have to face, despite *who* she'd have to face, regardless of how much Ivy might resist, she knew what they needed to do.

Liv looked up from the deed to her sister. "It's time to go home."

Home to Havenwood.

CHAPTER TWO

*B*reathing in the salty sea air, Liv let it wash through her and ease some of the tension that had built in her body during the long drive. She could finally hear the distant sound of waves crashing against the cliffs and echoing through the forest that framed the house and the back gardens. It added to the feeling that this place was significant.

And then there was that familiar something *more* that she could feel lingering in the air, humming around her. The kind of *more* she knew one couldn't see but felt. The thrum of it welled deep in her, calling to her. The power of the Terrabellas who had come before her, each of their ashes returned to this land, their essence and power returning to the earth from which they'd received it. Becoming one with it again. Ensuring Terrabella blood and magick was woven into every bit of life in this town, from the giant redwoods towering above to the tiniest speck of moss, and the earth it all emerged from.

It was the same magick that seeped into the old house. The same magick that flowed through her veins. A tangible gift from the generations of her ancestors who had built both the house and the town that it centered.

That feeling of welcome, plus a million memories, made this the only place that had ever truly felt like home.

She stood on the sidewalk looking up at the old Queen Anne-style

Victorian house and couldn't help but think that despite everything the last decade had thrown at her, everything she'd sacrificed, and after all the time away, she should have known she'd end up back here.

As if it had always been inevitable.

Though the house was technically part of the neighborhood, it was set apart, both by how far back from the street it stood and by its appearance. Liv looked up and down the quiet street. The perfectly manicured lawns, the antique lampposts that shined without a hint of wear, their eternal flames dancing steadily within. Every other house was in perfect condition. She turned back to her family home, the only smudge on an otherwise pristine canvas, standing out even more due to the perfection around it.

It had once represented something in this town. It still did—*she* knew that. She might be the only one, though.

It was clear it had been neglected.

From what she could see between the thick, leafless vines hanging from the gables and climbing the round tower that made up the left side of the asymmetrical house, the light blue color she remembered had faded to a dull gray.

Many of the fish scale shingles that should have covered the front of the second story were missing, the windows looked fogged over, and pieces of the decorative gables and spindles were cracking. Liv couldn't help but wonder how the ornate iron fencing that enclosed the front of the property had managed to survive the combination of decay and the Santa Ana winds that blew through the town every year.

The house had been lonely.

Thank Spirit they'd arrived at night...hopefully the darkness would soften the blow when Ivy saw it. She'd figured there would be a few things the house would need to get it back to what it had been when Terrabellas had dwelled within. She'd prepared Ivy for that. But she hadn't expected this. Not from this house.

But despite all the wear and tear the house still stood. A small smile pulled at the corner of her mouth. She supposed that the house considered itself too important, too regal, to succumb to something as trivial as time.

The modest porch still managed to support the small balcony that jutted out above it. Despite a few missing spindles, the balcony seemed mostly intact. Much like her vivid memories of gazing up at the stars from it.

The trellis that edged it was now covered in dead vines, but she remembered when they'd been thick and strong enough to support the weight of the boy who'd climbed them nearly every night to whisper dreams to those stars with her. To make wishes that would go unfulfilled.

Liv ignored the pain that lingered at the edges of the old memories, even the good ones—maybe especially the good ones. She'd make new ones. Despite what most would see when they looked at this place, she remembered what it had been. Saw what it could be. *Knew* what it would be.

She just hoped her sister would too.

The slamming of the car door reverberated through her, rattling her confidence. Liv sucked in a breath. *Here we go.*

Her sister appeared in the periphery of her vision, finally deciding to join her in front of the house, standing without speaking for longer than was comfortable. As Liv tried to see it through Ivy's eyes, she suddenly wasn't so sure arriving at night was the gift she'd originally thought it would be. One could argue the darkness didn't mask the rundown state so much as lend it an unnerving air.

"This is it, huh? The old place fared well while we were gone." The sarcasm rang loud and clear.

While we were gone. As if they'd just been on a quick trip or a vacation, rather than having left town in the middle of the night without a word to anyone. Over a decade ago.

"I know it's not exactly how we remembered it."

"No, I mean, if you're going to be dragged across an entire country by your sister, it better be for a gem like this." Liv forced herself to meet Ivy's glare with a soft look of her own. "Liv. What the hell are we supposed to do with a place like this? This can't really be what mom wanted for us." It was both an accusation and a plea.

No, it wouldn't have been, Liv thought. But maybe that was a good thing.

She could understand her sister's reticence about the house. She just wished Ivy could trust her and try to see that this was more than another move and an old house.

Outside of Havenwood, her sister's increasingly volatile magick was becoming impossible to hide or explain away while living in a world that had turned its back on all magick that didn't include parlor tricks and rabbits in hats. There'd been no safe way to teach Ivy to harness it, partly because it manifested so differently from Liv's own and partly because of the way their unpredictable life had made Ivy's emotions so volatile. This was their shot at building a stable life, something Ivy didn't realize how badly she needed.

Ivy shook her head at some silent conversation she was having with herself, and clearly not a positive one.

Biting down on the inside of her cheek, Liv pushed away the irritation she felt brewing. A week of cross-country driving would have that effect on a person. She reminded herself that her sister had only been a kid when they'd left the house and the town behind. Ivy hadn't had nearly as long as Liv to form the kind of connection to the house that was needed to see it past its current state.

She swallowed the guilt down to fester deep within her alongside a host of other emotions she didn't have time to deal with. This was the right call, she reminded herself for the hundredth time since they'd set out across the country, headed West as far as they could go.

She wrapped an arm around Ivy's petite shoulders and pulled her in. "You have to look past all this," she waved a hand at the dead bramble that had taken over the front garden and the house in general, "and see the heart of it, what it could be, *will* be again. This place just needs some love, and some Terrabella blood back inside it. It has good bones."

Shifting out of Liv's grasp, Ivy pushed the front gate open. Both sisters winced at the awful metal-on-metal grinding sound the hinges made before one of them gave way to rust completely, leaving the gate hanging askew from a single hinge. One that didn't look like it was going to hang on much longer, either.

Ivy turned back to Liv, a single eyebrow raised, and skepticism etched into her features. "Everyone knows *good bones*," Ivy made air quotes with her fingers, "is just what shady realtors say when a piece of shit house needs to be taken down to the studs."

Liv gently lifted the gate and moved it aside, waving her sister on. "Have a little faith. We've been in worse places." *Exclusively worse places,* she thought following behind.

She halted her steps at the sight of a single wayward dandelion pushing up between two stepping stones. It taunted her as it gently swayed in the breeze and unearthed a string of memories so potent she swore she could smell him on that breeze. She half expected to find him standing right behind her, but she resisted the urge to look, knowing it was pointless. Even if Jax was still somewhere in this town, he certainly wouldn't be waiting for her. She dismissed it as a symptom of nostalgia and continued up the path to join her sister at the foot of the porch steps.

"Ow! Dammit!"

"What?" Liv peeked over her sister's shoulder, which wasn't hard to do considering she had a good five inches on Ivy, who barely cleared five-one. It was just one of the differences between the two of them. Liv's dark hair hung nearly to her waist in the rare instances she wore it down, while Ivy's was a light brown that she kept shorter and always perfectly styled. Similar to their hair, Liv's skin was a few shades darker than her sister's.

The list went on, the fact that they didn't share the same father easily explaining away all of these differences. Except for one—their eyes. Liv's were luminously green, a distinct attribute *all* Terrabellas carried without exception, all but Ivy who had been born with one Terrabella-green eye, the other a dark swirling hazel.

Her grandmother had tried but never could explain how or why it had happened. But Liv knew magick wasn't inclined to explain itself. Besides, all it had ever done was make her sister even more beautiful.

"I…" Ivy examined her fingers. "I thought I got a splinter or something, but nothing's there." She glared up at the front door. "This kooky-ass house is already drawing blood."

Liv rolled her eyes, stepping around her whiny sister. "Maybe that's just its defense mechanism against intruders." *Or your shitty attitude.*

She ignored the muttered response of, "This house never liked me anyway." There was no point arguing, because she wasn't entirely wrong.

But it was because Ivy's magick had done so much damage to the house during the few years it had developed here, not because it chose favorites. Probably.

Liv's magick, on the other hand, had always flourished here. She had a reciprocal relationship with the land, enhancing it and helping it to thrive.

Okay, so maybe the house had some egocentric tendencies. But it was theirs, and she knew that no matter what, it was where they were meant to be. She'd become more and more sure of that, the closer they had gotten to home.

She paused at the old oak front door to run her fingers over the deep grooves of the wood grain and then traced the vine detailing of the stained-glass panels that accented the door.

The porch planks under her feet creaked ominously. She couldn't be sure if it was due to the age and decay of the wood or the impatience of the house, but either way, she didn't feel like finding out.

She reached for the handle only to remember it didn't have a lock, didn't require a key—at least not the traditional kind.

Shit. She'd forgotten about that little detail. What if after all this time it wouldn't open for her?

Ivy crowded in behind her, and Liv eyed her sister over her shoulder. "I knew you were a little excited."

Ivy rolled her eyes. "I just want to make sure the inside is inhabitable."

"Mhmm," Liv hummed skeptically. But she couldn't say that worry hadn't crossed her own mind.

When she set her hand on the tarnished brass handle a sudden rush of emotion coursed through her, catching her off guard, and taking with it any lingering doubt as it subsided. She pressed down on the lever and shoved once, twice. It felt as if the door had been secured with some type of sticky substance that finally gave under her repeated effort as if unsealing. Liv blew out a deep breath and crossed the threshold.

The moment both her feet hit the wide oak floorboards of the foyer a source-less breeze slid across her chest and shoulders and lifted the ends of her long hair.

The house decompressed as if it were letting out a sigh of its own, releasing the nostalgic scent of Palo Santo and the woods—*her woods.* A momentary warmth and deep sense of belonging overtook her, and she reveled in the moment as Havenhouse welcomed her home.

———

JAXON HAWTHORNE SAT HIDDEN FROM VIEW BY THE DARKNESS OF HIS rustic porch. He did his best to ignore the melodic tinkling of wind chimes hanging from the eaves as the current of magick hit them. But no matter how hard he tried he'd never be able to ignore the scent of *that* magick as it filled the air around him. It soothed something inside him, inviting him to lean back into the old rocker he was perched on, threatening to lull him into contentedness with false promises of happily ever after.

His fingers curled into the rough wood of his chair as he barely resisted the urge to rip the windchimes down as they mocked him, continuing to sway and chime gently even after the breath of her essence had subsided.

There was no point. He hadn't been afforded the luxury of forgetting the feel of her magick in the last decade, so why start now?

Jax exhaled a ragged breath, reaching for the magick within him, intending to use it to balance the magick in the air and free himself of her scent, but there was no point in that either. Now that the house had her back, the scent of her magick would engulf it and the forest beyond.

Jax sipped his whisky, then let the cool thin edge of the glass linger between his lips, the smoky scent of the liquid invading his senses and providing him with a brief reprieve from *her*.

The waning moon rose high in the sky above Havenhouse, giving off just enough light to cast the place in a subtle glow, without blotting out the stars. Stars that winked in and out, dancing against the pitch-dark sky, as if even they were celebrating the rare return of one of their own.

Generally, those who left this town weren't planning to ever come back. Those who intended to stay rarely ever left. He was unique in that way. And apparently, so was *she*.

Was it for good this time? Jax shook the thought off the second he felt the tell-tale lift of hope in his chest. It didn't matter. Couldn't. He'd spent enough time waiting for her. Looking for her. She'd not wanted to be found —a message it had taken him too long to receive. He'd known better,

16

known that there were no guarantees in the gift the Spirit had given his sister, but hope had kept him hanging on to Jade's vision for far too long. That vision that promised she'd be back.

But at some point, hope relented to pain. Pain that slowly morphed into something else, something ugly and bitter. Something he'd come to realize she wouldn't want if she ever did return.

So, he'd left, too.

When he'd left Havenwood it had been with the intention of staying gone, but those thoughts had been dictated by pride and pain. Time and maturity had dulled that drive over the past several years, the pull to come home only growing in intensity, no matter how much distance he'd put between himself and this place. Turned out he wasn't the kind of person who found it easy to leave his family, his duty, or his home, behind.

He'd been home for almost two years now, effectively living out the very life *they'd* always planned, but making it his own instead. If only slightly by default, as it wasn't like a small town offered many choices.

And it suited him just fine. He had what he needed to be happy. Or at least something that resembled it.

"You planning to go welcome her home?" Jax could hear the smirk on his sister's face, so he didn't bother looking up when she came to stand next to him, letting the screen door slap closed behind her.

"No."

"Okayyy…well, that was fast."

Jax relented, tipping his head to his sister. Sure enough, there was that smug-as-shit smirk curving the edges of her lips and creasing the corners of her eyes. Jax pushed a breath through his nose already regretting taking the bait. "What are you talking about, Jade?"

"Oh, you know, just how quickly you started brooding over her again. Nearly instantaneous. I thought it would at least take a few days. Looks like I owe Quinn twenty bucks. Damn empaths." She shrugged. "At least I did better than Logan. That loyal idiot gave you a month."

Jax's jaw shifted. "I am not brooding." Even he could hear the lie in the slow grumble of his voice.

"Uh-huh. So, you planning to sit here in the dark like a creep all night *not* brooding then?"

Jax didn't respond. The sudden realization that he didn't know what he was going to do next was a foreign sensation.

"You know I'm not always right about these things. Maybe it's just a coincidence." Jade's tone had softened slightly in an attempt to be sympathetic. But neither of them believed that.

"Coincidence? In Havenwood?" Jax turned fully to his sister. It was a question and an answer.

"Then what do you think brought her back?"

He exhaled through his nose. "How should I know? Why don't *you* tell *me*, isn't that how this is supposed to go?"

Jade shrugged again. "You know that's not how it works. Choices need to be made, and paths taken. Anything can change at any moment." Yeah, he knew that. Technically. Didn't make it any less frustrating. But she'd offered to keep these things to herself a long time ago. He hadn't wanted her to bear that burden alone then, and he wanted it even less now. He'd just have to deal with the aggravation of the uncertainty that sometimes came with Jade knowing what was ultimately unknowable.

Judging by the way she was currently clamping her lips together, he was also going to have to deal with the enjoyment she would get from watching him navigate whatever torture the immediate future held for him.

Jade crossed in front of him to sit in the other rocking chair. Her gaze moved out toward Havenhouse. She nodded slightly, causing her blonde curls to sway gently over her shoulders and across her back. Her blue eyes brightened infinitesimally. It was a quirk most people didn't notice, but Jax knew what it looked like when his sister withdrew into herself, into her magick. He waited for her to come back.

The tone of Jade's voice betrayed a rare bit of vulnerability when she asked, "Do you think she'll stay, Jax?" She turned to look back at him, the blue in her eyes shining even in the darkness. "We need her. Not just to have her back in our lives, but for whatever might be coming. I mean, first Quinn and now Liv, that's two more of the Six."

He had to turn away from the excitement that glittered in his sister's eyes. He couldn't answer that. Once upon a time, he wouldn't have been able to imagine Liv Terrabella ever leaving in the first place. Let alone the way she had. Back then he'd been sure he knew her, from the shape of her

18

soul to the feel of her lips. But he'd been wrong. He wouldn't dare to guess her plans now. He couldn't.

Jade was right about one thing, though. He looked around the town he'd thought he knew just as well. Something was going on...changing. He could feel the press of it all around him. He'd told himself he could handle whatever it was. But he felt that confidence waiver as he watched the only woman he'd ever loved set foot in Havenwood for the first time in over twelve years, and wondered what it might mean. For him and the town.

CHAPTER THREE

*S*pirit save me.

I. Get. It. The house is old and you hate it.

Liv moved around the kitchen opening cabinets, assessing the bleak state of their contents, and scribbling notes on a grocery list, all the while doing her best to ignore Ivy's latest scrutiny of the house. They'd been having some version of this same conversation multiple times a day since about thirty seconds after they'd stepped foot in the place.

Over those three days, they'd made their way through the two floors of multiple living spaces and all six bedrooms. Thankfully, the inside of the house was in significantly better shape than the outside.

The intricate woodwork that trimmed the ceilings, archways, and windows was still dark and rich. The decorative touches like the elegant wallpaper, paintings, and curtains all still hung. The chandeliers that dropped from the high ceilings with elaborate plasterwork, brass wall sconces, and an assortment of colorful Tiffany lamps scattered through the house, all still worked, though some needed new bulbs.

She'd removed sheets from the antique furniture still arranged just as they had been the night they'd last closed the front door. All of the pieces' luxurious fabrics were still in great condition, though not all entirely practical for day-to-day life.

There were significantly fewer notes to add to the hand-written list she'd started regarding the outside of the house.

Her sister's sole contribution to the endeavor so far had been to drop her apathy only when she found something worth criticizing.

"What is this room even for?" Ivy called from the other side of the house.

Liv didn't even have to look. "It's a library, Ivy." She rolled her eyes. "The shelves of books surrounding you might have been a good clue," she murmured.

"In a house?" Ivy's voice grew closer, coming down the long hall that split the house. Liv didn't respond. Ivy knew as well as she did that Haven-house had originally been not just a home for the Terrabellas, but also an inn for new arrivals in town.

As Ivy passed her in the kitchen, Liv realized where she was headed and stuck her head through the cased opening to see her sister standing in front of a set of French doors. She'd avoided the room so far, unsure if she was ready to face what she might find in there—the disrepair of the space, or the memories it held.

"And what the hell is this room?" Ivy jerked on the handles. "Look at all these windows." She cupped her hands on the glass of the doors and tried to see in. When it became clear she hadn't suddenly gained the x-ray vision that would allow her to see through whatever muck had clouded the glass, she tried the doors again. They didn't budge. Not even a rattle. Ivy groaned in frustration.

Liv couldn't help her small, satisfied smile. The house was either taking mercy on her or, more likely, trying to piss Ivy off in return for her near-constant criticism. Either way, she was grateful. She wasn't planning to put it off much longer, but she wanted to be alone when she entered the greenhouse for the first time after so long.

Liv turned back to the kitchen but froze when the abrasive edge of Ivy's magick grazed her skin, and she instantly knew she was too late to stop it. She jerked her shoulder toward her ear and cringed at the sharp sound of splintering wood.

"Shit!" Liv whipped back around.

Ivy shook her hands out in front of her. "I was trying to unlock it." Her eyes were wide with surprise, but no sign of regret.

The house creaked and the kitchen cabinets clattered open and closed repeatedly. A fire extinguisher she hadn't even known they had rolled across the floor, coming to rest against Liv's foot. She kicked it aside, moving to inspect the damage.

The wood was shattered around the melted, and now useless, brass latch where the two doors met. Scorch marks marred the wood, but by some miracle, none of the glass had cracked.

"Dammit Ivy. There isn't even a lock on the doors. It was the house messing with you."

"That's not my fault. How was I supposed to know that?"

Liv closed her eyes and took a calming breath. Period of adjustment, she chanted to herself yet again. Even if her sister was attempting to blame the house. "It's your magick, Ivy, that means it is always your," *don't say fault,* "responsibility. You know this. It's the one thing every witch must understand before they even think of using their magick casually. You have to be aware of your emotional state and know how it can influence your magick." Ivy said the words in tandem with Liv, rolling her eyes.

Liv sighed and crossed her arms. "I know you know this, but you need to actually *use* your knowledge if you're going to learn to control your magick. And there is no reason to use it for mundane tasks you're perfectly capable of handling without it. *Like opening doors.*" She knew the all-too-familiar speech wasn't penetrating. It was a waste of her breath. Even at nearly twenty-one, her sister still refused to take her magick seriously. Liv hoped being back in Havenwood would help encourage her to learn. Her magick couldn't be explained away in this town. And maybe Liv could focus more on teaching her and less on covering up her explosions.

"Yeah, yeah, I get it, everything is my fault, I'm a mess and shouldn't use my magick," Ivy droned, sarcasm dripping from her tone, and expression, for that matter.

Then, as was her habit, she immediately moved on from their conversation on her nearly blowing up part of the house with her untamed magick, instead taking a few steps away toward the center of the house where the sitting room opened to the foyer. Ivy spun in a circle and then threw her arms in the air, letting them flop back down to her sides dramatically. "Windows and shelves, that's all there is in this house. Where the hell are we supposed to hang a TV?"

Liv was running out of calming breaths to take and patience to find, and she wasn't letting this conversation go. "You're acting like you've never been here before. You weren't *that* young when we left. This is the same house you were born in, the same town you lived in for nearly ten years," Liv said, taking a few steps toward Ivy, running her fingers over the edge of the elaborate wainscoting that covered the walls hoping the house wasn't listening.

Liv closed the distance between her and Ivy, pulling her down onto a brocade upholstered love seat set up in front of a fireplace that took up nearly an entire wall in the sitting room.

"If we're going to make this work, you need to remember what we talked about. We're both going to have to make some adjustments." She placed her hand on Ivy's, grateful when she didn't immediately pull away. "And if you want a TV, you're going to have to put it in your room. On a stand. Not hung. With screws. In a two-hundred-year-old wall." She said it lightly, but she couldn't put anything past her sister—she'd learned that the hard way one too many times.

"Another point in the win column for *your* decision to bring us back to this place." Ivy turned her body away from her, taking her hand with her.

"Ivy, please. You know the same as I do, we needed to bring Mom's ashes back here... this is our home, where we belong. Plus, look at what just happened," Ivy didn't bother to look to where Liv gestured to the splintered and scalded door. "You need a place to learn, or at least some-where we don't have to create elaborate stories any time you use your magick. Short of you not using your magick at all." Liv raised her hands placatingly. "I'm not saying that's the answer or my desire," she rushed to say before Ivy could lose it. "I'm just saying we don't have a whole lot of other options, do we?"

Ivy shifted her upper body and opened her mouth to speak, but appar-ently, she'd used up all her acrimony for one day. Or maybe Liv had finally managed to get through to her a little. Unlikely.

With only a pointed glare to communicate her displeasure, Ivy got up and walked away, disappearing into another part of the house. The only other time Liv had made the mistake of suggesting maybe Ivy shouldn't use her magick at all, had gone over about as well as a sunflower in a snowstorm. A literal snowstorm Ivy had somehow accidentally conjured in their living room. So, she'd just done her best to clean up after Ivy's messes. Smoothed things over, and explained things away when it happened in front of nullies.

Ivy's magick had never been the same as the rest of the Terrabella's. Their grandmother had tried to work with her when she was younger but had died before it had developed very far. And their mother, with hardly any of her own power, certainly wasn't interested in helping…even before she'd started to lose her grip on reality. Liv had no clue where to start. She had tried to teach her sister the basics, things that would apply to any witch, but she'd never been able to get Ivy to take it seriously. It had gotten them nowhere. Now they were home, and she hoped things would be different.

The urge to go after her sister, to apologize and smooth things over, was as strong as it always was after one of their arguments. But while it may have been a little harsh, what she had said was the truth.

She didn't have the energy to endure another bout with Ivy's sharp tongue right now.

Though she'd done her best to hide it from her sister, Liv had experienced a veritable rector scale of emotions of her own over the previous seventy-two hours. She felt like some kind of human pinball bouncing from contentment to nostalgia so intense it threatened to crack her open, and then back over to something that felt dangerously close to hope before flying toward a suppressed rage that threatened to shatter glass whenever Ivy opened her mouth.

And despite all of Ivy's bravado and surface-level carelessness, she knew her sister was affected by being back in the house, too. Even if she pretended like she hardly remembered it. The truth had been evident the first night when she chose her room.

They'd made their way upstairs and the buzz of trepidation she'd felt hadn't only been coming from within her, but from her sister as well. Ivy had passed by her old room and Liv had assumed she was headed toward the master. Instead, she'd wordlessly slipped into the room that had last been their mother's.

Liv had also forgone the master that had last belonged to their grandmother, choosing her original bedroom instead.

One of them chose a room because of who it had once belonged to, the other forgoing one for the same reason. They were petals on the wind, driven by the same force, in opposite directions.

So, while it wasn't exactly pleasant, Liv understood that her sister was using the criticism as a safety net. And *that* knowledge was currently the only thing deterring her from throwing her sister out the closest window. That and the fact she wasn't sure she could get one open.

Liv let the tips of her fingers coast over the splintered wood and the still-warm melted metal. A sliver of light peeked between the doors. A faint iridescence shimmered in the light, and slowly the wood stitched itself back together. She wound a finger counterclockwise and the metal of the latch liquified before slowly reforming. The tingle in her fingers and up her forearms felt good...familiar, despite how rarely she used her magick.

Her limbs felt light, but her heart felt heavy as she cracked the door and slowly slipped in, leaving the door slightly ajar.

Liv took a few uneven steps deeper into the room she'd spent countless hours in growing up. Her eyes skipped around it, unable and maybe just a little afraid to settle on any one place too long. Her eyes closed and she turned her face skyward, inhaling the strong scent of long-since dried herbs that hung from thick wood beams framing fogged-over glass panels. The small bit of sunlight that was able to penetrate the glass landed on her face, and the tension in her chest lightened.

She opened her eyes again, feeling a little more ready. Slowly, she moved around the room, taking it all in. Dried-out plants in old pots, some cracked and overturned, were strewn across long shelves that lined the glass walls. Varying sizes of colored glass bottles littered between the pots.

Her eyes stung when she saw the stone mortar and pestle, remnants of herbs resting in the bottom like her Grammy had just gotten called out and would be back any minute to finish what she'd been working on. Liv reached out, dragging her finger over the cool stone and then down through the thick dust on the rough, dented surface of the workbench. A small, overturned clay pot rested on its side. Dried and depleted soil spilled from it. The carcass of a propagated plant lay in the spilled soil, its shriveled roots barely visible in the remnants of soil dried to them.

Liv's finger hovered over the sad little plant. Years of avoiding her magick in her mother's presence, and then more years of stifling it while they'd lived outside of town, caused her to hesitate. But the sad state of the plant urged her on. With little more than a soft brush of her hand, the pot righted itself, taking the soil and plant with it, as if the moment it had spilled over was moving in reverse.

Liv closed her eyes, finding that warm spark of life within her and pushing it out toward the plant. She opened her eyes in time to watch the soil darken and the small plant unfurl, green with new life.

A small smile tugged at her lips.

As she crossed back into the house, she didn't see the way the morning glory vines that had long ago found their way into the greenhouse, only to wither and dry over the years, slowly begin to awaken.

CHAPTER FOUR

*T*hey needed food, amongst a host of other things. She'd procrastinated as long as she could. It was time to suck it up and go into town.

She paused at the end of the front walkway. Surprised, and a bit confused, she stared at the dilapidated front gate that had previously been clinging to life, and which was now sitting upright and fully functional on shiny new hinges. Looking back, she took in the vines on the house, which were also showing some signs of new life. Maybe it was just the house responding to her and Ivy's presence.

The newly repaired front gate opened silently for her as Liv stepped through. Wary, she made the mistake of hesitating, and it smacked her on the ass and snapped closed behind her with much more force than necessary. *Message received.* "I'm going!" she hissed at the house. "So bossy." She looked around, hoping no one was around, she probably shouldn't let the first thing she was seen doing in town be her talking to inanimate objects…even if the house was anything but inanimate.

No one had the benefit of anonymity in a small town, but that was especially true for those who were descended from one of the six founding families, or simply "the Six" as they were generally called. Add to that the fact that they'd left town in the middle of the night, only to return a decade later just as abruptly. As annoying as small-town gossip could be, it was hard to fault people their curiosity.

Liv reminded herself that she was a grown-ass woman, and she didn't owe anyone an explanation, nor did she care what anyone thought about her. But it was a lot easier to think than to feel. Especially here, where she knew questions and theories were probably already being whispered. The longer she stayed holed up in the house, the more those stories would spin out of control. Better to just get on with it, she thought.

The smell of orange blossoms mingled with the salty sea breeze that chilled Liv's skin as she walked toward town. Houses slowly gave way to businesses as she got closer to the heart of Havenwood. The quaint downtown unfolded before her, and it was a relief to see that it was as storybook-perfect as she'd remembered. That her memory hadn't exaggerated its charm out of nostalgia and longing.

Compared to the easy-going sprawl of the neighborhoods surrounding it, this part of town was teeming with energy, the epicenter of life in Havenwood.

A large roundabout connected a web of cross streets. A graceful flow of foot traffic and the occasional car traversed the worn cobblestone road.

People milled about, ducking in and out of storefronts of varying architectural styles. Victorian-era elegance mixed with whimsical detailing, and charming craftsman's offered cozy porch dining. Spanish revival and touches of art deco lent punches of color against the deep green backdrop of the forest edging the town.

The businesses inside the buildings had changed over the years, each leaving their mark behind. Contemporary conveniences and intentional modernizations were skillfully woven in while protecting the heart of the architecture. Somehow it all came together seamlessly to create a vibrant amalgam that reflected and preserved the town's history perfectly.

At the center of it all sat the Glen, a small oasis of marble benches perched beneath tall pines, and the wishing well. The fountain was a memorial to the original place where the Six had supposedly converged their magick, creating the Umbra Aegis, the protective barrier that made Havenwood a refuge for witches and magick wielders.

The Umbra Aegis protected the town, not by hiding it from plain view, but rather by presenting it to those who needed it and weighing the intentions of those who attempted to pass into town. It didn't mean *nothing* bad could ever happen in town. People were people, witch or otherwise. But it did keep the knowledge of what went on in Havenwood from becoming widespread public knowledge.

Beside the Town Hall, which sat at the Northernmost point of the roundabout, The Glen was the hub of all community gatherings. Even now, with no events going on, downtown in general was buzzing with people.

Moving toward the Glen, Liv navigated small groupings of people walking and chatting on the street. Summoning her inner Elena, she smiled at familiar faces, and even a few unfamiliar ones for good measure. She offered a couple of brief platitudes when necessary. Her mother would be proud, she thought wryly.

She did her best to ignore the occasional lingering stares and whispers she left in her wake. And when one blue-haired woman sneered and turned away from her altogether, she channeled her inner Valeria instead and mentally flipped her off. Though, her grandmother would have done it right to the woman's face. With both hands.

Liv bounced between the contrasting personalities of her mom and grandmother, doing her best to hopefully find some way to exist in this town somewhere between the two.

By the time she crossed into the Glen her cheeks hurt. The act of smiling was beginning to feel foreign to her. She also suspected that her smile might be starting to edge closer to psychopath-trying-to-imitate-human-feelings, rather than the more approachable promise-I-don't-deal-in-poisons friendly neighborhood witch she was going for. Luckily, it didn't seem like anyone had noticed that she'd spontaneously forgotten how to work her face.

She approached the fountain, stopping at the brass plates that encircled it. They'd been inlaid in concrete on the two-hundredth anniversary of the town. Six brass plates, one for each of the founding families. She stood over hers, *Terrabella* proudly stamped across the middle of it.

A small sigil representing their Earth element was centered below it. She moved clockwise around the fountain reading each of the names as she went. *Sinclair, Wilder, Vulcani*—she hesitated on the brass plate that read

Stone, before forcing her feet to move on to the last marker. The one that rested beside her family name.

Hawthorne.

His name.

She sat down on the brick-hewn edge of the fountain between their names. She hadn't even been born when the plates had been placed, and yet they'd ended up side by side. It would have made for a romantic story if theirs had ended differently.

She looked away from the names to the water in the fountain. Copper pennies glinted, distorted by the ripples of the water. She knew more than one of those pennies were marked with her wishes—their wishes. Probably the ones covered in patina and buried beneath fresh wishes, ones that still had a chance. She pictured that version of herself, tossing those pennies. She clenched her fist as a light breeze circled her, drawing her out of the pity party. She decided it was time to back away from the fountain and stop letting this town drag her down memory lane.

As she made her way to the other side of the Glen her eyes scanned the people around her for familiar faces. She saw a few, but no one within acknowledging distance. Passing an abandoned easel, she subtly peeked at the work in progress. Whoever had been working on it was incredibly talented. Even in its incomplete state, the artist had captured the current sunset perfectly. Inspired, Liv sat on the bench a few feet away from the easel to watch the sunset for herself.

It looked like it was falling off the cliffs at the edge of town, plunging into the ocean below. The last of the rays painted the sky with pastel hues of purples, pinks, and oranges, the tall trees surrounding the town becoming dark silhouettes against the radiant sky. She'd been to a lot of places over the last several years, many of them beautiful in their own way. But she'd never seen anything that came close to a Southern California sunset. It was its own kind of magick.

"Hi."

Liv turned, surprised to see a little girl standing very close to her. "Hello." She looked to be around four or five, with blonde hair pulled back into a bun so tightly that Liv's scalp ached in sympathy.

"I like your eyes."

"I like your tutu."

"It's for ballet."

"They're for seeing."

"I hate ballet."

Liv's brows drew together, "I'm not really sure what to say to that."

The little girl studied her for a moment before climbing up onto the bench to sit next to her. Her little legs dangled several inches from the ground, swinging back and forth as the two sat there in silence for a minute. "If you hate ballet, why do you do it?" Liv asked.

"My mom says I need more dis-tah, dis-uh-." The little girl struggled to say the word and looked to Liv for help.

"Discipline?" The little girl gave a single sharp nod. "Is it working?"

She shrugged a little shoulder. "I eat my vegetables. Sometimes. And I follow the rules."

"Sounds like you have more discipline than some adults I know." *One in particular.*

"Buuut I'm also not supposed to talk to strangers." The little girl looked up at her.

"Well, I'm Liv."

"I know." She turned to her and regarded Liv intensely for a moment. "You don't look evil."

"I'm glad to hear that because I'm not."

"My mommy says you and all the women in your family are dangerous witches."

Liv was momentarily stunned silent, the confidence she'd constructed during her mostly successful outing wilting inside her. It was one thing for old women with long memories to harbor suspicion. But it was another thing entirely for those rumors to be perpetuated recently enough to be taught to someone so young.

"The only danger your mom needs to be worried about is the amount of Botox in her forehead." Liv's head whipped around to find a woman in paint-splattered overalls stepping toward them from behind the easel.

Before she could formulate any words, the little girl's mom was there, grabbing her daughter by the arm and yanking her away from Liv like she was in the middle of the street and Liv was a semi-truck headed straight for her.

The paint-splatter woman was coming around to stand next to her. Amber eyes turned up slightly at the corners giving her an almost feline look. Her skin was a patchwork of brightly colored tattoos flecked with dry paint and even with her hair thrown up into a messy bun, she was the kind of effortlessly beautiful she knew most women spent hours and fortunes to achieve. Somehow, she knew it came naturally to this woman.

"That was rude as hell." The painter propped a hand on her hip, genuinely offended on Liv's behalf. The simple act of decency probably shouldn't have elicited as much gratitude from her as it did, but she wasn't going to examine that at the moment.

"Small towns will always have small-minded people," Liv repeated the words her grandmother had said to her so many times growing up. It had become the mantra of her teenage years.

The little girl's mom took the time to pause her dramatic exit to glare at Liv and whisper-scold her daughter, before continuing to urgently drag her away.

A vague sense of familiarity came over Liv, not for the woman so much as for the look of suspicion and overall disdain that was pouring off her.

"That may be true. Or maybe someone just needs to help them expand their minds a little."

"Trust me, there's no point. It's fine. I'm fine." Liv turned to thank the pretty artist for caring, but her gaze was fixed on the angry woman's retreating back.

A light tingle rushed over Liv's skin, and a moment later a high-pitched shriek drew her attention back to the angry mom. Two pigeons swooped down on her, turned and did it once more before flying off for the trees.

The woman stood motionless for a moment before the shrieking, really that was the only word for it, started again. "My dress!" She released her daughter's hand, waving hers in the air as she looked around for someone to save her. Liv's eyes rounded as she realized the pigeons had pooped on the uptight woman's dress.

A small, satisfied laugh came from the artist as she sat down next to Liv with a sigh. "Ahh, a little dose of cosmic Karma. So satisfying."

One side of the woman's face slid up in a Cheshire grin. Her golden eyes twinkled with something that looked a lot like mischief.

"I'm Quinn Wilder." She stuck her hand out.

Slightly addled, Liv took her hand. "Wilder? As in *Wilder*, Wilder?" Liv asked.

"Yep. Apparently so." She shrugged a slender shoulder, giving Liv the impression that it was both something she'd also recently discovered and that it wasn't anything extraordinary. But it was to her. She'd never met someone from the Wilder line. She was pretty sure no one currently living had.

Liv's eyes narrowed in sudden understanding, "Did you just… make all that happen?" She gestured to where the pigeon debacle had just taken place.

Quinn only shrugged again and began picking at some paint under her nails. "Animals are very sensitive. They see straight to the soul." Her eyes locked on Liv's. "Those pigeons must not have liked what they saw in hers. So. Are you going to tell me who you are now?"

"Oh," Liv's cheeks warmed—she'd been so mesmerized by the enigmatic aura that radiated from Quinn she'd forgotten to speak. "Liv." She hesitated for a moment. "Terrabella."

"Ahhh, I see," Quinn replied, seeming to have gained some sudden understanding. Of what, Liv had no clue. "That would make you the owner of the amazing house out by the cliffs then."

It wasn't a question, but she nodded.

"You have to let me in there sometime!"

"Uh, yeah. Maybe sometime. We just got here, so we need a little time to you know…" Liv ran out of words.

But Quinn didn't seem to notice or mind. She just studied Liv intently for a second. Then her face suddenly lit up. "Come on!" She stood on long legs, grabbing Liv's hand on the way up, taking her with her out of the Glen.

"Where are we going?" Liv struggled to keep her legs under her as she tried to keep up with Quinn.

CHAPTER FIVE

*Q*uinn had brought her to Mac's.

Liv didn't know what or who to expect when she stepped into the bar. Finding that so little had changed—except for the fact that she was now legally allowed to be inside—was strangely comforting.

Like so many of the businesses in town, Mac's was housed in a building that had originally been something else, in this case, an old bank, melding a unique architectural blend from the early 1900s with classic pub style MacIver, the owner, had brought with him from Scotland.

The walls were the original brick, and the exposed ductwork weaving across the high ceilings was painted black, causing it to feel more like part of architecture, rather than an eye sore.

Liv took a moment to take it all in while Quinn moved effortlessly through the high-top tables toward the long oak bar that took up one side of the building.

There were only a few people in the bar, most of them tucked into the highbacked booths that lined the wall opposite the bar. The dim lighting cast them in shadows.

Brighter lights hanging over pool tables beckoned a few patrons to them like moths to a flame. She could feel the gaze of a couple in one of the booths, but she ignored them, silently thanking the man sitting alone in the corner, who hadn't bothered looking at her at all.

The heel of her boots felt loud on the old wooden floor as she walked to sit at the bar beside Quinn. Her butt had barely hit the stool when the sound of pots and pans clattering against a hard surface, followed by an all too familiar voice yelling in Gaelic, cussing judging by the tone, filled the entire bar.

A second later the swinging double doors that led to the kitchen slapped open violently. A small woman with bright blonde hair and a handful of French fries sauntered out, completely unfazed by the tattoo-covered, bear of a man who followed right behind.

"Dammit Jade, you're a bloody curse on a kitchen! I've told you a million times—stay on *that* side of the bar!

Just looking at the two of them made her heart clench. The shame and guilt she carried for the way she'd left them, and the excitement she felt seeing them again, blended into a potent amalgam of feelings that twisted inside her stomach.

Even though he was easily a foot taller than her, the woman spun on him, causing him to halt abruptly to avoid running her over. "Well, maybe if you'd pick up the pace, I wouldn't have to come back there and take care of myself." She stood on her tippy toes and popped a French fry in her mouth.

The man's eyes narrowed as he leaned down toward her, "Trust me, Sunny, my pace is flawless. No one ever has to take care of themselves when I'm *serving* them. Clearly, you've never experienced what the *right* pace feels like." He stood up straight again, looking down at her. "Maybe that's why you're so comfortable *serving* yourself," he quipped, a self-satisfied grin creeping up his face.

The blonde's eyes flared as she turned away from him and landed right on Liv.

Trepidation and longing leaving her unsteady and unsure of how to navigate reintroduction after more than a decade, Liv stood slowly. Then with a reticent smile simply said, "I'm home."

It was a stupid thing to say and sounded more like a question than a greeting, but at least she'd spoken actual words. That was a win considering she was pretty sure her heart was currently in her throat.

Jade froze mid-step, a half-eaten fry hung from her lips and then slipped to the floor as a smile as bright as the sun spread across her gorgeous face. The woman was sunshine in the most deceivingly sweet package. Just like the sun, she emanated light—and if you weren't careful, she could incinerate you. Fierce to the end, something Liv had always loved about her.

"Well, fuckin' finally." *And apparently as...direct as ever.* "I was starting to take it personally that you hadn't come around yet." Jade moved so quickly that Liv barely had time to open her arms to catch her in the hug, which was over nearly as soon as it'd started. She could have held on for minutes longer but considered herself lucky to have been on the receiving end of even a moment of Jade's affection, however fleeting. Coconut and sea breeze lingered in her senses, the smell of summer and Jade no matter what time of year.

"I'm sor—" Liv's words cut off along with her air supply as Logan wrapped her in his arms, which were much more colorful and *much* more muscular than she remembered. He swept her off her feet and into a near-crushing bear hug that went on for several beats longer than Jade's had. The laugh she released got stuck in her collapsing lungs, then came out with a wheeze as Logan loosened his grip but didn't set her back down. He leaned back just enough to look at her face.

"Hi, Liv." The childlike smile on such a towering man was the best contradiction.

"Hi, Logan." Her own smile was growing by the second.

"I missed you."

"I missed you too." And she realized in that moment how true it was.

Liv laughed again as he squeezed her tightly once more before setting her back on her feet, but kept her close with his hands braced just above her hips. "You turned into a damn smoke show, you know that?"

Liv smiled, running a hand up Logan's arm. "These are new," she said, shifting the focus away from herself.

"Oh, yeah. You like?" Logan flexed.

"She meant the tattoos, not your biceps, you idiot."

He winked at Jade. "I knew you noticed them."

Jade just flipped him off as she walked to the bar and sat down on a stool beside Quinn and Mac, the owner of the bar and Logan's grandpa.

"Down boy." Quinn smiled, from where she perched on a barstool watching the reunion. "At least make her a drink before you try to get in her pants."

Logan slipped an arm over Liv's shoulders, brushed a kiss over the top of her head, and led her toward the bar. She took a seat on the other side of Jade, who dropped the remainder of her questionably procured French fries directly onto the bar top.

She bumped her shoulder into Liv's and leaned in conspiratorially. "I missed you too," she whispered.

Logan scooped up the fries, laying a napkin down, and setting them back on top in front of Jade, who didn't even seem to notice the act. "So, what can I getcha, love?" he asked, flipping a glass and setting it on the bar in front of her. "I make a mean margarita." Logan waggled his eyebrows at Liv like he knew it was the exact thing that would tempt her.

"Logan's margaritas are worth your time, and you can trust me because the last thing I want to do is give the fool a compliment. Lord knows his ego doesn't need the extra stroke."

"I will never get enough strokes from the likes of you, Jade Hawthorne."

"Oh, for fek's sake." Mac shook his head with a sigh and scowled into his whisky.

"What he said." Jade rolled her eyes before turning back to Liv.

"I'd love to guys, but if I don't get to the store before it closes, things are likely to turn cannibal in Havenhouse."

Logan waved a dismissive hand at her. "Go in the morning. I'll make you something to take home tonight. It will be a lot better than whatever you manage in that kitchen anyway. That takes care of all the excuses. So, what'll it be?" Logan batted his blue eyes at her, something she was certain worked wonders one hundred and ten percent of the time. She shook her head as the last bit of her resolve dissipated.

"Okay. Just one."

. . .

LOGAN WAS RIGHT ABOUT HIS MARGARITAS. THEY WERE AMAZING, WHICH
was why she had definitely not had "just one". She'd had—well, however
many it had taken for her to catch up on at least a few years of what she'd
missed. The highlight for her being that Jade had a daughter! She could
only imagine what a little Jade would be like.

Quinn was also undoubtedly the most effortlessly interesting person
she'd ever met. And had also definitely been the one behind the pigeon fly-
by, as they were now referring to it.

Over the past hour or two, she'd also picked up on the fact that something had changed between Logan and Jade. The banter between them was
charged, and not altogether friendly, especially on Jade's side. But she
didn't ask. It wasn't her place. She knew that just because they'd been
happy to see her, a few drinks and some laughs didn't mean she was entitled to slip back into her place with them.

She also hadn't asked either of them about Jax, despite how many
times she'd been tempted. Being with his sister and best friend made it
impossible not to wonder about him. But she had to assume the fact that
they also hadn't brought him up was intentional, so she continued to bite
her tongue and attempted to force him from her mind.

Logan set another drink in front of her. Each one had gotten fancier
than the last. This one was light purple with a cinnamon and sugar-crusted
rim with a sprig of lavender resting against the side of the coupe glass.

"Made this one up just for you. I think I'll call it the Garden Fairy."

"What the hell! I've been here for six months and I haven't had a drink
named for me!" Quinn complained.

"You've also been here for six months and I've yet to see yeh pay for a
single one of yer drinks, lass. It's a wonder this one's libido hasn't put us
out of business." Mac thrust his chin at Logan.

Liv laughed, her smile finally feeling like her own again.

"It's beautiful. But I should head home. Ivy will probably wonder
where I am." More likely she and the house were waging war against each
other, and Liv wouldn't have a house to return to at all.

"Uh-uh. Nice try lady, but you're staying, at least until you tell us what the hell you've been up to *for all these years.*" Jade raised an eyebrow.

Logan started to nod in agreement as his eyes shifted up beyond her, crinkling at the corners in a slight wince. Before she could turn to see what he was looking at, she was wrapped in the warmth of a magick that was familiar on a biological level. Her magick surged to the surface of her skin to meet it so suddenly it took her breath away.

"Yea Liv, *stay.*"

The rich timbre of his voice was so close, flowing warm and molten, settling into her skin before finally penetrating her mind. The familiar comfort of it evolved into recognition of who it belonged to.

Shit.

CHAPTER SIX

*I*t didn't matter how long it had been, how much older they were now. It didn't matter how much deeper and sexier it was—she would have known that voice a thousand feet underwater.

Which coincidentally was where she wished she was now. Somewhere dark, and far away, where she could get her bearings and be better prepared for this. Or just avoid it forever.

She didn't turn around, and everyone else seemed as frozen as she was. As if the tension brought on by the two of them being in the same room again was so thick it had trapped everyone in place.

The fear that prevented her from turning to face him was such a contradiction to how good it had felt for that fleeting moment before recognition dawned. She wanted to go back to that moment and bask in the comfort of it just a little longer.

"I'm not a monster under your bed, Liv. I'm not going to vanish just because you refuse to acknowledge my existence." The words were low and gentle but carried with them a commanding edge.

The cool mint of his breath on the back of her neck sent chills down her spine that had her straightening. She imagined how close he must be. She wasn't afraid *of him*, but to see him. She felt every memory she had, every image she'd conjured of him over the years, every thought of what he might be like now, teetering precariously at the edge of the moment, and it would all shatter the second she turned to face him and the choice she'd made.

Liv steeled herself, taking one last deep breath, exhaling every ounce of vulnerability she felt, and securing the mask she'd perfected over the years. The one that convinced everyone she was *fine*.

But she was not fine. The delicious smell of sunshine on Pine trees enveloped her as a large golden hand settled next to her leg on the bar stool, she watched his long fingers wrap around the edge, and both too slowly and all too quickly he turned her seat until she faced him.

Him.

She didn't have to force herself to look into those all too familiar light blue eyes, his pupils framed in a shock of yellow, lined in impossibly dark and unfairly long lashes.

He looked down at her, from well within her personal space, before taking a step back.

"Hi, Liv." His smile was mostly in his eyes.

"Hi, Jax." The words sounded more stable than she felt. The rest of the bar faded from focus, seeming to exist outside them.

"We'll just—" Logan didn't bother finishing his sentence as he gestured to their friends.

"Oh, come on, this was just getting interesting," Jade complained as she let Logan drag her farther down the bar. Quinn followed along, that same conspiratorial smirk curving her lips.

Mac didn't move, but he also didn't seem to notice anything outside his glass.

Liv hardly registered their movements, or anything else outside wherever Jax had pulled her into with his mere presence. She forced herself to sever the intense eye contact, instead searching his face for any sign of the boy she'd left behind in the man standing in front of her.

He had the same golden skin as his sister, but for all her light and bright, he was her counter. His hair was so dark it looked black, but she knew his short, wavy locks would reveal shades of oaky browns in the sun. Just the right amount of matching scruff lined a jaw that was more chiseled than she remembered.

His simple black t-shirt stretched taut across shoulders that were just as broad, but more muscular and filled out with age. The rest of him had followed suit, the outline of the well-muscled chest beneath his shirt led to a trim waist and long legs covered in dark denim.

A million words danced on the tip of her tongue, as she looked up at him. Apologies, explanations, excuses... but nothing that seemed right after so much time.

Slowly she slipped from the stool to her feet and, just to prove to herself that she could, without giving herself time to reconsider, closed the distance between them. She walked into his arms as if it were instinct.

His arms closed around her too easily as she folded herself into him. Her cheek still fit too perfectly into the hollow in his chest, right beside his heart. The steady rhythm beat beneath her ear, painfully familiar.

JAX'S HANDS ROSE LIKE MUSCLE MEMORY—ONE TO THE BACK OF HER neck, slipping under her dark hair she'd restrained into a braid that hung long down her back. The other slid up her back and instinctively pressed her against him.

Her scent filled the air and spun around him, every bit as painfully intoxicating as he remembered, and *fuck* did he remember.

He felt the silent breath she released seep through his shirt, skitter across his chest, and soak into his skin. He forced his eyes to remain open when they wanted to slam shut. He wanted to drown in her.

He'd already kept her in his space a few beats too long, indulging and losing himself for a moment. Everything he'd sworn he'd feel, sworn he wouldn't, sworn he'd say if he ever got the chance died right there as his treacherous body invited her in like an addict begging for another hit of its own self-destruction.

Jax slid his hands down to her arms and took a step back, removing himself from her one reluctant inch at a time, like he needed to separate himself from her in stages.

He'd known she was back since the moment she'd crossed the border into town—watched as she'd walked back into Havenhouse for the first time in so many years. But being this close to her, for the first time in so long...he was a fucking idiot for thinking this little reunion wouldn't affect him.

His eyes scanned the woman who had once been his girl, taking in every facet of her that had changed. The little details he could see being this close to her again. The angles of her face had sharpened, while the curve of her hips had softened.

But so much of her was still the same. The olive tone of her soft skin. The sharp v in her top lip, the pout of her plump bottom one. He swallowed as his mouth filled with the memory of their taste.

The scattering of freckles across her nose and cheeks had faded slightly but were still there, just below *those eyes*. The eyes that had captured him as a kid, and still held him captive. Still haunted his dreams.

It felt like the combination—the totality of her—had been custom-designed just for him. To inflict as much damage as possible.

"Alright. So, the little witch is home, the flowers are sing'n, no doubt. Now can someone get me some bloody whisky, or shall I be drinking all yer tears?" Mac's grumbling shattered the moment they'd been encased in.

Quinn laughed. "No need for that. I gotcha handsome." She patted his hand as she walked behind the bar.

Jade suddenly appeared beside him and Liv, slipping an arm around each of their waists. Her excited eyes bounced between them. "So, are we all friends again, then?" Jade smiled too brightly, feigning like she didn't know she was being a little shit. He ignored his sister as Liv's eyes came back to his, something shimmering in their malachite depths, but an unfamiliar mask closed down over the openness he'd gotten a brief glimpse of. His shoulders stiffened and irritation sparked at seeing how easily she slipped it on.

"Yeah, of course. Friends." Liv smiled at Jade.

It was tight-lipped and the fakest damn thing he'd ever seen on her. It was gasoline on the spark of irritation that now flared in his chest hearing that word come out of her mouth. *Friends*? Was that what she'd reduced them to over the years? One flippant word. He was grateful for the burn—it shook him from the momentary lapse she'd tempted him into.

She could think of them as friends if that made her feel better. But in his experience with *friends,* as far as he knew, they usually didn't disappear in the middle of the night without a goodbye, and without a word for years on end. He had the strong urge to call her out, but it shouldn't, *didn't* he corrected himself, matter to him either way. He swallowed it down, with the heat from his chest crawling up his throat.

"So, Liv." Logan swooped in, placing a hand on the small of her back and guiding her back into her chair. "How is that batty old house treating you?" he asked, settling his elbows on the oak top bar, once behind it again. He should be grateful to his friend for lightening the energy in the room, but instead, all he felt was irritation at the casual contact between them.

JAX HAD BEEN LEANING AGAINST THE WALL NURSING A BEER FOR THE LAST two hours. He'd spent approximately one hour and fifty-eight minutes of that time internally threatening himself for a list of shit that all had to do with how he felt being near Liv. Watching the way the lacy edge of the silky black top she wore slid across her skin when she moved, was at the top of that list.

His mood had continued to descend as he'd witnessed her relaxing in the company of his sister and friends. Quinn may not have had cause for caution, but what about Logan and Jade? How was it so easy for them to welcome her back into the fold like she hadn't left them behind too? Jade would probably say he was brooding, but luckily for him, she was occupied.

He'd only been able to pry his eyes off of Liv for the last two minutes because he'd been monitoring the verbal sparring match his sister and Logan had decided to start, or resume most likely, on the other side of the bar.

"Uh-oh, looks like Tyson and Holyfield are at it again. Should someone break that up?" Quinn slid onto the barstool next to him. "Not it!"

He couldn't tell what they were saying, but judging by the look on Jade's face, Logan had dared breathe wrong in her direction. "As long as there's no blood, it's best not to get involved. Not worth the risk of losing a limb." He sipped his room-temperature beer without taking his eyes off them.

It hadn't always been like that between the two of them, but it had been for a long time. He'd been wrong for thinking it would stop once Jade got married. There had been a tentative truce, but that had only lasted as long as they were able to avoid each other, which wasn't long in a small town. Logan had softened when Cori came along. But lately, it seemed worse than ever.

If Logan were anyone else, if he didn't trust him so much, this shit wouldn't have gotten past the first minute. But he'd decided a long time ago to stay out of their bullshit as much as possible.

"What was it your dad used to say?" Her proximity caught him off guard, his body threatening to stiffen. *Everywhere.*

"They're like pit bulls, once their jaws are locked, the only thing you can do is wait for them to wear each other out?"

"Yeah, something like that," he said without daring to look at her. Just the casual mention of *before* ignited a riot of emotions in him. He'd had enough sorting through emotions in the last few days to last him the rest of his life. It was irritating. It was bullshit.

Jade made an abrupt break for the door, and Logan made the mistake of grabbing her wrist. Jade turned slowly, looking down at where Logan held her.

Liv winced. "That was probably a poor choice."

Dammit. Was her voice going to do that to him every time?

Jax pushed off the wall, taking a step in their direction. If Jade said anything, Jax couldn't tell, but whatever happened ended in Logan letting her go and throwing his arms up in defeat. They stormed off in opposite directions, and Jade was out the door immediately.

Logan chucked a dish towel on the ground before slamming both of his large hands into the swinging double doors and vanishing into the kitchen.

There was some banging of pots and pans then suddenly Logan reappeared. "We're closed!" he bellowed, before disappearing again. The few patrons seated at the bar murmured to each other, unsure what to do.

"Now!" He hadn't even bothered to come out for that one, but it did the trick. The few people left at the bar started moving.

"I think I'll go close out some tabs so Logan's tantrum doesn't bankrupt the place." Quinn hopped off the stool, kissed Jax quickly on the cheek, and then pulled Liv into a quick tight hug. "So glad to finally meet you, Liv." She said it with a genuine smile. And then she was gone, navigating tables quickly to stop the few patrons who'd been drinking at the bar before they left without paying.

Liv blinked a few times. They'd all gotten used to Quinn's affection over the last several months, but it had been a bit jarring to them at first too.

The awareness of the two of them being alone for the first time settled on his shoulders. He leaned back against the wall again. Sipping that same, now warm beer. It tasted like shit, but he needed something to do.

Liv moved in his peripheral vision. She pulled at the hem of her shirt that didn't quite reach the top of her tight denim jeans. The sliver of olive skin that peeked between had been fucking with his mind for the last two hours. "Does she work here?" Jax shifted his jaw. Small talk. That's where they were now. She felt awkward in the silence of his presence. That had never been a thing between them. But maybe that was to be their new normal.

"Sometimes."

Liv's eyes narrowed on him slightly. She glanced at Quinn who was coaxing what money she could out of some of Mac's drinking buddies.

"Okay. Well, I guess I should probably get going too." Her eyes came back to him. He evaded the green vortex that kept threatening to suck him in and gave her a tight nod.

"Bye, Jax." He only heard the sad smile in her voice, because he couldn't make himself watch her walk away from him again. Even if it was only out the door this time.

CHAPTER SEVEN

*S*he wasn't quite sure how to classify how her night had gone.

She'd run endless scenarios in her head of what it might be like the first time she saw him again. She'd done her best to be prepared for his anger, his venom, even his questions. Some of them, at least. She'd built walls around her heart over the last decade. They'd gotten her through so much, so she trusted them to guard her from the many different scenarios she'd imagined.

She knew why she'd left and that she'd done the right thing. Just like she knew he wouldn't understand and that it wouldn't make a difference. To him.

But the way he'd looked at her that first moment. The way he'd pulled her into him. Leave it to Jax to do the one thing she'd never have expected, never could have prepared for. He'd taken a battering ram to her carefully laid defenses. Then, as quickly as he'd pulled her in, he'd pushed her out again. He'd gone from, "Yeah, Liv stay," all broody and sexy like, to, well, to nothing.

"Ugh." He'd been so hot and then gone cold on her. Maybe she deserved it. But it was messy, so messy, and something she didn't have the energy to work out.

She walked through the deserted Glen back toward her house. She'd forgotten how quiet the town became once the businesses closed. Mac's seemed like the only place that stayed open after dark.

Her eyes drifted closed as she let the smell of the sea and pine trees mix and soothe her. She didn't need to see to find her way—muscle memory took over. She smiled when the leaves of a low-hanging branch brushed her cheek and her magick pressed against her skin in recognition of the tree's energy.

Alone, she sighed and let out a small tendril. The leaves of the trees around her rustled, the energy in them dancing over her skin and forcing a laugh out of her. All of the trees shuddered in unison, shaking loose dry leaves from the canopy above her. She turned in a slow circle letting them drift down around her. It felt like she was in her own little snow globe.

The tension left Liv's body, distracted by how the trees reacted when she let a little more of her magick slide out. It felt good…almost too good. "At least you're all happy I'm back," she whispered to the trees as she started walking again. Another branch slid across her skin. And then another and another. "Okay, okay. Hands to yourselves." She gently batted them away.

She was sure that the tequila was probably aiding in the feeling, and though she'd never fully understand her mother's choice to drown in alcohol, she came a little closer to maybe understanding why she'd started. Her brain felt quiet, her body light, almost like she could escape herself for just a little bit. Her mom had taken it far beyond that, though, to a place where control didn't exist. A state Liv had no interest in visiting.

Tall lamp posts dotted between houses, their flames' steady glow casting long shadows that seemed to dance rhythmically under her feet as she passed under them. She moved a little more into their light as the feeling of another's presence slowly moved up her spine. She ignored it for a few steps, forcing herself to maintain her casual pace.

But the feeling only grew stronger, chafing against the skin on her shoulders and neck. She glanced behind her, hoping it was something as innocent as someone else walking around at night. It was nearly ten, late but not so late it was impossible for someone else to be out. The idea that someone may have seen her playing with the trees in the Glen caused a flicker of anxiety. But no one was there.

She started walking again, rolling her eyes at herself. This was Haven-wood. Even if someone did see her it wouldn't be the end of the world. And no one was following her. It was probably nothing more than her own body reacting to the use of her magick.

The crunch of gravel was unmistakable. Her heart started to pound a little quicker in her chest as she picked up her pace. She didn't look back this time. The peace of the quiet town morphed into an eerie silence, broken by the distant echo of scuffing.

Liv's footsteps sounded like a drumbeat as her senses heightened. She drew her magick up. It pulsed an erratic staccato under her skin.

She fought to wrangle it into order, telling herself her mind was playing tricks on her, but with another glance over her shoulder again, her body prepared to take off in a run.

She pushed forward—and collided face-first into a solid wall. Before she could ricochet off and hit the ground, warm hands caught her.

She registered Jax's face, but it was a moment too late. Her unsteady magick had already burst out of her. Jax pulled her into his side, turning his body to take the brunt of her magickal assault on his opposite shoulder.

"Shit," he grunted. Every muscle in his body tensed and flexed around her as he held her tucked to his side with one arm. Liv searched his face, trying to gauge how much pain he was in, her skin prickling with a combi-nation of magick and adrenaline, quickly being replaced by regret and embarrassment.

Her magick was tied to the Earth below her, and that ability to draw energy from it was the only reason she'd been able to lash out like that without preparation. She hadn't thought she'd put so much power behind the blow, but she was rusty and afraid. Not a good combo.

He was in one piece, but her stomach bottomed out with the pain she saw in his rigid jaw. The muscle there feathered as he clenched his teeth and squeezed his eyes shut. Her adrenaline crashed into fear that she'd done real damage.

Then his eyes snapped open, and even in the dark, his blazing blue gaze was bright, drilling right into her. They stood like that for a moment, his warmth seeping into her and the smell of him mixing with the salty air working in tandem, coaxing her haphazard heartbeat back into a familiar rhythm.

Liv started to apologize, but then stopped, realizing he'd been the one following her. She pushed herself free from the cocoon of muscle Jax had locked her in. Then she shoved his chest with both hands for good measure. "What the hell Jax!" Not only did he not budge, but he had the audacity to look confused. Probably just to infuriate her further. "Are these kind of mood swings usual for you now? Spirit, save me! We are way too old for games, and that wasn't even funny." Liv resisted the urge to punctuate her anger by hitting him again, but like the first hit, it would only serve to harm her pride rather than him.

Jax inspected his shoulder. The t-shirt was singed in a few places, which probably didn't bode well for the skin underneath. She looked away.

"I agree. This isn't funny. But I'm the one bleeding. *You* attacked *me*. So, what. The hell. Are you talking about?"

Bleeding? Shit. Instinctually her body moved toward him to check the damage, then pulled up short. *Mad. Not concerned,* she scolded herself. "Well, that's on you for following me around in the dark and playing stupid games. I get that you're mad at me or hate me or whatever. I'm sorry I'm back in *your* town. But I have too much to deal with to add a stalker ex-boyfrie—"

"Shh." Jax cut her off.

She felt her eyes widen. *Oh hellll no.* Liv spun on her heels, stomping off toward her house. "Are you serious? Everyone in this town may bend the damn knee to you, Jaxon Hawthorne, but that has never and will never—"

Moving faster than Liv could react, Jax pulled her back into him. He grabbed the back of her neck when she resisted, forcing her to look at him and stunning her into silence. "Dammit, Dandy, will you be quiet? I wasn't following you. But that doesn't mean someone else wasn't," he hissed urgently.

She was momentarily frozen by his use of her old nickname and the feel of his lips against her ear. Then the sensation of a sticky unfamiliar magick slid over her skin and snapped her right out of it.

THE ROAR OF AN ENGINE KICKED UP FAST, BUT IT WAS ALREADY FADING before Jax could try to place it within town. The lanterns surrounding them flickered in a way he'd never seen before—in a way that shouldn't be possible—just as the sound of the motorcycle engine disappeared completely.

He didn't loosen his hold on Liv, and he didn't miss that she didn't try to break free immediately. Or the fact that she'd pressed in closer to him when she'd sensed the unfamiliar magick. Or how her body relaxed faintly in his hold.

A bright light cut across their faces. Liv all but launched out of his arms, pulling at her clothes that were already perfectly in place.

"Jaxon Randolph Hawthorne, is that you?"

"Randolph?" Liv's eyebrows pinched together.

That was definitely not his middle name. He couldn't see the woman against the megawatt flashlight she had fixed on them, but he knew who the croaky voice belonged to.

"Yes Mrs. Dottie, it's me," Jax answered, not taking his eye off Liv.

She shifted the light off their faces. The elderly woman stood under the light of her porch in a...yeah, that was a leopard print nightgown. He was never going to be able to unsee that.

"What are you doing out so late? What's going on out there? You've got Diesel all riled up and ready for an attack."

A little white puff of fur stood at her feet, its whole body swaying with the speed of its wagging tail. *Ferocious.*

"It's barely past ten o'clock," Liv mumbled under her breath.

The light swung over to Liv. "Who's that with you?"

Liv winced, shielding her eyes. "Hi, Mrs. Dottie, it's me, Liv... Terrabella."

"Oh, Olivia!" The old woman's voice turned markedly sweeter, no doubt smelling gossip in the night air. "I heard you were back. Welcome home, dear. I'm sorry to hear about your mother, have you imbued her ashes at the tree yet?"

Liv's mouth opened and then closed again, as she floundered for a response.

"Sorry, we woke you up, Mrs. Dottie. We'll be on our way so you and…Diesel, can get back to bed." Jax effectively ended the conversation before they inadvertently gave Mrs. Dottie any extra ammo.

The old woman eyed them, suspicion crossing her face. Then with a nod, she and her guard dog disappeared back into her house. The porch light flickered off, plunging them into near darkness again.

Jax pulled his phone out, sending off a quick message before slipping it back into the pocket of his jeans. "Told you I wasn't the one following you," he said, unable to keep from running his gaze down her body again as he walked past.

Someone *had* been following her, though. He heard Liv run a few steps to catch up with him. "Well, who the hell was it?" she demanded.

He shrugged, unsure. Why her? What did they want? What would they have done if he hadn't been there? He added all of those to the list of questions he didn't have answers for. He hadn't sensed anyone else when he'd slipped out of the bar less than a minute after her, too distracted watching her playing with her magick and the trees to notice anything else. And that distraction had put her in danger.

Danger she should have been able to get herself out of easily if her magick wasn't so covered in metaphorical dust and cobwebs.

"Come on."

She planted her feet and crossed her arms. It made her look like a child refusing to get out of the middle of the street. "Not until you tell me where we're going."

"Home. If that's okay with you, I mean?"

"But…shouldn't we go tell the cops or something?"

"The cops?" She really didn't remember where she was. "You mean Harlan? Or Grady O'Conner? And what exactly do you want to tell them? Even if I had something, you and I both know there isn't much they can do about anything that goes on in this town that has to do with magick. Or your fear of the dark."

That did the trick. He'd started walking while he spoke, and she moved on quick frustrated feet to catch up with him. "First of all, I'm not afraid of the dark." The words came out too defensive for him to fight his knowing smirk. "And did you just say Grady O'Conner is a deputy now?"

He raised a brow in confirmation as she settled into step beside him. He could see her mind trying to reconcile the version of Grady who still hadn't hit puberty at sixteen when she'd last seen him, with someone able to hold a position within law enforcement.

She was quiet for the length of a couple of houses. He could practically feel her mind swirling. It kept her from noticing when he slowed the pace of his steps down, and let himself indulge in the way the light from the lanterns played across her skin, highlighting the freckles that dotted her nose. He told himself it was a distraction from the pain in his shoulder.

"What are we going to do then?" Her question shattered the moment.

"We? Nothing." Two simple words...but he saw how they landed.

HE WAS SHUTTING DOWN ON HER.

She couldn't blame him. She knew she needed to find a way to clear the air between them now that she was back. It was the mature thing to do. Even if they couldn't find a way to be friends, at least they wouldn't have this *thing* hanging over them.

His muscles shifted under his clothes as they walked, his stride long and unhurried, two of hers matching each one of his. Every time they passed under a streetlamp it seemed to highlight the parts of *her* Jax that still existed, layered in perfectly with this grown version of him.

He was gorgeous in a way that forced her to hold in a sigh.

But he wasn't hers anymore—something she needed to remind herself as she continued to refer to the younger version of him as *her* Jax in her head. Even there it wasn't safe to claim him because this version of him, the one walking next to her...no part of him belonged to her anymore.

He stopped walking, and she realized they'd made it to her house without her noticing. He'd walked her home, and whatever that made her feel, she told herself it was just nostalgia messing with her head again.

She mustered the courage to face him again, but all she got was a flick of his chin toward her house. A dismissal. She knew he'd stand there, though, hands in his pockets, and make sure she got inside like he'd done a hundred times before.

"Jax, I..." She'd opened her mouth intending to apologize, but the singed holes in his shirt and the look on his stony face stole her nerve. "What did you mean when you said Harlan couldn't do much about *anything* going on in town? What's going on in town?"

Jax looked down at the street and then up at the stars above them. "Nothing."

Nothing? "Clearly, you meant *something.*"

"Yeah, maybe I did. It's nothing for you to worry about. I've got it under control." Jax reached out toward the iron front gate of her house. It swung open into his hand like the treacherous house was on his side. Liv's hand shot out instinctively, half covering his as she tried unsuccessfully to push it closed.

"Whatever it is, I deserve to know. This is my town, too."

A bitter smirk formed on his lips, as he shook his head incredulously.

Oops. That had definitely been the wrong thing to say.

Jax stepped so close she had to crane her neck to look up at him. His smirk dropped away. "Your town? Is that what this is?" The intensity in his eyes was unnerving and didn't match the calm tone of his voice at all.

She refused to show him the way it affected her. "Yeah, it is. It never stopped being my town. I just..."

"Just what? What the hell did you come back here for, Liv?"

It was such a simple question. And there was a simple answer she could give him: she hadn't had anywhere else to go. But that was only a half-truth.

"That's what I thought," Jax scoffed, and pulled his hand out from under hers. He gestured toward her house in dismissal.

"Be an ass if you want to, but I don't owe you or anyone an explanation for coming back to *my home*. Keep your secrets. I have enough crap to deal with."

Jax's tight-lipped smile was one she'd never seen before. "I will. And I'm sure you do," he said, then gripped her by her upper arms and lifted her off the ground like she weighed nothing. Liv gasped, unable to react before he set her firmly on her feet inside the fence line, and within the wards of her house. He turned away then, his long strides taking him toward the charming little craftsman across the street.

"Where are you going?" Liv yelled after him.

"Home!" He didn't bother looking back as he climbed the porch steps of the house directly across from hers.

"What?"

"I'm going home, Liv. Into my house."

She stood in silence for a moment as realization dawned and her stomach flipped.

"Oh, you can't be serious." She brushed roughly at a few errant strands of hair that had fallen from her braid. "Jax! Are you serious?

"Goodnight, *neighbor!*" was his only confirmation before disappearing into the shadows of his porch.

Jax lived across the street from her. Every day she'd been back, he'd been right there. The whole time.

"GOODNIGHT, *NEIGHBOR*," HE SAID, TURNING HIS BACK ON HER TO WALK UP the few steps to the porch of the place he'd bought a year before. At the time he'd beat himself up for being fanciful and romantic, but his better judgment always lost to his masochistic tendencies, at least when it came to her.

Now Jax patted himself on the back, though, because her little outburst when she'd realized she'd be living across the street from him told him something important.

She still cared enough to be pissed.

And he'd take her anger over her indifference any day.

He opened his front door like he was going to go in, then paused until he heard the slamming of hers.

From the safe distance of his porch, he allowed his magick to reach out and around her house, to check the wards he'd put on it years ago and had maintained since he'd been back. Then he went inside and climbed the stairs to his bedroom, crossing directly to the large window that looked out over hers. He told himself he was just going to close the curtains. At some point, he'd give up lying to himself.

Jax stood at the window, watching her make her way through the old house, lights clicking on and off, marking her progress toward her room. When the light in the front window over the library clicked on, he couldn't help but smile. He would have bet his substantial net worth that she'd choose the comfort of her old room over the available master. It didn't surprise him. And that realization, that maybe he still knew her, somehow didn't either.

He watched Liv's shadow move around her room as she got ready for bed. She passed the window, letting her long hair down. He warred with himself when he saw her reach for the hem of her shirt. The image of that sliver of olive skin rushed back to haunt him.

Every part of him went rigid, making it impossible for him to move away from the window.

He was relieved from having to either gouge his eyes out or become a peeping tom when she moved out of direct sight again. But he stayed rooted, hypnotized by her shadow as it moved around the room, tempting him, and stirring images and memories of her body.

When her light finally clicked off, he groaned in both relief and agony. Sleeping across the street from her was going to be a new kind of torture.

He gave her window one last glance, just in time to see a lone candle on her windowsill spark to life. Then he made a mental note to get her some curtains that weren't sheer.

CHAPTER EIGHT

*S*mall particles of dust sparkled in the sporadic spotlights of sunshine that passed through the newer panes of glass in the greenhouse. She avoided walking through them as she moved from the shelves back to the workbench, not wanting to interrupt their slow descent.

Liv set one of her Grammy's small tins on the workbench next to the fragrant oil steaming in a small cauldron. She stirred the enfleurage clockwise three times and then gently scooped the remnants of Rosemary, Eucalyptus, Myrrh and Sandalwood out of the oil and set them aside.

Her own principles about magick, the same ones she taught to Ivy time and again, had driven her out here. It was the right thing to do. Her magick had caused the mess, and, like the adult she was, she would be the one to clean it up.

Even if she had spent most of the morning trying to rationalize that he'd been the one to scare *her*. So, one could argue it was actually *his* fault.

She knew that logic was flawed. Even if he'd been an ass, her fickle mind challenged, and though it wasn't her job to worry about him. *Her* magick had done the damage to his shoulder. She winced. She really needed to stop thinking about his shoulders.

Maybe she'd just leave it on his doorstep…he'd know what it was for. And he'd know who it was from. Which was fine. Because they were adults. She wasn't avoiding him. She was respecting his space. Yeah, that was it.

Space he'd made significantly tighter by moving into the house across the street from her. What was she even supposed to make of that?

Probably nothing, considering she wasn't living in her house at the time, and hadn't given any indicator she'd ever be returning.

None of it mattered. Whether he lived across the street or two streets away like he had growing up, eventually they'd learn how to go about life as neighbors. Like adults. *Did real adults need to assert their adultness this much?*

She mixed a heavy-handed pour of the fragrant oil with the melted beeswax in the tin and left it to solidify, still not convinced she would ever take it over to Jax.

The sun had only been up for a few hours and the late summer air was already warm. It made Liv think of bonfires, tan lines, and cold seawater on warm skin as she wandered deeper into the wild parts of the gardens in search of more herbs and flowers.

After abandoning the salve, still unsure if she'd put it to use, she'd decided to go foraging for herself.

She'd had another nightmare last night. Really, the only justification she had for calling them nightmares was the dread they instilled in her. The images were never more than veins of darkness swirling in the shadows of her mind, but she was always left feeling like somehow the sightless darkness was watching her, touching her with invisible fingers. The impression of dense inky magick that she couldn't quite feel lingered vaguely inside her when she woke, unease clinging to her.

She'd added a small pouch of Rosemary, Thyme, and Mugwort under her pillow—that had been the most magick she'd been willing to try outside of Havenwood. It was becoming clear that she needed something stronger.

She'd felt Jax's magick sliding over her house shortly after she'd slipped the useless pouch under her pillow last night. It had caught her by surprise after their *encounter*—she wouldn't call it an argument, because that implied a familiarity she wasn't sure existed between them anymore. But feeling his magick settle into the wards that reached around her house had momentarily taken her breath away. And also confused the shit out of her.

The house, on the other hand, had shivered like it enjoyed the touch of Hawthorne magick strengthening the wards, preening under the fortification, welcoming a magick that hadn't even created it in the first place. Like the two were old friends. Which, in some ways, she guessed they were.

The gentle energy in the soil beneath her bare feet eased the remnants of anxiety the dream had left in her body. Waves crashed against the cliffs in the distance, the sound washing away the cycle of overthinking in her mind.

She focused on the crunch of dried leaves beneath her feet, some from the slow change of the season and some withered from abandonment.

Liv was surprised it wasn't in worse condition. She couldn't help but wonder if Jax's magick was somehow responsible for that too. As a Balancer, he was able to tap into any of the elements, including Earth. The realization that he'd warded her house with her inside was more than enough for her to wrap her brain around. But the idea that he'd think to care for her garden made her feel things in her body that her mind was too wise to acknowledge.

The nettle plant she'd been looking for was wilted when she found it, drying at the tips of the leaves, decay slowly spreading through it. She knelt in front of the plant and used a knife she'd carried out with her to prick her finger, letting a small amount of her blood drip into the depths of the plant. A small offering.

She didn't need it to bring the plant back to a healthy state but for now, it was all she had to offer. It felt wrong to take from it without giving something in return. The brown tips of the leaves fanned out into a lush deep green, and the rest of the plant filled out and expanded with health.

She used the knife to cut cleanly through a few small stems, carefully navigating the plant to avoid the sting of it. "Thank you," she whispered.

The garden woke to her presence as she continued weaving her way through it. Flowers opened as she brushed her hands over them and vines wound around her ankles in gentle hugs. Tree branches reached toward her, caressing her cheeks and arms, sighing in relief that they could finally rest into their natural rhythms of growth, and *thrive* rather than strain under the burden of merely surviving.

A sentiment she understood too well.

Liv only stopped when she felt the creep of weariness that came from sharing so much of herself with them. She owed them much more, but she'd have to pace herself. The flora surrounding her seemed to know it too, as they welcomed her deeper, shifting to create a path for her, but refraining from drawing on her. "I won't make you wait long," she promised the rest of the garden.

When she reached the edge of a small clearing, she stopped. Liv had been planning to come to this place since she'd come home but hadn't brought herself to do it yet. The plants had guided her here without her even realizing it.

A large Blackthorne tree stood at the center of the small clearing. Vines crept along the forest floor toward the tree, weaving themselves around it, thriving despite the thick, hard thorns that covered it.

Blackthorne, back more, mind the bite but beware the bark more.

Valeria's voice chimed in the distant recesses of Liv's mind as she regarded the stalky tree covered in beautiful white flowers. "Deceiving little beauty, aren't you?"

While the tree itself wasn't poisonous, it was covered in long, hard thorns, dubious in their own right, no doubt. But that was nothing compared to the bacteria that coated the bark, known to cause all kinds of trouble once upon a time. Hence the rhyme, a tool Valeria had often used to teach Liv the properties of the plants and species that dwelled in the expansive and wild gardens.

It was just like her grandmother to have such a plant. Not because of its uses but its history.

In the 16th century, the thorns of the Blackthorne had come to be associated with the Devil, and not long after, the Church had denounced it. A bush. It was soon associated with witches and, creative as they were, witch hunters had begun using the wood of Blackthorne trees for their pyres when they'd burned the so-called witches to death.

Liv almost laughed. Not at the history she'd pulled from memory, which wasn't at all funny, but rather how simply *Valeria* it was to have one growing in her garden. Leave it to her to take something like the rumor of the women in their family and rather than dispel it, lean into it fully.

Her mom had hated the tree simply for existing.

Liv, however, saw something different in the tree. The winter berries.

For anyone willing to take the time to get past the thorns and rumors, the tree offered a harvest of beautiful and delicious berries, completely worth the effort. To the right person, anyway. Most people never bothered to take the time, or the risk.

Not even Valeria or Elena. Which was just another example of her landing somewhere between the two women.

Growing up, her grandmother's approach to living had been the thing she'd most admired about the matriarch of their family. The freedom that came with not caring what anyone thought, the fierce independence, calm grounding, and unshakable confidence that could only come from true self-acceptance.

Her mother, on the other hand, had hated it. Having spent so much time alone in recent years, Liv had come to better understand her mother's desperate need to fit in and be accepted.

Ironically, it was the two women's opposing views that fed into the other's stubbornness, and the shitstorm that was their relationship. As well as the dark cloud over a large part of Liv's childhood.

The prouder and more obvious Valeria had been with her magick, the more Elena had grown to despise her own, what little she had. She'd resented her mother and overcompensated to fit in.

And the more that Elena had tried to blend in and reject her heritage and her mother, the more Valeria leaned into the very quirks that fed the rumor mill, which inevitably bled back into Elena's life.

Round and round the two had gone, spinning their family into a cyclone, neither pausing long enough to realize that while focusing on defending themselves and harming each other, they had sucked Liv in and trapped her in the dizzying eye of their storm. Years spent constantly having to choose between embracing her magick with Valeria and blending in the way her mom would have preferred, always having someone to disappoint, no matter what she did.

After her grandmother had died and they'd left Havenwood, it had been a hard decision for Liv to tuck her magick away. But she'd done it anyway. The last thing she'd wanted was to give Ivy a seat on the generational merry-go-round of mother and daughter fighting over magick.

The memory of the night they left Havenwood felt like a labyrinth of impossible decisions she'd had to make seemingly all at once. Seeing Jax for the first time in so long had brought the weight of those choices crashing back. But it didn't change the fact that she knew she would make the same choice again—for Ivy. Every time. Just like she knew Jax would never understand.

Abandoning the tree and the memories attached, Liv moved deeper into the secluded area of the gardens, stroking her fingers lightly over the blooms of pokeweed, foxglove, and daffodils. She could feel the warmth of the morning sun growing in intensity, but also the coming of fall on the cool breeze.

It was much too late in the year for any of these flowers to be in bloom —but then again, most of the plants in the garden weren't native to California or suited for the climate at all. Liv worked her toes into the earth under her bare feet, knowing that the magick of her ancestors literally wove through it, making all the impossible around her possible.

She stopped again before the ancient Weeping Willow, watching the dappled sunlight moving through the swaying branches as their leaves slid across the ground in the breeze. It was the guardian over the final resting place for all Terrabellas. The place where they had laid her grandmother's ashes. The place where they needed to lay their mother, as Mrs. Dottie had reminded her last night.

She'd tried broaching the subject with Ivy, once shortly after they'd gotten to Havenwood, and then again this morning in the brief time before Ivy had run out the front door, headed to the coffee shop. Both times she'd blown Liv off.

The curtain of draping branches parted for her, inviting her into the seclusion beneath its canopy. A single marble bench sat at the foot of the thick, gnarled trunk.

Valeria had brought her here on several occasions to bless the ground and honor their ancestors. She'd drilled into Liv that she shouldn't mourn those who'd gone before her. That it was a gift for the witches who'd been lain there, to return to that from which they'd come.

She just wasn't sure her mother would feel the same way.

Liv tried not to resent having to make yet another decision she wasn't equipped to make, alone. She tried and failed.

CHAPTER NINE

*L*iv jolted awake at the sound of a loud slap of wood on wood, followed by the melodic tinkling of the bells hanging from the front door. She sat up on the green velvet chaise in the library trying to make sense of her surroundings and to figure out how she'd gone from sorting through old books and dusting, to sleeping for—judging by the shadows stretching across the library floor—at least a couple hours.

She was just beginning to make sense of the sound that had woken her up when she heard Ivy's feet pounding across the floor overhead. Liv hopped up off the chaise to beat her sister to the door, nearly colliding with her as she flew off the last step of the staircase.

They both saw the old broom that usually leaned in a corner by the front door lying across the foyer.

"People!"

"Crap!"

Their words, vastly different, came in unison. The excitement on Ivy's face was in direct opposition to how Liv felt.

She raised her hands to stop her sister from racing to the front door.

"Wait!" She looked over her shoulder at the door and then back to her sister. "Wait." Liv reduced her voice to a whisper.

Ivy's eyebrows shot up in question. "Why?" she whispered back, most likely mocking her.

"Just let me see who it is first." Liv went into the library in the front corner of the house and climbed onto the window seat that followed the curve of the room. Slowly she slid just enough of the curtain back to see who it was. Scanning the front gardens, the path cutting between them and the sidewalk beyond, she saw no one. The only thing that caught her eye was the front gate that hung open. That had just moved to the top of her list of things to be fixed.

"Hi, I'm Ivy."

Dammit! Liv spun around, letting the curtain fall back into place as she launched herself off the window seat.

Ivy stood in the doorway, a bright smile on her face. Every self-preservation precaution Liv had driven into her little sister over the years, had gone in a blink. Yanking the handle out of Ivy's hand, Liv pulled the door open wide enough to fit herself halfway in front of her sister.

A woman who looked to be in her early forties with short dark hair stood on their porch, a piece of paper clutched in her hand. The fluttering edge of the paper betrayed the slight shaking of the woman's body, and though Liv didn't recognize her, she had a feeling the woman knew all about them. Or thought she did anyway.

The woman's eyes roamed over her and Ivy, before slowly lifting to bounce between theirs. She still hadn't said anything.

"Can we help you with something?" Liv asked.

The woman jolted slightly as if startled. "Emma, my name's Emma." The woman blurted the words.

Ivy's brows drew together, "Uh, are you ok?"

"I...you really are Terrabellas, aren't you?" Her voice cracked with a hint of disbelief, but it felt more like an accusation. Liv squared her shoulders, refusing to show any shame over her heritage no matter what some people in town whispered about them.

She stepped a little closer to the woman, placing herself further in front of Ivy. "Yes," she answered curtly, "is there something we can do for you?"

Emma swallowed and then looked down at the paper in her hand. She lifted it, pressing it to her stomach and running a palm over the sheet in an attempt to smooth the places where she'd crumpled it in her grip. Then she held it up, turning it to show them. "My husband. He's missing. He's been leaving town on and off for a while now, not telling me where he's going. But only for a night or two. He hasn't been home in a week, and I just need to know where he is. I, I was…maybe…" She fumbled over her words, stuttering. "Can you help me find him?"

The shake in the woman's voice was disturbing. Had the myths about them spiraled that much over the years? She was acting as if she were afraid of them. Needlessly. But then, the wariness—that was putting it nicely in some cases—some held for her family was never rooted in fact. At least not the kind that came with any sort of real proof.

That had been the line her Grammy had always whispered to her. She could see the conspiratorial humor dancing in her eyes like she was right in front of her.

"Oh, no. I'm so sorry!"

"We are both very sorry to hear that he's missing." Liv agreed, stopping Ivy before she could continue. "But we've only been here a couple of days. I'm not sure how…" Liv let her words trail off as Emma began shaking her head. She reached into her pocket and pulled something out.

"No. I mean I want you to *find* him." Emma opened her palm, revealing a small vile of deep red liquid.

"Uh, what is that?" Ivy's face scrunched, telling Liv she knew exactly what it was.

Blood. His. Why this woman had a vial of her husband's blood, Liv didn't want to know. But she did know exactly what she wanted them to do with it.

"Uhhh, yeaahhh. I am starting to understand your aversion to opening the door," Ivy whispered from the corner of her mouth.

Emma locked her eyes on Liv's. "Please."

"I'm sorry, we can't help you that way." Liv started to close the door.

"He's a witch, too. Not like you, and he wasn't sure which line, he only has a little in him, but maybe it would be enough?" Emma's voice gained a desperate edge.

Ivy softened, the porch light reflected off her bright mismatched eyes.

"Maybe we could try something?" she hedged, looking up at Liv, guilt lining the dainty features of her face.

But Liv couldn't give in to Ivy or Emma. People from Havenwood didn't go missing. Which meant he'd left, and if he did have magick and didn't want to be found, there was more than a good chance he wouldn't be. Which was most likely why this woman was standing on their front porch despite her obvious fear, rather than any of the other witches in town.

The blood would be her best chance at finding him, but blood magick wasn't played with. At least not anymore. Not openly. Because even in a town like Havenwood, where magick wasn't a secret and everyone was aware of how and why the town was founded, certain magick had been cast in a dubious light. One that made people uncomfortable.

Emma fidgeted with the neck of her sweater nervously, drawing Liv's eyes to the skin there. "I'm sorry, I don't know what you've heard, but we can't help you." The other woman opened her mouth, but Liv went on. "And if that bruise is from him, maybe it's for the best he's gone."

Emma's eyes widened, the trauma that swirled in them a silent confirmation. Her fingers flexed, hovering near the neck of her sweater as she fought the urge to drag the collar up and hide the green and yellow bruising. Liv could only imagine how bad it must have been when she'd first gotten it if the man who'd given it to her had been missing for a week.

"It wasn't him, I had an accident." She could tell Emma didn't expect her to believe the lie.

"Liv." Ivy tried again, only serving to make her feel all the more guilty. Her sister didn't understand what she was asking.

"I'm sorry." With an empathetic smile, Liv stepped back and closed the heavy oak door. She turned, pressing her back into it, but even through her shut eyes she could feel the disapproval on Ivy's face.

"Why didn't you help her?"

Liv blew out a heavy breath. "Because that's not the kind of thing we need to get involved in. That's not why we came back here. The last thing we need is people in town hearing that the Terrabellas are back and using blood magick."

"And you think we're going to win them over by refusing to help out a desperate neighbor?"

Liv's eyes opened. "Did you see her? The way she was shaking?"

"She was upset."

"She was *petrified!* And do you know why?" Ivy didn't say anything. "It's because of the stories they whisper about our family." They didn't just whisper, sometimes they said it right to your face. But Liv didn't say that—she wouldn't give the memories any power. "This town may have been founded by six magick families, but that doesn't mean they were all loved equally. Not by a long shot."

Ivy's face scrunched in disbelief, "You didn't want to help that woman because you're afraid of what people in town might think? I mean, the *entire* town can't possibly feel like that."

She was right. Of course, it wasn't the whole town. Liv would never have brought her back there if it was. But she also knew all too well that all it took was one person to say just the right, or *wrong,* thing to turn a peaceful life into something else entirely.

That was especially true for their family. They had a sordid history with blood magick, dating back long before Havenwood was ever founded. When the first Terrabella curanderas, were driven from their indigenous homes—not unlike their European counter parts—and first crossed the modern-day border between Mexico and America.

That history was only complicated further when her great, great aunt, Amapola, was suspected in the death of a man who'd appeared to have been poisoned. Never mind that *he'd* been suspected of beating his wife for over two decades.

No one could ever actually prove it, but it had been enough to cast a shadow of suspicion over her family line ever since. And risking sparking that again would only be a complication they couldn't afford.

Liv sighed. This argument was far too reminiscent of the ones she'd grown up hearing between her mother and grandmother.

"I'm sorry, Ivy. I don't like it either, but feelings can't dictate actions or supersede wisdom, especially not when it comes to magick." She rubbed at the pressure building in her temples.

Of course it had been hard for her to close the door on Emma's desperation, even if she couldn't understand why the woman would bother looking for a piece of shit who hurt her. But she was well practiced when it came to putting feelings aside to do what she needed to do. Just like she was doing right now for Ivy. She just wished for once her sister could see that, and they didn't have to battle it out.

Ivy scoffed, "Of course. I don't know why I'm surprised. Whatever you decide, that's the only right choice. Silly me for thinking that being back here would mean maybe we could finally stop hiding who we really are. Then maybe at least one part of this move would be worth it."

With her final blow landed, Ivy stormed away, the sound of her stomping feet reverberating through the house, up the stairs, down the hall, and punctuated with the jarring sound of her door slamming shut.

CHAPTER TEN

*T*he sound of singing and banging cupboards coming from the kitchen pulled Jax from sleep. There were morning people, and then there was Logan Sinclair.

"Morning sleepy head. Hope we didn't keep you up last night."

Jax sat up on the couch and planted his feet on the carpet of Logan's small living room. No one had kept him up. He didn't even remember falling asleep. The bottle of whisky between his feet probably had something to do with that. "We?" he grunted, rubbing at his face roughly, his mind slowly catching up.

The smell of coffee drew his attention to the kitchen directly to his right. Logan turned from the counter holding two cups of coffee, one in a mug, one in a disposable to-go cup…butt naked, every inch of his colorfully tattooed body on display. Something it was far too fucking early for.

Jax groaned, averting his eyes. "I'm grateful for you letting me crash here the last couple of nights. But boxers won't actually kill you, you know?"

Logan shrugged and glanced around the small kitchen, finding his pants in the corner and slipping them on. After decades of friendship, Jax had mostly stopped being surprised by what Logan did or what came out of his mouth. Mostly.

Being descendant from selkies came with the possibility of strong magick, something Logan had in spades, but it also came with the risk of more than a few quirks, which was a nice way of putting it—something else his friend had in spades. Most notably, the ability to charm anything more sentient than a rock (which he used frequently), the inability to take almost anything in life seriously, and a strong penchant for disappearing without a word, usually into the ocean.

"You know I love you. But you're aware that you're going to have to sleep at your place eventually, right?"

Yeah, he knew. But images of her shadowy shape cascading over the walls through her window and too sheer curtains from hell had kept him awake all night after their little encounter.

It was bad enough the scent of her magick seemed to be permanently embedded in his skin where it had hit him. He'd spent enough time in the shower the night he'd taken the shot of it on his shoulder that his water bill alone would probably be enough to fund the city budget. And the time in the shower hadn't been spent solely trying to remove her scent from his skin. It had been spent trying to exorcise her from his mind. Via his dick.

Unable to handle a repeat, he'd spent the last two nights avoiding his own house by couch-crashing with Logan, like a proper adult.

"Is that what this is about? You're trying to drive me away with your nudity?"

"Stop deflecting. Are you ready to tell me what happened the other night?"

"I did tell you. Someone was following Liv. They took off on what I assume was a motorcycle before I could find out who it was."

"Right. And what about the part where you and Liv were getting hot and heavy on Mrs. Dottie's front lawn? That's right fucker, I heard about that." Which meant everyone had. Great. Dicks and gossip before seven in the morning. What a wonderful way to start the day.

"That is not what happened. *At all.* Not unless you consider this *hot and heavy.*" Jax tugged the neckline of his shirt down to reveal the still-angry red skin where Liv's magick had glanced off his shoulder.

"Uh-huh. Well, lucky for our prodigal little witch, you were there to come to the rescue. Just like old times, huh?"

Old times. Since they were thirteen when Logan had shown up in town fresh from the stormy shores of the Orkney Islands.

Jax wandered into the kitchen. He didn't want to have this conversation at all, let alone before coffee. He reached for the to-go cup just to have his hand slapped away. "Get your own."

He narrowed his eyes, more offended by the denial of caffeine than his friend's nudity. Before he could ask what Logan needed two cups of coffee for, the answer walked into the kitchen wearing a pink bra and pulling jeans up over matching panties.

The mystery brunette smiled at Jax as she walked to Logan. She took the to-go cup in one hand and slid the other up into Logan's messy shoulder-length hair, rising to her tippy toes, and kissed him. The kind of kiss that really shouldn't have an audience. Or maybe that was just his preference.

A sudden moan left the woman as a surge of Logan's magick rolled out from him and over her, rippling out like a slow rolling wave. Jax barely reacted quick enough to slap it away before the edge of it hit him. "Fuck's sake," he grumbled, moving farther away as the woman all but had an orgasm standing in the middle of the kitchen, right between Jax and the coffee pot.

They finally disconnected. She reached around Logan and yanked her shirt down from where it was inexplicably hanging from a corner of the refrigerator. Then, with little more than a smirk, she walked out of the kitchen and through the living room. The sound of the front door closing followed a moment later.

Logan sipped his coffee. "Stop judging me."

Jax shook his head at the cocky grin on Logan's face. "That shit shouldn't be happening so close to where you keep food." It wasn't like Jax hadn't had his fair share of one-night stands. Just not in Havenwood. How Logan managed to pull the shit he did in such a small town was baffling.

He looked like the modernized version of a warrior, descended from the highlands of Scotland, about the same height as Jax's six-four, but the extra twenty or so pounds of bulk made him seem even bigger. Add in the tattoos covering most of his body and he should have easily been the most intimidating person Jax knew. And when needed, he certainly could be. But most that knew him understood that while the outside may give the impression of a grizzly bear, his insides more closely resembled that of a *stuffed* bear.

He gave love away so easily to his friends, but for all that, in the twenty-plus years Jax had been best friends with the guy he'd never once seen him in a serious relationship. He was incredibly loyal to those who he loved, though. Logan had a beastly side that slumbered beneath his big, beautiful exterior, but it usually only came out in defense of the few people he'd let close enough to know of its existence.

His magick was complicated, and some aspects were still a mystery to even Jax—things that he assumed Logan liked to keep between himself and the sea. Like the parts of him he hid beneath jokes and a smile that came much easier and more often than Jax's. He suspected that underneath hid depths of feeling his friend rarely spoke about.

Jax couldn't help but love the man, even if he was an enigma.

A stupid smile spread over Logan's dumb face. Jax stole his coffee off the counter. "I need this more than you do... you're clearly *wide* awake."

The mug froze halfway to his lips, his eyes narrowing and his head tilting in concentration. Logan caught on and waited. "Put a fuckin' shirt on," Jax told him.

Logan was about to have a couple more visitors, neither of whom needed to witness any evidence of Logan's late-night activities.

Jax sat back on the couch to finish Logan's coffee, finding it already empty. He grumbled and quickly scanned the room for anything out of sorts, only remembering the whisky bottle as the front door opened. Though he mostly frowned on using magick when he could use his hands or intelligence, he flicked a wrist, sending the bottle under the couch just as Jade walked into the living room with her six-year-old daughter, and Jax's favorite person, Cordelia, in tow.

"Uncle Jax!" Cori dropped her mom's hand and ran into the room. He caught her as she launched herself into his lap like it hadn't been less than a day since he'd last seen her. It took her no time at all to situate herself perfectly into the crook of his arm and make herself at home in his lap.

Cori looked just like Jade in every way, except for the deep red hair currently tied up in some kind of bun on top of her cute head. No one knew where that hair came from, considering neither Jade nor her not-soon-enough-to-be ex had red hair. But in every other way, including her temper, Cori was all Jade. Something he was usually grateful for.

Jax's under-caffeinated brain struggled to keep up as Cori launched into a string of stories. One bled into the next without so much as a breath between. It was part of why he enjoyed her company so much—she didn't need him to put on a show, fake a lighter mood. To perform in order to avoid having to explain every thought in his mind. And Cori was consistently herself. That was the more pleasant side of the stubborn streak she'd inherited directly from her mom.

The signs that something was shifting within the town's magick were subtle; the sudden arrival of several newcomers to town, including Quinn who also happened to be a Wilder, the flickering streetlamps whose flames should be steady and eternal, the return of the Terrabellas, to name a few. All things that anyone else would dismiss as coincidence. Anyone but him. He looked down at Cori…making sure this little witch would have a safe place to be free settled heavily on him. He would do anything to ensure nothing would ever force his niece to hide any part of herself.

The thought brought an uncomfortable realization about another witch who'd most likely been doing just that for far too long.

He'd seen Liv stifle herself when they were growing up whenever her mom and grandmother got into one of their fights. But at least back then she'd had her forest to get lost and free herself in. He doubted she'd have risked giving in to her magick since she'd left Havenwood—even in a forest, knowing her. Not that he did. For any witch who'd once been so free and in tune with her magick, going without would be a huge sacrifice, and probably have side effects. Especially for someone as powerful as Olivia Terrabella.

And he'd thrown it in her face in more ways than one.

"Ah! There's the wee bonnie lass!" Logan turned on an extra thick accent as he scooped Cori out of Jax's arms.

"Mother of magick!" Jade waved her hand in front of her face. "It's like a magickal bomb went off in here. What the fuuu-nky chicken were you guys doing?" She caught herself part of the way through the word she'd meant to say, pivoting.

Jax blinked a couple of times. "What did you just say?"

"Mommy got busted for her potty mouth," Cori reported.

"Hey! Didn't we just talk about having each other's back no matter what? Besides," Jade put her hands on her hips, "I only got busted because someone else," she eyed her daughter accusatorially, "got busted at school for responding to being pushed off a swing on the playground with some spontaneous pyrotechnics. Something I would have happily gotten her out of. But when the principal tried to talk to her about appropriate emotional expression and asked her if she had anything she wanted to say, the little flamethrower decided to turn the waste basket into a bonfire." Jade tried to glare, but it was half-hearted.

Logan held Cori under her arms in front of him, the rest of her little body dangling high off the ground. "Did you do that?"

Cori shrugged a shoulder, then mimed zipping her lips closed.

Jade feigned exasperation. "Oh sure, now you get it."

"Don't worry, I know better than to believe a word your mother says. We all know who the real hothead is. Just like we all know you're an angel. I bet you can even fly!" Logan tossed Cori into the air toward the couch. Jax caught her on a breeze of his magick, bringing her down slowly, then let her hit the couch with a plop from a foot in the air. Cori's giggles filled the room.

"Anyway, somehow all that turned into *me* getting a lecture about setting a better example, blah, blah, kids have soft brains, and some other condescending bullshit. So, I'm trying to be a good example. Starting with my mouth." Jade held her hand up before Jax or Logan could get the words out. "I'm aware. It's not going well. Progress over perfection, okay?" She dared them to contradict her with her eyes.

"Oh, and then to make my visit to the school a little brighter, Nina-Pinterest-perfect-Peters cornered me about parent volunteer hours, and some other bull shiiii-p crimes against mothers, and now I have to *bake* something for a fundraiser." Jade's face scrunched up the way it had when they were kids and he'd used his big brother influence to convince her eating a grasshopper would make her powers come in faster.

"Oh, the injustice. I don't know how you make it through a day," Logan mused sarcastically. "But I suppose I could be convinced to do the baking for you." He plopped down on the couch, sandwiching Cori between the two of them.

Jade poured herself some coffee and opened one of Logan's cupboards, adding far too much sugar to it. When she turned around, her eyes drifted over the three of them but lingered on Logan for just a second before she quickly looked away. "I'm perfectly capable of making some cookies," she nearly snarled.

Jax couldn't help but wonder if she'd passed the glaze-eyed brunette on the sidewalk heading over. If she had, there was no way she'd have missed the remnants of Logan's magick clinging to her body.

Just like he didn't miss the way Logan had watched her moving around so comfortably in his kitchen. Logan saw Jade nearly as well as he did. So no doubt he also saw the tinge of bags under her eyes. Felt the slightly sharper edge she had to her lately. It was a pretty good bet it had been at least part of what the two of them had been arguing about the other night. But he wasn't going to bring that up, not when there seemed to be a tentative—no doubt short-lived—peace between them.

"You working today?" Jax knew the answer. It was the same most days lately. But it seemed like a safe topic to break the silence the room had fallen into. And maybe also better than focusing on the overly complicated nature of the relationship, or relationship that never was, between his best friend and his sister.

"Yeah, I'm shorthanded again since summer break ended for the girls who were helping me. Oh! How did it go after I left Mac's the other night?" Jade hiked her eyebrows up and down as she took a sip of coffee.

For fuck's sake. Jax let his head fall back on the couch.

"Well, if you don't want to tell me what happened I guess all I have to go on is the scandalous story I heard on my way over." That smug-ass grin was getting really old.

"Mrs. Dottie told Mommy you were messing around with someone named Liv in the middle of the street. Don't you know it's dangerous to play in the street Uncle Jaxy?"

Logan barked a laugh. "That's right, little firefly." Jade shook her head at Logan's new nickname.

"What? Would you prefer pyro pixie?"

"I'd prefer we not make light of her nearly burning the school down. Don't distract me." She pointed at Logan, then turned back to Jax. "So?" Jade drilled him with her eyes. He wasn't getting out of this one.

"Sorry man, I tried." Logan leaned back onto the couch, crossing his legs at the ankle as he set them on the coffee table. Getting comfortable in preparation for every juicy detail.

Jax shook his head at him. "You're worse than any of the women in this town."

"Someone was following Liv," Logan answered Jade for him. "And he just happened to be nearby to come to her rescue."

Jade ignored the humor in Logan's answer. She stepped closer, concern drawing her brows together. "Who was it? What did they want?"

Jax rubbed the back of his neck "I don't know. On either account." Between all the questions he'd been fielding and the thoughts in his head, the words were starting to get really fucking old.

"I told the sheriff about what happened. He's going to have Grady and a few of the other deputies be on the lookout for any strangers on a motor-cycle, but I'm not holding my breath. This has magickal implications at the least, and that's just not something the nullies he's got working for him are equipped to deal with."

"The timing isn't ideal."

"He's not wrong," Jade said, uncharacteristically agreeing with Logan. "Especially with so many new faces in town." Her eyes shifted to Cori who was currently filling one side of the living room with bubbles she'd made with her magick. *Why couldn't she use that kind of magick at school instead of the flames?*

"What did Liv say about it? Did she have any idea who it might be?" Jade probed further, looking back at Jax.

"Not that she was willing to share with me."

Her eyes narrowed. "Well, did you give her the chance? Or were you playing the tall, dark, and emotionally stunted role again? Don't bother answering that."

Logan and Jade may not know every detail of what happened that night, but they knew him well enough.

No, he admitted only to himself, he hadn't given her much of a *real* chance to explain. But it wasn't his fault, it was her damn magick. He'd sensed it as it built inside her and had been all but drugged by it as it filled the air around him, which was why he hadn't reacted quickly enough before she'd let it out.

That had been what he'd had to grit his teeth against, much more so than the pain. The intoxicating smell and feel of her magick all around him and sinking into his skin. He'd have taken another hit from her in that moment, just to experience it again. His body was a damn fool when it came to her. The last thing he needed was to be engulfed in her essence when he should be focusing on, well, anything else.

"As far as I could tell the only thing Liv wants from this town is for it to leave her alone."

"The town, or you? Because that's not the impression I got."

Jax just looked at his sister, not having an answer for her.

"Do I need to remind you about my vision, Jax? It was *all of us*, six in total. Liv included. Not to mention the timing of her coming home. You said it yourself the other night: there's no such thing as a coincidence in Havenwood."

"Do I need to remind *you* about choice, and how your visions work? We can't base any of our plans on that. The town is too important." A small glimmer of hurt flashed across her face, too quick for most to notice. But not him, and definitely not Logan.

"Alright." Logan stood up, "It's too early for this. *You* need to get to work." Logan took the coffee cup from Jade's hands. She opened her mouth to protest, but he replaced it with a to-go cup before she could get a word out.

"Did you just give me one of your..." she glanced at Cori, "nighttime guest souvenirs?"

She'd definitely seen the brunette.

Logan turned to Cori without answering. "And you," he scooped Cori up off the ground, "need to get to school. We don't want to add truancy to

78

your rap sheet. How about Uncle Jaxy and I take you on our way to work this morning? Maybe you can introduce us to this swing-stealing kid."

Jade walked up to Logan and Cori. "Thanks." The word was barely audible and seemed almost painful as it came out. "Hey, you!" Jade stood on her tippy toes trying to get closer to Cori in Logan's arms. "No flames today."

Cori rolled her eyes. "I know, Mom." Damn, if that was already starting at six, Spirit save them all when she became a teenager, Jax thought.

"Uh-huh. Prove it. Daddy's going to pick you up from school today."

"Really?" Cori asked, her face lighting up.

Logan's eye pinched at the corners in a small wince.

"Yep." Jade's tight smile didn't reach her eyes. She didn't look at Logan. Cori leaned down so her mom could kiss her on the forehead. Even with Logan lowering slightly, she was still barely able to reach.

Jade brushed a hand over Jax's shoulder and walked out without looking at Logan again.

"Uncle Jax?" Cori looked at him, her deep blue eyes focused on his. "Who's Liv?"

"Alrighty then." Logan shifted the little girl, tossing her in the air.

"Put me down, walrus! Release the human!" she squealed.

"You're a witch, and it's a seal if anything."

"Witches are humans too, fish breath."

"Ah, but not all humans are witches, are they lassie?" He tossed Cori in the air again before placing her on his shoulders. "Come on. Maybe if you don't get arrested for arson at school today I'll tell you the story of two little witches who fell in love."

Jax picked up Cori's small yellow backpack and slung it over his shoulder, trailing Logan and Cori out the door.

CHAPTER ELEVEN

"*H*ello!" Liv froze at the sound of the sweet familiar voice. A small bolt of panic dropped into her stomach—even distorted by the murky glass, Liv knew it was Sandra Hawthorne standing in her garden.

Be normal! her brain commanded as her body refused to move.

"Uh. Yeah. Hi, I'm in here."

The sight of a genuine smile spreading over the older woman's face eased the tension in her shoulders and chipped away a little at her initial trepidation as their eyes connected through the glass.

Sandra glided through the open doors and immediately wrapped Liv in a full-body hug. The good kind of hug. The type where you can tell the other person truly means it. Two arms, squeezing tight, smashed chest-to-chest and cheek-to-cheek. Cinnamon and vanilla radiated from her, cocooning Liv in familiar comfort.

Sandra released her but kept her hands on Liv's shoulders. "It's about darn time. Do you have any idea how long I've been waiting for you?" Sandra's shoulder-length hair swayed gently as she shook her head. Her brown hair, now lightly streaked with gray, showed the years since Liv had left, but did nothing to diminish her beauty.

"If I didn't know any better, I'd be tempted to think you were avoiding me." Sandra's gaze lingered on Liv's face a heartbeat too long, slightly probing. There was no telling how much Sandra could ascertain from just that quick scan. That particular gift of hers was one of motherhood, not magic, but it had always left Liv feeling both self-conscious and thankful, knowing someone cared enough to look closely. She just hoped this time Sandra didn't see too much of the truth.

"I'm sorry. I know I should have come over." Excuses lingered on the tip of her tongue just waiting to be vocalized but she held them in. She may not have consciously realized it until that moment, but she had been avoiding Sandra. And now, standing in front of her, in her light, she knew it had been pointless. She may want an explanation, but even if Liv could never give her one, she knew Sandra was too good to hold it against her. There had been a time when she'd felt like a second mother to her.

"Well, yes. But that's not exactly what I meant." She hesitated, pursing her lips for a moment. "Never mind." Sandra moved on without clarifying.

Her soft hand brushed Liv's cheek as she smiled softly, causing light lines to form at the corners of her knowing eyes. "Well, didn't you turn out beautifully," she said, then kissed her head. Liv moved a few steps away to inspect the workbench, getting some distance rather than crumbling into the other woman and their old relationship like she wanted to. "No wonder you've got my son all up in knots again."

Liv blinked. *In knots?* What did that mean? Was that a good or bad thing?

She patted the bag hanging off her shoulder tucked under her arm, shifting the conversation to lighter topics in that effortless way she had. "Isn't this a lucky surprise? I was just planning to drop some lunch off for Jax."

His mom was making him lunch. She wanted to count it against him in some way, but she couldn't. Because it was Sandra, and knowing her, it was unbidden, and just an excuse to check up on her son.

"I saw him dropping Cori off at school this morning and figured he hadn't bothered to make any for himself."

"That's Jade's daughter, right?" She rushed to fend off the image in her mind of Jax walking down the street holding the tiny hand of a little girl before it had time to fully materialize and rearrange her insides permanently. Starting with her ovaries and moving south.

Sandra radiated pride. "Yes." Liv momentarily wondered if the color that glowed from Sandra's face may have been sucked directly from her own.

"That's thoughtful of you. Making him lunch, I mean."

"It's nothing. Jade's got a lot on her plate right now, and you know how she is, she'll burn something down before she admits to needing help. Jax is the only person she allows to do anything close to it. And I'm pretty sure he usually has to trick her into it. Like a good brother." She rolled her eyes and laughed at the same time. "So, this is just my small contribution to the effort." Sandra patted her bag again.

You know how she is. Just a passing phrase, but the familiarity it implied was heavy. She wanted to laugh along with Sandra as she mused on about her kids so casually, to relate to it with her...but she couldn't.

She'd missed so much.

"How's being a grandmother?" she asked instead, trying not to fall into regret.

"Well, I'm convinced she's perfect, so it's wonderful. She's in kindergarten, but sometimes she seems closer to sixteen than six, and more than giving Jade a run for her money. Between you and me, it's been an absolute delight to watch Cori give it to Jade, just as much as she did to me when she was that age. Nature's justice." Sandra laughed.

"Anyway. What are you working on here?" she asked. Her eyes scanned the various plants and tools Liv had scattered across the wooden surface where she'd been working on yet another dream spell that probably wouldn't work—unless she was desperate enough to charm the thing with her magick. She wasn't sure why she was still trying to tough it out. The lack of sleep was wearing on her.

Sandra picked up the small tin of salve that had been sitting on her workbench for three days now, leftovers from what she'd ended up just leaving on Jax's porch. Somewhere in those days, she'd finally stopped lying to herself about "not wanting to disturb him" and admitted she'd chickened out. She hadn't seen the tin on his porch when she'd gone out the next day, so he'd gotten it—which was what mattered. Even if she had a sneaking suspicion he wouldn't use it, not with even just a hint of her magick attached to it.

Sandra unscrewed the lid and inhaled the salve deeply. "It smells wonderful."

"It's for…" Liv hesitated to say burns. If Sandra didn't know about what she'd done to Jax yet, she would soon. And it would take her about three seconds to put two and two together. Singeing the shit out of her son probably wasn't the best topic to reconnect over.

"…treating troubled skin." Okay, maybe that hadn't been her intent when making it, but it also wasn't a lie. If it had been, she had no doubt the older woman would have known and called her on it immediately.

Sandra rubbed some on the back of her hand. "Oh, it feels wonderful. You Terrabellas have such a gift. It's a wonder we all haven't dried up and turned to dust not having access to the magick that comes out of this place." Sandra took a little more salve from the tin and then twisted the lid back into place. "I can't tell you how many times I tried to get Valeria to open a shop in town so people wouldn't constantly be tracking her down at home."

Liv smiled at the memory. "I think a storefront may have been too formal for her."

"Yes. That's exactly what she always said." The way Sandra looked at her made it clear she didn't believe it, though. Liv had similar thoughts growing up. And now she couldn't help but wonder if it wasn't a choice her grandmother had made to spare her mother. The idea that Valeria would have made that sacrifice without her mother ever realizing it, let alone giving her credit for it, didn't sit well.

"If it wouldn't be too much trouble, do you think you could make me one of these?"

"You can have that one." The words came out of Liv's mouth a little too quickly as she easily fell back into the habit of wanting to please Sandra. The thought that maybe it wasn't good enough, that the rust on the small magick she'd used would be evident to such an experienced witch. All similar doubts she'd had before her porch delivery to Jax.

"I should say no. Not to rob the intended but…I don't think I will. How much do I owe you?" Sandra reached into her bag.

Liv stayed her hand. "Nothing."

"Oh, I couldn't possibly. I know how much effort and time goes into these."

"No, really. I'm just getting my bearings back. It probably won't be any good anyway."

Sandra relented. "Well, alright. On one condition. Promise me you'll come over soon so I can at least pay you back with a home-cooked meal. You may be exceptional at cooking things up out here, but I do seem to remember those skills never quite transferring to the kitchen. I think I still have a burnt pan or two as proof."

Liv laughed at the truth in it. And the fact that Sandra had held onto a memory of her at all.

"The ladies at book club are going to be so jealous to hear I got my hands on some Terrabella Magick." Sandra eyed her over the edge of the tin of salve as she smelled it again and smirked.

"Oh…" Liv hesitated, "if you wouldn't mind, maybe just keep it between us for now?"

The older woman considered her for a moment. "Of course. It will be our secret," Sandra agreed as she twisted the lid back onto the tin and placed it in her bag.

Liv watched Sandra look around the room, a moment of silence passing between them before Sandra's eyes finally came back to her. "I have to admit that my visit isn't entirely as coincidental as I may have let on."

Liv tilted her head. "What do you mean?"

Sandra let out a heavy sigh, the weight of which made Liv's stomach tighten with apprehension. "I need to ask you a question, one that I've been carrying with me for quite some time…since the night you left." While Sandra let out another smaller sigh, Liv's breath seized in her throat. "And I must ask that you be honest with me, no matter your answer. Can you do that for me?"

Liv nodded, unable to speak around the breath seized in her throat. Sandra considered her, then went on in a quiet voice. "That night when you came over to see Jax but found me instead… the things I said—Liv, I am so sorry love, not only was it incredibly insensitive of me to do on the night of Valeria's ash laying, but in all this time, I've worried that my stupidity played a role in why you chose to leave us."

Liv opened her mouth to quickly assuage the guilt she saw welling in the tears brimming Sandra's crystalline eyes, but the other woman wasn't done. "I also have to confess: I've never been able to bring myself to admit to Jaxon, or anyone else for that matter, what I did."

"Stop." This time it was Liv who spoke before Sandra could descend any further into the trap of guilt Liv knew all too well. She took a step forward, gently taking one of Sandra's hands in both of her own, looking down at them.

She couldn't believe the woman had spent all these years carrying around a burden that wasn't hers in any way. "All you did that night was provide me with the confidence and clarity I needed to make my own decision." Liv forced herself to meet Sandra's eyes, so she could be sure her words were received, finding the older woman surveying her intently, no doubt using her motherly intuition to sniff out any hint of a lie in Liv's words—but she wouldn't find one.

"That's just one example of the many things you did for me, and I'll always be grateful to you for that. But leaving was my choice, no one else's." And it was the truth. She'd been given a choice and she'd made one. One that, despite how much pain it might have caused, she didn't blame anyone else for, not even her mother—at least not most days. "I'm so sorry you've spent all this time carrying that around with you." Liv's words got smaller before trailing off altogether.

Sandra dropped Liv's hand and instead placed a gentle palm on her cheek, her eyes bright with tears but fierce. "You have nothing to apologize for, do you hear me?"

Sandra wrapped Liv in yet another hug, and this one lingered as she smoothed a hand down Liv's long hair and squeezed her once before releasing her.

Sandra stepped back, sniffling a little, and then straightened herself up again. "Well, now that's taken care of, and since Jax isn't here after all, I should probably go track him down before this becomes dinner." She indicated the bag on her shoulder again, where she had Jax's lunch tucked away.

85

Liv nodded then caught herself. "Before you go," Sandra stopped before she could make it out of the greenhouse, "can I ask why you would have thought Jax would be here in the first place?" It's not like he was exactly a fan of hers lately.

"Oh, you know how he loves old houses," Sandra tilted her head up, looking around the greenhouse again, "loves his plans and projects," she replied, clarifying nothing as she walked toward the exterior doors of the greenhouse.

She paused in the doorway, "I'm so glad you're home and finding yourself again." She dipped her chin to the mess on the workbench. "Your grandmother would be so proud of you." The way she said it was so genuine it hurt a little. "It was so great to finally get to see you. Don't forget dinner. And *soon*, Liv." The look Sandra gave her was one that only a mother could give. The implied threat of "or else" not veiled at all.

"Deal."

Once Sandra was gone, Liv looked around the greenhouse, noticing for the first time a few repaired wooden beams, and the random panes of glass that looked significantly newer than the rest.

CHAPTER TWELVE

*T*hree nails burst from Jax's gun in quick succession. Two more than needed to do the job of attaching a single shingle in place against the siding of the house.

"So, that makes four of the six then, huh? That's gotta be the first time we've had that many descendants in... Well, I don't know, a long ass time. Right?"

"I don't know." Even though he did.

The guy had been his best friend for going on twenty years. Even if the direction he was taking this conversation wasn't as obvious as the neon signs that hung in his bar, Jax would have known what Logan was digging for.

"Annnd, do you think it means something?" he pressed.

This was why he'd told Logan he didn't need help today, even though he was already running behind on this project. But he'd shown up all the same, his long hair still dripping with seawater. It wasn't that Jax didn't appreciate his friend's help. He did. He more than owed Logan for the way he'd helped with their family business all these years. But this morning he'd wanted something Logan was incapable of giving.

Silence.

He wanted to get lost in the work. Jax enjoyed what he did. Enjoyed doing something he knew he was good at. Working with his hands gave him a break from his mind. It was peaceful and predictable, just like this town. Or at least it had been until recently.

"Maybe." One more shingle, two more nails.

This had become Logan's new thing over the last few days—tiptoeing around any subject that might lead back to *her*. Coddling him like he was still that same heart-sick teenager rather than a thirty-one-year-old man.

Whether via Logan's coddling, his sister or mother's prying, or nosey townspeople, all roads of conversation seemed to lead in the same direction the last week—to Liv. *Wasn't that a thought?* A thought that itself led right back to bright green eyes, black lace, and dangerous-as-hell curves wrapped in too-tight denim.

No one had talked to him about Liv in years. But since word had gotten out about their little late-night show, it was like every thought they'd been storing up had been given the green light.

No, I don't know why she's here. No, I don't know how long she plans to stay. Why yes, she does still have those beautiful green eyes. Thanks for the reminder. As if he could forget.

The sound of the nail gun popped into his ears repeatedly. "Shit Jax! Watch what the hell you're doing with that thing."

Jax's vision focused to find the sleeve of Logan's shirt embedded behind the head of the nail he'd just driven into the siding.

"Sorry," Jax mumbled, pulling a set of pliers out of the back pocket of his worn-out denim jeans. He yanked the nail out of the shingle, freeing Logan's sleeve. "Finish this up, I need to check something." He practically threw the nail gun at Logan before storming down the side of the house back to the front.

Jax leaned over the makeshift table they'd constructed out of a couple of sawhorses and some plywood, bracing his hands on either side of the plans that covered the surface. He shoved at the measuring tape weighing the papers down and pulled the pencil out from behind his ear, crossing out changes he'd just made, unmade, and then remade several times over the last few hours.

He closed his eyes in an attempt to gain control over his mind. There was no room for it to be clouded by anything that wasn't completely necessary.

Jax had finally stabilized here, figured out and built the kind of life he wanted. The last thing he needed was any complications. Not that she was a complication. Rather, she didn't need to be. If he could maintain his distance and level head, eventually the town would move on to the next hot topic and the people in his life would drop it. He'd learn to co-exist.

He'd have to, because she had roots here too. She had just as much of a right to be here as any of them did.

No matter how much it fucked with his mind.

There was plenty of other shit to focus on, he reminded himself. Four descendants out of the six founding family lines were present in town—the most at once in over fifty years. And there was an unexplained shift happening in the town's magick.

He wished he had the luxury of acting as if it were nothing. It seemed to be what most people in town were doing. But even though it seemed inconsequential, the lanterns flickering—or going out all together, as three had just last night—really shouldn't be happening. The flames were intrinsically bound with the town's magick...they should have been steady. Of course that had landed on his plate, because the Hawthorne line was made up of Balancers. Any time the question of magick behaving oddly came up, the town came to them. Him, because Jade needed to focus on balancing her magick before she tried to fix anything—there wouldn't be anything left to fix if she melted every lantern in town.

He was also running behind on more than one project. Undesirable by his standards, unacceptable by his father's. There'd been an influx of work to fix up the few vacant homes in town due to the uptick in newcomers. Another thing on his "what the fuck is happening" list.

People left this town relatively often, mostly to seek a life somewhere more mundane or less secluded. It was part of why there hadn't been a representation of the full Six in, to use Logan's words, a long-ass time.

People found and settled in the town far less often. It wasn't unheard of, but it wasn't a regular thing. As far as he knew, town growth hadn't been at this rate since around the time of the founding.

That, combined with the possibility that someone had been following

Liv the other night, was leading him to question how well the Umbra Aegis was functioning. It worried him, but with so much going on it had been added to the "deal with when necessary" pile in his mind.

"How's it going, son?" The unmistakable gruff voice of his father came from behind him.

"Perfect timing," Jax mumbled.

His dad wasted no time taking up a crossed-arm stance over the plans laid out on the table. "What's this?" His dad pointed to a recent change. "That's not what we talked about. That style of trim is all wrong for this house."

"It's not wrong if it's what the customer wants," Jax replied as he walked to the other side of the yard to pick up the measuring tape he'd flung off the table. His dad followed him back across the lawn, standing behind him as he climbed a couple of rungs of the ladder to measure the width of the eaves.

"It's not right for the period of the house. Did you tell them that?" *Scrutinizing. Always scrutinizing.*

The measuring tape slid back in with a sharp snap. Jax jumped down from the ladder, landing in front of his dad.

"Yes, Dad, but Mrs. Dade was adamant that this was what she wanted." He walked back to the plans to mark down his measurements, even though he knew he wouldn't forget them.

"Well, it's wrong."

Jax held in a groan.

It had been two years since Jax had technically taken over the restoration company full-time, but the man still made regular appearances at all his job sites to check his work and order him around.

His dad had built the business from the ground up. He'd seen the need for it within the town, and he'd also had the desire to preserve their history, rather than see it torn down and turned into something generic and cookie-cutter.

Jax knew the checkups weren't about his dad not believing him. He'd spent every summer absorbing the never-ending knowledge his dad had, committing it to permanent memory. And he knew it showed in the way he'd maintained the standard of work his dad was known for.

The man just didn't like change.

Truthfully, Jax had never thought he'd see the day Warren Hawthorne would retire. He was sure it hadn't been his dad's idea. Just like it hadn't been his dad who told him about the accident. That had been his mom. The guilt of not being here when his dad needed him because he'd been selfish and only thinking of what he wanted at the time, which was just to be as far away from Havenwood as possible, ate at him. His dad never would have been on that ladder if Jax had been there.

He still remembered the sound of his mom's voice when she'd called and asked him to come home, not that he'd needed much convincing. Although, Sandra Hawthorne had a way of getting what she wanted, and convincing you it was actually what you wanted, before you even knew what was happening. Sometimes he wondered if maybe there was magick at play there, despite her instance she hadn't been gifted by the Spirit.

Speaking of the woman. "Leave him alone Warren. He's doing a great job." His mom walked toward them, with a miniature, red-headed clone of his sister in tow.

That made it official—he'd seen every member of his family today and it was barely past noon.

Logan wrapped a large arm around Warren's shoulders, making the older man jump. "Hawthornes!"

"Dammit, what have I told you about that sneaking shit?" Jax's dad flicked Logan in the forehead. "No man your size should be able to move so silently. It isn't natural."

Logan chuckled as he walked over to Sandra. She handed him a to-go coffee cup and a brown sack. Logan beamed at her. "Thanks, Sandi!" He kissed her on the cheek.

Jax's mom set down another coffee and brown bag smack dab in the middle of the plans he'd been working on.

"Where are you coming from and where's mine?" Warren asked.

She shrugged, pulling out another lunch for him. "Oh, you know, here and there."

His dad eyed her suspiciously and then kissed her. Far too hard for the public, and their age.

Jax averted his gaze, landing on his unusually quiet niece. "Hey, Firefly." Logan's nickname from that morning suited her. He crouched in front of Cori.

"Hi, Uncle Jaxy," Cori responded morosely to the ground.

He gently grasped her chin to lift her droopy head. "What's the matter?"

Cori let out a sigh beyond her years. "Nothing. I just didn't have a very good day." Her bottom lip wobbled slightly but she sniffed the tears away. Another inherited trait from her mom.

He could feel Logan step a little closer behind him as he looked up over Cori to his mom in silent questioning. She shook her head slightly, lips tucked in a tight line, raising a brow as if to say, "Take a wild guess."

But Jax didn't need to guess. Her dad had flaked. That jackass didn't deserve to call himself a father. Didn't deserve Cori, had never deserved his sister.

He kissed Cori's cheek as he stood up, crossing his arms over his chest.

His mom rubbed Cori's little shoulder. "Her father said he's just running late and promised he'd be by to get her as soon as he could." She pumped positivity into her voice for Cori's sake, but no one bought it, least of all Cori.

Jade was still at work, no doubt.

"We were just passing by on our way to the Historical Society meeting. I wanted to see if there was a day this week you boys could come over for dinner?"

"She's already had a bad day, and now you're going to subject her to a meeting?" His dad shivered. "How about you stay and help me keep these guys from ruining this house even more than they already have?" He bumped Cori with his leg, getting little more than a light nod. "Oh, and ask that uptight bunch if they can use their powers for good for once and force the Dades to use the right trim." His dad shoved a thumb over his shoulder toward the house.

"Mhhmm. Sure, honey." His mom agreed absently as she dug around in her way-too-large bag.

Logan stepped around Jax and lifted Cori into his arms. "I've got to get going too, got a delivery comin' to the bar. You know," Logan shifted Cori so they were face-to-face, "I have a few new flavors of ice cream comin'.

Dinnae suppose you know anyone keen to taste test for 'em for me do ye?" His brogue slipped through as it tended to whenever he was more focused on controlling what dwelled inside him than he was on controlling what he presented on the outside.

Cori's face brightened and her hand shot in the air. "Me! I'm the best taste-testerer ever!"

"Well, the job is yours, *if* your gramps says it's okay." Both Logan and Cori turned pleading eyes on Warren.

He shrugged. "Fine with me, I'm not the one who has to get her to bed later."

"Perfect." Sandra clapped her hands. "And dinner?" She looked between Jax and Logan.

Logan beamed at his surrogate mom. "I'm free any night you're cooking."

"Good boy. And how about you?" She turned a lifted brow on Jax.

"She's got that look in her eye." His dad leaned into him. "Better weigh your options quickly. Give in to her demands and endure whatever she's scheming or deny her and risk the wrath." He spoke out of the corner of his mouth.

"I vote for the option that gets us food," Logan piped up.

"Jaxon?" His mom urged as she finally found what she'd been looking for and pulled out a small black and silver tin. She opened it, dipping her fingers into the contents, and began rubbing it on her hands.

"Whatcha got there, Mom?" He'd recognized the tin the second she pulled it out of her bag. It was identical to the one he'd found waiting for him on his porch the other night after work.

He'd known where it came from even though there hadn't been a note left with it. He'd seen those same tins inside the Terrabella greenhouse when he'd occasionally been drawn over to Havenhouse to do the odd repair over the years.

Initially, he assumed the small gift was just a result of Liv's guilt over the damage her magick had done to his skin.

But then he'd opened it. On the surface it could have been just another skin ointment, except for the hint of her magick entwined within it, working with the natural properties, and amplifying them. He could smell the familiar soothing scent of it from a few feet away where his mom was currently rubbing the same balm into her hands.

"What? This?" His mom feigned ignorance as she lifted the tin in question. "Oh, nothing. Stop deflecting, Jaxon." She slipped the tin back into her bag

It was far from nothing. He'd considered throwing it away— knowing even a hint of her magick near him was a bad idea, but then he'd imagined her taking the time to make it and caved at the thought of her tapping into her suppressed magick… for him.

Rubbing the silky salve into his chest and reveling in the earthy scent of it, mixed with the cool, tingling feel of it on his skin, had become his new nightly indulgence. The faint scent of her magick lingered within, a maddening siren song attempting to lure him across the street for a more potent hit, straight from the source herself.

That kind of thinking was exactly why having her magick around him was so dangerous, and not just when she was firing it off at him.

His mom flipped her wrist, checking the time. "Shoot, I'm late. See you boys at dinner." By the time he realized she'd been the one deflecting, his mother was already halfway down the block.

"You ready, Firefly?" Logan dropped Cori down beside him.

"Super ready!" Her answering smile set at least one thing right in Jax's world.

"See ya later on?" Logan asked as they started to walk away, and Jax shrugged. He wasn't sure where was safe for him in this town right now.

Logan stopped at the edge of the lawn. "If he shows up, tell the, d-o-u-c-h-e," he spelled the word out, "he can come get her from me." Warren gave Logan a subtle nod.

Jax could hear Cori trying to sound out the word Logan had spelled as they disappeared down the sidewalk. His dad watched them go for a moment, too, before he turned his attention back to the plans and micro-managing him.

"How about the other projects? How are you managing with those?" He grabbed a long tube with plans for other projects.

Jax took them back, setting them down firmly on the table. "Dad. I know you're bored. But this is retirement. Enjoy it! Go golfing. Get a coffee. Join a bowling league. Hang out with Mom!" *Whatever gets you out of my job sites.* "You don't have to worry about this stuff anymore. I've got it covered."

"Alright, know-it-all. What about our favorite green-eyed girl? You got that covered too?"

Jax's head dropped back between his shoulders, and he groaned at the sky.

CHAPTER THIRTEEN

*L*iv glared at the house across the street as she walked out her front gate. She still couldn't believe that Jaxon freaking Hawthorne had bought the house across the street from hers—not that she'd seen even a hint of him living there in the past few days, besides his mother's visit the day before. She still didn't know what to make of that, which was becoming somewhat of a trend when it came to him.

Turning from the house, Liv made her way into town and did her best to evade the memories that seemed to be waiting around every corner. She focused on the storefronts instead, taking in everything that had changed, and everything that hadn't.

She paused in front of a business she hadn't seen before. Beautiful deep turquoise tiles and warm wood trimmed the huge windows that made up the Art Deco storefront. Black and white checkered flooring peeked out underneath the entrance to the enchanting shop. Liv took a step closer to the windows, her eyes drifting slowly over the displays that featured an artfully arranged array of books, stationery, and art.

She glanced up at the tall gold lettering that ran above the windows. It simply read, "The Bookstore". The name was to the point, if not a bit lackluster for such an alluring shop. Liv took another step closer, wanting to take in every detail.

"Hey!" Jade broke into Liv's daze, half of her body peeking out of the door. "Are you going to stand there all day fogging up the glass? Or are you going to come in and rescue me from stocking?"

Liv nodded enthusiastically, following Jade through the heavy Oak door, and entering into a shop so whimsical it felt like being transported into the pages of a romance novel, where everything was always dreamier than real life.

The scent of old leather mixed with fresh ink on paper engulfed her as she moved deeper into the shop.

A few people milled around inside. A couple of them looked up from what they were doing to asses her. She gave one man who didn't immediately avert his eyes a small smile. He dipped his head to her and then looked back to the book in his hand.

"You work here?" Liv asked. It was a dumb question for obvious reasons, but she couldn't stop looking around. How did a person get any actual work done?

Jade walked through the store, moving books around and putting things back in their rightful spot before walking back behind the counter.

"Yeah. Well, kind of. I own it. This place, the empty shop next door, the two apartments above them. In other words, the whole building." Jade shrugged like it wasn't a big deal.

"Wow, that's amazing! *This place* is amazing, Jade." It really was. The way it made her feel…it wasn't her gardens, but it wasn't far off. "Do you live upstairs?"

"No." Jade picked up a stack of greeting cards and put them back in their correct places. "That had been the plan once upon a time, but well, I got pregnant with Cori not long after I bought it, and a nine hundred square foot, one-bedroom apartment isn't exactly family-friendly."

"I didn't realize you were married," she blurted, then immediately wished she'd been more tactful. It didn't take a husband to make a family. Liv knew that—believed it. She'd never known her father and had spent several years being raised by her grandmother alone when her mom had run off, only to return a few years later, a three-year-old Ivy in tow.

"*Was* married. Technically I guess I still am, but not for much longer."

"Oh." Liv wasn't sure what to say to that. The matter-of-fact way Jade had put it out there hadn't given any hint as to how she felt about it.

"I'm fine," Jade said, reading Liv's mind. "I shouldn't have married him in the first place. I was young, and small towns plus unwed mothers. You can fill in the rest."

She could. She hadn't lived that exact life, but she knew very well what it felt like when everyone around you knew something about you and felt entitled to have an opinion about it. It was understandable that Jade had married the guy.

Jade amazed Liv the more she thought about it. Her old friend had accomplished so much, all within this small town. Owned a business, multiple technically, got married, and had a family. And, maybe bravest of all, she'd also decided to end that marriage and face becoming a single mom. But if anyone were going to conquer so many mountains before they were even thirty, it would be Jade.

She'd done so much, and Liv had missed it all.

Liv hadn't expected time to stand still, but it felt like everyone had lived a full lifetime while she'd been gone. And even though she'd had the same number of years, she had much less to show for that time.

But she wasn't Jade. She didn't have the luxury of taking risks. Or the kind of support required to chase big dreams.

"I knew I didn't love him from the start. Not because I knew what it felt like, but because I knew what it looked like. I'd been surrounded by it with my parents and…" Jade trailed off as she looked at her, something passing in her eyes, and Liv knew exactly what she hadn't said. Her and Jax. Jade turned away and started scribbling something on a piece of paper. "I guess I just thought maybe it could grow into that. But it never did. For either of us, apparently," she added, not looking up from her paper.

Letting the slightly uncomfortable conversation fade naturally, Liv continued to wander around, enamored. When the shop was empty of other customers, Jade disappeared through a doorway behind the counter, reemerging a moment later with a box more than half her size in her arms. She set it down, then repeated the same revolution until three heavy boxes sat on the floor.

"Speaking of living situations, how's yours going?" Jade asked, seeming to hold in a laugh.

"Well," Liv started as the first box opened on its own. She watched as books filed out of the box, one after another lifting into the air above her head. "The house seems happy to have us home. Maybe me a little more than Ivy. They're still having a hard time warming up to each other." That was an understatement. The fried door had just been the beginning. The house had retaliated, helping Ivy "unpack" by throwing her belongings out a window. In return, Ivy had let a couple of squirrels into the house, which had been promptly locked in her room. With her inside. Liv was hoping that Ivy would realize there was no winning a war against your own home. She wasn't holding her breath.

Jade laughed as she shelved each of them in their rightful spot with casual flicks of her wrists and the occasional swirl of her finger. The scent of her magick-filled air felt warm on Liv's skin, the light scent of coconut surrounding her. "I really need to come over soon."

"Maybe you can just stop by next time you visit your brother. Which is what I think you were probably getting anyway. Thanks for the heads up on that, by the way."

Liv fought with some tape to open the second box. Jade pretended not to notice. When she finally got it open, she saw it was filled with delicate stationery. Looking around, she found a shiny wood table with a gold inlay stacked with similar items on it and began refilling the stock by hand.

"Yeah, sorry about that. I was hoping to be there for the big reveal." Jade's laugh was cut off by a ringing phone behind the counter. She checked the caller ID and made a low groaning noise in the back of her throat, appearing to debate for a moment before answering.

"You better not be calling to tell me what I think you are." No greeting, just straight to the point.

"You're her dad. That's why they called you." Jade's face twisted into something between confusion and disgust.

"I don't give a shit how important you think your job is. It's not more important than my job, and it's certainly not more important than *your daughter.*" Jade's free hand clenched into a tight fist.

Liv moved to another set of shelves, out of Jade's direct line of sight. She couldn't avoid overhearing Jade's conversation, but she could at least give her the illusion of privacy.

"That's not true." Her voice dropped into a lower more subdued tone. "You can't blame me for this. There is a learning period for every young witch. We've talked about this, the magick is a side effect of her emotions, not the other way around. The outbursts are coming from something else, and you constantly breaking your promises isn't helping."

"AARON!" Jade pulled her phone away from her ear and looked down at it. "Mother fucker," she seethed.

Liv approached the counter slowly, "Is everything okay?" Clearly, it wasn't. Jade radiated anger, causing the bookshelves to shudder around them. She closed her eyes, inhaling and exhaling deep breaths, and the shelves began to settle. So much magick in such a little body. It had always amazed Liv that her friend could contain it at all.

"Just an asshole doing typical asshole things." Jade looked at the time on her phone and then around the room like she was searching the shop for the answer to an unasked question.

"Uh, do you think you could maybe watch the shop for me? The school called. Cori had another *incident*." Jade rolled her eyes. "Apparently, the school thought the absent father was a better point of contact than the hot mess mom. I have like five minutes to get there if I want to avoid yet another parenting lecture from the principal. I'll be back as soon as I can, I promise." It was obvious by the way Jade, the most direct woman on earth, over-explained, that she was uncomfortable asking for help.

"Of course, I can," Liv said with an easy smile she hoped conveyed that it truly was fine.

"Thank you so much!" Jade kissed her on the cheek before running for the shop door where she paused. "If anyone comes in just…" she searched for an idea, frantic energy pouring off her, "just do your best." And then she was gone.

JAX REFUSED TO LET THE QUEASY FEELING IN THE PIT OF HIS STOMACH reflect on his face. Logan didn't even seem to be trying, his eyes darting around the cave tucked into the cliffside, taking in the sigils and markings drawn on the rocky walls. In blood.

Harlan Jennings, the town's sheriff, had called Jax that afternoon and had asked him to come to a crime scene. When it came to magick, no one in the six-person sheriff's department would know what to make of any of this.

He'd followed his request with, "I think we might have a dead body." Seeing the crime scene now was proof of how underqualified the man was to deal with a real crime. Harlan had been sheriff most of Jax's life, and in all that time he'd rarely had to deal with much more than unneighborly disputes, missing pets, and town hall meetings that occasionally got a little too heated.

A little heads up on the state of the body would have been nice, considering Jax wasn't exactly familiar with dead bodies, himself. But he had a feeling Harlan hadn't gotten any closer to the body than where he stood now at the mouth of the cave. Because there was no way around the fact—the body was dead.

Jeremiah's body. He forced himself to use the man's name, if only in his head.

"Does he have any family in town?" Logan asked, his mind going in the same direction as Jax's. They knew this man. Not well, as he'd only moved to town a couple of months before, and from what Jax knew, he worked somewhere outside of town most of the time. But he'd seen him in passing at the coffee shop and around town from time to time.

"We're not sure. Grady will ask around soon, but I wanted to get your thoughts before we risked word getting out." Harlan shifted on his feet and pulled at the sides of his belt, his rotund midsection fighting back. "Do you think he did this to himself?"

Wishful thinking from a small-town sheriff.

"Seems unlikely he slit his own throat then spent some time finger painting on the walls with *his own blood*." Logan shivered, his eyes still darting around in avoidance.

101

Jax skirted along the edge of the cave to get a closer look at the markings Logan had alluded to.

"There are a few sets of footprints farther back in the cave," Logan noted.

Jax lowered into a crouch to look at the power more carefully. Between his feet, an opaque substance sat on the sand. Gently he picked it up, pinched it, and rolled it between two fingers. It was wax.

Straightening, Jax walked the perimeter of the circle, finding several small pools of the same waxy substance. One at each of the cardinal points.

"There were candles here." Jax indicated the spots just inside the undisturbed halo around the body.

Neither Logan nor Harlan responded. They just watched as Jax's mind began to work and his eyes raced over the sigils again.

He bent down over the body, closer this time. If they'd found him sooner, maybe he could have walked through the man's memories. There would be a lot of risk to it—he'd never walked a dead person before. But morbid as it might be in this case, he'd always had a hard time controlling his desire for knowledge. Especially when it came to magick.

Regardless, it had been too long. The ember of magick the man once had was long gone, returned to the source now. Jax hesitated to cross into the circle, created with unknown magick, but took the chance. He rubbed the edge of the man's shirt between his fingers and turned his head toward Logan. "Tell me about the tides last night." Harlan stood, hands on his hips watching the two of them, trying to follow Jax's line of thought.

"I headed out a little before high tide, maybe three a.m., and stayed until the tide drained around seven. The waves were so clean." Logan's eyes went bright with excitement recalling his time in the ocean.

"Jeez boy, when do you sleep?" Harlan shook his head.

Logan rubbed his tattooed hands together, "I'll sleep when I'm dead. Oh. Shit. Sorry man, way too soon." He looked down, apologizing to the body, then quickly turned away again. "Dammit! I looked. This shit better not give me nightmares, Jax."

"His clothes are dry." Jax glanced from Logan to Harlan, who wasn't grasping what he was getting at.

"It was a full moon last night. High tide would have had this place flooded."

Jax nodded at Logan's insight. "Exactly."

"What the hell are you doing? Get your hands off the body." Jax didn't stand but turned toward the opening of the cave. A broad frame filled the space, the bright, mid-morning sun behind the figure, casting him in shadow and masking his identity.

"It's okay Declan, they're with me." Harlan clapped the man on the shoulder. "I asked Jax to come down and take a look around to try to make sense of what's going on here."

The figure stepped farther into the cave, where Jax could see him a bit better. He wore dark cargo pants and tactical boots. He was tall, though shorter than Jax, and a bit more muscled. A shadow of a beard covered his jaw, and from what Jax could tell, the man looked to be a little older than him, maybe in his late thirties.

"Is letting civilians tamper with evidence par for the course here?" The air around the stranger vibrated with authority, instantly irritating Jax. *Civilians? Who talked like that?*

Jax stood carefully, stepping back around the circle as *Declan* came toward him, skillfully maneuvering around the crime scene and avoiding anything that might be evidence. His eyes shot over to Logan before coming back to Jax. "Isn't that why we have deputies?"

We? Jax caught the look on Harlan's face as his eyes darted to him and back to Declan quickly. Who the fuck was this guy?

"Well, Declan, this is Jaxon *Hawthorne*." The emphasis on his last name made Jax cringe inside a little. A common enough occurrence, but he hated it anyway. But Declan either didn't know the background of his family name or didn't give a shit.

"Jax, this is Declan Stone." The lift of one eyebrow was the only outward sign he allowed of the surprise he felt flicker inside. There hadn't been a descendant in the Stone line in town for well over a hundred years. They'd been the first line to leave Havenwood. That made five of the Six in town now. He quickly added that to the "what the fuck is happening" pile.

"Short of a few others in town, he's the most qualified to understand what all this is about," Harlan continued, trying to justify Jax's presence to Declan.

"What are you, a professor of the occult or something?" Declan asked dismissively.

"Or something." Jax met the glare the other man shot him with an unaffected shrug of his shoulder, casually communicating that his air of dominance which probably worked on most, wouldn't work here.

A vein pulsed in Declan's neck as he turned back to Harlan, "If only a few people around here would know how to commit a ritualistic murder like this, wouldn't that make him a suspect, not a consultant?"

Harlan opened his mouth but couldn't formulate a rebuttal quickly enough.

Logan scoffed, voicing Jax's thoughts. "Who the hell even are you?" Declan gave Logan his direct gaze for the first time, though Jax had no doubt the man had been acutely aware of every breath each of them had taken from the moment he'd entered the scene.

"Declan is uh, he's a new addition to the department. Declan, this is Logan Sinclair," Harlan said, trying to mitigate the growing levels of testosterone filling the small cave.

"Let me guess, another expert?" Declan's voice dripped with sarcasm as he looked Logan over.

"He's, uh, good with the ocean. They're sort of a package deal." Harlan explained, waving his hand between Jax and Logan. Jax really could have done without his assessment. They were thirty-year-old men, and Harlan was making it sound like they were little boys running around with walkie-talkies, tracking each other's every move.

Declan ignored the comment entirely, turning his back on Jax and Logan to face Harlan, who still hadn't moved much further than just inside the mouth of the cave. "I don't suppose anyone has bothered to check the body for ID?" Declan accused, a subtle southern drawl rounding his words.

"Not yet. When it comes to things like this, I've learned not to cross the lines... or circles," Harlan looked pointedly at the black powder surrounding the body, "that are out of my league. This is definitely out of my league.

"His name is Jeremiah," Jax said to the other man's back.

Declan looked over his shoulder at him, then back at Harlan. "So, your *expert* knew the vic too?" More sarcasm. If it hadn't been directed at him and used to insinuate he was a murder suspect, it may have made Jax like him. At least a little. But that wasn't to be the case today.

"No one in Havenwood uses ID. No need. As I said, the *vic's* name was Jeremiah. He moved to town a couple of months ago and is renting the backhouse over at the San Roman's place, and spends a lot of time outside town for work." Jax spouted off the report like it wasn't information most people wouldn't be able to recall of someone closer to a stranger than an acquaintance.

He stepped toward Declan, sick of this stranger wasting time on baseless accusations. "It's a small town, everyone knows everyone and all that. Except for you, that is, Declan *Stone*."

Logan, having moved in that silent way of his, placed a large, tattooed hand on one of each of their shoulders. "Hey guys, relax, you're stressing the sheriff out and I don't think the ol' boy can take much more today."

Declan held Jax's glare for a moment before he shrugged off Logan's hand. "He may have needed your help," Declan flicked his head toward Harlan, "But I don't need a couple of co-dependent, amateur sleuths stomping around, fucking up my crime scene. You're officially trespassing." His words were precise and radiated that same air of authority he seemed to think he had.

Jax was putting the pieces together, and he didn't like the picture it made. He was about to ask for clarification on what role, exactly, Declan held that made him think anyone should give a flying fuck what he said. He needed to make Harlan give up the secret he'd somehow managed to keep, but Logan spoke before he could.

"Hey! You absolutely do not have to twist my arm to get me out of this den of depravity. Think we could both use some whisky to wash down the murder, anyway. Right Jaxy?" Logan squeezed Jax's shoulder and dipped his head toward the cave entrance, imploring him to heed Declan's demands. It went against Jax's nature to leave something unresolved—the crime, and the answer to why this stranger had such a stick up his ass. But it was a rare day that Logan was the levelheaded one in their friendship.

Jax let his posture relax. "Right." He looked away from Declan to

Harlan. "Sheriff." He dipped his chin to the aging man as he moved to leave the cave, Logan right behind him, all too ready to get into the sun and away from the body.

"Oh, and Sheriff," Jax paused at the mouth of the cave. Declan and Harlan both turned to look at him. "Whoever did this knew what they were doing. Those sigils were most likely used to keep the tide out and to preserve the ritual site for as long as possible, to maximize its effects. Also, your *vic*? He died between three-thirty and seven this morning."

CHAPTER FOURTEEN

*L*iv did her best to unpack the rest of the books from the remaining box. Not understanding Jade's stocking system, if she had one, meant wandering the aisles and shelves until she either found the same title or a similar genre.

Holding a few copies of the same book, she lifted her chin slowly to the highest shelf. Of course, that was where they went.

She scanned the shop for a ladder, but why would Jade have one when she had her magick? Liv looked toward the front door, to the books in her hands, and then back up to the top shelf. With one last glance at the front door, she closed her eyes and blew a breath through her nose.

The weight lifted out of her hands, and she opened her eyes to watch the books lift into the air, much slower and less gracefully than when Jade had done it, but they were getting there all the same. Just as they reached the edge of the highest shelf, the bells on the front door chimed and a breeze flitted in through the opening door. Liv's head swung to see Jax standing just inside the shop, his bright eyes locked on her, causing her to momentarily lose concentration on the heavy books floating above her head.

They started to fall at the same time Jax lunged forward, his magick darting out toward the falling books, catching all but one.

Liv half-ducked, half-fell onto the floor, the book striking her in the side of the head. "Shit!"

Jax was already there, crouching next to her on the floor when she opened her eyes. Gently, he pulled her hand away from where it pressed into her skin. "Let me see." His voice was deep, the words low. The heat from his body coasted over her as he crowded her front, the bookshelves at her back. She focused on the concentration and what looked a lot like concern on his face, the combination momentarily distracting her from impending embarrassment, and she gave into the urge to just look at him. His jeans were dirty and worn in a way that made them look like they were made specifically for his body. Well-used work boots were tucked under his jeans, and the T-shirt he wore showed off his tan, muscular arms. He smelled like fresh-sawn wood and *him*. Not his magick but his skin, his sweat. A scent that was not helping stabilize her lightheaded state one bit.

After a moment her sanity returned and she pushed her heels against the floor, slipping out of his reach. She lifted her hand, touching her head then looking at her fingers. No blood. She blinked a few times. No concussion. "I'm fine." Probably.

Jax looked at her, a single dark brow lifting as if to say, *clearly*. Could eyebrows be sarcastic? Because it sure seemed like it. Jax shook his head, any sign of possible concern from a moment before easing from his face.

She moved to pick up the offending book a little too quickly. Her body swayed forward and there was Jax again, his hand shooting out and pushing her back down to sit on the floor. Okay...so the concussion was back on the table. His other hand snapped to the side and the book flew to its spot on the top shelf. While the books had moved gracefully like a gentle dance, under Jade's magick, this one cut through the air like a knife, snapping itself and the others into place. The showoff didn't even bother to look when he did it.

"What the hell are you doing?"

"I was trying to put the books away," Liv said, stating the obvious.

"I can see that, kind of." The corner of his mouth barely twitched. "I mean why? What are you doing here? Where is Jade?"

"There was an incident at Cori's school. She asked me to watch the shop until she got back." His eyes showed the briefest moment of surprise before lifting over Liv's head.

"Well, hello guys," a raspy feminine voice said from behind her. Liv turned to see Quinn standing a few feet away, looking down at them with a crooked grin on her face. Jax stood up and Liv followed, but quite a bit slower. A dull ache was beginning to bloom on the side of her head. She resisted the urge to rub it, trying to salvage the small amount of pride she had left.

Jax ignored Quinn's insinuation. "Is it ready?"

"Yes. It's right over here. Hi Liv!" Quinn smiled as she moved behind the counter. "What brings you in today?"

"She's covering for Jade. Cori got in trouble at school again." A small piece of Jade's one-sided conversation she'd overheard suddenly gained context, and she didn't like it at all.

Quinn's laugh came from her throat, "That little one needs a hazard sign glued to her forehead." Then she disappeared into a backroom, returning with something thin and square, wrapped in brown paper. She set it on the counter in front of them. "Would you like me to unwrap it so you can make sure everything looks right?" She moved her fingers to lift the tape keeping the paper in place. Jax's hand moved quickly to stop Quinn's.

"I'm sure it's perfect," he said, sliding her hand off, taking the package from the counter, and tucking it tightly under his arm. His eyes shifted away like he was willing the conversation to end. Now Liv really wanted to know what was inside that paper.

Jax handed Quinn some money. "Thank you for your patronage, Mr. Hawthorne. I hope you enjoy your purchase," she said smugly.

Jax made a noise that was maybe supposed to be an affirmation but seemed more like a "shut up" in the form of a grunt.

The bells on the front door rang as Jade walked in.

"Uncle Jax!" A blur ran through the shop, colliding with Jax's legs in a bear hug.

He bent down and lifted her with one arm, setting his package on the counter. Liv's fingers tingled with the desire to peek. But she turned her attention to the little girl in Jax's arms instead. Then had to internally scold her ovaries again. The little girl's face was so much like Jade's, if it weren't for her mane of fiery red hair, she could have been a clone.

"Hi, Quinn." Cori waved. "Is Boo-Boo home?"

"He is. But he's sleeping right now."

"Oh, yeah," Cori whispered as if she were trying not to wake someone, or whatever a "Boo-Boo" was. "Because owls are nocturtle!"

A laugh bubbled up out of Liv before she could cut it off. Jade and Quinn both smirked but Jax didn't seem to find it funny—if anything, his scowl deepened.

Cori's inquisitive bright blue eyes landed on Liv. "Who are you?" Right to the point, too. Just like her mom. Liv was pretty sure she loved the little girl already.

"This is Liv, she's an old friend of mine and Uncle Jax's." Jax's eyes pinched at the corners, but he didn't contradict his sister. Liv decided it was time to stop trying to decipher his every shift in mood.

"You must be Cori. It's nice to meet you. I've heard so much about you!"

"Woooowww. Your eyes! They look like a cat's! Can you see in the dark, too?"

Liv laughed again. "I wish. Unfortunately, they're just standard human eyes."

"Uncle Jax. I saw a delivery truck outside Mac's...do you think it's more ice cream?"

"Are you serious? We just left *another* meeting with your teacher and you're trying to get ice cream? Absolutely not." Jade leveled Cori with a look that reminded Liv of the one Sandra had given her just the other day.

"You said triple scoop if I didn't burn the school down. That was the deal, and I didn't!" Cori reminded Jax, ignoring her mom.

"We never said triple scoop."

"Hello?" Jade waved her hand between Cori and Jax. "I said NO scoop. Not burning a school down seems like a really low bar, Jax."

"It was sarcasm."

"She's six."

"She's also your daughter. It's basically her first language." He had a point there, even if she didn't want to agree with him.

110

Cori shrugged. "Deal's a deal."

"No. That deal was not approved by me. Deal voided. As a matter of fact, no ice cream period until you can make it a week without setting any fires! Period!"

"What?! That's not fair." Cori's face drooped. "It's not all my fault, Mom. It's just so hard *not* setting anything on fire when Colby Peters is around. He's mean to everyone, and it makes me so mad!" Liv had the sudden urge to go find every scoop of ice cream in town just to win back her little smile.

Jade stared at her daughter for a moment, her face softening. "Single scoop."

"Double," Cori negotiated.

"I think we should quit while we're ahead, Firefly."

Oh shit. *Firefly?* A nickname? Spirit save her. And all her lady bits.

"Okay deal. Let's go before she changes her mind. Bye Quinn, bye Liv! Bye Mom."

"Bye baby." Jade's eyes narrowed on Jax, "I'm letting you know right now, if she comes home like some kind of sugar-possessed demon she's sleeping at your place. And I shouldn't even have to say this, but I'm going to anyway. NO POWER TOOLS."

"Noted." He nodded and moved toward the door, but stopped short. "Oh, come by my place when you're done here, we need to talk," he said to his sister.

"Is it good or bad?" Jade narrowed her eyes at Jax.

"Secrets, secrets are no fun, Jaxon," Quinn added.

He ignored both of them, turning to Liv. "Try to avoid any more magickal mishaps if you can. I think we've had enough injuries for one week." Then he walked out, leaving Liv oscillating somewhere between embarrassed, confused, and desperate to know what he wanted to talk to Jade about.

"Everything go okay at the school?" Quinn asked Jade as she walked behind the counter.

"Yeah. No big deal," Jade said, coming to stand next to Liv on the opposite side of the counter. But the heavy sigh she released said otherwise.

Quinn looked at Jade and nodded gently before turning to the cash register and typing a few numbers in.

Liv followed Quinn's lead and changed the subject. "Do you work here, too?" she asked.

Quinn smiled. "Sometimes."

That had been what Jax said about her working at Mac's. "Exactly how many jobs do you have?"

"Right now? I don't know. I like to do a little of this, a little of that. I started walking Mrs. Dottie's guard dog in the mornings. Then there's this place, if Jade can bring herself to ask for help."

Jade gave her a look that screamed, "Ha-ha very funny," as she fidgeted with some pens in a jar on the counter.

"And sometimes Mac's when Logan needs someone to cover. Different kinds of art on all kinds of canvases." She winked at Jade, but Liv didn't get the insinuation. "Just kind of depends on the mood."

"Wow. You have like seven jobs. I don't even have one."

"Speaking of that…how would you like one?" Jade asked.

"Here?" Liv's face lit up.

"Yeah, why not?"

"I mean… are you sure?"

"See, this is why I have seven jobs and you have zero. If she's asking, she's sure," Quinn quipped.

"I'm sure. I wish I could say today was an isolated incident, but Aaron's made it more than clear that I can't count on him to do even the bare minimum. I need someone I can depend on, plus," Jade looked around at everything Liv had stocked, "pretty sure you put everything in the wrong place, but it works way better than the way I had it."

Liv beamed. "Okay!"

"Good." Jade nodded as she thrust a set of keys at Liv. "You can open for me tomorrow."

CHAPTER FIFTEEN

*L*iv walked into the quiet house, the stillness communicating Ivy's absence. Maybe it was an overreaction to let that fact worry her, but there it was anyway. Another rotation to the twist that had formed in her stomach the moment some women had come into The Bookstore while she was training, asking questions about what Jax "knew".

Jade had brushed them off well, acting as if she didn't have any information to share, but it had become quite clear that she just wasn't willing to share with the "Whispering Wives Club" when she turned to Liv and told her the truth—and granted her wish, revealing what Jax had needed to talk to Jade about the night before.

They'd found the body of a man, someone from the town, in the caves by the beach.

For the last several hours all she'd been able to think about was whether it was the man in the picture stuck in her head. Whether or not it was the husband of the woman she'd refused to help.

She chewed her already raw lip as she headed straight down the long hallway to the back of the house. Before she was even fully in the kitchen the lid was already coming off the tin of Chamomile tea on the counter.

"Don't suppose we have anything a little more on the alcoholic side?" she asked the empty kitchen. Liv snatched the chamomile tea bag out of midair before it could land in the mug that already had a steaming teapot poised to pour hovering over it.

The teapot hit the counter with a distinctly annoyed clank.

"I wonder if all magickal houses are so testy?" she wondered with a small halfhearted laugh.

She'd stopped trying to understand how the house could intuit needs and produce things seemingly out of thin air a long time ago. But it was times like these she wished it took requests.

After searching every cupboard and failing to find anything alcoholic, she settled for some stronger tea. Between the dreams and now the gnawing dread that she may, however inadvertently, have contributed to this man's death, and having no clue where Ivy was or when she'd be home, there was no chance she'd be sleeping tonight, anyway.

Liv leaned against the counter, sipping her tea, and attempted to let it work its inherent magick. On the outside she was calm, but on the inside an old familiar battle resumed. On one side of the battlefield Logic, trying to convince her she couldn't have known something like this could happen in Havenwood. She wasn't responsible for that man's death. *She hadn't even asked his name.* That she couldn't keep tabs on her sister at every moment. That she was fine, and that calling her or tracking her down would only cause more distance between them.

But on the other side of the battlefield, Feelings, Guilt, and Fear fought back hard. Replaying for her images of all the people she'd let down, every instance she'd failed, and everything that had already gone wrong, and still could. *Because of her.*

For a few minutes, the house was still and silent, as if whatever aspect made it sentient had left the room.

A sudden thud sounded from down the hall. Followed quickly by another, and another. Liv followed the sound out of the kitchen and through the house to the library. A few books littered the floor. Liv bent down to pick them up, turning one over to see what the house was trying to tell her. Nothing about any of the titles made much sense to her. "I think you've been alone too long. You might be losing it." *You may not be the only one,* was her immediate thought that she didn't voice, but also couldn't avoid.

The curtains framing the front window parted to the side, drawing Liv's eyes. New tendrils of green ivy, littered with a few delicate white buds swayed lightly on the other side of the window. Beyond the reemerging front garden, Jax's house sat perfectly framed in her window.

She looked down at the title of the book in her hand, *Gifts of the Spirit, Volume II: Second Sight and Other Intellectual Giftings,* and then back to Jax's house, slowly realizing what the house was suggesting.

"No."

Liv put the books back on the shelves and walked out of the library. The rug in the hallway slipped from under her feet, causing her to stumble and her tea to slosh over the side of her mug. "Oh come on. You're *my* house. You're supposed to like me better than him." The rug under her feet started to slowly pull backward toward the front door, taking her with it.

Liv leaped to the side, off the rug, and back into the library, "Stop. I can't." But even as she said it, she lowered herself onto the window seat, her eyes shifting to Jax's house again.

The distance between their houses felt so far. Like that walk would take all her effort. But the need to know, the possibility of at least one answer, was so tempting.

He'd been very clear. He didn't want her getting involved in what was going on in town. Which felt like reason enough not to go over there. But if it was Emma's husband, she was already involved, and not just because of the guilt. The whole point of bringing her sister here was to keep her safe.

She had assumed the danger her mom spoke of—the reason they'd left Havenwood in the first place—was little more than delusion or paranoia brought on by her drinking. It was a big part of why Liv had chosen to leave with them, to make sure Ivy was safe—not from the danger, but from their mom.

After their experience at the cabin, she'd brought Ivy back to Havenwood under the same instinct, keeping the promise she'd made to her mom the only way she knew how, despite knowing how her mom had felt about Havenwood.

Now, Liv feared she had been too quick to dismiss her mom's concerns and had inadvertently delivered Ivy to the very danger her mom had warned about.

Before she'd even fully committed to the decision, the front door opened with a flourish. "Gloating is unbecoming, even on a house," she called as she put down her tea and stomped out the door.

Something hit Liv on the back of the head as she stepped out onto the front porch. "Ouch! What the hell?" She turned around to find a lip gloss rolling across the wood planks.

Liv sneered at the house...but still moved to pick up the little tube. Maybe a bit of gloss wasn't the worst idea.

The wood floorboards creaked and shifted slightly under her feet. Once she was a safe distance away, she turned back to the shabby front porch. "Maybe you should worry a little more about your face than mine."

Mumbling to herself on the short walk across the street, cursing her nosy house and rehearsing her words to Jax, she suddenly felt like the distance between their houses wasn't far enough.

She was very grateful that she had the only sentient house in the neighborhood, since she'd spent several minutes standing on Jax's front porch, talking herself in and out of knocking.

The asshole probably knew she was out there the moment she'd stepped onto the property and was just standing on the other side of the door, letting her stew.

She adjusted the hem of her skirt and pulled her sweater a little tighter around her as the cool breeze followed the setting sun. This time of year in Southern California, you can experience two different seasons in one day: summer during the warm, sunny hours and fall in the chilly evenings. It made dressing for the day a tricky endeavor.

When she finally knocked, the door opened almost immediately.

Yep. *Asshole.*

And that was her last coherent thought as a very shirtless, very grown-up Jax appeared in the doorway. His wide shoulders nearly filled the space. All that height he had on her left Liv at eye level with skin. *So much golden skin.*

His hard chest, the ridges of ab muscles that tapered into thick oblique muscles split by a dark trail of hair. That was a new addition to grown-up Jax as well, she thought, as she traced the path of the happy trail all the way down, down, down, until it disappeared into the waistband of his low, *so* low, sweats.

"Good evening, neighbor."

Oh, this is what people meant when they said, well, fuck me. Good to know.

She didn't want to meet his eyes. She didn't want to see the cocky grin she knew would be there. Which put her in a tough spot, because she was also sure continuing the one-sided staring contest she was currently having with his crotch wasn't doing anything better for her pride.

Well, what did she have to lose now?

Liv let her eyes slide back up his body just as slowly as they'd slid down, enjoying the way his abs seemed to tense one by one as she passed over them. Like they could feel the intentional perusal.

By the time her eyes made their way up to his, the yellow ring around his iris looked like a fire eating up the blue.

And the shit-eating grin was on her face instead.

He cleared his throat, shifted, and ran a hand through his slightly disheveled, damp hair.

He'd just gotten out of the shower.

She tried not to picture it. How could she, anyway? She didn't even know what his room looked like, let alone his shower. Did any other women in town?

The stray thought was a cold bucket of water over her entire body.

"Whatever conversation you just had in your head, I think I prefer where it started more than wherever you ended up." He didn't smirk, just looked at her intently. "I've got something on the stove, and since I doubt you're here to borrow a cup of sugar…"

He pushed the front door open farther with the arm that wasn't leaning against the jam, making room for her to enter the house.

She ducked under his extended arm doing her best not to inhale for the brief moment they were in close proximity.

Even if she'd succeeded, it wouldn't have mattered. The foyer of the craftsman made her feel like she was drowning in him. Not just his scent but *him*. His magick, his essence. And beyond that, the delicious smell of whatever he was cooking.

Her eyes swept over his home like they had his body. The same warm wood that encased the large front window was used for the banister that traced the stairs to the second floor, and on the floorboards that accented the sage green walls perfectly. Built-in bookshelves stacked with well-worn books framed the fireplace, and a wingback chair and small sofa sat in front. The low sound of mellow blues flowed from a record player tucked into the corner, proving that not everything had changed. A pair of boots that looked like they'd been kicked off and a couple of books strewn on the couch made the space feel even more comfortable than the warmth of the wood.

It was completely him.

Liv followed Jax through a cased opening into the kitchen. More wood, windows, and light countertops made the space feel warm but airy, even with the growing darkness outside.

Jax walked over to a small speaker on the counter and turned it down, but not all the way off. The music that drifted around the kitchen filled the silence between them as Jax leaned against the counter expectantly, and she tried to figure out where to begin.

Those seafoam eyes that had always seen too much bore into her. She should have thought about this more before coming. Taken the time to craft her story. Pick which pieces she was willing to give him. *Too late now.*

His eyes shifted to the whisky he'd just poured, debating whether to dump it down the sink or his throat. It'd gone warm in the time it had taken her to knock.

She was in his house, standing there in the center of his kitchen, a plaid skirt skimming the middle of her thighs, a thin sweater he didn't know if he loved or hated for hiding some of that olive skin from him, and all that dark hair thrown up in some kind of messy thing on the top of her head. Unruly strands hung around her face as if they refused to cooperate. She wore no make-up except a layer of something shiny on her lips that did just enough to draw his eye.

Down the throat, then.

He moved to where he'd been making dinner before he'd felt her on his porch. The sensation had been as corporeal as feeling her eyes on his back right now.

"Have you eaten?" he asked, trying his best to be gentle before he started demanding answers.

"I'm fine, thanks though." The hint of hesitancy in her voice grated at the patience he was clinging to. He wanted to know why she was there. In his house. In their town. In his fucking dreams every night.

He looked over his shoulder and his eyes caught on the flush creeping up her neck. He knew that flush would slowly make its way to the apples of her cheeks, and with the right touch to the right place, it would spread lower. He wasn't the only one affected by her being in his space. He'd missed having that effect on her. The sudden thought that someone else may have had a similar effect on her in all these years—more than one someone, most likely—filled his mind.

He turned back to the knife in his white-knuckled grip. "That wasn't what I asked. Have you eaten?"

He could feel her loud sigh as the breath coasted over the skin of his bare back and had to stiffen to keep the goosebumps at bay. "No, Jax. I haven't eaten. I'm not hungry."

Also not what he'd asked. He pointed toward the stools behind the island. "Sit." He wasn't trying to be bossy or short, but the way she was standing in the center of his kitchen made him feel unsettled, like she might bolt right back out the front door at any moment. Before she told him why she was there.

Thankfully she didn't argue and sat down. "What do you need, Liv?" he asked as he set a kettle on an empty burner and finished cooking his dinner. Maybe giving her his back would make it easier for her to get the words out. And maybe it would make it easier on him if he didn't have to look at those long legs her skirt accentuated. The sweats had done their job, but they weren't going to do him any favors when it came to hiding what those legs were doing to him.

"The body—" she started.

"You don't need to worry about that," he said, cutting her off as he crossed the kitchen to stand over her.

She narrowed her annoyed eyes at him, the bright green peeking through long dark lashes. Jax wondered if she realized the green on his walls was one of the lighter shades that wove through the green of her eyes.

Focus.

He set a mug of Earl Grey tea with too much honey and a sprig of lavender in front of her and watched surprise bloom on her face. Was she surprised he remembered? As if he could forget. Or was it really so surprising that someone would do such a small thing for her? The thought that no one else had been taking care of her was simultaneously pleasing and infuriating.

"Thanks." She gave him a small smile, and he, for whatever reason, couldn't turn away until she took the first sip. He watched her eyes close for the briefest moment when the warm liquid hit her tongue, and her throat work as she swallowed.

She looked back up at him and pulled the corner of her lip between her teeth. "I'm already worried about it, Jax. I need you to give me some answers this time."

He moved back to the stove, needing to look away from her familiar habit.

She was quiet until he returned to the island with a plate of creamy pesto chicken and asparagus. He stood at the edge of the island, setting the plate of fragrant food a little closer to her than him.

He took a bite of his asparagus and then used the empty fork to point at her. "I'm a little confused as to why you'd want to know about the body badly enough that you'd come over here. I thought you had enough crap to deal with," he said, using her own words against her.

"I do, but…" She hesitated.

"Get to the point. I'm on pins and needles here."

"What does that saying even mean? Have you ever thought about it?"

"Most signs point to an early nineteenth-century playwright, John Poole. Stop stalling." He wouldn't be distracted by her ramblings, no matter how much he'd once loved that particular quirk of hers. Now it felt like an irritating reminder that there were parts of her she was withholding.

Liv snatched a piece of asparagus from his plate and stood to pace the kitchen. He watched the fabric of her skirt shifting against her thighs as she moved.

When she sat back down in her seat across from him, he inched his plate closer to her. Without thought, she picked up the fork. He hid his pleased smirk by rubbing at the few days of beard growth on his face.

After she'd finished all of his asparagus, half his chicken, and all of her tea, she finally let out a long sigh. He wasn't sure if it was from contentment or resignation—either way, it was a small victory for him.

"Ok, you've fed me. Now can we talk about the body? Please?"

The desperation in her tone was unsettling. He looked at her, really looking, trying to gain some insight. But she'd tucked herself away behind that too-practiced mask.

He sighed, too, and allowed his tone to soften. "What's going on, Dandy?" Her eyes pinched slightly before shifting away from his use of the nickname. He'd used it on accident the other night, an old habit, returning too easily in a charged moment.

But this time it was different.

His mind did what the Spirit had gifted it to do, bringing forward old images of them tucked together tightly on the little balcony outside her window, making wishes on dandelions she summoned up to them from the garden below. Night after night he'd scaled that trellis of vines, and every night she'd spent tucked between his legs, pressed against his chest, with each dandelion that drifted into the sky, they'd built the life they'd imagined for themselves. But really, *she* had always been his wish. He remembered the moment he'd realized it, that whatever life she wanted, he'd make it happen. Because all he needed was her.

He'd had less than a year after that before she'd disappeared. Just enough time to put some of those plans into action for them. Not enough time to convince her to live them out with him.

Jax cleared his throat and the images from his mind. "Did you know him?"

She nodded but then caught herself. "No, but I may have met his wife." Her voice cracked, and her face lost some of its color. "A woman showed up on our porch shortly after we got back in town. She said her husband had been missing for a week and asked us to help her find him."

Jax hadn't heard anything about a missing man, or even a woman looking for someone. He needed to find a way to get some insight into what, if anything more, the sheriff's investigation had turned up.

"She said he was like us, at least in a way—that he had a small ember of magick. Not enough to do much with, and she never mentioned what line it came from." She shook her head. "I was so quick to shut her down, I never even asked her his name."

Liv didn't try to justify why she'd turned them away or lessen the burden of guilt that was so clearly clawing at her. She sat in it, because she thought she deserved it.

"And now you think the body might be him, and somehow you're to blame for that?" Jax knew she didn't owe anyone her magick, and yet here she was taking the blame for something she had nothing to do with.

"I'm sorry Liv, I can't tell you if it was this woman's husband or not. All I know is that his name was Jeremiah, and that's not going to do us any good."

"I may not know his name, but you saw his face, didn't you?"

He nodded, trying to figure out where she was going with this.

"So did I. A picture, I mean."

Jax's body stiffened. Was she asking him to do this? She didn't look away, even though they both knew this was a bad idea.

"It's really that important to you?" She pulled her lips into a tight line and didn't look away. He knew the answer anyway. "What if it is him? Or what if it's not? Have you thought about that?"

"Yeah, I have, but either way I need to know, Jax."

He took the empty plate and silverware to the sink to rinse them, using the act to buy him a moment to think.

Could he even do it? Technically yes, but with her? It had always been different with her, a different intimacy to their magicks mingling that way. It would be… intense.

He relented and turned to face her, bracing his hand on the edge of the counter, his grip tight enough that he thought it might crack the stone counters as the thoughts bounced around in his treacherous mind. *Needed to know. Needed him.* She wouldn't put it that way, and he shouldn't want her to.

"Fine. But first I need to know something."

Her eyes rose to meet his, trepidation glittering in their viridian depths as she waited for him to go on.

"Why did you come back? No bullshit. No distraction or play on words. Why now?" It wasn't the question he really wanted to demand the answer to. Quite the opposite. But he knew he had a better chance of getting this one without sending her running off than he did with the one he didn't voice. Not why did you come back... *why did you leave?*

Her face shifted, tinged in anguish like she knew exactly what he was thinking. And of course, she did. Besides Jade, she'd always been the only one who could take one look at him and know exactly what he was thinking. As if his eyes were nothing more than magnifying glasses on his deepest thoughts.

He didn't give her the relief of hiding it. Maybe it was emotional manipulation, but if she knew he wasn't asking the question he wanted to, maybe she wouldn't refuse him the answer to this one.

The corner of her lip disappeared between her teeth again as she searched for an answer, those green eyes never leaving his.

"After my mom died... we didn't have anywhere else to go."

He waited. There was more. She was trying to see how little she could get away with sharing. And as much as his patience had already been tried lately, he was content to wait her out in silence.

She sighed, propped an elbow on the counter, and leaned her forehead onto the tips of her fingers.

"One day, not long after my mom died, I don't know, eight months ago maybe, the deed to Havenhouse just showed up out of nowhere at the cabin we were living in at the time. And then it kept showing up, all over the place, more or less every day. No matter what I did to it or how I tried to avoid it."

He tried not to laugh as he imagined the stubborn personality of the house imbued into the deed, chasing her down. "It went on like that for a few months, and I continued to ignore it. Until one day it became clear it wasn't..." she paused, considering her words, "a good idea for us to stay there in that cabin anymore."

"Then the deed showed up again and well, I couldn't deny it anymore, could I? And even if I'd wanted to, like I said, we didn't have anywhere else to go." She looked down at her lap and traced the lines on her skirt with her dainty finger. "Nowhere I would feel safe like I had here."

The words hung between them for a moment. *Feel safe.* That had been his role in her life once. He wasn't sure what had scared her, but he wanted to find it and remove it from her world, just to remind her he still could.

"And that's why you wanted to know about what's going on in town, to see if you actually are safe here after all."

It wasn't a question, but she looked up and shrugged. "Yeah, I want to believe this is still the safest place for us..." she said, letting her words trail off.

"But?" he pressed.

"But, I can't afford to be wrong."

He nodded slightly, pressure building in his jaw. Part of the reason it had taken him so long to accept she wasn't coming back was that he didn't believe she'd wanted to leave in the first place. It dawned on him then that, even after all these years, somewhere inside him he'd still held that belief.

But she'd become a woman in all those years, one who could have come home at any point. It had taken fear and having no other option for her to do it. If another opportunity suddenly became available, or if she no longer felt safe here, who was to say she wouldn't disappear again?

What she was asking though, having her magick embedded in his skin, after she'd accidentally lit him up that night he'd walked her home...it would be nothing like weaving his consciousness with hers.

The way his traitorous magick writhed restlessly within him at just the thought of doing this with her was a warning bell in itself.

Jax ran a hand through his hair. He hated that the idea of her leaving again felt so unacceptable, but if this was what she needed to stay, he could do this for her.

He sighed. "I'll go change."

CHAPTER SIXTEEN

*I*t shouldn't take this long just to put a shirt on.

She could hear Jax's footsteps on the floor above her when he'd first left her sitting on the couch directly across from the tempting front door, but it'd been silent for at least two minutes. Two long minutes of willing her body to stay put while she pictured him sitting on the edge of his bed, in the bedroom she had to fabricate images of.

Maybe he was giving her a few minutes to think—to be sure she wanted to do this. On the other hand, this could just be his way of making her suffer a little, knowing her anxiety was growing by the minute.

Liv jerked her legs up, folding and unfolding them under her as she shifted on the couch, the plush material starting to feel scratchy. She pushed a rough breath at the hair hanging around her face that had suddenly become incredibly irritating.

When that didn't work, she yanked her hair tie out, stiffly pulling all her hair up high on her head again, looping the band one twist tighter than usual. The pressure on her scalp was a welcome, if momentary, distraction from what she was about to do.

She heard Jax's steps moving down the stairs and nearly groaned in relief. She'd been grateful he'd gone to change out of grey sweatpants (and not much else) before they did this, but the sight of him as he walked down the stairs in his dark jeans, and the way the white t-shirt hung on his torso but sat taut at the width of his chest and arms, wasn't much of a relief.

He shoved the old steamer trunk that functioned as a coffee table away from the couch and came to stand in front of her. "You ready?"

She had to crane her neck to make eye contact with him from where she sat.

Nope. "Yeah."

Liv ignored how evident it was that he did not want to do this. She needed to know. Jax lowered to his knees in front of her. Even though they'd done this before, it still felt like a first. It took all her effort not to fidget as he settled and leaned in toward her.

"You remember how this works?" Pinpricks of awareness danced across her skin where his breath touched her.

She hadn't even realized she'd closed her eyes until they popped open to find his face hovering close to hers. Arguably closer than he needed to be. She nodded, not trusting the stability of her voice.

Their eyes locked, bright green on icy blue. Did she feel his magick or see the veins of gold moving in his irises first? She couldn't be sure, but in the next moment, all her awareness was focused solely on him. His magick moved slowly up her body as he eased into her, and her into the process.

She squeezed her eyes closed tight under the feeling. It didn't hurt. That would've been easier to tolerate.

"Relax, Liv." The words were stiff but his thumbs were gentle at her temples, brushing over fine hairs and across her hyper-sensitive skin. Neither of which was helping her to comply with his request.

She could feel the tension in his body, in the places it touched hers. Regardless of how he felt about her now—which was anyone's guess at this point—sharing this wouldn't be easy on him either. She shouldn't have expected him to say yes to this request, but some part of her had, other-wise, why would she have come at all? And what did it mean that even after all this time she still knew he wouldn't say no to her if he knew she needed it? Or that he hadn't?

The feel of Jax's fingers brushing against her skin reminded her it was absolutely not the time to examine the nuances of their… interactions.

His magick was trying to slip into her mind's eye, gentle and coaxing, as if it were attempting to charm her into allowing him in. She did her best to relax into her body and focus on the smooth circles he was stroking on the side of her face rather than wasting energy in the attempt to keep certain memories hidden.

Little by little the pressure of his magick increased in her mind and built into the air around her until she was engulfed in him. Drowning.

Her chest began to rise and fall in shallow breaths. She gulped for air, but at this proximity, all she got was a mouthful of his minty breath and his intoxicating magick.

There was a burning in her chest. It was too much...*everything was too much*. His hands on her, his breath on her, his magick on her. All of him on her, working itself inside to her most hidden parts.

People thought sex was the zenith of intimacy, but they hadn't experienced allowing someone into their memories—the place where you were laid bare. There was no telling what he might find around some dark corner of her mind. Everything was archived there, whether she could actively recall it or not. Nothing was off limits. It required the utmost trust...or desperation.

They both exhaled when she felt him push past the barrier in her mind. She wouldn't be able to control what he could see now that he'd entered the halls of her memories.

Liv had never met another Memory Walker, but she'd read about them. It could be a dangerous gift for a less skilled witch. There were all sorts of things that could go wrong when one shared consciousness with another. There was a danger, too, of the Memory Walker getting lost in someone else's memories, and not being able to return to their consciousness.

Most Memory Walkers weren't powerful enough to search out specific memories the way Jax was. If the Walker wasn't able to control what memories they saw they could be bombarded by whatever the holder of the memory threw at them. But even for Jax, there was always a risk.

Suddenly the small shallow breaths weren't enough, and what they were doing was far too much.

"Breathe."

Easy for him to say, he wasn't the one having to lay himself bare. So much had happened over the last decade, and if he saw it... if she opened her eyes and found even an ounce of pity in his eyes, this entire move would have been for nothing, because there was no way she would be able to stand seeing him every day.

This was a bad idea. She wasn't this desperate—*shit*. She felt it right before he did.

His hands slipped to cup the base of her head, his thumbs pressing a little more firmly into her cheeks.

She couldn't relax, she couldn't do this...but she also couldn't move.

"You're holding on too tight. Let go, Dandelion." It was a whisper of a voice. She couldn't tell if it had been in her mind or ear, but the effect was the same. Something unlocked and a memory unraveled between them.

Emma stood on the porch clutching the image of her missing husband. The mixture of apprehension and desperation on the woman's face was even more striking now that Liv was removed from the situation—rekindling the guilt of turning her away, heavier now with the weight of the unanswered question hanging over her. Was it him? Was he the body Jax had seen?

She looked on as the anxious woman lifted the fluttering piece of paper, the one with the image of her husband at the center. That was it, that was all they needed.

As the memory began to fade and the edges of it darkened, Liv prepared herself, her mind and senses, to be free of Jax.

She waited, but Jax's presence within her wasn't easing, and she couldn't feel his physical presence outside of her anymore—something wasn't right.

The sound of a heartbeat filled her ears, and her awareness of the world around her, outside of her body, faded away entirely, leaving her solely in the presence of her consciousness.

Panic was just beginning to rise within her when the ability to control her mind was stolen from her, and she was suddenly ripped from one memory and plunged into another.

Deep in the gardens of Havenhouse beneath the old Willow tree, Liv rubbed the tips of her fingers together. Remnants of her Grammy's ashes were mixed in with the soil coating them. More dirt dusted her knees and dress, but she didn't have the energy to care, let alone brush it off. Her eyes drifted to the freshly upturned dirt just beyond her toes where now lay all that was left of the force of nature that had been Valeria Terrabella.

She tilted her face skyward at the sound of light rain hitting the dense canopy of trees above her. Too few drops made it through. She needed it to pour down on her, to wash the soil and ash from her hands and the sorrow from her being.

With what felt like the last of her energy, she forced the sky to open up, and the branches above her bowed and parted, letting the rain fall directly on her face to mix with her tears. A slender branch of the Weeping Willow reached out, brushing across her back in comfort before drifting to hang again.

The energy of the plant life surrounding her joined in the longing. Time slowed as she held her hands out and watched as black silt dripped from her fingers, taking a small part of the pain with it.

The earth below her bare feet hummed with the power of her ancestors, Valeria's melding with all those who'd come and gone before her. She knew it was a gift, both for her and her grandmother.

Everyone else had gone hours ago—this part was meant only for Terra-bellas. For her alone, it seemed. It would have been nice if her mom had stayed, let Ivy stay, to speak the words of their line over the matriarch. If not for Valeria, at least for her.

The words swam clearly in her mind, but when they found their way to her tongue, they came out ragged.

"From Earth, we're born, to Earth we're bound. In her depths our power found. When at last, to ash we burn, to Earth our ashes, we return. In cycles of life, our power refined, and thus our endless journeys entwined."

She repeated the words twice more before stepping through the veil of the Willow tree's branches.

She slowly waded back toward the house, her black lace dress thor-oughly soaked through as wet dirt gave way to scattered stepstones.

Grief felt like a heavy anchor wrapped around her heart, squeezing like *a noose, and dropping through her center as she moved. Attempting to weigh her down, making every step harder than the last. Her body was listless with exhaustion from carrying it around with her, and it had only been a week.*

Muddy footprints marred the oak floorboards in her wake as she made her way through the old house. She left them.

All the drapes were pulled closed, the faint warm glow from a single lamp in the corner of the sitting room the only source of light.

The house was mourning too.

The sound of dishes clashing against each other felt abrasive as it echoed through the stillness of the house.

She found her mom in the kitchen throwing things haphazardly into a box. A few more boxes were stacked near the back door.

Elena looked over her shoulder at her and then went back to what she was doing. "Take a box, whatever you can fit in it is what we can take."

"What are you talking about?"

"We're leaving."

"What?" The word was little more than a confused breath.

Elena froze, turning to her, green eyes that should match her own, but grew more foreign every day. "We. Are. Leaving." How could her eyes be so cold and so frantic at the same time?

Elena returned to throwing random items into boxes.

"Where are we going? For how long?"

"As far as we can get for as long as possible."

Her mind spun, fighting through the haze of sorrow trying to make sense of her mom's words. She couldn't leave.

"But—but we're the last Terrabellas, we can't just abandon our home. Our lives are here." Him. He was here. They had dreams to fulfill, and promises to keep.

Elena didn't bother to look at her, "Then stay here alone. You're old enough. It's your choice. But Ivy and I are leaving. Tomorrow, so you better make up your mind quickly. Does a town that doesn't even want you mean more to you than what's left of your family?"

Liv left the kitchen, her pace quickening as she made her way down the hall to the front door. She had to get to him. He'd know what to do. Jax would fix this, make it okay, make her okay again.

She reached the front door, then froze at the small sleepy voice.

"Sissy?"

She turned to see Ivy standing in pajamas that hung loose on her tiny frame.

"Hey." Liv knelt in front of her sister, resting her hands on Ivy's arms, gently sliding them up and down. "It's late, go back to bed."

"Mom had another loud dream. I think something is wrong with her."

"I know. But that's not for you to worry about. You know I'll take care of it right?" She pulled the pajama top that had fallen off Ivy's shoulder back into place.

Her sister nodded sleepily.

"Good. Go back to bed." She tucked a wayward strand of Ivy's brown hair behind her ear and kissed her forehead as she stood up.

"Where are you going?" Ivy asked.

"I just need to go out really quick." She opened the door, but instead of the porch that should be there, it was only swirling, inky, blackness.

It undulated in front of her, beckoning her to step closer. No words were spoken, but somehow she knew what it wanted—for her to join it. It was the way out. She just needed to walk through that door, and she'd be free, of what she wasn't entirely sure anymore. But when she tried to proceed, to heed its call, something held her back, something refused to let her go.

"Open your eyes." The deep voice came from within her. "Open your eyes, Liv." The voice registered, but she couldn't obey. Why couldn't she open her eyes? What the hell was happening?

"Olivia!" His voice boomed through the recesses of her mind in a shock that felt like a tidal wave washing through her.

She gasped as his magick suddenly whipped out of her, dragging her out of herself, and back into her physical body.

Jax's hands were still braced on the sides of her face, his eyes searched hers. "Are you okay?"

She blinked a couple of times, forcing her vision back into focus. It took a minute before she could tell, but taking inventory of her body, she found she wasn't in pain. She was just having a hard time getting her breathing back into a steady rhythm. "I'm fine. What happened?"

He sat back, surveying her. "I don't know. You pulled me into a memory, but then when I tried to back out it was like something was holding me there." She could see the questions dancing in his eyes. A question she wasn't willing to answer. Her chest was too tight, and the room was beginning to feel too small.

"I'm sorry," she said as she stood up, moving toward the front door. She wasn't sure what for, but she needed to get out of his house, needed air that wasn't laced with him.

Jax stood up, too. "Will you fucking slow down?" He pushed the door closed just as she'd gotten it open a crack.

"Was it him?" she asked before he could say anything else.

"Are. You. Okay?" He said the words slowly like she couldn't understand simple English.

"I—I don't know." It was probably the most honest answer she'd given him up until that point. But *she* hadn't pulled him into anything. There was nothing about that night she wanted to relive, let alone with him. "Please Jax, just tell me the truth. Was it him?" Her voice cracked as she looked up into those too blue eyes, eyes that now held the exact pity she'd feared they would.

Her body practically vibrated with the need to get out of that house, but she needed the answer he was holding hostage, so she forced herself to hold his eyes despite what she saw in them.

Finally, he relented. "No Liv, the man that was found in the cave was not the same man on that picture. But—"

She didn't let him finish, and this time when she yanked on the door, he let it open.

She didn't bother to check if it closed behind her as she ran down the steps and across the street. She didn't look back. Didn't hear his footfalls behind her through her racing thoughts.

The front gate opened before she got to it. She threw it closed behind her. The front door swung open, welcoming her in and wrapping her in the comforting familiarity of her home. Finally able to take a breath without drowning in him, clarity began to return, and the rock in her chest slowly loosened.

But her relief was short-lived. The reality of what it meant replacing the relief she'd gained at finding out that her self-preservation hadn't inadvertently led to a man's death finally sunk in.

Her anxiety began to kick up again just in time to feel Jax's presence at her back.

She threw her hands up in frustration. "What is the point of a gate or door?!" She wasn't sure who she was yelling at, Havenhouse, Jax, or the world. She moved toward the front door to invite him to get the hell out but he stepped in front of her.

"Will you fucking slow down for one second so I can figure out what the hell is going on?"

"That's the whole problem, Jax, I don't know what's going on. I have no clue what happened when you were in my memories, how or why you were pulled into that one, but it wasn't meant for you, and I certainly don't want to talk about it. On top of that, the body you saw wasn't the man on the flyer. Which is good, obviously." Her hands were moving as wildly as her mind was racing now. "But that means not only was someone killed in our town, but someone else might also be missing. At best." Her words came out in quick bursts, in an uncomfortable but also uncontrollable display of vulnerability. The chandelier above her began flickering, possibly in response to her emotions, but more likely expressing its displeasure with the way she was speaking to its new favorite.

"I'm aware of what it might mean. *Might,* Liv."

She shook her head. "And the dead body? Whoever was following me? We still have no clue what that was about. Those things happened. Even if he isn't missing, none of it should be able to happen. Not here!" It was a fact. Or at least it should have been, but the words fell from her lips like a plea instead.

Jax's jaw clenched and unclenched. "Liv…" Her name was a weary sigh as he reached his arm out, as if he might touch her but caught himself before he could.

The skin on her arm prickled with the touch that could have been.

The play of lights and shadows in the foyer distracted Liv from the swirling torrent of thoughts she was descending into, drawing her to the front window just in time to witness the headlights of an unfamiliar truck pulling up to the curb. Breaking off her conversation entirely, she stepped onto the front porch just as a dark figure made its way around the truck to open the passenger side door, and her sister tumbled out.

CHAPTER SEVENTEEN

*H*er sister's laughter resonated through the dark street as she swayed slightly, leaning into the stranger's arms for support. Liv's heart sank at the sight—Ivy was drunk. Hopefully just drunk.

Memories flooded Liv's mind—memories of having to track down her sister at dingy crash pads and smoke-filled house parties. The worse their mom had gotten over the years, the less self-preservation her sister demonstrated. Never seeming to grasp the potential danger she repeatedly put herself in—or maybe she just didn't care.

Liv hoped that wasn't the case, because it would undermine the whole point of coming back to Havenwood. She'd believed being home would mean Ivy would be safe, that she could afford to give her sister the space she so desperately wanted, and secretly that she might finally get a break from constantly worrying every time Ivy was out of her sight. But considering what was going on in town, and the fact that her sister could sniff out trouble like a damn bloodhound, that expectation seemed futile.

The random guy with his hands all over her sister would've been intimidating to look at even without the black ink creeping out of the collar of his black leather jacket, up his neck, and over the shaved sides of his head. Who even did that?

It wasn't usually in Liv's nature to judge people, but her sister had a type—tall, dark, and waving more red flags than the beach during rip tide.

The two of them started making out, completely oblivious to her presence. How was it that in the couple weeks they'd been back, and she'd been preoccupied with the house and reuniting with people in town, her sister had somehow found the time to not only meet people but find some random guy to make out with?

Icy fingers ran down her spine as cold grew inside her, a muted roll of thunder sounding in the distance, but Liv barely registered it through the torrent building inside her.

Just as she was about to finish descending the steps, warmth seeped into her, gently easing the storm inside, enough that she didn't leap out of her skin when Jax spoke from just behind her.

The smell, the feel of him hit her again a moment before his voice did. "Damn, she makes friends fast. Who is he?" The gravel of his voice was a low rumble close, too close, to her ear.

Liv stiffened, not wanting to show that he'd caught her off guard. "If you don't know, how should I? Why are you still here?" She fought the desire to turn from Ivy to look at him.

"Because, when you're done playing sentry to your sister, you're going to give me some answers."

She looked over her shoulder just enough to know what answers he wanted. Maybe he even deserved some of them. But rather than allow the challenge in his pale blue eyes and stubborn set to that stupid chiseled jaw to melt her into submission, she decided to focus on how infuriating it was that he thought doing her a favor entitled him to *anything* from her. And maybe it enraged her, too, that he would be there to witness whatever came next.

"I think we've shared enough for one day. Go home, Jax."

She needed to focus on what she was here for, and who she was here for—neither of which was him.

Rage only slightly banked, she descended the porch steps. Consistent as ever, Jax ignored her, following behind.

Liv cleared her throat obnoxiously, and still, it took Ivy and Random

Guy a moment too long to break apart, for him to remove his hands from where they roamed her little sister's body with too much familiarity.

When Ivy finally noticed her sister she dropped her head back and moaned her annoyance into the night. Random Guy peered around Ivy, focusing his intense gaze solely on Liv for longer than was comfortable. His hair was slicked back from his face, and just as black as all his clothes. She couldn't say he wasn't attractive, but in the kind of way that fire was fun to look at—until you got too close, and it burned the shit out of you.

Liv registered and chose to ignore the protective steps Jax took to close the distance she'd managed to put between them.

"I think it's time to call it a night, don't you, Ivy?"

Her sister took a few short steps toward the front gate. "I think you're my sister, not my mom. I don't have one of those anymore, remember?"

She remembered. Just like she remembered that their mom might have only died recently, but she'd been having to act as Ivy's only parental figure for far longer. If she still believed in wishes, she would have made a hundred to have the opportunity to just be a big sister to Ivy.

But she didn't have that opportunity. Not through wishes made on dandelions, or alone in the dark.

I DON'T HAVE ONE OF THOSE ANYMORE. JAX WATCHED AS THE BLOW LANDED, probably deeper than it was even intended to. But Liv schooled her face so quickly, shoring herself up, protecting Ivy from the effects of her own words. Keeping her secrets and hiding herself from everyone, including him.

The man dressed in head-to-toe black reached for the gate only to yank his hand back. Jax could feel the hum of an unfamiliar type of energy ripple lightly on the wards he'd placed on Havenhouse. When he tried to dig a little further, his magick stalled, as if it were attempting to wade through sticky muck and mire.

"I'll make sure she gets inside when we're ready." His words were weighed down by a heavy accent—Scottish maybe—not a local, but the stupid grin and dismissive tone made it clear that the smug douche knew exactly what Jax was doing. He recoiled his magic and stepped in front of Liv before she could respond.

"She wasn't talking to you, and I think you're ready now." He took a few more steps toward the gate. Part of him hoped the guy was enough of an idiot to push him. He ignored the magick rolling beneath his skin—he wouldn't need it for this. After all, he preferred not to use his magick for what his hands were capable of. Or fists, in this case.

Showing some modicum of intelligence, Smug Douche course corrected and turned back to his truck, stopping in front of a fuming Ivy on his way.

"I gotta go anyway, love." Ivy wavered slightly as he grabbed her face for a quick, hard kiss. "But I'll see you soon," he added as if speaking to Ivy, but with his eyes fixed on Liv. Then he jumped into his truck and peeled away from the curb, taking the feel of inky darkness with him.

LIV DIDN'T WAIT TO WATCH HER SISTER STRUGGLE WITH THE GATE. SHE ALL but ran toward the house, knowing what was coming and hoping they could at least make it inside before Ivy lost her shit on her.

She made it to the porch.

"I didn't even want to come to this lame-ass town! Or live in this shitty-ass house, but here I am! And when I finally find *one* redeeming quality about it, you can't even let me have that! You really need to get that stick out of your ass. Or maybe get laid. Something! Can you help her out with that?" Ivy threw an arm out, waving it from Jax back to her.

When Liv turned around she nearly collided with Jax, who had apparently taken up a side hustle as her shadow. He gazed down at her as she craned her neck to look up at him. "Is that true, Liv? Do you need my help?" He cocked his head to the side as if he were truly curious, and not baiting her. She took a moment, just a brief one, to let herself be sucked in by what she saw in his eyes. The slight tilt to his lips might have hinted at humor as if he were only trying to break the tension between the sisters, but what she saw in those eyes suggested something else entirely. *Shit.* Why did everything about him call to her so strongly?

She so did not have time for this. Liv pushed him to the side and looked at her sister, who was trying and failing to keep her balance as she attempted to take off her heels. She looked more like an angry baby deer struggling with the cobblestone walkway.

As Ivy got closer, recognition finally seemed to hit her, seeing Jax under the porch light for the first time. She narrowed her eyes, fighting time and booze to place him. Liv saw the moment it clicked for Ivy, her eyes rounding in excitement. "Oh my gosh! Jaxon Hawthorne, is that you?" Ivy found her legs and ran up the first few steps, nearly killing herself as she hooked a toe and tripped over the last step. And, in an illustration of her entire youth, Jax was there in time to catch her. "It is you!" Ivy straightened and threw her arms around his neck, practically climbing him to reach.

"Hey Ivy," he greeted her back, wrapping her in a hug and steadying her on her feet as he released her again. She gripped onto Jax's biceps to steady herself and then squeezed. Liv rolled her eyes so hard she nearly saw stars.

"Damn Jax, you're like a real man now." Ivy smiled up at him as he used one of his large hands to keep her from slipping back down the steps.

Liv crossed her arms, quickly growing tired of feeling like some awkward bystander to a long-awaited reunion.

"You're looking pretty grown up yourself, little one." He tilted his head to the side. "And maybe a little drunk too?" Jax chuckled through closed lips, eyeing Liv over her sister.

Liv shook her head. Of course he found the whole thing amusing. Maybe if she'd been granted a different life, it might be to her, too. If she could play the role of the big sister and take Ivy inside, make her some greasy food to absorb the booze, and put her to bed.

"Maybe just a little, teeny, tiny bit," Ivy whispered, pinching her pointer and thumb close together. "Don't tell Liv, she gets so pissed when I have any fun at all." Ivy swung her arms across her body wildly.

"Is that so?" Jax looked at Liv with one arched eyebrow. "Well, that doesn't sound like the Liv I know."

Knew, she thought, as her eyes narrowed on him slightly.

"Oh, yeah, that's because she's not her anymore. Nope, not for a looonnnggg time. Not since mom went you know." Ivy twirled her fingers next to the sides of her head.

Liv cut her off before she could say any more. "That's enough, Ivy. Go inside."

Ivy turned toward the door a bit too quickly, swaying slightly, and again Jax was there to steady her, of course. "You good?" he asked, looking at her like he cared. *He still cared.* Much more of this and Liv would be too full of swallowed emotions to eat for a week.

"Yep." Ivy turned pointedly to Liv. "Right as fucking rain, actually." She gave Liv what was clearly the dirtiest look she could muster as she pushed past her and disappeared into the house, punctuating her exit by slamming the door hard enough to make the old windows rattle.

CHAPTER EIGHTEEN

*a*nd then they were alone again. Jax stayed Liv's hand on the door handle before she could flee into the house.

"Look Jax, thanks for sticking around for the show. But can we please just call a truce for the night?"

"You lied to me, Dandelion." He gave her a half grin, hoping to disarm her a bit. He wasn't ignoring her request, he just wasn't willing to grant it.

She stood up a little taller, pulling her hand out from under his. "No, I didn't."

"You certainly didn't tell me the whole truth."

"Maybe not, but I did tell you I don't owe you any explanations." Of course, she was going to make this as difficult as possible.

"What did she mean when she talked about your mom?" Shortly before Liv returned he'd heard about Elena passing away from his mom. How she'd found out, he had no clue. But that had been all the details he'd gotten. Ivy had implied that there might have been more to it than that.

Liv closed her eyes and sighed heavily. She looked tired. Not just from the day, but more than that. From carrying the weight of several years alone, from the sound of it. It pissed him off, but for the wrong damn reasons.

He should be mad that she'd made that choice, if anything. Not mad at himself for letting it happen.

She leaned a hip against the porch railing and sighed again as she looked out into the front garden. He looked, too, giving her a moment to choose to tell him more. It was starting to fill out nicely. The orange tree had leaves on it, and from where he stood he could see that the brittle vines on the trellis he'd climbed so many times were starting to show proof of life again.

"You know what Elena was like. She was never happy. Especially after whatever happened with Ivy's dad." Her tone was dismissive, but he did know. Even if forgetting had been within his control, he'd never have been able to. It was more than being unhappy—Elena was miserable. And she'd taken every opportunity to spread that misery around, targeting Liv most often. The memories still stirred anger in him.

"Let's just say it got a lot worse once Valeria was gone, and then spiraled from there. Bad enough that eventually, she needed real help. Help I couldn't give her. But I guess they couldn't either."

"I'm sorry you had to go through that alone." It didn't take an idiot to see that Ivy wouldn't have been any kind of support to her. They both knew it.

He also knew there was more to the story than she was giving him. He'd watched her cater to Elena for years. What he'd seen tonight between her and Ivy didn't seem too far off from it. And from what he could tell, she was still burying her own needs so far down under someone else's, that she didn't even know what they were anymore.

He'd let her drop it. For now.

"Thanks." Her eyes softened slightly, and then she made a move for the door again.

Again, he stopped her. "Not so fast, Dandy." She started to roll her eyes. "The memory I got pulled into? That was the night you left, wasn't it?"

He watched as that mask slid back into place, covering up what she was feeling and costing him the few inches of ground he thought he may have gained with her.

"Stop doing that." The words sounded more like a guttural plea than the command he wished they'd been.

"Doing what, Jax?"

"Stop hiding from *me*." She was shutting him out again. He could feel it. This time she was doing it while standing mere inches from him, rather than by disappearing in the middle of the night. He wasn't sure which was worse.

"I'm not hiding. I just don't want to waste time digging up the past with you when we have more than enough to deal with in the present. And for the love of Spirit, stop looking at me like that!"

"Like what, Liv?"

"With all that—" she gestured to his face, "*pity*." She started to pace, her frustration getting the better of her.

"Pity? I don't pity you. I'm trying to understand how you expect me to solve this damn puzzle when you won't give me all the pieces."

She turned back to him after a moment and spoke evenly. "I'm not expecting you to do anything. Certainly not with memories that weren't yours to see in the first place."

Her mask slipped for just a moment before she tried again.

"Look Jax, I appreciate what you did for me earlier. Thank you for coming over here to check on me and staying through all of that." She gestured around her like she could encompass where the scene with Ivy had gone down. "But it's unnecessary." She sounded like she was trying to cordially get rid of an annoying neighbor without offending them so much that it would be awkward to share a lawn. It was the equivalent of calling him her friend. *Again.* But she wasn't done yet.

"Despite what you think you know, or whatever you see when you look at me like that, I don't need you to recuse me. I came back here to try to create something stable for us. For Ivy. All I want is to find a way to create a normal life. So, let's just focus on figuring out whatever the hell is going on around here so I can do that, okay? Because other than that, we're fine." She gestured to the house where her intoxicated sister had likely passed out somewhere. "I'm fine. Just like I have been the last decade." She finished off her little speech, and something snapped inside of him.

"Twelve," he all but growled at her.

"What?"

"Twelve years. You keep saying ten. It's been twelve years, three months, and five days, Liv. That's how long you think you've been fine." *Without me*, he tried not to think.

Her mouth dropped open, and he wasn't sure if it was shock at his comment or she was revving up to say something, but he wasn't done. "Which anyone who bothered to look close enough would see is complete bullshit. Other people might buy this act, but I am not one of them." He took a step closer to her. "You have stuffed down, denied, and forgotten more magick than most people could ever hope to possess in their entire line! You've buried who and *what* you are so deep under your guilt and responsibility, you don't even recognize it. Do you even feel it anymore? Or is it suffocating slowly inside you, leaking out just enough to keep you from exploding? Because it will—this can't last." He stopped, chest rising and falling now as he stared at her, and waited.

Her green eyes flared brightly. *Good. Give it to me,* he silently urged her. Too far in now, he was going chip away at that mask she was wearing with whatever tool it took, even if it was her anger, even if it made him the bad guy.

"Are you done?" Her words weren't small, but they were aggravatingly controlled, with hardly any feeling.

"Are *you* done? Done pretending to be whatever *this* is?" He gestured to her, then quickly turned away, running a hand down his face and across the shadow of scruff that lined his jaw.

She didn't take his bait. When she spoke again it was with that practiced calm that forced him to turn back to her. "You don't get to show up and demand answers from me after all this time like you have a right. You don't, Jax. You don't have a right to any part of me anymore. Just like you don't get to stand there and judge me about things you don't know shit about." He opened his mouth to speak but stopped when she lifted her eyes to his. "Because you don't *know me* anymore." She patted a hand over her heart as she said it.

It was enough to send him over the edge if her words hadn't already done that. She was wrong. This could be her truth, but that didn't make it *the* truth. She'd closed him out once before. Left town, left him. She'd chosen then, and he'd let her. Let her shun every dream they'd ever had and ruin everything.

Her chest rose and fell with the effort she was exerting to maintain control, to hide from him. He balled his hands into fists at his sides to keep from reaching for her. The sound of his heart thrummed in his ear like a chant: *touch her, touch her, touch her.*

His mind replayed her words, insisting he choose self-preservation just this once when it came to her. His body begged him to storm down the porch and leave this girl, *woman,* behind him for good this time. He'd always been too indulgent where she was concerned, always choosing more of her in whatever form he could get. *Stupid. Indulgent. Masochist.* His head countered his heartbeat.

Jax exhaled a ragged breath, frustration coursing through him, laced with anger at himself for pushing her.

Liv didn't speak again, just chewed on the inside of her cheek as the two of them waged a silent war. His silence demanding her answers, and hers refusing to relent to his goading.

The pressure started to build in the air around them, followed by the distant roll of thunder, not totally uncommon for late August. But he could feel her on it, laced in it, and *fuck him* it was irresistible. It only took him a quick glance at her to know she wasn't aware she was even doing it.

He pulled her into him. She sucked in a small, surprised breath, pressing a hand into his chest between them. He knew she could feel his heart, his very essence beating.

"You're right, I know fuck all about what's gone on in your life. I don't even know where you were when that deed finally found you. I don't understand why you're so hell-bent on sacrificing every last piece of your-self to make sure everyone else is taken care of, or why you'd ever settle for *normal,* as if that was ever something you were meant to be."

He wrapped one of his hands around her hip, pulling her closer to him and willing her to stay in place. To keep her from fleeing. He took advan-tage of their proximity, wrapping his hand around her back and pulling her a little closer, so he could inhale the intoxicating scent of her hair and skin. He relished the way her eyes shined, and her body softened just a little in response to the way he shamelessly indulged in the scent and feel of her.

"You may be right about me not knowing exactly what's going on around here—that's become abundantly clear."

Jax splayed his other hand across her jaw, tilting her face and forcing her to meet his gaze. He used his thumb to swipe away the lone tear she let fall. They let the moment carry on a few heartbeats too long, long enough for his heart to sync back to hers like it was sighing in relief. *Home. Home. Home.* An old promise.

An old lie.

A new punishment.

"But you're wrong. I'll always fucking know you Liv, twelve years or twelve lifetimes; whether we're eighteen or eighty, it won't ever matter."

He released her suddenly, stepping out of her space and down the porch steps.

"You're the one who doesn't know you anymore, Olivia *Terrabella*. And until you can get your head out of your ass and remember who the fuck you are, *we're* not figuring shit out. And you can keep your pretty little ass in that house and stay the hell out of my way."

CHAPTER NINETEEN

*L*iv shifted the Tupperware under her arm and looked down at the flowers in her hands, flowers from her garden, and suddenly became self-conscious. Did it make her look like she was trying to kiss ass? *Hi. Thank you for inviting me into your home even though I disappeared for twelve years. Here, have some free flowers.*

She stood at the bottom of the porch steps to the Hawthorne home, Jax's childhood home. She felt a twist in her gut at the thought of Jax's words the other night, and his warning to stay the hell away from him. The thought made her seethe, even as she wondered at her own choice to respond to his directive by accepting the dinner invitation from his mother.

So much for keeping my pretty little ass in my house, she thought.

Through the screen door, she could hear the low hum of music, voices laughing and talking over each other in the way that only family could, while still somehow carrying on a conversation. A young voice yelling about something and the low gravel of a reply. She couldn't see them, but she could picture it all the same, and it made her heart ache a little.

A home. Maybe not hers, but it had been as good as hers for several years growing up. And it was something she'd missed desperately.

Most of her adult life had been a blur of big cities, where her mom had thought they could blend in, and rural middle-of-nowhere towns, where she'd thought they could hide from whatever haunted her, and supposedly hunted them all. Liv had allowed it based on the hope that the next town might bring her mom the peace she needed to settle in. But it had been a fool's hope.

The old cabin had been the closest they'd gotten. They'd spent nearly two years there. And that was only because it's where they'd been when Elena's mental health had gotten so bad she'd been forced to seek professional intervention.

Liv's thoughts rotated away from the painful memories to safer ones, like rethinking her outfit choice yet again. She'd already changed five times when the house had finally had enough and thrown the short, deep plum shift dress and nude sandals she currently had on at her. The dress was simple and comfortable but showed a good amount of leg. Too much leg?

She fingered her wavy hair, wishing she'd remembered a hair tie. In a rush because of all the outfit changes, she hadn't had time to do her hair, so she'd left it down to air dry.

"Rethinking your dinner plans before you even get inside?"

Liv startled, finding Warren Hawthorne sitting at the far end of the large wrap-around porch in one of the Adirondack chairs. "Didn't mean to scare you."

"I just didn't see you there, and no," she smiled as she climbed the steps toward him, "not changing my mind just—" She shrugged, unable to come up with a quick lie.

He didn't demand an answer like his pushy-ass son would have.

"What's in the dish?" Warren stood up slowly, stretching out his back as he went. Growing up, Warren had always been kind and welcoming to her. Jax had idolized him in a way that had made him seem like a giant of a man. He still had a gruff sort of indomitableness to him, but age had made him slightly more human. Seeing him show any sign of something as trivial as back pain still felt far beneath him.

Liv looked down at the dish in her other hand and back up at him. "Mexican wedding cakes." She shrugged again, trying not to set expectations for the dessert too high.

He tapped the lid with a dry calloused finger. "Valeria's recipe by chance?" The smile grew on her face at the mention of her grandmother.

"I'm not sure. To be honest, the house did most of the work." It was a good thing the house couldn't hear her taking any amount of credit, considering when she'd come downstairs after getting ready, they were already cooling atop the oven. All she'd done was wrap them up and carry them over here. But hey, that was the most important step, wasn't it? And something the house couldn't do. Probably. The full extent of what that house was capable of was anyone's guess and seemed to change based on its current mood.

"I'm pretty sure that was the secret to Valeria's recipe as well. The only cooking you want a Terrabella to do should involve plants and magick. Lots and lots of magick." He winked at her. "Let's have a taste. You know, just to be sure that kooky old house hasn't completely lost it in your absence." He cracked the lid of the Tupperware, pulled out one of the crescent-shaped desserts, and popped the entire thing in his mouth. Liv watched him chew as he nodded his head this way and that, pretending to be deep in contemplation.

"You know," he started before he fully finished chewing, "I may have eaten more of these than even your grandfather throughout my life. Which I think makes me a good judge." He took the Tupperware out of Liv's hands. "House or not, you did well, Olivia." He walked past and held the screen door open. "Welcome home, by the way."

And a small piece of her loosened.

"Look what I found on the porch," Warren said to no one in particular as they stepped into the foyer of the Hawthorne house. It was just like she remembered it. The scent of wood polish and dinner cooking in the air. The vintage coat rack standing in the corner, a little yellow backpack hanging where they'd hung theirs after school once upon a time. The beautiful, Tiffany-style pendant light overhead casting a warm glow over the family photos on the walls.

"Liv! There you are."

"I was talking about these," Warren lifted the Tupperware of cookies, "but yeah, her too." He drifted into the living room and down the hall that led toward a small den, cookies still in hand.

"Hey! Where do you think you're going with all those?" Sandra called after him, but he'd already disappeared around a corner. She rolled her eyes and moved in for a hug. "So glad you decided to take my invitation." Liv inhaled deeply in Sandra's warm embrace.

"Yeah Mom, like any of us had a choice." Jade walked toward her, skillfully balancing a half-full glass of wine as a flash of red darted between her and the wall.

"Liv!" She barely had time between Sandra releasing her to dip and catch Cori as the little ball of fire collided with her chest, wrapping her arms around Liv's neck. Hug complete, Cori took Liv's hand in hers and tugged. "Come look at the castle Papa and Uncle Jax built me."

"I have a better idea." Jade stepped in front of her. "Why don't we let our guests eat before we give them a grand tour of the palace? Besides, once we let Liv outside, we may not be able to get her back in."

Sandra laughed as she walked by them toward the kitchen. "I'm surprised she's even got shoes on!"

Liv marveled at how their seemingly simple comments made her heart swell. It was the little observations, learned habits, and casual familiarity families had. It was being known, being seen. And above all else, being accepted.

Cori's face drooped as she let go of Liv's hand. To cheer her, Liv brushed her little cheek with her fingers. "I promise I'll eat fast, and then we can sneak out there and you can show me anything you want."

"Okay!" Cori took off through the living room and cased opening that led to the large room where the kitchen and dining area were.

"Come on." Jade waved her through. "Wine is this way."

Liv trailed behind her friend, taking in the rest of the familiar house. It was a Craftsman, like the one Jax had bought across the street from hers but, larger. The Hawthorne's house was open and airy, with cream walls and accented with warmer wood, rather than the heavier and more masculine mahogany in Jax's.

It was meticulously decorated and filled with mementos, heirloom furniture, and photos.

She passed through the opening into the huge room where the kitchen was separated from a large dining area by a butcher block island.

French doors at the back of the room opened out into the grand backyard.

"No Ivy?" Sandra asked as she entered the kitchen, glancing up from the vegetables she was chopping on the island.

Jade patted the stool next to her.

"Um…" Liv hesitated, holding back a cringe. "No. She had to work. I'm sorry if you went out of your way for her for dinner." Liv hated lying to Sandra, but at least Jax wasn't there to call her out on it. The truth was, she had no idea what Ivy was doing. Besides giving her the cold shoulder.

The most she'd seen of her sister had been the back of her body vanishing into one room or another as she expertly balanced avoiding her while still managing to orbit her enough to make sure Liv didn't forget she was mad. As if that were possible. And to make matters worse, Liv had been playing her version of the same game with Jax, all but sprinting in the opposite direction whenever she got so much as a glimpse of his truck headed down the street or a whiff of his magick on the breeze. Except at night when she lay in her bed and felt his wards falling over the house, and she could revel in the feel of it where no one else would know.

"You have nothing to apologize for—well, unless those aren't for me." Sandra eyed the flowers she was still clinging to like they were some kind of floral emotional support pet. "They're beautiful," Sandra said when Liv thrust them at her. She took a moment to inhale the flowers deeply, closing her eyes, before placing them in a vase she pulled out from a cabinet. "I'm so glad that the gardens finally have you back." She handed the vase back to Liv, motioning for her to place them on the large dining table behind her.

Just as she set them down, Jax appeared in the archway connecting the kitchen to the hall that led to the bedrooms and powder room. She felt his eyes everywhere they moved over her. Having mastered dodging him, she hadn't seen him face-to-face since whatever the hell had happened between them on the porch the other night. And while she still hadn't been able to emotionally unpack that conversation, she also didn't know what version of him to expect tonight.

"Here you go, Liv."

She turned back to her seat next to Jade, who—like the savior she was —set a large glass of wine down in front of her. Liv took a sip, or maybe gulp was a more appropriate word. She tried not to squirm, but she could still feel Jax's eyes on her back.

"Hey, Hawthornes!" Quinn sang in her sultry voice as she glided into the kitchen. She looked effortlessly stylish as usual in bell-bottom jeans, a simple white tee tied into a knot, and a sheer green kimono with white embroidery thrown over. The chunky heels and stack of gold bracelets on her arm set it all off perfectly. If Liv thought her hips and ass could fit into any of Quinn's clothes she'd demand to be taken to her closet immediately.

Quinn walked straight to Sandra, giving her a light kiss on the cheek and handing her a bottle of wine. "Thanks for the invite. I think the kid who delivers for the Dades' restaurant was starting to get the wrong idea about why I order out so often. I found a flower and his number in the bag with my last order."

"Of course, sweetie. You're always welcome. I love having a full house," Sandra said with a smile.

Jax's eyes finally left her back only to reappear in front of her as he silently took over the vegetable cutting for his mom, who set Quinn's wine on the table and then drifted toward the living room.

"Are we sure your gift of the Spirit is Emp-a-thy," Jade over-enunciated the word, "and not just empty? Like, maybe there's just an abyss inside you where all the calories you eat go to die, allowing you to eat like a frat boy and still look like that?" She pointed to Quinn with the hand holding her wine.

Quinn sighed, "According to the most recent rumors I've heard, this," she waved her hands over the front of herself with a flourish, "is the result of a deal I made with gypsies, designed to lure the husbands of the Pilates Club into my wicked grasp."

Everyone laughed except Jax, who was too busy staring daggers at Liv to experience joy, but she focused on Quinn. "Um, what?"

Quinn shrugged. "Pretty sure that one was started by Pigeon-Poop Lady."

Liv nodded in understanding, the feeling of gratitude she'd had for Quinn when they'd first met returning.

"Pigeon-Poop Lady?" Logan walked into the kitchen and Liv couldn't help but smile at how he'd tried to clean himself up for dinner. Usually his hair either hung down around his shoulders in a mess of curls and knots thanks to seawater and a clear lack of brushing, or it was pulled back with a hair tie, still a mess of curls and knots. But it looked like he'd at least attempted to brush it before pulling it back into what resembled a bun that night. He wore a short-sleeve button-up shirt with well-fitted jeans. *Very* well-fitted jeans if she were being honest. Her smile widened to a grin when she made it down to his shoes—or flip-flops, rather. Logan was generally barefoot as much as she was.

"What exactly did I just walk in on?" Logan asked as he walked behind them, kissing Quinn and then her on the tops of their heads. Jade stood up before he could get to her, moving to the other side of the island near Jax. *Damn,* she'd kind of wanted to see if he would kiss her, too.

"Oh, nothing. It's just my and Liv's origin story." Quinn winked, coaxing another laugh from her.

"Speaking of Gifts of the Spirit," Quinn started, circling back to Jade's earlier comment, "Do you have one?" she asked turning to Liv.

Not everyone did. The Gift of the Blood was the magick that came through your ancestral line. It worked more closely with DNA. How much any one person got couldn't be precisely predicted, case in point her mom, and it could manifest to a varying degree based on the person, case in point her sister. The gifts you received were always intrinsically tied to your ancestral, elemental line.

There were no guarantees when it came to Gifts of the Spirit, though. No one was promised one, no matter how much power they had, and they weren't genetic in any way. Though it did seem that in the rare occurrence that one family was blessed with multiple members who'd received a Gift of the Spirit, they tended to fall within the same Center.

Her grandmother had taught her that the Centers were Head, Heart, Gut, and Hands, though Liv was pretty sure those categories had been the work of witches attempting to understand Spirit, more than the Spirit operating within any kind of boundaries. Jax's ability to Memory Walk would be Head, as would Jade's visions. If Quinn was an Empath, like Jade had implied, that would be a Gift of the Gut, even though Liv had always thought it would make more sense as a Gift of the Heart. She supposed that just because someone could pick up on the emotions of others didn't mean they understood or even cared about them.

Jax paused his chopping to look up at Liv. He raised a single eyebrow at her, and it felt like a challenge. Did he think she wouldn't tell Quinn? He'd accused her of hiding herself and denying her magick.

It dawned on her then…he thought she was ashamed of it, of herself.

It would be that simple to him. Because he'd never had to live with someone who resented him for something he had no control over. Or in a town that whispered about you behind your back no matter how much good you did with that gift. Or a mom who hated her magick so much she chose to slowly waste away rather than let you use your gift on her.

Liv made a point of looking away from him to Quinn, her chin lifting ever so slightly. "Hands," she said proudly. "My Gift of the Spirit is Life." Liv lifted her left hand, "Both giving," she wiggled her fingers, then raised her right hand, "and taking," she wiggled the fingers on her right. Then she turned a sickly-sweet smile on Jax, who immediately went back to chopping.

Of course, her Gift of the Spirit wasn't that black and white. It was limited, and nuanced beyond what even she knew, especially after all this time. But she wasn't going to give Jax the satisfaction of saying that part out loud.

"Wow." Quinn's eyes sparkled. "Have you ever used it?"

"I had the same goldfish for ten years."

"Oh yeah! How is old Hercules?" Logan asked.

"Finally had to let him go to that big fishbowl in the sky," she told him, laughing at her lame joke. You could only push a life so far beyond its natural timeline before it started to have major consequences.

"Aw poor little dude," Logan lamented.

"You mean he's sleeping with the fishes?" Quinn added. Liv fought to keep the wine in her mouth.

"Those are some pretty bad dad jokes," Jade said peering around Jax's arm to inspect his work.

Jax paused and glared down at her. "Can I help you?"

"Uh, pretty sure Mom said chopped, not macerated into baby food. Maybe you should step away from the knife."

. . .

A LITTLE WHILE LATER, LIV LOOKED UP AT ALL THE PICTURES THAT LINED the narrow hallway. She'd excused herself to the restroom, not because she needed to go, but because she needed out from under the weight of Jax's gaze. Then she'd gotten lost in the old pictures, distracted to still see herself in them. Her eyes drifted to a larger one in a wooden frame. It was taken from a distance, without them knowing. She and Jax were standing in their bathing suits with their fingers interlaced at the edge of the water. Jade and Logan were a few feet in front of them, water splashing up around them. All of their faces were forever frozen in laughter, captured by the moment and the photo.

She wished she could remember the day, or what they were laughing at, exactly. It was a blessing they'd had so many days like that, playing and laughing in the sun and the water. Singing and dancing in the sand, under the moon, around bonfires at night. She just wished she could remember the exact moment. Her eyes started to sting with tears she didn't understand.

Maybe because of how much had changed since the day in that picture. Maybe the joy on their faces made her miss something she didn't even remember how to feel. She reached out and ran a finger over the smile on her face, and let it trail over their linked hands and up to Jax's face.

She jerked her hand away from the picture at the sound of a throat clearing. Jax took a couple of steps closer to her. Close enough that she felt trapped, his body all but filling the small hallway. He looked at the picture she'd been studying, and then back to her.

She swallowed the lump in her throat and fixed a casual smile on her face, intending to move past him, but he didn't move out of her way.

"You remember that day?" he asked, lifting his chin toward the picture. They were the first words he'd spoken directly to her all night.

She looked at the picture, feeling the heat of his body as he drifted a little closer. "Looks like we were what, like sixteen or seventeen? I guess that would make Jade like fifteenish? But no. I wish I did, but I don't remember the exact day."

"Seventeen." The low timbre of his voice seemed to bounce off the close walls, and he pushed a harsh breath through his nose. "Must be nice."

"What must be nice?" she asked, looking up at him as he looked at the picture.

"Not remembering." He looked down at her then. He was so close she felt like she might tip backward trying to meet his eyes. It would be worth it, she thought. She'd tried giving him time, she'd tried having an adult conversation, and now she'd even tried ignoring him altogether...no matter what she seemed to do when it came to him, nothing worked. She couldn't exist in this constant state of tiptoeing around the grudge he was clinging to, and she certainly wasn't going to let him get away with any more glib, walk-off comments like that.

"Dammit, what the hell is your problem, Jax? When are you going to let go of this shit?" The question shot out of her like a whispered hiss. "Because if that's really how you feel, you're welcome to forget I exist. No one's stopping you."

Her body went stone-still as he ate up the meager distance left between them, taking her by the arm and guiding her into the bathroom. He kicked the door shut and trapped her against the door before she even knew what happened.

"Yes," he breathed raggedly, "actually someone is stopping me. Do you think I don't wish I could forget every moment we spent together? Or even have it dulled by time? I do. And I've tried all sorts of shit to try to forget. But all that's come of it is the realization that I don't have that luxury, don't deserve it."

His words were hushed but she felt the gravel of them roll through her where their chests were pressed together. Their breaths mingled in the small space between them. His words may have been intended to sting, but the way he was leaning into her, one of his long legs wedged between hers, their torsos pressed together, and how he had her caged within his arms, was communicating something else entirely.

"This is my punishment. I'll be haunted by every vivid detail of every memory of you. The sound of every one of your laughs." One of his hands clenched on her hip, the other still pressed firmly into the door above her.

"The way you smell." His head dipped down and he inhaled deeply as he dragged his nose up the column of her neck.

"I remember every kiss we ever had." His eyes drifted over her lips, then the hand above her head dropped down. He dragged his thumb back and forth over her bottom lip, pulling at it, just the right side of rough. His eyes tracked the movement of her mouth and his own opened slightly. "The way you taste, Dandy, like it's right here on my fucking tongue right now." His eyes closed for just a moment and she swore she could feel a slight vibration in his chest, like he was humming in satisfaction.

Holy shit. Her body was melting into the door, held up more by Jax's leg and grip on her hip than her own feet.

"I remember every wish you ever made, and I remember every promise. Every promise you broke." His voice shifted, the edge of desire she'd felt from him a moment ago disintegrating into something achingly vulnerable. Their chests rose and fell against each other, their heartbeats meeting for just a brief moment before being pulled apart again.

The raw intensity in his words transformed as his face pulled into a light sneer. "And luckiest of all, I remember the way it felt standing on the dark porch of your empty house the night you left. I remember all of it like it was yesterday. Like it was five fucking minutes ago. That's my fucking problem." The derisive way he said the words burned like acid in her throat. She couldn't speak as the truth of it hit her.

His Gift.

But was it a gift at all if this was what it had developed into? If this was how it tortured him now? It hadn't been like that before, and she wanted to ask him when it had changed, but she knew better. "I'm sorry Jax." She swallowed around the lump forming in her throat. "I wish you could understand."

"You didn't give me that chance though, did you Dandy?"

What had looked like desire—or maybe even something more than that —burning in his eyes just a moment ago had vanished. The set of his jaw hardened with resolve, and as quickly as he'd pulled her into the bathroom, he slipped out again. Leaving her standing there in the wake of his truth, her breathing halted, mind reeling, and heart racing.

157

TOUCHING HER HAD BEEN A MISTAKE, BUT NOT NEARLY AS MUCH AS pouring all his truths out to her had been. The pain in her eyes when she'd realized the way his so-called *Gift* had morphed into his hell would haunt him.

Right alongside the damn dress that would no doubt take center stage in his dreams right alongside olive skin and black lace, he had no doubt. The color made her eyes shine like polished gems. Or maybe that was all the wine and laughter.

The dinner table was filled with mostly empty serving trays, plates, and wine glasses. The cacophony of voices, laughs, silverware on plates, and corks popping out of bottles hummed around Jax, but it was little more than background noise to him. He was too focused on the place where the side of her bare knee pressed against his. She'd hesitated when his mom had ordered them to the table, hovering at the edge as everyone started grabbing seats. His dad had all but pushed her into the chair, saying, "It's still yours."

He'd said it under his breath, but Jax had still heard it.

So he'd spent the entire meal half-convinced that even through his jeans he could feel her skin on his, and trying to keep his eyes from wandering down to those damn legs. Why did everything she wore make them look so good? He clenched the silverware in his hands to keep from slipping one under the table to see if the skin there was as smooth under his fingers as her lips had been.

It didn't help that somehow Logan's massive ass had ended up in the seat next to him, taking up any space he could have used to shift away from her.

The only benefit of sitting next to her was that he didn't have to watch her laugh and smile all night. The meal was almost over, and then he'd be free. She'd no doubt go back to avoiding him like she'd been doing the last three days. And he could go back to checking the wards on her house multiple times a day and watching her window from his at night. Solid plan.

He grunted when a sharp elbow hit his left side. Logan's eyes shifted from his down to the fork in his hand. The fork that had started to melt. He slipped it down between them before anyone else could notice, but Quinn's eyes were already on him, and she looked like it was taking every ounce of effort to hold in her laughter. For fuck's sake, she'd probably been pelted with every emotion he'd felt during this misery of a dinner.

"So, Liv," his mom started. "I heard you had a very eventful walk home not too long ago."

Jade coughed around the wine she was sipping at the same time Logan's knife slipped out of his hand and hit the plate below with a loud clank.

"Oh, I do think I heard something similar," Quinn added, batting her eyelashes obnoxiously at him and Liv while sipping her wine.

"Mom. Please." He rubbed at his temple. He'd been momentarily stunned stupid seeing Liv standing in the middle of his parents' kitchen tonight. Surprised to see her and surprised by the way it made him feel to see her in his childhood home again. But at least he finally knew why his mom had been so insistent about this dinner, taking meddling to a new level even for her.

His mom looked around innocently. "What? All I was going to say was that one of the ladies in my archery club said that she heard someone was stalking Liv and that if Jax hadn't come along you may have been abducted."

His dad wiped his mouth and beard roughly with a napkin, shaking his head but keeping his mouth shut, making his allegiances clear.

"That is not even close to what happened." Though as far as gossip went for this town, it was closer to the truth than they usually got things. Maybe on another night, he would have humored his mom with the full story, but he wasn't in the mood to make light of town gossip or contemplate the idea of someone *taking* Liv.

"Yeah. I mean, I was fine." For Spirit's sake, he never thought he'd loathe a word, but here he was never wanting to hear the word *fine* ever again. "But," she started again, and then those fucking emeralds she called eyes turned up to him, "I do think I was probably lucky Jax showed up." Her full lips tilted up at the corners so slightly it felt like it was only for him, and it hit him like a slap across the face considering how much emotion he'd seen on her face not an hour ago in the bathroom. Now here she was, *fine*, all signs of emotion tucked away neatly so she could perform for everyone else's sake.

"Well, I'm glad you're okay." Liv turned back to his mom at her words, taking her eyes with her. "I never thought I'd say this, but for now I think it's safer if you all take some extra precautions, especially at night. If you work late, I'm sure Jax would be more than happy to walk you home, Liv."

"Real subtle Mom," Jade mumbled from the other side of the table. Their mom narrowed her eyes on Jade. "What?" Jade said defensively. "This is still Havenwood. I'm just saying, you don't need to get yourself all spun up about it." She topped it off by doing a really poor job of hiding her signature eye roll. More dinner table fun then. Great.

"Don't dismiss me, Jade Adelaide. Maybe I'm not the one overreacting. Maybe you need to be taking this a little more seriously."

"I'm not *not* taking it seriously. But if nothing else, we are still witches."

"Not all of us," his mom said, eyeing their dad pointedly.

His dad held his hands up, leaning back a little in his chair. "Hey, don't bring me into this."

"Too bad. You *are* in this. Not everyone in town has power to call on. People in Havenwood look to us and take cues from us to know how they should behave. What about them? Would you have nullies walking around as if there were nothing to worry about?"

"Well, now wait a minute." His dad had entered the race. "When you started walking to job sites and my appointments with me you said it was because you wanted to start spending more time together. Now I'm starting to think you were manipulating me." His dad sat up a little straighter. "You're making it sound like I'm some helpless creature walking around the streets needing your protection. I'm still a man, Sandi, magick or not. I've been taking care of you for over fifty years, for cryin' out loud. That's not about to change now, and I don't need anyone in this town thinking any different."

Jade deliberately ignored the death stare Jax was sending her way for getting them into this. She never could let it go when their mom toed the line between mother and s'mother.

"Nah, Warren you don't need to worry about all that toxic masculinity shit," Logan chimed in, because clearly he'd been an abhorrent monster in another life. "Everyone in town knows the truth. It takes a real and secure man to marry such a powerful witch, let alone one of the Six. Uphold tradition and take *her* last name; embrace the bad, not just use the good that comes with that sort of power. Most men are too weak—their pride is bigger than their stones and it shows."

It was a poorly veiled jab at Aaron, Jade's soon-to-be ex. One that was the absolute truth. Everyone at the table knew it. Including Jade. Her skin pinkened even as her eyes narrowed and jaw shifted, silently daring Logan to look at her.

Quinn leaned forward in her seat toward Liv. "Gird your loins lassie, this place is about to blow."

Unable to help himself, Jax looked down at Liv. Her shoulders were shaking ever so slightly, and her lips were tucked in as she fought to hold in a laugh.

"I bet you don't even want to spend more time with me. That's why you joined all those clubs as soon as I retired." To his mom's credit, she didn't so much as blink when his dad leveled a suspicious glare at her. "Wait a minute! Did you trick me into retiring, too? Dammit Sandra, that's it! I unretire!" Warren declared, standing up from the table, completely ignoring Logan's interlude.

Jax felt his eyes go round—like hell he was going to unretire. That wasn't even a thing. But before he could throw his hat into the ring of chaos it was Jade's turn—*again.*

Quinn grabbed the half-empty bottle of wine from the center of the table, filled Liv's glass, and then took a swig straight from the source as she leaned back in her chair to take in the show.

"What the hell would you know about relationships at all, let alone with a witch? Or stones for that matter?" Jade snapped back at Logan, looking about a breath away from lighting the whole table on fire. Jax was half-tempted to push her over the edge just to put this dinner out of its misery.

At least until Liv's hand shot out and gripped his thigh as she fought the laughter that was filling her from the inside.

The entire awareness of his body centered at that point where they were now connected. It was the first time she'd intentionally touched him in twelve years. Not that she was even aware she'd done it, which somehow made it both better and worse. Better because it had been a reflex for her to reach for him, worse because if she was going to touch him, he wanted her to be as wildly aware of it as he was.

Liv looked down at her hand and then up at him, a flush immediately blooming on her face as she withdrew it. It was an awful idea, one that conflicted with the way he'd left her in the bathroom, but he wanted to reach down and stay her hand on his leg. He didn't get the chance.

Energy rippled out from Logan, causing the hair on Jax's arms to stand on end. He returned the favor of a stiff elbow to his side, but the animal in him must have been at the steering wheel because Logan didn't even flinch.

His mom stood up as well. "You absolutely will not unretire. I want to enjoy you before all that's left is an overworked and calloused corpse."

"Papa's going to be a corpse?" Cori stood just inside the open French doors, her eyes the size of saucers.

"Hey! I was just about to come find you," Liv said as she rose from her chair and approached Cori. "How about you show me that castle now?" She took his niece's hand and the two of them disappeared into the backyard.

"Wait, I want to see a castle, too." Quinn unwound her legs from where she'd tucked them under her and followed Liv and Cori outside, the bottle of wine in tow.

CHAPTER TWENTY

*L*iv's fingers moved above her face as vines with bright pink flowers crept in the windows and wove between the strands of twinkly lights that crisscrossed the ceiling of Cori's treehouse—or tree castle, rather.

Cori and Quinn oohed and aahed, lying on a giant yellow bean bag next to her. "Now do purple, Liv!" Cori squealed. Purple blossoms joined the pink and white that were already blooming on the vine. When she was done, they all three laid back and admired her work, Liv and Quinn discreetly passing the bottle of wine back and forth.

It really was the cutest little space, Liv thought. She could tell Jax and Warren had taken their time building it to fit Cori perfectly. But her favorite part was the unique construction. The structure was supported by the thick branches of the large olive tree in the Hawthorne's backyard, but the treehouse itself had been designed in a way that it was built around the tree rather than into it, with additional beams added for support. Not a single nail penetrated the tree itself. And she could tell sitting there how happy the tree was to have them all in it, and how much it cared for Cori.

"Wow! I love what you've done with the place," Jade laughed, peeking her head in through the treehouse window.

"Too bad there isn't a bed. I might move in," Quinn said as she sat up.

Jade crooked a finger at Cori. "Speaking of, time for bed, your majesty."

Cori sat up and crossed her arms. "But mooommm," she whined.

"How about we both head in and I'll tell you one of my secret stories," Quinn whispered.

"How about three stories." Cori shot back.

"How about, get your buns down that ladder or no stories?" Quinn countered with a lifted brow and a poorly suppressed grin.

Cori's eyes narrowed for a moment before brightening again. "Okay, deal." She crawled toward the slide that shot out of the round turret of the castle to the grass below. "Night, Liv," Cori squealed as she launched herself down the slide.

"Sweet dreams, Cor," Liv called after her.

"That's what I thought," Quinn said, crawling to the slide right behind her. She stopped and kissed Liv on the cheek. "Goodnight."

"Night." She smiled after them.

"I'll be inside in a minute," Jade said, climbing into the treehouse from the opposite side where the ladder was. She plopped down on the bean bag next to Liv with a sigh. "Now this is a castle." Jade's eyes roamed the small space, taking in all the new additions Cori had requested.

"I just supplied the flowers, but it was all Cori's design."

"I'm pretty sure that's exactly what Jax said when he built this thing. It was great before, but this is exactly what the space was missing." She turned slightly so she could face Liv. "I guess you and Jax just make a really good team."

Liv leveled Jade with a stare, "Wow, inherit that subtlety from your mom or does it come naturally to you?"

"Okay yeah, not my best work," Jade agreed with a laugh.

A silence settled between them as they watched the lights above them imitate the stars. It wasn't an uncomfortable silence, but one with a weight that gave Liv the impression her friend was considering her words.

"I tried to hate you for a while. I wanted to, or maybe just felt like I should if I was being a good sister. You know?" Liv didn't rush to defend herself. She knew this conversation was probably overdue, no matter how hard it might be. "It was so hard to watch Jax fade away in front of my eyes the longer you were gone. It was even harder when he left, though. When I couldn't tell how he was truly doing. It felt like I lost both of you the night you left, and I couldn't understand why you'd want to leave us."

"I never wanted to leave you guys," Liv whispered, her eyes lining with tears for the second time that night.

"I know," Jade rushed to say. "And I can't imagine how hard that must have been for you. Having to choose between giving up everything you had planned for your life—your dreams, maybe even your only chance at real love—and taking care of the one person who needed you, the person you were responsible for."

Jade looked directly at her. "But I think what most people don't under-stand is that a choice like that isn't something you only had to make once, the night you left. You had to make it every day for all those years you were gone. Most people wouldn't have the strength or that kind of selfless-ness. I didn't get that, not back then."

The tears slid from Liv's eyes in a steady stream. Not just for herself, for being understood, but for the truth of the words she could see reflected in Jade's own glassy eyes.

Liv nodded. "I'm still sorry I hurt you," she said, hoping the words were enough. Jade looked back up at the ceiling, blinking any sign of the tears away. Then she reached over and interlocked their fingers, squeezing once.

"There is nothing to forgive."

Liv took a deep breath. "I don't think Jax feels the same way. I know it's selfish, but I wish he could just try to understand why I had to go. As hard as leaving here, leaving him was, coming back here might actually be harder." She discreetly wiped at a tear that managed to slip free. "I wasn't naïve enough to think anything would be the same. But facing the changes in him has been the hardest thing I've ever done. The way he looks at me... I don't know. I guess despite it all I just never thought he could hate me this way."

"Oh, you beautiful idiot," Jade lamented as she sat up.

"Look, I'm probably about to break every sister code known to man, but for the record, I did try to give you and Jax a little space, hoping he'd tell you himself. Turns out we all underestimated the depths of my brother's ability to brood. She made a face as if that were an understatement.

"Whatever it is, you don't owe me anything, I don't want you getting in trouble with Jax."

"I fear no man," Jade replied dismissively. "Besides, it's for his own good, and you deserve to know. Anyway, not long after you left, I had a vision, and you were in it. Changed a little, but I still knew it was you. Now I realize the change was that you were older, *this* old." Liv rolled onto her side to give her full attention, to find Jade already looking at her.

"You, Jax, and I were standing at the edge of the cliffs out in your forest. There were others there too, six of us in total, one of which I now know was Quinn."

Liv felt her eyes widen slightly. Of course, Jade's visions weren't a sure thing, but for her to have one all those years ago, to have at least a piece of it coming together now felt substantial. "Who was the other? What were we doing out there? What does that even mean?"

"I don't know, I couldn't see his face. As for what it means, only Spirit knows. I stopped trying to understand her, and my visions, a long time ago. That's a fast lane to becoming the batty old lady who wanders around town, giving prophecies and living with a hoard of feral cats. No thanks, I'll pass." Jade shivered. "Besides, I've learned, that if they're meant to, these things tend to reveal themselves at the right time. All I know is that we were using strong magick. I swear I could feel it flowing through me." She shook her head slightly as if she could still feel it all these years later. Liv suppressed the list of follow-up questions she had about the vision and let her friend continue.

"Anyway, you know how Jax was—still is, always making sure I don't have to carry the weight of knowing things alone, adamant I share any vision I have with him, and back then I listened to him." She smirked conspiratorially, momentarily lightening the mood. Liv's lips curved, at the memory of how protective Jax had been of Jade growing up, how it had felt when that extended to her too.

"So, I told him about seeing you come home," Jade continued, "and then he made me show him. I'm pretty sure he replayed his memory of my vision every day for the first several months you were gone. Hanging onto it with every ounce of hope he had in him—until he used it all up. That's when he left, too."

Liv pulled her knees into her chest and wrapped her arms around them. She'd suffered through her memories all these years, but she couldn't imagine the added pain of hanging on to hope like that.

"And that's why he hates me?"

"He doesn't hate you Liv. More like he hates that he doesn't."

She was about to argue but their moment in the bathroom earlier came rushing back, the desire she'd tried to convince herself she hadn't seen. "I…I don't think I understand."

"Ugh," Jade groaned, "I swear the two are so determined to sacrifice yourselves to your misery you can't see the forest for the trees."

Liv's face pinched in confusion. "I'm not miserable."

"Oh, please. You both are. Look Liv, once Jax accepted you weren't coming back, I think it was too painful to stay here, so he went to try to make some new dreams to try to replace the old ones." Liv squeezed her eyes closed tightly as she was confronted by the ripple effect her actions had.

"But while he was gone things happened around here, things that his idiotic brain thinks he could have prevented if he hadn't left. He nearly lost his shit when he found out I was pregnant and had a quicky wedding at a courthouse outside town." Jade gave a playful wince, then continued, "Not because he was unhappy about having a niece, but I think he had some dreams of his own for me. Dreams that didn't include settling in Haven-wood and certainly didn't include Aaron." Liv knew Jax wasn't the only one who had assumed Jade would have left this town to travel the world as soon as she graduated college. It had been all Jade talked about at one time. But Liv didn't point that out.

"But he didn't come home…not until my dad fell off that roof and broke his back. As soon as my mom called him, he abandoned the insanely lucrative position he had at an architecture firm in Europe and didn't skip a beat taking over everything for my dad, and then insisting on taking over as Praefectus for my mom, so she could take care of Dad."

"That must have been a really hard time for him. For all of you."

"Yeah, for sure. But I think it was hardest on Jax. He carries this asinine belief that if he'd never left, done more, been more, he could ensure nothing bad had ever happened to anyone…ever." Jade rolled her eyes at the impossibility of the idea. "So, now he thinks it's his job to make sure everyone around him has everything they need before he even thinks about himself."

"Sound familiar? Probably not, but it should." Jade eyed her pointedly. "My point in all of this is that no, he doesn't hate you. He's scared. You remind him that he can't control the entire world. You remind him of what it feels like to want something so much, and the risk that comes with that kind of hope, that kind of…love. There. I said it." She blew out a breath like she'd just had the weight of the world lifted from her and collapsed backward onto the bean bag.

Jade's words hung in the air between them, the shock of them hitting Liv like a wave. Her mouth opened and closed, no sound escaping as she tried to find something—anything—to say in response, to deny the possibility, if only for her own sake.

But she was too late.

The tiny spark of hope was already there. It was dangerous, she knew. To entertain the idea was to invite the kind of pain she'd promised herself she'd never feel again. The thought of Jax's seemingly erratic mood swings around her stemming from some inner turmoil, as Jade suggested, seemed far-fetched at best. Of him carrying any feelings for her, after all this time… she fought to keep herself grounded, because it probably wasn't true. But the what-if of it all echoed in her mind, quickening the beat of her heart as it attempted to take root there.

JADE'S WORDS STILL PLAYED THROUGH HER MIND IN THE LAST HOURS OF the night as Liv sat on the small balcony beneath her bedroom window, looking between Jax's house and the moon high above her. She almost ducked out of sight when the lights in her bedroom behind her flickered, but she resisted.

He appeared on his porch a moment after she felt his magick cascading over her and weaving with the wards surrounding her house. He started to turn, to go back in, but stopped mid-stride. Like he could feel her gaze. He turned back, his eyes lifting to meet hers. They stayed locked like that for too long for it to be meaningless before he retreated into the shadows of his porch again.

CHAPTER TWENTY-ONE

*T*he same overgrowth of brittle vines that grew up and over the house and greenhouse also spread through a majority of the front gardens. New life had been trying to root here since they'd been back, but it was either being choked out or denied by lack of sunlight—a tangible consequence of the absence of a Terrabella in the house for so many years.

Liv knelt in the dirt, clearing space around an Autumn Crocus that was trying to find space to bloom. When Autumn Crocus bloomed near a grave it was a sign that the dead were happy, and since the magick and ashes of long gone Terrabellas wove through the entirety of the land here, it felt like a gift.

She rolled her shoulders, where tension had been building the last several days. The result of a particularly fun combo of more nightmares, and not knowing where she stood with her sister, or her illusive neighbor for that matter. The closest she'd gotten to seeing him since the dinner at his parents' was at night when she felt his magick in the wards around her house, which had become a nightly habit of his. Just like her waiting for it out on her little balcony had become a habit of hers.

She'd begun to see the small repairs she found in the house in a new light. Originally, she'd assumed the house might be repairing itself as some kind of emotional reaction to it not being lonely anymore. But after her conversations with Sandra and Jade, she'd begun considering that maybe someone had been making those repairs before her return. And maybe the house hadn't been all that alone, at least not since Jax had been back.

The scent of him in the magick had been a large part of what had driven her out into the gardens this morning. The way it moved through the house like it belonged there. It slid over her as sentient hands trailing feather light touches over her skin before draping itself around her like a favorite stolen old t-shirt that was worn in just right.

Goosebumps prickled over her arms at the thought.

She groaned in annoyance, at herself and him. She wanted to know if he'd found out anything more about the body or Emma's husband. She'd also noticed the lanterns acting up again on her way home from work last night.

Stop. She commanded her defiant brain. The whole point of being out here was to spend a little time not thinking about Jax or being avoided by Ivy. She sat back and watched the Autumn Crocus as it seemed to stretch in relief now that she'd given it some breathing room.

Colchicum autumnale, a member of the Naked Lady genus. She'd probably been too old to laugh as much as she had when her grandma had taught her about the flower, but even now it made her smile. She almost always preferred the Latin name for plants to the common. They usually captured the nature of the flower more accurately. Plus, using them gave her an excuse to use the knowledge Valeria had drilled into her.

The garden had always been the best place to come when things got complicated. It helped her work through whatever mess was in her head. The second nature of the work was like her own personal form of meditation, since actual meditation tended to feel more like her own personal form of hell.

She'd only tried it a couple of times over the years but the quiet and stillness only ever seemed to amplify the sound of her thoughts, which was not something she needed help with.

No, it was being with nature that brought her balance, Liv thought as she wiggled her toes in the dirt and was rewarded with the light trill of energy coursing from the earth into her skin. No matter how small or rundown the place they'd lived in had been, she'd always managed to form a little greenspace she could retreat to when things got too heavy with her mom or Ivy. It brought a sense of calm, which was something she'd needed then, and could use right now.

She'd decided to start clearing the invasive vines from where the roots seemed to originate, back between the side of the house and the gate that surrounded the front of the property. The fact that she'd be hidden from sight back here if anyone passing by looked at the house was just a coincidence.

Liv eyed a section of dead vines that overflowed from the garden, snaking up the trunks of a pair of Orange trees, *Citrus sinensis*. Decaying fruit littered the ground around them, and stunted oranges peeked between the cords of the vine.

She wrapped the vines around her arm and yanked, sending dirt flying, and a few of the roots sprang free with a satisfying snap. It had minimal effect in the grand scheme of what she would need to do to get the gardens back in shape, but it felt good all the same. Her mind began to quiet as she sank into a rhythm, lulled by the repetition of the work.

"Liiiv? Ow, shit."

Liv could only faintly hear her sister cursing the house. She stopped, pushing her long dark hair out of her face and searching the area for Ivy. "I'm back here!" she called from below her bedroom balcony, where she'd followed the vines to their roots.

The sound of footsteps and rustling leaves came from the back of the house. Using her elbows to push long stems and leaves aside and sending rays of sunlight dancing around her, Ivy emerged holding a mug in each hand. She ducked under the low-hanging branch of a Boysenberry tree that needed a trim, the bitter smell of coffee that followed her robbing Liv of the scent of upturned soil.

Ivy looked around before her tentative eyes landed on her sister. The sunlight caught on the brilliant green and rich brown of her eyes, beautiful but different from every Terrabella before her. Liv had wondered a hundred times as she caught Ivy staring into the mirror if it bothered her or not but never asked, not wanting to risk implying Ivy should feel something she hoped she didn't. She liked that her sister was unique.

Ivy came closer, shoving a mug in her direction. "Here. I thought maybe you could use this, too."

Liv resisted the urge to tilt her head back from the intrusive smell as Ivy let the cup hover in front of her face.

It was her sister's form of a peace offering. Taking it meant agreeing to ignore what had happened between them the other night, agreeing not to bring it up, and just moving on like it never happened. Liv hesitated, not just because she hated coffee, always had, but because this time was different. Taking the coffee this time felt like it would be a silent approval of her sister's choices—choices that could have much more dangerous consequences than they had in the past.

But she also worried what would happen if she didn't take the offer. Was their relationship so fragile it could be broken by a cup of coffee?

Apparently, she thought, because the next thing she knew she'd wiped her hands off on the back pockets of her jeans and accepted the mug from her sister, even going so far as to take a tiny sip of the tawny liquid.

"Thanks." Liv set the mug aside in the dirt and tentatively went back to work, trimming back some plants to give a small cropping of Bindweed access to the sun.

Ivy surprised her when she settled down on an old pebble-textured steppingstone nestled under the dangling branches of an Aspen rather than going back inside.

The tree shivered in delight at Ivy's proximity. She looked up at the tree. "Hello to you too." And that was the most attention she'd *ever* seen her sister pay a plant.

Liv worked in silence for a few moments, debating whether or not she should push her luck with Ivy's mood and broach the subject of placing their mom's ashes out under the Willow. It didn't feel right keeping her in the urn. Even though their mom had very little power, it still needed to be returned to the Earth. Part of Liv believed that her mom wouldn't truly be set free from the pain and sickness she'd been plagued with in life until she was returned to the Earth as well.

When Ivy stood up, Liv assumed she'd head back to the house, but her sister took a few small steps around the garden, also barefoot.

"Wouldn't it be faster to just use magick?" Ivy asked, watching Liv struggle to dislodge the root system of a particularly stubborn vine.

"Magick isn't a loophole to hard work. Plus, I enjoy. The. Work." Liv grunted as she tugged. Ivy was right, though. Technically, if she wanted to, all she'd need to do was pull the metaphorical plug, lean into that innate *knowing* that was a constant low-grade thrum flowing out from the depths of her soul and rising to simmer just below her skin, and simply, *let go.*

Self-indulgent and lazy. Elena's words forced themselves into Liv's mind.

"Yeah, you look like you're having a blast. What about some good old-fashioned weed killer, then?"

Liv dropped the vine. *You've won the battle, not the war,* she silently told it. "Those poisons kill indiscriminately and wreak havoc on the regenerative properties of the soil."

Ivy rolled her eyes. "I'm just saying, there has to be a faster way to clear out all these weeds." She gestured to all the plants growing at her feet.

Liv sat back on her heels. "There's no such thing as a weed. That's just what people call a wild plant they don't think is pretty or perfect enough to fit the image they deem worthy of growing in their perfect little flower beds. But everything has beauty if you look close enough—sometimes it's just in their use, not their leaves."

Her sister cracked a smile. "I feel like maybe you've been holding that one in for a while."

Liv laughed. "Yeah. It was something Grammy used to remind me of a lot." Whenever she'd had a particularly rough day at school with the other girls. Or anytime her mom saw her using her magick and walked out of the room, giving her the silent treatment the rest of the day. Or week.

Ivy looked away from whatever emotion she saw pass over her face. "So you're telling me that's not a weed?" Ivy challenged, indicating a small grouping of plants nestled amongst fallen leaves and larger plants.

"That's *Stellaria Media.*" Ivy looked at her with raised brows like she was speaking a foreign language, which she was, but it should have been one that Ivy understood. One Liv should have done a better job of teaching her. Even if this was the most interest Ivy had ever shown in flora, or being outside in general.

"Chickweed," Liv clarified. "Technically yes, it's growing wild here, but it's more than welcome. That little guy can cure all kinds of things, from constipation to asthma and even rabies. Plus, it's pretty. Soon it'll get tiny, white, star-shaped flowers all over it."

Ivy made a face that said she was mildly impressed by the unassuming plant. "Fine you win that one." She surveyed the ground around them. "What about that." Liv took a step toward where her sister pointed, enjoying Ivy's sudden interest.

"Conium Maculatum." Liv gave Ivy a sly smile. "Hemlock."

Ivy's eyes went round. "Isn't that like, crazy poisonous!?"

"Everything is poisonous at some point." Liv leaned closer to her sister and whispered, "It's all a matter of dosage…and intent. At least that's what Aunt Amapola used to say." Ivy swatted at her sister and they both laughed. "But really, all plants ever did was uphold their right to exist. It's people who decide how to use them."

"Alright fine, no weeds, no weed killer." Ivy smiled again, a sight that Liv hadn't seen enough lately. Her sister was beautiful on her worst day, but when she smiled, she was stunning. A stunning *woman,* and it may have been the first time Liv had consciously made the distinction.

"I still think this is too much work for one person," Ivy added.

Liv just shrugged. "Some of these plants have been here since the house was built. Their roots are deeper than ours here, and they'll flourish faster because of it. They just need some care and space to grow, and I don't mind helping them get that."

Ivy's eyebrows rose as she nodded her head and lifted her cup to her lips. "Where can I get some of that?" The words were mumbled at half volume, but Liv could see her sister's smile over the rim of her mug and in her eyes.

"Ha, ha." Liv went back to pulling out vines and Ivy walked back toward the front door, still smiling. It was the first conversation in weeks that hadn't ended in a fight, and Liv couldn't help but breathe easier. Progress.

. . .

"EXCUSE ME. LIV?"

She jumped at the sound of her name. Two hours had passed since her sister had gone inside, and Liv was covered in sweat and dirt, but happy with the progress she'd made. Now Gideon Finch, the elderly owner of the antique shop in town, approached her from the gate, which had obligingly let him in.

"I'm sorry if this isn't a good time," he said, coming to stand next to her.

"It's fine," Liv relented, trying to wipe some of the dirt off her hands as she turned to face Gideon. He had to be getting close to eighty. He still looked handsome, if a little tired, in his signature three-piece tweed suit, though, and through the subtle wrinkles of his ebony skin, it was easy to imagine what a gorgeous young man he must have been.

"What can I do for you, Mr. Finch?"

"None of that now, Gideon. And well, it's Jane, my wife. You remember her?"

Liv nodded. "Yes, of course."

"Well, you see, she's had a terrible cough for weeks, fever on and off. She's absolutely miserable. I was just hoping—"

Following where he was going, Liv started to shake her head. "I'm sorry, Mr. Finch, I can't help you. Maybe a doctor…"

"We've tried." Gideon returned the favor of not letting her finish. "I even took her to one of those city doctors, outside town, but they all say she's just getting old and needs to slow down. But my Jane, slow isn't in her vocabulary, and not being well enough to leave the house…" Gideon paused, letting out a breath that seemed to weigh more than he did. "She's fading into this illness and more so into depression. It feels like I'm losing her before my eyes."

"Please, Liv. I'll pay you. The Terrabellas have always had a gift for this kind of thing, I just know you're the one who can give her what she needs." The crack in his voice was enough to break her heart on the spot.

But what he was asking for wasn't just some herbs mixed up into a glorified tea. He was asking for magick.

Gideon's face was etched with desperation, the exhaustion of days spent worrying evident in the dark circles under his weary eyes.

For once, Liv didn't think, just turned and walked deeper into the garden. Slowly she moved through the different beds, searching for what she needed. Gideon walked behind her, giving her space but watching her work with rapt attention.

Once she had what she needed, Liv cupped the flowers and herbs in her hands and whispered the words her grandmother had taught her over them.

"From earth below to skies above, by powers old, by powers new, may wellness bloom within you. With gentle touch and soothing balm, banish pain, restore, and calm. Healing powers now amassed, may wellness reign through you from me, for the intended I decree, as I will so mote it be."

Liv opened her palms, allowing the plants to lift into the air a few inches, spinning in a tiny whirlwind that shimmered faintly. Even with her eyes closed she could feel Gideon's eyes on her, but using her Gift of the Spirit felt so good she forgot to worry. She repeated the words twice more, then opened her eyes when she felt the warm smooth weight drop into her palm and smiled at what she'd created.

SHE HANDED THE TINY VIAL OF LIQUID TO GIDEON ALONG WITH A SMALL satchel of herbs. "Simmer these in a pot of water for three hours, then add three drops of this to the tea. She should take it three times a day for three days. After those first three days, place the damp herbs under her pillow and in her socks for three more nights. Come back if she isn't feeling better by the seventh day." Liv closed Gideon's hand around the supplies and gave him a tight-lipped smile when she saw relief settle onto his face.

"I can't thank you enough, Liv. How much do I owe you?"

She didn't hesitate. "Nothing." Taking money for this would only encourage more of the same, and that was a commitment she wasn't ready to make. Yet. "You just focus on Mrs. Finch. Remember, three times three, then three more."

He nodded and then pulled her into a quick tight hug. He smelled of leather and dust, probably from his shop, she thought, as she walked him back to the front gate and watched him hustling down the street, moving quickly for someone his age, and visibly lighter than he'd been just moments ago. She'd done that, she realized.

Gideon wasn't even out of sight when the prick of tingles sparked at the nape of her neck and spread an awareness down her spine. She could have run back into the garden without looking, but she knew he'd consider the intentional avoidance a victory, and her pride wouldn't allow it.

Liv turned and looked directly across the street.

Jax leaned a broad shoulder into the post of his front porch. A picture of effortless, smug satisfaction with the tips of his fingers slipped into the front pockets of his dark jeans, his full attention unapologetically fixed on her.

She could feel the weight of those pale blue eyes everywhere they moved across her skin, over her dirt-covered body as they both stood still, separated only by the narrow, lamppost and tree-lined street. The barely-there smirk that had one corner of his full mouth slightly lifted and the tilt of his head as he studied her told her all she needed to know. He'd been watching her.

And judging by the look on the sharp angles of his stupidly perfect face, he was more than pleased by all of it.

His words floated across the street to her. "Well done, Dandy."

JAX WATCHED AS SHE HEARD HIM, TRANSFIXED BY THE FLURRY OF emotions that passed over Liv's face in that single moment before she stormed off around the side of the old house. He knew he was an ass for being so pleased to see another hole poked in her defenses.

But watching her do what he knew she was meant to, seeing her relent little by little, was quickly becoming his sole obsession.

Watching her wage that internal war with who she truly was and who she thought she needed to be for everyone else wasn't always easy. And he'd be the first to admit he didn't exactly navigate it with the most tact. But the small glimpses of her peeking through that mask were a sight to behold. One he didn't mind pissing her off to witness.

178

A<small>N HOUR LATER SHE COULD STILL FEEL THE LIGHT EFFERVESCE OF THE</small> magick below her skin from the little she'd used on the spell for the Finches.

She wondered if he could feel it too. If that had been what had drawn him out onto his porch. Or if he'd been there the whole time.

"Well done, Dandy."

That's what he'd said before she'd forced herself to look away. Before she confused that look on his face for something like pride. She shivered, remembering how the deep gravel of his amused voice compelled her body to react in a way she only ever did for him. The sensation threatened to break the already fragile grip she had on the last vestiges of her precious self-control.

He continued to see too much. More than what happened out there on the street, but also what was happening inside her, gradually building since she'd come back to town. It was infuriating.

And it was really fucking hot.

Rather than giving him the satisfaction of seeing how he affected her, she'd retreated to the back gardens where she'd worked off the buzz of her emotions in solitude.

Now she stood, looking up at the old greenhouse she'd spent so many hours in growing up. People always said that the kitchen was the heart of the home.

Well, she thought, if the heart was in the kitchen, then this greenhouse was the soul of theirs. And this soul needed saving.

The same heavy and invasive vines she'd spent her day waging war on in the gardens stretched over the greenhouse. Those vines sucked up every available nutrient around them, making it impossible for almost anything else to thrive in the garden.

They were also slowly destroying the framing of the greenhouse, causing the glass panes to crack, and preventing enough sunlight from getting in.

Removing it would hopefully be a constructive way to burn through the overabundance of frustration she had coursing through her right now—both of the sexual and standard variety.

Liv stood with her hands on her hips, examining the greenhouse carefully, tracing the vines from their roots to where they crisscrossed and wound. With her attention fixed on methodically planning where to start, she didn't notice the way a hush rolled in from the cliffs, through the forest surrounding the house, and then over the garden around her, like a wave of silence.

She didn't feel the inky darkness slinking at the edges of her property line, or how it slipped through the wards undetected.

She didn't notice as it slithered over the foliage and across the ground, encroaching on her. She didn't hear the low hissing as plants withdrew into themselves, branches retracted, and flowers closed and shriveled in its wake. She didn't feel it as it watched...and waited.

Silence.

CHAPTER TWENTY-TWO

"*A*re you planning to spend the entire night watching my sister from across the bar?" Jax all but groaned at Logan.

"Are you planning to spend the rest of your life in love with your ex and pretending you're not?"

"Clearly, the pair of yeh are planning to spend eternity being eegits." Jax choked on the whisky he'd been sipping for the last thirty minutes. MacIver had just appeared behind the bar with nothing on but a pair of loose boxers, an undershirt, and a burgundy robe thrown over with matching velvet house shoes.

"Sitting here with yer thumbs up yer asses, instead of over there with them." Mac stabbed a thumb over his shoulder toward the back of the bar where Liv, Jade, and Quinn, along with some other townspeople, were playing pool.

"I've come across a few intellectually challenged creatures in my day." He set a large plate of nachos on the counter and bent to grab a beer from the lower fridge. "But the two of you truly take the cake." Then he disappeared through the swinging kitchen doors again.

Jax looked at Logan, who was still staring at the doors his grandfather had gone through. "He walked here like that."

"He sure did." Logan looked at Jax. "And then called *us* intellectually challenged. The worst part is, I think he's right." Logan picked up a rag to wipe down the bar where Mac's nachos had left cheese and crumbs behind. "About you at least."

The cracking of pool balls ricocheting off each other pulled their attention to the back of the bar. Jade broke, sinking a couple of balls, while Quinn and Liv talked to Grady O'Connor and Leo Riviera, two of Havenwood's finest—or medium-ist if he were being honest.

Grady was so entranced by Liv that he wouldn't be surprised if he was drooling. The only thing keeping him from ending up on the receiving end of a blinding spell was that Jax couldn't blame the guy. The way she leaned on her upended pool stick, her hips subtly swaying to the deep bass of the slow song from the old jukebox, was impossible to look away from. Like she was casting a spell of her own.

To his surprise, her gaze slowly but deliberately drifted to meet his, as if she could feel his eyes on her, the way he'd felt hers on him every night when she watched him checking the wards on her house. For a moment the connection hummed like a live wire, sparking between them. But too soon her attention was stolen by his treacherous sister, who said something that made the rest of them laugh.

He strained to hear the sound above the hum of music and people talking. It was probably for the best that he couldn't—the sight of pure joy on her face was dangerous enough to his ability to leave her alone.

He could see the golden embers in her eyes sparking to life one at a time every time she let a little more of herself out. It unwound something inside him to witness it, and then twisted it right back up, not be the one who'd caused it.

He turned back to the bar, fixing his attention on his whisky instead.

"Why don't you just go over there and free the rest of us from the sexually frustrated misery on your face."

"What are you talking about? And why does everyone keep making comments about my face? Maybe I'm just thinking. It's not like the only thing going on in this town is her coming home. For shit's sake, I'm just sitting here, drinking with my best friend, same as always. Or at least I would be, if you would do your job as well as you antagonize and irritate me." Jax looked at Logan dryly, nudging his empty glass toward him.

Logan leaned back against the line of fridges behind the bar and crossed his arms over his wide chest. "That wasn't very nice. I'm going to ignore your rudeness though, because I think that may be the first time you've called me your best friend out loud." Logan winked and kissed the air between them. "And because clearly, you're in denial. You're not the same as *always,* but you are the same as you've been for a long ass time." Logan took his empty glass, setting it aside. "Which is the problem. Call it what you want to call it, but you've spent too much of your time barely living." He punctuated his statement by setting a fresh glass of whisky in front of Jax, a little harder than necessary.

"Where is all this coming from?" Jax asked, grabbing at the drink. "I've done more living than anyone else in this town."

"No, what you've been doing, my friend, is distracting yourself. Meanwhile, somewhere deep inside you've been waiting for her all along."

Logan placed both his hands on the bar and leaned in close, ensuring this conversation was only for them. "You may have convinced yourself you let go of Jade's vision of Liv coming home, and maybe you even believe that. But you'd be the only one. You bought the damn house across the street from her, you sadist." Jax had been waiting for someone to bring up that little fact.

"You know I'm right. Which is why you've been even more of a cranky ass since the moment she set foot in this town. You don't want to feel whatever you are. You're scared." Logan lifted a hand when Jax opened his mouth to argue that point. "I know I don't have any room to talk, but it's not the same." A brief, loaded silence passed between the two of them as they acknowledged a truth that only the two of them shared.

Jax took a sip of his drink, needing a break from the intensity in his friend's eyes. Logan relented.

"I'm not even saying you're wrong for resisting whatever's being dug up between the two of you. But I do think it's time you decide if you're resurrecting something or just kicking around old bones. For both your sake, because you may think you're protecting yourself, but this looks a lot more like punishment to me."

Jax looked up, caught off guard by his friend's words. The wisdom in them prompted Jax to confess the thoughts that had been plaguing him, the reason he'd been holding back. "Let's say you're right, and I stop holding back. What if she decides to leave again? And even if she doesn't, what makes you think she wants anything to do with me?"

"Come on man, we both know she didn't want to leave when she did. She felt like she had no choice."

"She could have come to me." And as he said the words, something about it clicked in his mind. The memory she'd pulled him into. She'd opened the door that night, and in that moment, he knew she'd at least intended to do exactly that.

Now he just needed to know what had stopped her.

"Yeah, well, maybe she should have, but I think you're missing the point," Logan said, mixing a drink and sliding it down the bar to another patron with a practiced flair.

Jax waved him on with his glass. "Well, don't stop now."

"She *did* have a choice this time. She could have gone anywhere, but she came back here. Maybe she doesn't even realize why. But I think we both know, and maybe you need to show her."

Jax ruminated on Logan's words, relenting to the truth in them. The truth he'd either been too dumb to see or too scared to accept. Until now.

When she'd needed somewhere safe to go, she'd come back to Havenwood. Maybe not just to the town, but to *him*. Because even after all this time, whether she realized it or not, she knew deep down he'd always keep her safe. And understanding that set something right inside him, something that he hadn't known had been misaligned for so long.

"When did you become an expert on relationships?"

Logan laughed loudly. "Only the messy, fucked up kind."

Jax smiled and sipped his drink. "Anything else?" It was his way of thanking Logan, and they both knew it.

"Yeah." Logan's face changed, uncharacteristically devoid of all humor. "Be sure. Because at the end of the day, you're not the only one who lost her, and you're not the only one who's finally got her back. And I'll not have you fuckin' it up for the rest of us." The lightness returned with his crooked smile. "Ye kin?"

"Yeah," he said, "I *kin*." Jax mimicked the hint of a lilt in Logan's words, subtly pointing out the brogue that had risen to the surface again.

He did get it, though. No one wanted to lose her again. He needed to make sure they didn't. That he didn't.

Logan ignored him. "Besides, it's in my best interest you at least give it a shot with her. Worst case scenario she turns you down, you go catatonic or disappear again, and I don't have to look at that face you make when you're stewing anymore. Best case scenario you two kiss and make up, you give your molars a break, and maybe you loosen up that death grip you have on all my glassware."

Logan winked and went to clear tables, leaving Jax to his thoughts.

This time he didn't fight the urge to watch as Liv stepped to the table to take her turn. He stared as she hinged at the hip, eyes scanning the table, debating her shot. She stretched her tan-toned arms out to aim. When her tongue slipped out and dragged across her plump bottom lip, coming to rest in the corner of her mouth while she lined up her shot, it felt like the room contracted, like it was holding in a deep breath—or was that just him at the images flooding his mind as his eyes tracked over her body.

He wanted that body stretched out over him the way she was now. His hands wrapped around the curve of her hips, tucked into his own the way they hugged the edge of the table. He knew her ass would be more than what he could fill his hands with as she moved over him. He wanted to rip off the tight jeans that hid those toned legs he wanted wrapped around him while he drove into her.

The sound of Quinn cheering as Liv sunk her shot in a corner pocket released him from the lustful haze he'd fallen into, but the way she slowly unfurled from the table threatened to pull him right back under. Anyone else would have missed the little smirk that ticked at the corner of her mouth, and he almost did. *Almost.* He didn't miss it though, and the sight of it told him she knew exactly what the fuck she was doing.

She set her stick down and met his gaze, pure heat in her eyes for just a moment before she chickened out and turned away.

He tracked her as she walked toward the back corner of the bar and disappeared into the dark alcove that led to the restrooms and the back exit. She was running from whatever it was that was finally happening between them. That was fine—it only solidified that she was feeling it too. And this time she wouldn't get far. This time, he would chase her.

"Christ. Sure, nothing's going on. I just suddenly need a cold shower because of all the nothing happening between you two right fuckin' now." Logan said, reminding Jax he wasn't alone here in the bar.

He didn't bother denying it, though, as he stood up and headed after her. "Fuck off."

"Yeaahh, buddy!" Logan cheered as he walked away, followed by the sharp crack of a towel snapping behind him. "Go get that girl, Magick Daddy!" A few patrons laughed, but Jax barely noticed, focused only on chasing down his girl.

Liv walked out of the bathroom and came face to chest with a wall of Jax. She took a small step back, but his hand stopped her, wrapping around the back of her neck to hold her in place and surprise the crap out of her. He used his hold to tilt her head up to him, and the look in his eyes made her want to run and melt at the same time.

"You should be careful how you look at me, Dandelion."

She couldn't hold back the shudder that ran down her body at the sound of his rough voice. "I wasn't looking at you any sort of way," she claimed, though they both knew she was lying. She'd felt the weight of his stare all night, causing her body to be all but engulfed in flames. Giving in to the feelings he ignited in her for once, she'd decided to give him a little taste of his own medicine and had low-key been pretty proud of herself for the uncharacteristic display she'd put on for him. Even if she'd run away to the bathroom immediately after.

She certainly hadn't expected him to call her on it.

Jax guided her a couple of steps to the side of the bathroom door just as it swung open, but she couldn't see who came out around the cage of his body. With his leg tucked between hers, she could feel his hard length pressing into her thigh and shivered.

For Spirit's sake, what was happening?

"You're playing a game you need to be sure you're willing to win," he said low in her ear.

Her mouth opened but no words came out. He'd knocked her

completely off kilter. And who could blame her—she was lucky she didn't get whiplash from his change of moods. It left irritation warring with desire.

"I'm not playing any games, Jax." Liv pressed against his chest and wiggled herself out from under him. Knowing she'd only been able to do so because he'd let her only served to piss her off more. "Maybe I smiled at you, but that's only because I thought maybe you'd finally come around to the idea we could be friends." Okay, that was a total lie, but she didn't care. "If anyone is playing games here it's you, and honestly, I'm done. Fuck being friends. I'm officially getting off your merry-go-round of moods."

She took the first escape she could find, throwing open the emergency exit sign, silently thanking the Spirit when it didn't trigger any alarms, and took a deep breath of the cool air.

She spun back toward the door when she heard it fly open, smacking the brick siding of the bar, and slam back shut. "I said I'm done, Jax!"

He didn't care, because he didn't stop. He came straight for her, colliding with her body and lifting her off her feet by her ass with one arm, never missing a stride. A moment later her back met brick, her front met his, her head landed in the cushion of his other hand, and his mouth crashed into hers with the force of twelve years of frustration, twelve years of pain, twelve years of longing. And deep inside her something cold and hardened cracked open, filling her with warmth.

She melted into him, wrapping her legs around his waist, sealing any space left between them. Her arms wound up his back, her fingers digging into the hard muscles there, and her mouth opened wider, welcoming his tongue. Reveling in remembrance of his taste.

Her body ached at the feel of him, hardness tucked against her core. Her legs clenched around him, lifting herself so she could slide down it again. His groan into her mouth echoed against her own soft moan.

She didn't know how long the kiss lasted, but her chest burned with a need for oxygen when he finally pulled back just far enough to see her face. He brushed the hair out of her eyes, his own glassy and bright, the yellow ring electric as they bore into her with the most intensity she'd ever seen from him.

"We've been all sorts of things to each other," he said, slow and low, mere inches from her face. "Any one of which I'd be more than happy to revisit with you. But we have never been anything as ordinary as *friends*."

His hand slid out from behind her head and cupped her chin, firmly but not painfully. "But you need to be sure that's what you want. Because the next time I kiss you, I don't plan on stopping. Ever. The next time I kiss you, I'll be inside you, in every way." He shifted slightly, his cock brushing hard against her core at the same time his magick brushed against her skin. Liv gasped as her magick bloomed inside her, rising with force against her skin to meet his. She shuddered again, the sensation moving over her entire body, her entire being. "And once that happens, because *it will happen*, there is no going back. No hiding. No secrets. No running away. Do you understand?"

She wasn't sure she was even capable of rational thought after that kiss, let alone those words. She certainly couldn't speak. So she just nodded her head, though what she wanted was to concede, to give him whatever he wanted right then and there. She just barely managed to cling to the morsels of her self-control.

His mouth pulled into a pleased grin, one that sent tingles through her body and directly to her core. Suddenly her purpose in life was centered around doing whatever she needed to keep it on his face.

"Good." He let her body slowly slide down his until she was standing on shaky legs. He tucked an errant strand of hair behind her ear and pulled the hem of her shirt back into place. Then he took a couple of steps back from her. The cold air she'd come out here for now felt abrasive on her hot skin.

"Come on, Dandy," he reached a hand out for hers, "I'll walk you home." She looked down at his outstretched hand, his long fingers, waiting so patiently in the air between them, and couldn't help but wonder if she deserved it. But she took his hand, their fingers slipping back into place, fitting perfectly like they always had.

CHAPTER TWENTY-THREE

*J*ax dropped a stack of wood planks on the ground in front of what barely passed as wood, let alone a porch. "Where do you want this, Uncle Jax?" Cori trudged up the path, his leather tool belt slung over her shoulder, weighing her down as she fought to keep it from dragging on the ground. The corner of his lips twitched at the sight.

"I'll take it. Why don't you go help Logan carry those boards? He could use your muscle."

She gave him a serious nod and set out for the job.

Logan had already loaded an obscene amount of wood onto his shoulder. Jax shook his head and wondered how his friend ever passed for merely human.

Logan—and Cori, who was "helping"—dropped the rest of the boards on the others, causing a reverberation so big the ground shook. If Liv wasn't already awake, that should do the trick, Jax thought.

He was prepared for the fight she was going to put up about this and had already decided he didn't give a shit. He'd been working on the old house mostly in secret for the last couple of years, only stopping once she'd moved back in… more or less.

But as he'd told her, no more hiding. For either of them. Because even though she'd been shedding little layers, revealing her true self little by little, she hadn't fully let him in yet. He'd tried to fight it, but now he was all in, and he needed to show her it was safe to release the grip she had on those tendrils of doubt once and for all. If this was going to work, they'd have to learn to try again, and to trust. So, he'd go first.

He preferred to be prepared for all situations, so he'd brought reinforcements. Liv might be willing to try to turn down his help, but he doubted she would do the same to Logan. And if he was wrong there, well, that's what Cori was for. He'd use every tool at his disposal to break through the last of her defenses, including the spellbinding charm of one Cordelia Hawthorne.

The second set of boards had no sooner hit the ground than the front door flew open. Jax readied himself for a fight, only to find Ivy standing in the doorway instead of Liv. Well, there went all his well-laid plans.

"Jax?" She rubbed at her eye and pushed at her hair. "What the hell are you doing?"

He jerked his chin to the porch in front of her. "This thing is a hazard to the health of anyone who even looks at it, and I figured you guys might prefer a porch to a plunge."

Ivy looked around at the rotting wood. "Yeah, that would be ideal. Liv think so too?" Her raised eyebrows suggested she found it hard to believe her sister would've approved of his venture.

"She likes porches." It was an evasive non-answer. Because he knew she more than liked porches. She'd dreamed of a huge one that wrapped around the house and had plenty of room for an oversized porch swing. He just hoped she wanted it bad enough to let him be the one to give it to her.

Because as much as she liked porches, he also knew she would probably like the idea of anyone thinking she needed help a lot less.

Logan and Cori brought the rest of the supplies and set them down next to the wood.

"Well, good morning," Logan all but purred at Ivy.

She rolled her eyes, but Jax saw the blush that crept over her.

Cori beamed up at Ivy. "Good morning!"

"Oh, good morning! And who might you be?"

"I'm Cori, which is short for Cordelia, it means heart of the sea. I'm here to help keep Liv from killing Uncle Jax."

Ivy's eyebrows raised to near her hairline at Cori's loquaciousness, but she smiled. "Well, that's a beautiful name." Then she turned skeptical eyes on him. "She doesn't know you're here, doing all this." She circled her finger in the air, indicating the porch and all their materials.

Ivy took Jax's silence as answer enough and sighed. "Good luck with that. I'm going to go hide—I mean, get ready for work."

Jax's resolve remained unshaken. Despite Ivy's ominous words, he knew what he was getting himself into.

"Jax?" Ivy paused at the door, her face a little more somber. "Thanks."

He shrugged, making light of it, one of the tactics he'd planned for dealing with Liv. "No big deal."

"It will be to her. Which is why she'll hate it. So, just…thanks."

Jax gave her a small smile and a nod, and she closed the door.

"Uh, what the hell? We're here too." Logan feigned offense on his and Cori's behalf. Then he let a small set of pink safety earmuffs snap down over Cori's ears. "You said she wanted a porch," he accused.

"Yeah? She does." Jax turned back to the materials.

"She just has no fucking clue she's getting one." Logan groaned. "Whatever. I'm on board, but you'd better not get our asses handed to us. Remember what I said about fucking this up for all of us."

Cori looked up at Logan, "I heard that."

"No, you didn't."

"You told me to go get her. Now you just need to trust me to do it."

Logan glared at him for a moment, then turned, grabbed a crowbar, and headed up the porch to start working.

They made it through all the prep work without catching sight of Liv. Lulled into a false sense of security, Jax kicked on the saw and the three of them fell into a steady rhythm. Jax cut through boards, settling into the familiar practice of working with his hands. Logan placed the boards and let Cori secure them with the nail gun whenever they thought Jax wasn't looking.

He'd just brought the miter saw down on a thick support beam when the saw suddenly cut off.

He pulled off the sunglasses he was using in place of protective goggles and turned to look back at where he'd plugged the cord into an outlet by the front door. His eyes tracked the cord up long brown legs to where it was held in slender fingers, and then up to Liv's beautifully confused face.

Her hair was tied up in a slightly crooked high ponytail, wispy strands falling loose. It was messy and reminiscent of sleep. She'd just gotten out of bed. Jax's mind moved to her bed as the delicate scent of her hit him. He swallowed hard around all the images that conjured in him.

He smiled in an attempt to get ahead of her. "Good morning, beautiful."

"Wh-what is all this?"

She looked around, taking in everything they had laid out, and what they'd set the foundation for. Her eyes lifted to meet his. "You're building me my porch?"

"I figured this would be easier than having to rescue whatever unlucky soul happened to breathe wrong on the old one next." He smirked up at her, trying to keep it light. It was like trying to feed a baby deer. No sudden movements.

"Uh, hello? We're also building the porch, Liv." Cori stood off to the side with a hand on her hip, Logan hovering behind her like the personal guard to a little overall-clad queen.

"Did you bring your niece here to manipulate me into not kicking you off my property?" Liv demanded, seeing right through him. He liked that.

"No, that's why he brought me." Logan winked at her.

She fought hard to maintain her annoyed façade. But he'd spotted a hole in her defenses and was tempted to cry victory.

He rubbed at the back of his neck, feigning innocence. "It may have crossed my mind that you'd have a harder time denying what we both know you want if she was here." The double entendre hung between them.

Her eyes held his for a beat, then scanned the front yard and the porch again, spotting the blueprints near his feet. She motioned with a hand for them. He walked up the porch steps and handed them to her over the gap of space between them, then watched as her eyes traced the lines carefully. They softened, the green going unnaturally bright, but her lips tightened into a hard line. He'd been ready for her to push back, maybe even be angry with him for inserting himself again. But not for this, not for what he saw shining in her eyes.

He could also practically hear her mind as it spiraled, so loud he thought he could hear the gears moving.

"It's just a porch, Dandy." Jax's words cut through her thoughts. She stared up at him, and they both knew the lie for what it was, but she nodded anyway.

"I can pay you, at least for materials." She regretted the words immediately but felt like she had to say them. She knew he'd fixed a few things around the house, but that was different. A spindle here or there, even the glass panes on the greenhouse, those were little things. Not to mention they'd all been before she was back here, living in the house.

Logan hissed, sucking a breath between his teeth, but she kept her eyes locked on Jax. The muscles in his neck tightened, and she thought she could actually feel the temperature around him go hot, even from where she stood on the other side of the chasm that had once been her porch. It felt oddly symbolic. But the last dregs of her pride and guilt wouldn't let her take the offer back.

The tip of Jax's tongue appeared for a brief moment before disappearing as he dragged his teeth over his lower lip. She knew it was an angry tick, but it forced all her attention to his lips and the memory of them on hers. A bolt of lightning shot right through her and down to her lady bits at the memory.

Liv squeaked, jumping back into the house as Jax crossed the porch framing and was through the door in one long stride. "Can I talk to you?" It wasn't a question, as he used her upper arm to maneuver her out of sight of the others.

"I think Uncle Jax is going to use some bad words."

"I think you're right, Firefly." Cori and Logan's words floated through the open door right before Jax pushed it closed. He leaned heavily into the palm still on the door, his body looming over her.

"I don't need your fucking money, Liv." He leaned down into her space. The proximity made her brain go foggy. "I'm not doing this out of pity, or to try to trick you into something you don't want. Because we both know you do." He lifted her chin when she tried to look away. "You take your time. As long as your body keeps reacting to me like this," he trailed a finger across her cheek, along her throat, and down her chest, tugging down ever so lightly on the neckline of her shirt as he pulled away, "I'll do my best to be a patient man."

Holy-panty-melting-goddess-of-all-sexy-things this man was so hot. Even when he was mad. Which was making it hard for her rational brain to regain composure.

"There aren't any strings to this, for me or Logan—"

She cut him off. "I know."

"You know?" His brows pulled together.

"Yes, I know."

"So, then what, exactly, is the problem?"

She said nothing because she didn't know how to put it into words. She was too busy working through it herself.

"Dammit, Dandy, it's like a compulsion, the way you have to make everything as difficult as possible." His words were softer, and his forehead brushed against hers like he couldn't help but touch her.

"I'm sorry, I'm not trying—"

"Stop apologizing," he snapped, pulling back. "It's not me you're making things difficult for, it's yourself. Please tell me what is the made-up fucking problem with me building this for you?"

"That. That it's just…just because. Just for me. And we both know it's not just a porch, it's… I know that porch, Jax." The porch he'd drawn on a set of blueprints when he'd just been a boy who loved her and the weird old house she lived in. When she'd been young and brave enough to dream with him. When they'd made plans for the day when the house would be passed to her and it would be theirs, together.

"It's the one you drew for…me." She caught herself before she could say *us*, no matter how badly she wanted to.

He didn't deny it, just looked down into her eyes. A million thoughts passed through them, and she knew every one, felt each one herself.

After everything that had happened behind Mac's the other night, it had been all she could think about.

But even if she let herself admit that what she wanted was him, she couldn't make those promises again. Not until she was sure she could stay here and keep Ivy safe. Because just like before, she knew he would sacrifice too much to follow her, and just like before, she couldn't let him do that.

But she could let him do this.

"Are you going to let me finish it or not?"

She rolled her bottom lip between her teeth and looked up at him through her lashes. "Fine." She smiled, then. "But I want a porch swing, too."

He leaned harder into the arm propped above her head until she was half convinced he'd kiss her. His eyes dropped knowingly to her lips. "Whatever you want." The words coasted over her mouth, but his lips never touched hers. Instead, he pushed off the wall and walked out the door.

"CORI, PUT IT OUT."

"No!"

Liv looked up from where she was crouched in the front garden to see Jax standing over Cori, who had a small fire blazing around her little fist. She stomped her foot and the fire flared slightly, matching her mood.

Liv had been out there most of the day, sticking to the gardens, working around Jax, and trying to ignore the butterflies that swarmed her anytime she felt his eyes on her. Despite all the silent flirting, they'd managed to make a lot of progress on their respective projects. They'd worked continuously through the morning, only stopping briefly when a lunch spread had appeared in the middle of the garden, compliments of the house. She wasn't surprised when all the dishes turned out to be Jax's favorites.

But it was pushing into the later afternoon, and she had a feeling their little witch was getting bored and tired.

"Cor, if your mom shows up and sees you within ten feet of anything with a motor or a blade, let alone that miter saw, you and I are done-zo, kid. Throwing a fiery tantrum isn't going to change that."

Logan stepped up next to Liv just as Cori whined, "Logan let me use the nail gun."

"Way to throw me under the bus, kid!" he called out to her. "Not all of us can remain stalwart against those damn baby blues," he mumbled after, more to himself than her.

"Put it out or it's back to kinder-jail for you." To Cori's credit, she didn't back down from her uncle's glower.

She knew Jax could have snuffed Cori's fire out himself. He was teaching her, Liv realized. Teaching her that her magick was her responsibility, and most importantly that he trusted her to handle it and take responsibility for it. A twist of guilt pinched in her stomach. Cori wasn't the only one learning.

Cori's little fist of fire flared again at the mention of Jax taking her back to school.

Liv approached them. Following Jax's lead, she knelt close to Cori, showing she wasn't afraid of her fire. "Hey, I was wondering if you wanted to ditch the stinky boys and help me out instead?"

Logan sniffed his armpit and shrugged.

Cori sized Liv up, debating her motives. Too dang smart, she thought, but then again, she'd expect nothing less from Jade's daughter.

Liv glanced up to Jax, who was already watching her, then back to Cori. "My Grammy and I built a faerie garden out here somewhere. If you help me find it maybe we could bring it back to life again for the faeries?"

"Sure!" The fire disappeared in a blink, and when Cori took Liv's hand it was no warmer than normal.

After cutting back and clearing the severely overgrown front garden beds they began to unearth little cottages, doors, toadstools, and other remnants of the tiny village she and her Grammy had created for Ivy what felt like a lifetime ago.

After they'd found and set several of the little pieces around where they thought they fit best, Liv pulled an envelope of wildflower seeds out of her pocket and showed it to Cori.

"We can plant these, and over the next few months the faeries will help them grow. We can also leave little gifts out for them, little treasures and thank yous." I'm pretty sure there should be a Polly Pocket buried around here somewhere," she said looking around like it might be there, waiting for her to rediscover it.

Cori looked delighted. "Orrrr," Liv smiled conspiratorially, "do you remember the little trick I taught you at your grandparents'?"

Cori's eyes widened with excitement, and she nodded and took the seeds. She shoved a tiny little finger into the dirt, making a shallow trench around the small faerie city and spread the seeds into it, covering them with the displaced dirt. A small cloud formed and suspended from her palm, and rain began falling from it, watering the seeds. Cori laughed loudly, "I'm doing it!"

"You sure are!" It was amazing to see her use her magick so freely, taking so much joy in the little things she could do and create with it. She was only six, and yet she knew it for the gift it truly was. Something maybe Liv had forgotten...or had never fully grasped in the first place.

The rain cloud now gone, Cori rubbed her palms together then lifted them over the seeds, and a warm glow flickered, fighting to break through. "Don't force it," Liv whispered next to her. "Just think of the sun on a warm day." The glow emanating from the little hands steadied. A moment later, tiny sprouts began to shoot through the dirt. Cori giggled as they kept growing, some unfurling and others growing larger and larger. Liv and Cori stood up and stared in wonder, laughing and cheering as some of them grew taller than Cori.

"That's beautiful, girls." Jax's voice came from right behind her.

She looked up at him over her shoulder. "That was all her." Sweat from the last dregs of summer heat had his thin t-shirt clinging to the outline of his chest muscles. The musk of his skin mixed with the scent of his body wash, and she had the sudden urge to make sure she wasn't drooling.

"It's true." Cori nodded, quite proud of herself. "Logan! Come look at this!" She yelled, running across the yard.

"I was talking about the way you look when you laugh like that," Jax said as his hand slid around her hip. He pulled her back against him. "I can't decide what I like better, the way you look when you laugh, or the way you look when you know I'm watching you." The scruff on his chin slid across her cheek roughly as his words flowed over her. The combination made her feel lightheaded.

"Well, um..." She cleared her throat. "Let me know when you decide, I guess." Her words were uneven, and she could feel the small laugh that vibrated in his chest against her back for a moment before he stepped away.

A sharp whistle broke the moment and drew their attention over to Logan. He flicked his chin toward the street. "Incoming."

Quinn and Jade were a couple of houses down, headed their way.

"Shitsicle."

"Cordelia!" Jax whisper-scolded as she ducked behind a large White Sage bush.

Jade didn't even bother looking toward the bush. "Brother. Why the hell is my kid here doing manual labor instead of at school where I left her this morning?"

The only sound came from Liv and Quinn as they fought to hold in their laughs.

Logan walked halfway through the garden and crossed his arms over his chest. "We plead the fifth."

"It's cute that you think this is a democracy." Jade gave him an acrid smile. "It isn't."

"She charmed the principal into calling me instead of you," Jax said unapologetically.

Jade looked around Jax toward Logan. "Wonder where she learned to do that?"

He didn't look the least bit sorry. "Wonder where she learned *shitsicle*."

The two of them glared at each other for a couple of heartbeats. Liv, on the other hand, tried not to let the realization that Jax was Cori's emergency contact, and the one person she'd wanted when she got in trouble, short out her brain. Or her ovaries, for that matter.

Cori popped her head out from behind the bushes. "Hi Mama."

"Hello, payback." Jade let out a sigh and her anger seemed to melt away at the sight of her worried daughter. "So, another rough day huh?"

Cori's little head drooped as she nodded gently.

Jade knelt in front of her. "Hey, did you do it on purpose?"

Cori shook her little head. "No. I promise I didn't, but my teacher sent me out of class anyway."

"Well, that's all that matters to me. Intent. Remember Cor, it's all about what's going on in here," Jade pointed to Cori's heart, "and in here." She tapped Cori's temple. Then she stood up, her face going hard. "As for your teacher, you let me worry about that. I'm always on your side, right?"

"Right." Cori smiled.

"So, tell me something you learned with Uncle Jaxy today," Jade urged her, clearly telegraphing to her daughter that all was well.

"I learned about the safety on a nail gun!"

Logan slowly inched his way back toward the porch.

"Okay," Jade breathed. "Maybe something else. Anything else."

Cori thought for a moment. "Oh! I learned how to grow flowers." She closed her eyes. *"Don't force it,"* she hummed serenely. Liv felt a touch of pride, and they all laughed

Jade kissed Cori's forehead. "Then as far as I'm concerned, you went to school today. You learned something about nature and yourself. We'll figure out the rest as we go."

Cori gave her mother an adoring look and then promptly ran off, yelling, "Uncle Jax! Logan! We're not busted!"

"Never said that!" Jade called after her.

No one else seemed to react to the scene the way Liv did. Her heart both swelled and ached at the same time. The way Jade had reacted to Cori struggling with her magick, the way she'd soothed her daughter, absolved her of guilt over something she didn't have control over. The way she knew Jade would fiercely rise to Cori's defense. Not because Cori hadn't technically broken a rule, but because she was *her daughter*. That was how a mother should treat her daughter, and she was glad Cori had that.

But it chafed at her wounds. Seeing how Jade had just reacted, and how Jax had handled his niece earlier, she couldn't help but see more ways she'd gone wrong with Ivy. And how her mom had gone wrong with both of them.

Quinn moved up close to her, giving her hand a gentle squeeze, no doubt feeling the emotions she was unintentionally exposing.

As if she'd summoned her with her thoughts, Ivy appeared at the front door. Liv would've assumed her sister would see the missing porch and find another way around. Instead, she took a step and then gracefully floated over the porch altogether, landing softly on the pathway.

Liv tried not to gape as she approached them, but *how,* and *when* had she learned how to do that?

"Looks great, guys," she said happily to Logan and Jax.

She greeted Jade, who introduced her to Quinn. "Your tattoos are amazing. Where did you get them done?"

"Most of them I picked up here and there. Some I did myself."

Ivy beamed at Quinn. "Can you do one for me? I've always wanted a tattoo."

"Sure. I work out of my apartment a couple of nights a week. Don't tell my landlord," she said, shielding her mouth from Jade, who just rolled her eyes.

Ivy's smile lit up her face.

"Where did these flowers come from?" Ivy asked, noticing the fairy garden.

"I did that!" Cori ran back over to stake her claim. "Well, Liv helped me, but it was mostly me."

Something flashed across Ivy's face, but it was so quick Liv wondered if she'd imagined it. "Well, they're absolutely beautiful. Certainly better than I seem to be able to do." Who was this person doling out compliments and making small talk?

"But aren't all Terrabellas supposed to be able to grow stuff?" Cori asked Ivy innocently. Liv fought a wince.

"That's what they say, but guess that bit of magick skipped me," her sister said breezily.

"Where are you headed off to?" Jade asked before Liv could say something that might offer a more positive view of Ivy's magick.

Ivy smiled proudly. "Work."

"You got a job?" Liv asked, learning it for the first time. "Where at?"

"Yep, a little shop down by the pier on the other side of the cliffs." Outside of town was all Liv registered.

"You didn't need to do that."

Ivy sighed. "I *wanted* to Liv. I'm twenty. I need a job."

"I don't know if that's such a good idea. I'm sure we could have found something in town."

Quinn and Jade shared a look, no doubt noting the growing frustration on Ivy's face.

"Yeah, I could have." The sound of a loud engine echoed down the street, causing Liv's body to tense.

"That's my ride. Bye." Liv's stomach dropped as Ivy jogged to the curb just as a black motorcycle pulled up in front of the house. The driver had on a black helmet, and the tint of the front visor hid his face, but the tattoos on his hands and fingers told Liv it was the guy from the other night.

Jax was moving past her before Liv could even get a word out.

"Ivy!" he barked. She ignored him, pulling on the helmet the driver handed her as she got on behind him.

"I already have one overbearing sibling, Jax. I don't need another one. Oh, and neither of you needs to be waiting for me on the new porch tonight, either," she yelled over the loud idling engine. She flipped down her visor and they pulled away from the curb.

Jax wrapped a hand around the back of Liv's neck in comfort.

Jade's face was scrunched in confusion. "What the hell was that?" Liv wasn't sure if the question was for her and Jax's reactions or Ivy taking off with a veritable stranger.

"I don't know. But we're going to find out," Jax answered for the both of them. And even though unease dominated her, she didn't miss Jax's use of the word *we,* or the way it seemed to unfurl through her body and wind around her heart.

CHAPTER TWENTY-FOUR

*L*iv tossed and turned, kicking at the sheets tangling around her legs as she emerged from the same dark dreams just to be plunged right back into them again. When she was finally able to pull herself from sleep, all she was left with was that familiar feeling of unease and the impression of darkness clawing at her.

Her mind and body felt sluggish, but she gave up on sleep anyway.

Creeping out of her room and down the long hallway, she passed the unlit wall sconces that had always remained on. Carefully she skirted the wall, avoiding the floorboard just outside Ivy's room that tended to creak under pressure. Under the dim light of the foyer chandelier, she slipped down the stairs and toward the back of the house.

The sky was black and everything around her was silent and still, as if she were the only one awake in the world.

Not aware of when she'd decided to, Liv found herself walking through the greenhouse and out into the back gardens. She thought to stop near her tea garden to pull some dandelion and chamomile for tea, but no, she needed to keep walking.

The patio turned to step stones, cold and rough under her feet, then plants and dirt. A heavy marine layer hung in the air, prickling at her skin, but the cool touch felt nice on her still over-heated body. The old t-shirt she wore tickled high on her thighs as a breeze fluttered around her, and she kept walking, weaving deeper into the garden.

The twinkling lights ended, and the dark sky above transformed into trees and tall plants that created a tunnel of flora. The faint notion that she'd gone far enough danced at the edges of her mind. It lingered there as she moved farther and farther through the dense gardens at the edge of the property surrounding the house.

With a hand on the gate that marked the property line, Liv paused, one foot on the property and one in the forest that lay between the house and the cliffs. A faint urging to turn back pulled at her.

And then he was there, standing in the trees just beyond the Terrabella property line. Jax smiled at her. It wasn't the Jax that she was getting to know again, but the younger version of him, the one she'd been forced to leave behind. He beckoned her to him, and then turned from her, walking farther into the trees.

He promised her everything, and all she had to do was follow him. No voice made those promises, just a sense of knowing, moving through Liv's body, propelling her forward.

Pine needles and small rocks pressed up into her bare feet, and thick dense fog came in waves, whipping around her legs as she moved through the moonlit dark, following *her Jax.*

She felt none of it.

Her name was a soft cadence from his lips when he stopped ahead of her. She stumbled, falling on her knees into thorny undergrowth and sharp rocks. And suddenly he was right there, lifting her, stealing away any pain. Just like he'd always taken the pain away when they were younger.

Step after step he led her deeper into the woods until the sounds of waves crashing against the cliffs grew from a soothing distant melody to a roaring warning, engulfing all other sounds. Still, the only thing Liv recognized at that moment was Jax, the way he'd been before... from before she'd left. That smirk that had always been just for her playing across his young face.

Jax woke up to a sharp wave of magick washing over him. He peeked at the clock on the nightstand as he slipped out of bed. Not even four in the morning.

He walked to the large window that looked out over Liv's house. It was dark and quiet, no different than any other on the street. He rubbed at his face, questioning whether he'd felt what he thought he had.

If it had been his wards reacting to something he'd be able to tell, he reasoned. Still, the what-ifs plaguing his mind urged him to go over there and check on her. He knew if she was there, and she was fine, he'd risk crowding her too soon after laying all his cards on the table. He'd seen the way she'd hesitated to take his hand the other night at the bar, to accept his actions that day, weighing what he was asking of her. Despite how badly he'd wanted her to say yes right there in the moment, he'd also been glad that she was taking his words, and what they promised, seriously.

Jax groaned. The woman had insisted she was *fine* so often that it had him questioning his gut.

Just as he was about to turn away from the window a cacophony of caws, trills, and screeches rang through the air, followed by several flocks of birds exploding into the night sky from the forest behind Liv's house.

He was moving immediately. Barely stopping to yank on a pair of sweats, he flew down the stairs and out his front door, shoving his feet into a pair of work boots by the front door, not stopping to tie them as he made his way across the street.

The gate flew open in front of him. The trees to the right of the porch shook and rustled, demanding his attention. He trusted the trees, following them as they shuddered and swayed, guiding him deeper into the gardens and, he hoped, toward Liv.

When he came to the gate mounted in the stone wall marking the end of the Terrabella property he hesitated. This was the end of the house's guidance and the boundary of his wards. He stepped across the line and into the abyss of fog that swirled in front of him, masking the forest entirely.

THE YOUNG JAX STOPPED AND TURNED TO HER. HIS MOUTH DIDN'T MOVE, but what he wanted was clear in her mind as he reached a hand out. *She could have the life she always wanted with him. All the pain of the past could be undone like it had never happened. All it would take was a simple trade. Her power for the future. All she had to do was take his hand and every one of those dandelion wishes would be theirs.*

The life they'd dreamed of passed before her eyes like a movie. It was perfect—it hurt how perfect it could have been.

Just release the burden of your magick and it's yours. It's ours. Just let go. Come to me.

Her magick, she'd have to trade it. But it was part of her. Even when she'd shoved it down, deep within her, it had always still been there.

But it's not more a part of you than I am. We can have it all. We can go back, and start from the beginning. We'll make it right. We'll make it perfect. Just let go, and every obstacle will be removed. It sounded too good to resist. She took a step toward him.

That's it. Take my hand, make the trade, and it will be undone. The people who stare, the ones who fear you, the sister who doesn't appreciate you, the mom who resented you, the magick that makes you unlovable. No more pain. No more.

No more? No more Ivy? No more magick? And her mom? Even if she was already gone, that wasn't what she wanted. Even if it meant no more pain. The pain she could handle—she *had* handled. *Her* Jax would know that wouldn't he?

Spray landed on her skin—was it raining? Her name rang through the distant sound of crashing waves as more cold water splashed on her face.

Her hand fell to her side as she took one step back from the younger version of Jax.

His face contorted into an unrecognizable sneer. *Weak. So weak and selfish. You can't even give the one thing that's cost you the most.*

Images of her mother wasting away appeared in her mind. *Your mother hated your magick so much she chose to drown in booze and pills just to escape you.*

The images changed to a loop of Ivy walking away from her, yelling at her. *You failed her, and you'll keep doing it.*

JAX KEPT GOING, MOVING THROUGH THE TREES, IGNORING THE BRANCHES that slapped at him and the persistent fog that seemed to push back against him, cold on his skin. Too cold.

He stopped, his chest rising and falling. He needed to focus, not let his fear and desperation get the best of him. Tunneling down into himself, accessing the balance of elements within him, he called upon the warm southwesterly winds. They blew in off the sea and pushed at the fog, forcing it to dissipate.

The force of her magick hit him like a punch to the face through the brief opening the wind had created for him, before it regrouped quickly, even as another strong gust whipped around him.

The first wave began as little more than an acute frequency humming under his feet. Then the vibrations seemed to be coming from all directions. He braced himself against a tree as the ground cracked beneath his feet.

He took the opportunity given to him, either by Liv or the magick of her ancestors. He called the wind again, using the force to drive the fog into the crevasse in the ground. The fog roiled and resisted but bent to his will.

The shaking stopped momentarily, and the earth sealed shut, taking the sentient fog with it. As it cleared, what he saw had him lunging forward, scrambling across the ground, and praying to whatever god or goddess would listen that he could make it to her in time.

THE IMAGES BEGAN TO FLASH MORE RAPIDLY, DISORIENTING HER. PAIN laced her legs as something pulled at her. She squeezed her eyes shut but the images and the words wouldn't relent.

She saw her friends, saw Jax as he was now, just ahead of her.

You're incapable of being enough for any of them. Young Jax hissed the words in her mind. *Since the moment you were born with those eyes and that power, you've been wrong. Your mother chose to die rather than let you touch her with your magick, rather than spend another moment near you.*

Liv clutched at the sides of her head. "No," she chanted the word. "No, no, no."

You know it's true, that's why you let her die in that facility. You're self-ish, you dragged your sister here even though she didn't want to come because it was what you wanted. Forcing her to face all that you have that she doesn't, rubbing your magick in her face.

And he, the one you think you love, all you'll ever be is a weight around his neck, keeping him from his dreams and from finding happiness. How could he ever love someone like you?

Let go of your magick! Or spend forever alone. Alone like you've been for so long.

Somewhere in the distant recesses of her mind, she heard her name become a desperate chant.

"Liv!" He yelled her name over and over into the night, into the storm that was building at her beckoning.

She stood mere feet from the cliff's edge. Thick ropes of inky fog crept up the cliffside like malevolent serpents, wrapping around her ankles, slithering up her legs, and coiling around her torso. Her hands pressed into the sides of her head, her eyes clenched shut as dirt and debris were sucked into a cyclone circling her. The ground shook under him as he fought to keep his balance, to get to her.

Every time he made a move to get closer a new surge of the dark fog attacked, and Liv's body swayed. As if it was daring him to move any closer.

Wherever she was, he needed to reach her. But she needed to fight through it if he didn't want to lose her to the sea. Jax swore, unsure how to fight against the invisible and unknown force holding Liv captive right in front of him, but just out of reach.

CHAPTER TWENTY-FIVE

Quinn's magick surged and danced within her veins, in both alert and recognition of the storm brewing overhead. It still amazed her that the faint flutter she'd carried within her veins all these years had been this incredible gift, just waiting to be discovered. Unleashing it felt like the moment heavy, dark clouds finally relented to their purpose and released the torrent stored within them.

She sensed the next convulsion a moment before it hit and watched as Logan bent his knees and widened his stance, using his preternatural senses, which she perceived weren't that different from her own. Unfortunately, the magick caught Jade off-guard before anyone could warn her. Logan's arms shot out with the instinct to protect riding him hard, gripping her friend around the waist while they all rode it out.

"Shit!" Jade swore as the world seemed to sway and blur around them. Each quaking session packed more vengeance than the last. The ground creaked below them, threatening to break open.

The wave slowed and then stopped. Quinn shoved down a completely inappropriate laugh as she watched Jade push Logan's hands off her—even in the face of danger the woman was incapable of playing nice. The range of emotions that carried on between the two of them was confusing, often overwhelming, occasionally set-something-on-fire hot, and *always* intense.

They either needed to sort their baggage out or she was going to have to hit the road again, just to get a little peace.

Residents from nearby houses began filing out into the street, yelling at each other and generally panicking, as if the quaking had shaken all the common sense right out of them.

"We've got to do something. These people have no clue what to do in case of an earthquake." Jade said, parroting Quinn's thoughts as she scanned the street.

"This is California, how is that even possible?" she asked. "Aren't earthquakes basically part of a balanced breakfast for you guys?"

"We don't have earthquakes in Havenwood. Magick town and all."

"No, we don't have natural earthquakes," Logan corrected Jade— because he was apparently unable to help himself from stoking the fire within their already volatile friend.

A loud cracking sound filled the air. "Look out!" someone called from a house a couple of doors down. Logan moved with unnatural speed in the direction of a young redwood as it gave out under the force of the quaking and began tilting toward the small crowd in the street.

His forearms tensed and the veins weaving his muscles bulged under the heavy downward pressure as he used inhuman strength and magick to redirect and gently lay the tree down safely between two houses. Quinn fanned herself. Again, inappropriate timing—but pissing off Jade *was* fun.

She was still adjusting to the fact that she could freely use her magick here. Sure, a few wide eyes landed on Logan, but most of the residents were not only aware, but had become quite dependent—too dependent, in her opinion—on the magick that protected Havenwood. A dependency that had left them incapable of coping with any sort of natural phenomenon. Not that this was exactly natural.

"Split up and get these people somewhere safe. Preferably back in their houses. Tell them to get under something heavy or into a doorway, not near anything that could fall," Jade ordered, taking charge as always. It was so interesting how pressure and chaos almost seemed to center Jade. It was a rare trait in her experience—which, when it came to people's emotions, was vast.

Logan stopped Jade as she started to move toward the forest behind Liv's house. "And where the hell are you going?"

"To find Liv. There isn't going to be anywhere safe left if she whips herself into a full *Tempestas Venefuror*."

Tempestas Venefuror, Quinn chewed on the words, drawing on the Latin she'd been teaching herself. Storm of fury? Something like that, she thought. Still fairly new to so much of this, it was hard to keep up with the parts of being a witch that weren't solely intuitive.

"The fuck you are," Logan snapped, and Quinn felt a jolt of fear shooting through him, quick and hot, like a shot of lightning. "Jax is the only one capable of handling her. If you go in there the only thing you're going to do is become a distraction or start a damn forest fire. Your ass is staying out here." *With me,* Quinn almost willed him to say, because she knew that was what he truly meant.

Jade opened her mouth to argue even as the trembling ground shook harder, and the wind started to whip around them. *Unbelievable.* Only these two would refuse to lay their weapons down amid a cataclysmic event.

"Save it, Sunny," he growled. "You can yell at me all you want later when everyone is safe. But I swear to the Gods of the Seven Seas, I will strap you to my back like a damn baby koala if you don't listen to me."

Quinn held back a laugh, half-convinced he'd do it, and backed him up instead. Logan was right—they needed to focus. "I have to agree with the big guy. Sorry."

The rage on Jade's face wasn't about Logan or her betrayal of "girl code"…or at least not all of it. There wasn't much Jade hated more than not being in control, and control was the one thing she couldn't get a handle on lately.

"Fine," she snarled at him. "But Olivia Terrabella has more suppressed power built up in her than this town has seen in ages." She pointed toward the forest where they sensed the power coming from. "If Jax can't get through to her and she levels this whole town to the fucking ground, you're the one I'm telling them to burn at the stake first."

"Oh." Quinn winced. "Too soon."

"Sounds good," Logan said, sarcasm evident. "You guys just stay right here and play defense with this shit." He gestured to the weather that was beginning to kick up and join the party. "I'll start with parts that require people skills."

Jade rolled her eyes at Logan's back, not arguing when he walked off to use that dangerously effective charm of his to convince the neighbors, and every other nosy townie, to consider their safety over their need for gossip. They all complied with hardly any pushback and, from what Quinn could tell, very little magick on Logan's part. Damn selkies could get just about anything they wanted out of anyone they wanted it from. It would be a nice power to have, she thought, if not for whatever dwelled within Logan. He did a good job suppressing it, but she'd gotten a feel for it when it'd slipped through the cracks of the cage Logan kept it locked in, deep within him, and she did not envy the effort it must take him to keep his baser instincts under control.

Logan had beguiled all but a few bystanders to safety, and more importantly out of sight, by the time a police cruiser pulled up. He met the two officers as they got out of the car, one the unmistakable shape of Harlan, the town sheriff. Or former sheriff, rather. Which meant the other was most likely the new sheriff she'd been hearing so much about. But between the dark, the distance, and with noise all around them, she couldn't make out any of his fetures, or what they were saying. She could, however, feel the panic rolling off Harlan wane as Logan briefly spoke to him.

The other man moved just enough to survey his surroundings. Something about him piqued Quinn's curiosity. She opened herself up to him— something she rarely did, as it was hard enough to block out the constant barrage of emotions radiating all around her without her seeking them out —but all she found at the other end of her reach was quiet. Sweet, peaceful, quiet. Not devoid of feeling, but…but she didn't know. She'd never encountered someone who felt like that endless quiet.

"Alright, Wilder." Quinn blinked reluctantly, turning her attention from the stranger back to Jade, who had turned toward the tumultuous sky over the forest. "Just like we practiced, but you know, slightly higher stakes." Jade winked at her and then made a wide swooping motion with one hand, clenching the other into a tight fist. "Deep breath and let the magick lead you from there." Jade pulled her outstretched arm toward herself, attempting to balance the magick in the atmosphere. Her long blonde curls flowed behind her in the wind, her sapphire eyes bright with the fear she was pretending not to feel and all the power she held in that lithe little body.

Quinn exhaled and joined Jade, bringing her hands together in front of her center, as if she were in prayer pose. She closed her eyes for a moment in concentration, then, turning her palms away from each other, she threw her arms out wide.

She did her best to block out everything that was happening around her, as well as what she could feel from the last few humans lingering on the street. It was more difficult to block out the animals. Unlike human emotions, which were sometimes dampened or suppressed for all sorts of reasons, animal emotions were raw, unrestrained, and honest, her connection to them deeper than humans because of it.

She could feel the animals' confusion and fear all around her as birds flew overhead and smaller animals scurried away from whatever was happening deep in the forest. It had been the animals that had first alerted her to what was happening, and how she'd gotten to Jade before the first tremors even began.

Slowly, the emotional mayhem faded into the background of her mind. Quinn's magick didn't so much as flow out of her, but rather filled the space around her, rising up undulating like her own zephyr, awaiting her command.

Following Jade's lead, Quinn freed her magick and her body moved intuitively. Her arms swept through the air around her as if conducting an orchestra featuring the Seven Winds, the song they played a familiar one only she could hear, thanks to her lineage. Quinn pushed away those thoughts and focused instead on the electrical zip that coursed through her as she inhaled the erratic winds.

Together, she and Jade worked to stabilize what they could between bouts of quaking Earth, something none of them had close to enough power to rival Liv with. Maybe not even Jax...

CHAPTER TWENTY-SIX

"*L*iv, I *need* you to hear me. Please listen to me. Use your magick to get that fog away from you and come over here to me." Liv lifted her head to him slowly, the embers in her eyes alight in a way he'd never seen. Her long hair blew wildly around her in the wind and stuck to her damp skin.

"If I just give it to him, I can have everything I always wanted." Her voice was disembodied and sounded almost childlike. She turned her head, looking out across the cove of cliffs. "If I give him my magick everything will be like it was supposed to be. I won't have to fight anymore. *We* won't have to fight just to be happy. I won't have to be alone anymore. I'm so tired and I'm so tired of fighting, of being alone."

The words hit him like a gut punch. He knew she wasn't herself, but he also knew that truth was at the root of her words. "I know Liv. Baby, I know, but you don't do things the easy way. You're too strong and too damn stubborn." Liv blinked, his words seeming to break through, but her head turned again as if she were listening to someone else pulling her in the opposite direction.

Another pulse of shockwaves rippled out across the ground with her at the epicenter. The world around him groaned, matching the anguish he saw on her face.

"Liv! Look at me!" Those ethereal eyes came back to him.

"Come here to me." He yelled over the sound of shaking earth and cracking trees. "We'll figure the rest out together, Dandelion. You and me, right? That's what we said all those years ago, that's what we can have now. But right now, I need you to fight one more time. Just a little more. Please Dandy, then I'll fight for you. I'll fight *with you*. Every day."

Her ethereal eyes turned to him and lingered. "No." He could barely hear her from within the swirling debris, but her voice grew stronger with each word that followed, as she spoke into the night. He saw it the moment she broke free of whatever had her.

"I don't need easy." She heaved the words. "I don't want anything else you have to offer. This life, this power—they're *mine*." Jax watched in awe as Liv flung her hands out and, with a small surge of magick, pushed against the cyclone of rocks. A howl rang through the air, but the rocks shattered and fell, leaving Liv standing, her eyes still glowing but clear as they settled on him. He could sense her relief in the way that the shaking of the earth ceased.

But she couldn't see what he could.

"Jax!" The shock in her voice nearly ripped his heart out.

He shot forward, wanting to lunge for her, but as he pushed at the fog with his magick, her body swayed toward the edge of the cliff. Her eyes went wide as part of the cliff gave way under her feet.

"Fuck!" He roared at the fog, the sky, at everything around him. All the magick between the two of them and he couldn't figure out how to get to her. He'd just gotten her back. He had barely gotten started showing her how he planned to love her.

THE OBSIDIAN CORDS TURNED TO BARBED SPIRES THAT DUG INTO HER SKIN. She screamed as she was yanked off her feet into the sky, forced to look down at the ocean raging below her. Angry waves slammed into the cliff-side, revealing jagged rocks beneath the surface as they washed out.

"Look at me, Dandelion. Keep those beautiful eyes on me." She could see the fear Jax fought to reign in. "You can do this," he said, his voice forcibly calm, and so full of confidence in her. "Trust yourself. Do what comes naturally. Think about what you want and then do what comes naturally."

"I don't—I can't. Jax! I can't!" she pleaded.

"Yes. The fuck. You can. Look at me!" he yelled when she looked down again. The fog tightened, the voice gone, but the demands were still clear. If it couldn't have her magick it would take her life.

But she forced her eyes up to Jax. He was so sure. Everything she saw there, she wanted to *feel it.*

"That earthquake, that cyclone of earth, *you did that.* You did that without even thinking. *Fight!*" he demanded.

Everything hurt, but the pain she could tune out. The pain wasn't new to her. She'd lived with it for years as she shoved herself down and hid her magick away.

She turned inward and reached for what she'd kept buried. She remembered her own words—*don't force it.* Then, on an exhale, she let go.

Everything went still. The pressure in the air dropped, and the power in her built. A bright strike of lightning tore through the sky and the earth shook, rolling and rumbling.

———

JAX'S BREATH LEFT HIS BODY AS LIV LIT UP LIKE THE RAYS OF THE RISING sun. The shriek of the fog pierced the night, it writhed and hissed as she plunged her hands into its depths. Vines shot from the ground, rising to meet her as the fog tried to dissipate, only to be forced back together at her will as she balanced the magick in her hands, draining it rather than allowing it to retreat to wherever it came from.

With a final movement of her hands, she released what ashen material remained into the wind.

The world around him, all that had just been a torrent of chaos, went still and silent.

The vines that had gone to her aid gently escorted Liv back down to the solid ground in front of him.

Liv looked down at her iridescent skin, behind her to where all signs of the power she'd just brandished had vanished. She lifted her arms in front of her, examining them as the magick that had erupted from her slowly receded inside her.

Jax couldn't move. He stood still, taking in all she was, the aura of her magick crackling around her mesmerizing him.

They stayed like that for another two heartbeats.

She took one tentative step toward him. His chest heaved. She took one more. His body vibrated with the effort it took to wait.

Then she launched herself at him. He caught her like an immovable wall, wrapping her in his arms as a shuddering breath of relief left him.

At the same time he pulled her up, she jumped, locking her legs around his waist, and their mouths together. He held onto her by her ass, her arms wound around his neck, and her fingers dove into his hair. Their tongues stroked and twisted, hands grappling and bodies desperate to get closer, closer, closer. Equal in their wanting.

So wrapped up in each other, neither of them noticed the moon-white owl that swooped low above them, then out over the ocean and into the night sky.

Her magick hung in the air around them still, feather-light but potent, just like he remembered. Every one of the memories of her that had haunted him for years became a gift in a single moment. He didn't deserve her, but he'd meant what he said. He'd fight every day for her.

JAX TURNED, PRESSING LIV'S BACK INTO A TREE AND DRAGGING A HAND UP her side roughly. She moaned into his mouth as his shaft pushed against her, separated by only the thin layer of his sweatpants and the material of her underwear.

He thrust hard, hitching her up higher. Her head fell back and her mouth dropped open at the feel of him, and he took the opportunity to dive in again. She bit into the flesh of his bottom lip and sucked, then opened for him just as he went to slide his tongue into her mouth, like she knew his next move, like she remembered—because oh, her body did.

He angled his head and hers, still in his hands, then moved those hands down her body, pulling her closer.

After a few long moments he pulled away slightly, his bare chest heaving, the blue of his eyes clear and striking. "You know what this means." The words came from deep in his throat.

She nodded, biting down on her lip. His eyes dropped to her mouth, and the sound that vibrated up his throat settled between her legs. She pressed her lips to his and across his chin to his neck as she ran her hands up over his bare chest and shoulders. She remembered exactly what this meant, and she might still have worries, but she knew what she wanted. And she didn't want to fight it anymore.

"Say the words." He squeezed her ass hard.

She gasped against his throat and then licked the side of his neck up to the spot that made him crazy below his ear, where she swirled her tongue. "No going back," she breathed against his ear. He groaned and ground into her instinctively.

Maybe some girls wouldn't find being pressed to a tree in the woods a fantasy, but for Liv, it was perfect. The rough feel of the bark of the tree on her back, the smell and sound of the sea crashing, the way it all mixed perfectly with the smell and taste of Jax. Just kissing him again like this was a whole body and soul experience.

One she wanted to revel in.

The heat he made her feel inside mixed with the warmth of him pressed against her, and with the cold, wet coastal air pressing on her skin, was an overwhelming combination, like her skin didn't know how to feel. She shivered against him.

HER BACK ARCHED OFF THE TREE, HEAD TILTING BACK, GIVING HIM FULL access to the column of her neck. She wasn't the only one—he remembered too. He couldn't wait to remind her how well he knew her body, show her how much better than *fine* she could be.

When she shivered in his arms again, this time he knew it wasn't him, but the cold setting in and the adrenaline wearing off.

He pulled her off the tree, and her little groan of disappointment was a pleasing stroke to his ego. "We need to get you warm." She nodded as more shivers moved through her body.

She hissed the moment her feet touched the ground, clearly noticing the cuts that marred her legs and the bottom of her feet for the first time.

Jax lifted her back into his arms and turned to leave the forest, and all the dark parts of this night, behind them.

He looked down at her as she laid her head against his shoulder, letting him carry her, letting him take care of her even in this small way. He knew that one small thing was the biggest hole he'd blown in her walls yet.

Wordlessly he carried her through the forest that was beginning to come to life around them, night slowly giving way to dawn.

THEY STOOD IN THE EMPTY STREET, LOOKING AROUND AT WHAT WAS LEFT behind in the wake of Liv's magickal meltdown.

"Damn, our girl went full." Logan pushed his hands out from his head while making an exploding sound.

"Always so eloquent." With a simple flick of her wrist, Jade set fire to a large branch that had fallen in the middle of the street. Within a moment it had disintegrated into ash and been carried away on a breeze.

A large white owl screeched as it dropped out of nowhere, far too close to Logan's head for his liking, and landed on Quinn's shoulder. She nuzzled the thing for a moment then turned to them with a smug smile. "I don't think we're going to be getting an audience with the lovebirds any time soon."

"What? Why?" Jade asked.

"They're currently making a different kind of magick." Quinn wiggled her eyebrows suggestively. "And they are doing a damn good job." She fanned herself.

"Ugh." Jade groaned. "They've waited twelve years, but they couldn't wait ten minutes and help us clean up?" Her complaints were half-hearted at best.

Logan held up his hand to Quinn for a high five. "You're a quick study!"

"Thanks!" she said, turning to him with a bright smile and pools of silver swirling in her eyes where gold should be.

He dropped his hand. "But I'll never get used to all that business." Logan grimaced and gestured to his eyes with two fingers.

"You're a natural with the elements, but don't be surprised if you start to feel like you could eat a house soon," Jade warned.

"I already feel like that."

"*You* hardly even had to use any magick on anyone. You just used all that." Jade waved a hand at his face.

He grinned. "I know, just wanted to see if you noticed." Clean-up done, the three of them began walking down the street just as the sun crested over the tall trees. Logan slung an arm around each of their shoulders, guiding them toward the bar. "Come on, I'll feed you both."

CHAPTER TWENTY-SEVEN

*H*e didn't set her down when they reached his front porch, or when he slipped through the front door he hadn't taken the time to close before, or when he kicked it shut behind him. He didn't set her down as he kicked off his boots, either.

He didn't set her down as he moved toward the staircase.

She bit the edge of her bottom lip as he ascended the stairs. "My first aid kit is up here." He smirked at the flash of disappointment that crossed her face.

"I think you can set me down now you know?"

"I could." The truth was, he didn't know if he could, not with that image of her at the edge of the cliffs burned into his mind. She'd freed herself out there, in more than one way, and captured all of him in the process.

He walked down the short hall into his bedroom with her still in his arms. Her green eyes darted around the space, lingering on his bed as he passed it. He couldn't wait to have her spread out on it, under him, over him, every way. But that would have to wait until he could be sure she wasn't just high on adrenaline, magick, and memories. Once he was inside her again, he knew that would be it. For the both of them. He knew they were inevitable—he just needed her to catch up.

JAX CARRIED HER INTO THE ENSUITE, WHERE HE FINALLY RELENTED AND SET her down on the cold granite counter between the dual sinks.

Liv looked around, taking in the small details he'd paid special attention to. A large glass shower with multiple heads and matte black fixtures took up one corner, but her eyes fixed on the opposite corner, where a large clawfoot tub sat just below a large, arching, and beautifully restored stained-glass window. Leafy vines of several shades of green glass wove across it, bordered by a repeating pattern of white and yellow flowers... dandelions. Her heart clenched.

He followed her gaze, mistaking whatever he saw on her face to be about the tub. "Next time." His lips curved up on the side. She watched him intently as he leaned down, pulled a first aid kit out from a drawer, and set it beside her. Then he knelt in front of her, his broad shoulders forcing her legs apart slightly. She inhaled when he grasped her right ankle, lifting her leg to inspect the nicks and cuts across her knees and shins. His eyes flinched when he got to the bottom of her feet. They were the worst off, she could feel that now. Even for someone who spent as much time barefoot as her, there were limits.

She looked down at him kneeling in front of her, fussing over her small wounds, and let herself lean into the moment. Into how good it felt to let go and know she could trust someone so completely. That she didn't have to be the one doing the caring, for once, and that the vulnerability wouldn't come back to bite her in the ass. She couldn't remember the last time she'd felt like that, but she did know it had been with him.

"Good news, you'll keep your feet. Bad news, this is going to sting."

She hissed when he sprayed the antiseptic, clenching her jaw, and then moaned lightly in relief, leaning back against the mirror behind her when Jax blew cool breath onto her cuts, easing the stinging.

"Better?"

"Mmhhmm." She could barely think with him between her legs, not with the heat radiating off him and the feel of his breath sliding across her skin.

He placed a couple band aids where the cuts were deepest and rested a hand on each of her ankles.

She watched his blue eyes coast over her as his hands slid lightly up her legs. "I looked for that shirt for weeks." His words came out deeper than usual.

She blushed when she realized what she was wearing, her words breathier than she'd have liked. "Don't let it go to your head, it's just comfortable."

The space around them warmed and the tension went taut. His hands slid up another inch. "It's definitely going to my head." His grip on her legs was a little firmer as he inched his hands a little higher, excruciatingly close, careful to avoid any of the scrapes.

"Jax—" Her voice shook, and she squirmed slightly on the cold granite.

He shook his head, "I'm going to break my own rules, Dandy. But after seeing you on the edge of that cliff tonight—" His voice cracked, and then the fear that flashed in his eyes disappeared as his pupils dilated and his hands slid higher. "I just want to give you everything you want." His hands moved, inching higher still, pressed slightly outward, baring more of her to him as his focus dropped between her thighs.

"But you are going to give me what I want too, eventually," he said, his eyes raising to lock with hers.

"And what is it you want?"

"Everything, Dandy. Every part of you. I'm trying to be patient. But we both know it's not a particular strength of mine." It felt like a challenge, a question, and a promise all in one.

Her mouth went dry, her back arched slightly at his words. She said his name again, but this time it was a plea.

She shifted again, suddenly needing the cold of the granite on her thighs. The look in Jax's eyes bordered on feral, and she wanted to release him from the binds he had on himself. From the way he held himself back, just waiting for her word, despite how much desire she saw there. A desire that was all for her.

JAX WAITED. FELT LIKE HE HELD HIS BREATH EVEN THOUGH HE COULD FEEL his chest moving too quickly. He needed to hear her say it, needed her to voice the want, to choose it for herself. So she would know, tomorrow and every day after.

His hands glided a little higher over the smooth skin of her legs, exposing even more of the green material peeking between her thighs, and he couldn't take his eyes off her. He swore under his breath at the sight she made in her panties and his old t-shirt, her hair a tangled mess. Finally, she put him out of his misery on a breathless whisper.

Her tongue darted out to wet her lips. "Yes Jax, I want—"

"I know exactly what you want." He'd heard all he needed to. In one quick motion, his hands slipped from her thighs to her ass, cupping it and yanking her down to the edge of the counter.

Liv gasped, stoking the fire inside both of them. He was so hard he was surprised his cock hadn't pushed its way through his sweats. He wanted to learn her all over again, every inch of her. Wanted to take his time, but knew it was unlikely either of them possessed the ability tonight.

He licked the inside of her thigh, gauging her reactions, tuning into her. Forcing himself to slow down, he worked up her thigh little by little, running his hands all over the soft skin of her legs, wanting to touch every millimeter of her body.

THE SENSATION OF HIS ROUGH HANDS ON HER BODY MIXED WITH THE gentle licks and kisses was already grating away at her ability to focus. She could sense how much he wanted to touch her, and it made her feel so desired, ratcheting the fire in her veins, in between her legs, to a level she thought previously impossible without spontaneously combusting.

Jax inched higher on her thighs until he reached the apex and, without removing her panties, pressed his lips right where she wanted him, needed him, moaning into her.

"Mmm baby, I can't wait to taste you."

"Oh, *shit*. Jax please." The dirty words and the heat of his breath sent ripples of electricity through her body to her core.

"You never have to beg me, baby. Unless that's a game you want to play. Do you want me to make you beg, Liv?" He spoke against her, the vibration of his words driving her crazy. She rolled her head against the mirror.

"No, not this time. Another time. Because there will be another time, Liv. Another and another. On and on, forever. Until they lay us in the ground and we're nothing more than fertilizer for your pretty flowers."

Her eyes opened and this time she nodded. "Yes."

Jax hooked a finger into each side of her panties. "Lift that perfect ass for me." She did as she was told. He slid her panties down her legs and off, tucking them into the pocket of his sweats.

Too slowly, Jax lowered himself down between her thighs. Liv squeezed her eyes closed, bracing for that first touch.

"Eyes, Liv."

She forced them open and found his gaze under hooded eyes and thick lashes, already locked on hers. She took in his broad bare chest and cut torso, him perched on his knees before her, telling her how much he wanted her, showing her, touching her reverently, as if she were a goddess to be worshipped. It made her feel powerful and treasured. She could come from a breath, she was sure of it. But she didn't have the chance to find out.

Never breaking eye contact with her, Jax gripped her hips and lifted her to him as he leaned in and ran the flat of his tongue from her opening and up to her clit, humming a deep groan over the sensitive swollen bundle of nerves.

She threw her head back, moaning, pushing against his hold on her.

"You taste even better than I dreamed. And I did Liv, I dreamed of you, of this. So many times. I'm going to show you every single one, in my mind and then on your body."

She basked in his words, the dirty praises he rained over her between strokes of his tongue and the circling of her clit.

The friction of the scruff rubbing high on her thighs as she alternated spreading for him and clenching around his face was just the right amount of sweet pain. Somehow it was all too much and not enough at the same time.

IT TOOK ALL HIS SELF-CONTROL NOT TO COME IN HIS PANTS AS LIV whimpered his name when he brought one of his fingers to her entrance, circling it a couple of times with just enough pressure to drive her crazy without entering her pussy. He matched the movements of his finger at her entrance with light circles of his tongue around her clit, building her pleasure higher and higher.

Her body bowed, her hands grappled and clawed for purchase on the granite counter until she finally slid them into his hair, gripping hard, desperate for him to give her what she wanted.

If he'd believed in revenge, he might have kept her like this forever, teetering right on the edge of the sweetest torture, punishing her for robbing them of more than a decade of this. Making him wait so long to taste her. But he'd been designed to serve her, always edging on too desperate to give her everything she ever wanted. Nothing had changed.

She writhed against him, demanding more with her body and her breathy pleading. "Such a good girl, telling me what you want."

He rewarded her, giving her what she needed, finally sinking his finger into her. They both moaned, both experiencing the pleasure and relief of him finally being inside her in some way.

He pulled all the way out and then pushed back in again, crooking his finger up this time. Stroking that sensitive spot inside her as he latched onto her clit and sucked it into his mouth, working his finger and tongue into a steady tandem rhythm.

Her hips rolled against his hand and mouth as she finally released all sense of self-awareness, every trace of modesty, and unleashed on him, grinding into his face. He watched every second of it, sure that it was actually giving him life.

"That's my girl," he spoke the words against her, one hand moving in and out of her at a steady, slow pace, the other drifting up and down her thigh, stroking every piece of skin he could reach from where he knelt before her. "That's my girl," he said again, loving the way her pussy clenched his fingers at his praises. "Are you ready to come for me?"

She nodded erratically.

"I want to hear the words, Liv. Give me what I need and I'll give you what you need."

"Please, make me come, Jax!" She panted the words. "Jax, Jax, please." His name was a siren song on her lips, promising him everything he wanted, or luring him to the sweetest demise, he wasn't sure which—and, for this moment, he was willing to take either.

She was clamping down on him so tight, teetering right on the edge, it took all his willpower not to rip his cock out and plunge it into her. But he wanted this first time to be about her, to take care of her, break her apart, and then put her back together again, the way he knew only he could do for her.

Jax withdrew his finger, but before Liv could protest thrust it back in, adding a second. They moved in long deep strokes as he increased the pressure on her clit, working in a steady rhythm. Her legs locked around his head, and then she was shaking, whimpering, and moaning his name as she came on his tongue.

He carried her through every rolling wave of her orgasm, loving the way she looked as she received her pleasure like a gift. He loved the way she felt, too—tight and wet in one hand, soft, warm, and pliable under his other gripping her thigh.

Finally, her body drooped listlessly against the mirror behind her. Slowly, reverently, he removed his mouth from her and ran his hands lightly across her oversensitive skin, eliciting shivers, taking every bit of her until she was barely clinging to consciousness. Wordlessly, he scooped up her languid body and carried her into his bedroom.

He laid her listless body down, admiring the sight of her in his bed, then slipped in behind her. Before he had a chance to pull her into him, she rolled to face him.

He watched as she worked herself into his body like she was trying to crawl into his skin, fitting perfectly against him.

He slipped his hand beneath her shirt and lightly traced her spine. Her skin pebbled under his touch, reacting to him even in her sleep.

In that moment he knew that no matter what the source of the darkness had been that had almost taken her from him, it would never get that chance again. That he would sacrifice anything to keep her here, right here, part of him, no matter who or what he had to take on to make that happen…including Liv herself, if it came to that.

CHAPTER TWENTY-EIGHT

The floorboards creaked in the room above, signaling to Jax that his little flower was awake. He leaned against the kitchen counter, smirking over a much-needed cup of coffee as he listened to her move around his room, feeling her frazzled energy even before she appeared.

The blush covering her neck and cheeks when she entered the kitchen while unnecessary, considering that what they'd done a few hours earlier was barely a prelude to the list of dirty things he planned to do with her, was also quite entertaining.

Liv pulled at the hem of her shirt—well, his shirt, technically—attempting to cover more of herself.

"I hardly see the point of that. I've already spent plenty of time up close and personal with everything under there," Jax said, setting his coffee aside to pull her in close. He loved the way she instinctively came straight into his arms, likely not realizing she did it, which made it even better.

Liv chewed on her lip and looked up at him. He kissed her until he felt the trepidation melt out of her body.

Jax kept her close when he broke the kiss. "How do you feel?" he asked, running a hand through her long hair, lifting a strand to inhale its scent. He'd taken the tie out while she slept so he could see the way the onyx strands looked spread out across his sheets.

Her eyes sparkled at the affection. *Good.* He never wanted to hold back on any urge to touch her again after spending so long not being able to. He also wanted to make sure she understood that there would only be steps forward from here, not back.

She considered her answer for a moment. "Good. Actually, really good." She smiled and rested her chin on his chest as she looked up at him.

"A good release can do wonders for a person." He smirked when she blushed. "I meant the magick you worked out of your system, but my pride prefers what you were thinking much more." He handed her a mug of tea.

"Thank you." Her eyes lit up, then narrowed in concentration when she took a sip, and then another, working out what she was tasting.

"Where did you get this blend?"

He shrugged. "Just some stuff I had around."

"Jasmine?"

He nodded. "For tranquility."

She sipped again. "Cinnamon and Lavender?" She cast suspicious eyes on him as she started to put the pieces together.

"Healing and purification."

"And I suppose the same goes for the hint of rose? If it didn't taste so good and I didn't know better, I might be a little suspicious of the fact that all the herbs you chose for their "healing purposes" are also known for their association with lust." Or love, and they both knew it.

"You were always better with plants and spells than me." Judging by her face, she didn't miss the smirk he was fighting to hold back.

"Uh-huh."

"I have to go by the town hall meeting before work this morning, but I have a feeling that we're not going to be able to avoid giving Jade and the others some answers for very long. You up for that?"

Jax could see the shame and guilt trying to work their way back into her. He took the tea out of her hand, set it on the counter, then lifted her chin. "No. Don't let the shit in your head win like that." He tilted her head to the side. "No more hiding, remember?" He whispered the last words against her neck, then trailed kisses and licks up the side of her neck where he'd found she was still especially sensitive.

"Mmhhm," Liv agreed, sinking into a lustful haze. He slid a hand just under the hem of her stolen shirt. He ran his fingers lightly across her still-sensitive skin and around to cup her bare ass, then pulled her close, so she could feel how hard he was. "I'll be over after work, okay?"

"Okay." Her words were breathy. She stepped back as he regrettably let her go.

"Have you seen my um…" She hesitated.

"These?" He pulled the silky emerald panties out of his pocket.

Liv reached for them, but he was quicker, tucking them back into his pocket. "I think I'll keep these. You know, for insurance purposes."

Her eyes widened, the green nearly electric in the bright sunlight shining through the large kitchen windows. "What? No. Insurance of what?" Liv stammered, her frazzled energy entertaining.

"Insurance that you come back. That you don't run away again. For next time." He couldn't resist running a hand up her thigh again.

She leaned into his touch like she didn't have a choice. Then she tried to slip her hand into his pocket but he caught her, shifting to the side as he slowly pulled her hand out so she could feel how hard she made him. The breath she took in only made him harder.

It was going to take all his focus not to spend the entire day with a hard-on picturing her on his bathroom counter last night.

He shook his head and placed the tea in her hand instead. "Have a good day." He lifted her jaw, kissed her hard, and then walked out of the kitchen toward the stairs.

"Jax! You aren't seriously going to make me walk home in a t-shirt with no panties! It's daylight! Everyone in town will know by noon."

"Good!" he called back, and laughed when the only response he received was the slamming of the kitchen door.

CHAPTER TWENTY-NINE

*J*ax leaned against the wall just inside the back door, trying not to take pleasure in the aggravation quickly overtaking Declan Stone as he attempted to navigate his first town hall meeting.

The room was a symphony of chaos. Raised voices bounced off the brick walls amplifying the sense of disorder. Some shouted, while others waved their hands around, desperate to be called on—the result was a cacophony of unintelligible chatter that left no room for the very answers they were demanding.

If the guy hadn't been such an ass, Jax might feel bad for the way he'd been thrown to the wolves.

Harlan had given the man a quick introduction to the thirty or so in attendance and announced his immediate retirement, confirming what Jax had already put together—there was a new sheriff in town.

Then Harlan had left the building, leaving the new Sheriff Stone to inform the gathered townspeople about the ritualistic murder that had taken place right outside their border. His first moments in office had been used to rip down the curtain of their perceived perfect paradise. It was a dick move on Harlan's part, no doubt. But survival of the fittest and all that.

Personally, Jax had appreciated the direct way the new sheriff had informed the room about the murder. But most people needed a level of gentle finesse that, so far, Declan did not seem to possess.

"How can you be sure it was a murder?" one voice called out.

"Because that's my job." Declan's derisive tone made it clear how dumb he found the question to be.

The man was clearly not used to being in the public eye in any way. He'd probably applied for the job assuming being in a small town would mean less crime and therefore less attention. If that had been the case, he was already learning the hard way that small towns might mean less crime, but it didn't mean lower expectation or visibility—quite the opposite.

These meetings were open to the public, but Jax attended because, as Praefectus—it was expected, not because he enjoyed them. But if they weren't discussing someone's death, this would have been one of the more entertaining experiences he'd had in this building.

It helped that, for once, he wasn't the target of the rapid-fire question and demand sessions.

The low hum of chatter began to pick up again. These people needed some placating and assurances of their safety if the new sheriff expected to get out of there sanity intact. "Also—" Declan interjected loudly, then waited as the noise quieted again, the crowd waiting for reassurance.

At least the man can read a room.

"There was also a laceration to his throat."

Or maybe not.

Jax dragged a hand down his face as Declan shuffled through some papers he had on the podium and continued to throw gasoline on the dumpster fire that was this meeting. "Though we haven't determined if the wound was deep enough to have been the cause of death. Preliminary evidence shows signs that suggest poisoning, as well."

A collective gasp rang through the crowd, igniting another round of shouted questions, and indistinguishable chatter.

Jax was pretty sure he could hear the sheriff's blood pressure rising from the opposite side of the room. "Hey!" Declan slammed a hand into the podium. "One at a time." His scolding wrangled the entire room into silence. That would be a handy trick if he lasted, Jax thought.

Allen Tanka, the middle-aged man whose family ran the single grocery store in town, stood up to speak. "When do you expect to have some real answers for us?"

Declan's brows drew together, giving Jax the impression he didn't expect to have answers, at least not ones he was planning on sharing with anyone. Including him, most likely. That was not going to work.

"How do we even know if you're qualified to handle something like this?" Allen went on.

"I was hired to be sheriff specifically because I'm qualified for the position—including handling murder investigations. Which I should be getting back to now." Declan nodded once like that would be the end of it and began tucking his papers into a file folder.

"That's not what I'm asking," Allen continued, stubbornly ignoring Declan's attempt to end the meeting. "You may be a Stone, but that doesn't mean you know anything about this town. Do you have magick?"

Oh, now this is getting interesting. Jax studied Declan's face and body language as the other man hesitated to respond for the first time. "I am a Stone, and I'm familiar with this town's history." He paused, lifting his hand like he might rub at his face, but he caught himself, dropping his hand and fortifying his resolve. "No, I don't use magick. But—"

"Obviously we're directing these questions to the wrong person." Nina Peters shot to standing, not bothering to let Declan finish as she turned her attention from the sheriff at the front of the room to face Jax at the opposite end.

Dammit.

"Things like this aren't supposed to happen here. Aren't you the one who's meant to ensure that?" It was more an accusation than a question.

Jax pushed off the wall, intentionally avoiding Declan's glare. "Yes." He made no excuses.

In most towns, something like a murder would be the sheriff's responsibility. And if murder was something that happened in Havenwood, maybe that would be the case. For the most part, Jax remained completely detached from whatever petty infractions usually took place in town, leaving them to Harlan and the few deputies he employed. But when it came to the magick that coursed through the town and the Umbra Aegis—that was the responsibility of the Hawthorne line. His responsibility.

"Well then?" Nina planted her fists on her narrow hips, eyeing him expectantly.

He couldn't tell them the truth: that he didn't know where to fucking begin. The feeling of failing everyone was eating away at him.

This wasn't something he was prepared for. The role of the Praefectus had been mostly symbolic since the founding of Havenwood. The presence of their magick in the town serving to bring security in a "just in case" kind of way. Which was more or less how he'd been trained by his mom. He was powerful and well-versed in the town's history. He understood the magick as much as anyone could, but it wasn't like it came with a user's manual where he could find information on how to troubleshoot the system. And it certainly hadn't come with training in ritualistic murder.

Still, he'd be more equipped than the sheriff—past or present.

His mind raced for something that would satisfy the room, finally settling on, "I'm working on it."

"You're working on it? Is that supposed to be enough?" another person called out from the audience.

Fuck. His frustration with himself was getting the better of him. It wasn't the pressure of eyes on him, day in and day out, or the weight of expectations. Those were all things he was used to growing up here. It was the stakes.

It was desperation.

And he didn't have any more to offer them than Declan did—less, it seemed, if what the new sheriff had said about poisoning turned out to be true.

Jax searched the crowd for the source of the voice, finding dozens of expectant eyes boring into him. "I understand you're scared, but it's being handled. In the meantime, if you need to travel outside town, take safety precautions and—"

"Exactly what kind of safety precautions do you recommend for earthquakes and 'natural' disasters, Jaxon?" Nina asked, using air quotes around the word "natural." Heat surged through him at the thinly veiled accusation, clearly directed at Liv. His muscles tensed as he fought back his anger. Reminding himself that if Nina were truly convinced Liv had caused the storm, she wouldn't have bothered to veil it at all.

"Yeah," Allen piggy-backed off Nina, "not all of us can protect ourselves with magick, that's supposed to be your job."

"Actually, that would be *my* job." Declan drew the collective attention of the room back to him. Jax didn't delude himself into thinking the new sheriff was trying to save him in any way—the man wanted his authority made clear. Declan Stone had already proven he was unwilling to share, and the last thing Jax needed was a sheriff-sized obstacle impeding him.

"I don't mean to undermine you," Jax lied, all eyes bouncing back to him, "but seeing as the crime scene took place just *outside* the town line," Jax emphasized the point, hoping it would bring a small amount of comfort to the townspeople, "that would also make it outside your jurisdiction. Luckily, the obvious magickal implications make it mine." He may have pulled the argument out of his ass, but it was a sound one.

"Sadly," all attention rebounded back to Declan, "you're mistaken. The forests and beach surrounding Havenwood are unincorporated and protected land which, if you understood how jurisdiction worked, you'd know, makes it well within *my jurisdiction*. Which is lucky for all of us considering, unless I'm mistaken, I am the only person in this town with investigative experience. Certainly, the only one with any experience in homicide. Or am I wrong?"

The only sound in the room was that of rustling clothing, and the shifting of chairs as the townspeoples' attention volleyed between him and Declan.

Jax found the other man's cool confidence grating, if warranted. He ran his tongue across his teeth and did his best to keep his growing irritation from his voice. "I think you'll find your experience will only take you so far here." He'd been moving steadily toward the front of the room as they spoke, and now stepped closer to the stage, lowering his voice so the whole room wouldn't hear. "You won't be able to solve this murder without understanding the magick and intentions of the ritual. For that, you'll need *my experience." My job, my responsibility, my birthright, my burden to bear.* "I assume solving this is more important than your pride. Or am *I* wrong?" Jax took a couple of steps back toward the end of the aisle, which split the room into two sides.

Declan came out from behind the podium to the edge of the short stage, not bothering to keep his voice down in his frustration. "And understanding the magick means jack shit if you don't have the skills necessary to understand a crime scene. If you can't understand the crime scene, you can't catch the killer. That seems a hell of a lot more important than anything else. I think the victim, and the people still living in this town, would agree."

More murmurs rolled through the room as confusion took hold. Jax realized their argument was only serving to create more insecurity and doubt, news of which would engulf all of Havenwood by the end of the day.

This was a waste of time. Jax didn't need Declan's permission to do anything in this town, and the people in this room didn't need to worry about some clash of the Titans. They needed their sense of safety restored, and he needed to get the hell out of this building before he cracked a molar.

"You're right, Sheriff. I'll let you take it from here then. Good luck with your investigation." Jax gave the man a tight-lipped smile and slipped his hands into his pockets as he headed for the exit. He was certain he looked like exactly what he was: the poster child for peaceful acquiescence, with just a hint of condescension, and absolutely zero intention of keeping his word.

CHAPTER THIRTY

*Q*uinn placed a hand on Liv's wrist with a momentary look of concern. "That's so crazy! I'm really glad you're okay."

"Thanks." Liv went back to meticulously stirring the hot liquid she had on a burner in front of her. Sandra had asked her to make a couple of calming candles for her goat yoga class. That woman seemed to be part of every club and class the town had. Liv didn't know how she handled that much people-ing on a daily basis.

She added a few drops of Cedarwood oil, trying to focus on the relaxing intentions she had for the candle and not on the errant thoughts about Jax and the things they'd done the night before. If she wasn't careful, she could accidentally imbue the candle with the wrong emotions, and then they'd have a class full of horny women and goats. Liv set the ladle down, deciding not to risk it.

"Where was the last place you remember walking before you were on the cliffs?" Jade asked as she poked around the greenhouse.

She shook her head slowly. "It felt kind of like I never woke up from the dream I was having. It wasn't so much a feeling of being controlled or overtaken, but more like I was being convinced, and seduced by my memories and desires. Then there was this intense knowing, that if I just kept walking everything I wanted would be mine."

"Oh, what was it?" Quinn's eyes rounded in excitement again. Liv decided to ignore that question.

"Maybe we should wait for Jax and Logan. I don't feel like reliving most of that more than I have to."

"I can't believe Jax didn't call for us, or at least me. It would've helped if I could have seen or felt the power around you for myself, rather than just yours whipping up the storm." Jade mumbled some swear words, which was essentially her way of pouting.

"But mostly she's just glad you're okay and that you were able to call on your magick like that," Quinn added on Jade's behalf, remnants of concern lacing her words.

Jade waved a hand as if that were a given. "Yeah, obviously."

"So, if you don't want to go back through what happened out there on the cliffs, how about you tell about what happened after!" Quinn urged, the impish sparkle returning to her eyes.

"What? I...nothing happened." *Wow, real convincing.*

"You definitely had an orgasm."

Liv's skin went hot at Quinn's observation. She'd had orgasms in her life, but what she'd experienced last night felt more like something they hadn't found a word for yet. She'd spent all day bouncing between thinking about that and everything he'd said to her out there on the cliffs. Everything she'd been able to do. Even though she'd saved herself, she knew having him standing in front of her, reminding her of the power she held inside her, had given her the confidence to do it.

But he'd also reminded her multiple times that there was no going back from this. He'd said it with his words and with the way he'd touched her. He'd practically tattooed it on her skin with his hands and mouth and on her heart with his words.

When she'd washed the post-orgasmic haze away in the shower her mind had started to work overtime on her again, trying to convince her that his words were said out of fear and lust. And debating whether she'd be able to hold up her end of the bargain. Her stomach seized at even the thought of leaving him again. Leaving any of them. She blinked, clearing her mind, not wanting to get caught up in that endless cycle of overthinking again.

"Stop looking at me like that," she told Quinn.

"You're glowing! I can't help it! I want some of that glow. It's been so long. Give me every detail right now. Those architect hands have to be magical. I mean they are *literally* magickal. Come on pleassseee."

"Pleasssseeee don't." Jade mimicked Quinn's plea with one of her own. "I'm happy for you and all, but I do not need the play-by-play of anything that involves my brother."

"What if I use a code name?" Liv joked.

Quinn jumped on her slip-up immediately. "So, you admit it! You did have sex!"

"Well, it wasn't sex, exactly. But…okay yes, I had an orgasm. Yes, his hands are magickal. I think I left my body at one point. Sorry Jade, but things happened to my body that I may never fully recover from…ever. Are you happy now?" She took a breath, glad to have gotten that all out.

Both Jade and Quinn stared at her, mouths open a little, blinking.

"I think that's the most words I've ever heard you say at one time," Jade finally said.

"Also, he wouldn't give me my underwear back. Okay, that's it. Promise."

"Why is that so hot?" Quinn asked.

Liv opened her mouth to respond, but Jax appeared in the open French doors that led from the house into the greenhouse. She didn't know how he'd managed to slip into her home so silently, but she had a strong feeling the house itself had a hand in it.

The cocky grin on his face told her he'd heard most, if not all, of what she'd said, and the fire in his eyes was promising her so much more to come. And she wanted it. All of it.

"Marco!" Logan's voice echoed from somewhere in the back of the house. "Where you guys at?"

Liv had moved them all to the library, trying to salvage the energy of the candles, but it was a lost cause. There was no salvaging them after Jax had showed up looking at her like that, still in his worn-in jeans that fit him way too well, and that tight white t-shirt.

He'd come straight from work, and the idea that he'd wanted to see her as soon as possible, plus the light scent of sweat on his skin…well, there was no chance those candles hadn't been corrupted by her lusty energy. She'd have to toss them…or save them for personal use.

"MARCO!?" Logan's voice shocked her out of her thoughts just as Jax slipped behind her, straddling the chaise she was sitting on, and pulled her back between his thighs.

"What are you thinking about, Dandy?" he practically purred against her ear.

"Fucking POLO you idiot! The house is a square for Spirit's sake." Jade yelled, saving Liv from having to admit her thoughts or lie.

"I'm aware." Logan appeared in the opening of the library, biting into an apple, clearly having found the kitchen. The smirk on his face said he'd known where they were the whole time.

"Oh. I like this," Logan pointed to her and Jax with his apple. "'Bout time," he said around a mouthful as he leaned against the wall.

Jade closed her eyes to take a calming breath. "Can we *please* get on with this?"

"I second that." Quinn raised her hand, dropping to sit cross-legged on the floor next to Liv and Jax.

"Thank you," Jade said with a smile to Quinn. Then her eyes snapped up, landing on Jax and Liv. "What the hell happened?" she directed to Liv. "Why didn't you call me?!" That one was to Jax.

"Whoosah, tiny tornado," Logan said, placing his hands on Jade's shoulders and pushing her down into an armchair. She pushed a breath out her nose while she shrugged his hands off her.

Liv smiled at her. "Love you too."

"Yeah, fine. Love you. Now, *please. Begin!*"

So, they told them. Well, mostly Jax told them, with her filling in the small details she could clearly remember. The visions of younger Jax and how it seemed to be after her magick more than anything. Most of what that distorted version of Jax had said to her once it dropped the charming façade.

"Jax would never say shit like that," Logan grumbled from behind the chair Jade was sitting in.

"She knows that." Jax's words were clipped, and she wasn't sure if the tension that had his fingers flexing against her thighs was from Logan thinking he needed to clarify that for her, or from having his identity stolen to torment her.

By the time Jade had finished telling her and Jax what they'd seen and dealt with while she was in the forest, she found herself in the cocoon of Jax's arms and thighs. She'd recoiled so far into herself under the weight of the guilt of what she'd caused, she'd had to lean into Jax to remain upright.

Quinn's hand squeezed her leg from where she sat on the floor next to her. But she didn't say anything, she didn't even look up. Quinn just kept a hand on her in quiet support, responding to whatever she was picking up from her. The little act made her feel seen. Silent support that didn't call any extra attention to her.

"Is there anything else you can tell us? Anything about the magick that stood out or felt familiar?" Logan asked.

"I'm just going to say it if you're all going to beat around the bush. Your sister's sus-as-hell boyfriend. That fool has dark and deadly written all over him. Not to mention *the motorcycle*."

"Yeah, I mean, I love me a bad boy, but he's pushing the line even for me. And didn't you say you guys heard a motorcycle the night you were followed home?" Quinn said, seconding Jade's train of thought.

It was an understandable leap. So much so it wasn't even really a leap. But it also wasn't the case.

"It wasn't him," Jax said before she could.

"How can you be sure?" Jade challenged, standing up to pace the room.

"I felt his magick the first night he brought Ivy home. There was maybe something slightly similar between the magick I felt coming from him and the fog. But it wasn't the same. The fog wasn't natural, but there also wasn't a magickal signature on it," Jax explained.

"What does that even mean?" Jade was getting more and more frustrated with each moment and every unanswered question.

A light breeze blew in through the open library window, bringing with it the faint scent of sandalwood and saltwater, reminding Liv of driftwood on the beach. The suncatcher hanging from the ceiling swayed, sending rainbows flitting across the room like tiny butterflies. And the tension in Jade's shoulders was released.

Liv did her best to explain. "He means that there isn't anything distinct about the magick that you could use to describe it. It just leaves you with this feeling…or maybe it's a knowing. Either way, you can't describe it, but you know it when you feel it."

"That's exactly it. You remember that?" Jax's voice vibrated in his chest behind her. She turned her neck to look up at him when she nodded. His eyes were already on her, baby blue with a shock of yellow in the center. They reminded her of the sky on a sunny, cloudless, Southern California day. He waited patiently for her explanation.

"I think it followed me here."

CHAPTER THIRTY-ONE

*J*ax's dark eyebrows drew together, and his arms tensed around her instinctively. "I need more than that, Dandy."

Liv sighed, looking around the room at her friends, trying to work out where to start. How to let them into the mess she was pretty sure she'd created, or at the very least made worse. Concern was written all over their faces, and she knew it wasn't just for her. Just like she had Ivy, they all had people they cared about, and if she'd brought something dark here with her, they at least deserved to know what she'd done.

Jax's warmth around her, the weight of it, the steady rise and fall of his chest behind her, and the patient silence of her friends around her all urged her on.

"I've been having these dreams since before I came back to Haven-wood. Not every night, but more often than not. There is this consuming darkness…it moves, and even though there is only darkness, it still feels as if something is weaving itself into my mind. I can tell it wants something from me, even though there are never any words or voices.

"When I wake up there's just this lingering feeling, almost like remnants of something real left behind, something I can tell is of the same source. It doesn't feel like any other dream I've had."

"That's because it's not. That's a nightmare." Logan's face was scrunched into something between concentration, anger, and being thoroughly creeped out.

"Yeah, I guess I just never wanted to call it that because it's so intangible."

"If it's real to you, it's real, period," Jade said adamantly.

"Why didn't you tell me?"

She looked back up at Jax.

"When, exactly, would I have done that? When you were ignoring me, or when you were telling me to 'keep my pretty little ass in the house'?" He didn't argue, but that little muscle in the side of his jaw twitched in annoyance.

"And, from what I've heard, your mouths have been a little too busy for talking lately." Quinn grinned up at them from the floor.

"Anyway," Jade said, steering the conversation back on track, "even if your nightmares are somehow connected to what happened last night, why would you think it followed you here?"

Now for the part that she'd be avoiding all along. She could feel herself wanting to shut down and close off, but she forced herself to look at her friend's faces. They'd all shown up at her house to check on her. They wanted to figure this out because they wanted to help her. Whether this was all in her head or not, it didn't matter to them.

"When we left twelve years ago, my mom said it was because this town didn't want us, and she wanted to find somewhere new. We lasted a year in that first place. When we left there, she said it was to find somewhere "safer". We made it six months in a small town in Georgia before she became convinced that something, or someone, was following us.

"From there the paranoia just kept getting worse. She couldn't relax enough to sleep, and the lack of sleep just made her more paranoid. So she started drinking to help her calm her nerves and sleep. Soon she was drinking more than she was sleeping.

"The cycle just kept compounding. I literally watched her wither away in front of my eyes. I tried to help her, but she didn't want my hands, let alone my magick, anywhere near her. She'd always resented my magick, but she grew to hate it. Hate me for it. I did it anyway, in small bursts when she was passed out. But it was only just enough to keep her alive most of the time." Liv paused, letting her mind catch up with the words that were flowing out of her now. Jax's arms had become steel bands around her as she'd shared the cliff notes version of what her life had been like in the years they'd been apart.

"One day I came home from work and found her in her room, bleeding from wounds she'd given to herself. She was barely conscious. And even still, she tried to fight me away when I used my magick to heal her enough to stabilize her to get her to a hospital. The whole time she was rambling on and on about digging it out of her, and making the voices stop."

"Geez Liv. I had no idea it was that bad. Why did you keep following her?" Quinn asked.

"Because of her sister," Jade answered for her.

Liv nodded. "Ivy was young, and she wouldn't leave my mom. She'd started to struggle too, in her own ways. Her emotions were erratic and her behavior and magick followed suit. She already resented me for not healing our mom. I was afraid if I forced her away from Elena it would just make everything worse. Plus, my mom wasn't capable of keeping a job. She wouldn't have been able to support herself." Liv shrugged. "I didn't tell you guys sooner because I didn't want to look too closely at it, at how it started for her."

"How did it start?" Jax asked.

"With the nightmares." She didn't stop to let that sink in. "They started for her around when my grandmother died. Everything went to shit so quickly after her death, I don't even know exactly when they started. I used to wonder if Valeria was helping my mom keep them at bay. If the mere presence of her power did. But now I have to wonder if maybe she passed them on to my mom when she died." Liv laughed sardonically.

"All along my mom was telling the truth. I never believed her. Never." She looked around at her friends, their eyes filled with emotion. Empathy, but also pity. "Even when she nearly killed herself to escape it. And she died in a psychiatric facility I had her put in, for all I know, that was probably a consequence of me using my magick on her even though she didn't want me to." She took a deep breath, ready to just have it all out.

"I never believed her, and the last thing she asked of me was to keep

Ivy safe. And now, for all I know, this *thing* has been with us all along and either I brought it back here with us, or I delivered her straight to it. Now it's got its claws in me, and if I end up like my mom, what will happen to Ivy then?" There. She'd said it out loud. Everything she'd been through, everything she thought, everything she feared. She covered her face around Jax's arms, hiding the tears that were burning her eyes but wouldn't fall.

"No." Jade's voice was suddenly close to her. Her friend pulled Liv's hands away from her face as she sat at the foot of the chaise, her gaze steady. "None. Of. This. Is. Your. Fault." Her words were fierce, leaving no room for argument. "Just like what happened to your mom isn't your fault. Just like any decisions your sister has or will make aren't your fault. You're not the great conductor of life. You're a witch. A powerful one, but not *that* powerful. You were alone, and you did your best to take care of people who never bothered to return the favor. That's it. Okay?"

Liv pulled her lips into her mouth and nodded her head. Jade's words felt harsh, but they were hard in her defense, even if that defense was of her to herself.

"And you'll never do it alone again. Okay?" Jax turned her face to him. His eyes were shining, and his body practically humming.

Liv nodded. The urge to feel helpless and coddled pressed on her, but instead she chose to let herself accept the care these people, her people, were offering. She reminded herself it didn't make her weak. She didn't have to hide the hard that was behind her. And because of the people in that room, she didn't have to face the hard that was in front of her alone.

Jade stood up. "Alright, one thing at a time. First of all, I think we need to check the wards around here."

"I already did," Jax said, his grip on her not having loosened at all.

"Of course you did." Logan squeezed Jax's shoulder as he started to walk out of the library.

"Well then," Jade turned and gave Liv a smile that made her nervous in a, *oh crap what is she thinking* kind of way. "I think we need to do a cleansing. Of the forest around this place," Jade circled her finger in the air, "and on you." She pointed at Liv.

"Oh!" Quinn unfurled her long legs and stood in one fluid movement.

"A girls' night?" she said, looking between her and Jade. The two of them standing side by side made Liv both excited and very nervous.

"Okay. Sure."

CHAPTER THIRTY-TWO

*N*either of them had spoken in the minutes since the others had left. Liv could feel the tense energy coming off him in waves as his mind worked, sorting through everything she'd said. Within the firm hold of his arms, her body rose and fell with the rhythm of his breaths. It was soothing to rest against him, to let his body support hers while she let him work through it.

Jax moved his hands to her hips and turned her so they faced each other on the chaise, both straddling it, her knees tucked inside his, the short skirt of her dress stretched taut across her legs. His hands wrapped firmly around her thighs like he needed to hold her in place.

"Something tried to take you from me. It almost did." There was a harsh edge to Jax's voice, and he didn't try to hide the range of emotions he was feeling, though the clench of his jaw told her it wasn't comfortable for him. *No more hiding.* That was what they'd agreed, and he was showing her how.

She'd given up so much truth, told their friends all of what they needed to know—but Liv knew that wasn't all he needed. All *he* deserved.

She climbed into his lap, letting her legs hang over his thighs. The way his hands instinctively came up to brace her back soothed some of her nerves. He'd been very clear about where he stood when it came to them, but she hadn't fully met him there. Not yet.

"We said no more hiding." His words were low but not gentle.

"I'm trying." It was all she could say.

He exhaled a ragged breath, pulling her closer, resting his head against her chest. She left him like that for a moment while she steeled herself for what came next, and then whatever would come after that.

Jax didn't loosen his grip on her when she slid her hands against the sides of his face, bringing those beautiful eyes up. He exhaled as her magick rose to the surface, and Liv dropped her forehead to his. "I'll show you the rest," she said against his lips.

He leaned away so he could see her face.

"Are you sure?"

She smiled. "We used to do it all the time."

"That was a long time ago. And last time I wasn't able to keep out of things you didn't want me to see."

"No more hiding." She held his eyes so he would know she meant it, and know she trusted him to see what he needed to. It wasn't about trusting him not to look where she didn't want him. But trusting him enough to know that no matter what he might see there, he'd still want to be here, with her, after.

He brushed a strand of hair away from her face, and like her thoughts were written all over her face, told her all she needed to hear. "Nothing in there will change the way I feel about you, or the fact that you're mine for good this time." The determination in his words penetrated something deep within her. The resolve in his eyes and the stubborn set of his jaw reminded her of the promises he'd made when they were young, the ones she'd let him make and then had been too scared to believe in when the time came to count on them.

The moment might be small, but it felt significant, like when he'd been on his knees, cleaning her wounds, kissing up the inside of her thighs, telling her what it meant if she took him up on his offer. Accepting or turning down what was being offered then, and now, meant so much more than just the physical act.

This time she didn't need to think. This time she wouldn't let guilt and fear control her or hold her back. This time she would trust him and take the risk of letting someone in—fully.

She nodded and lowered her lips to his.

It started as a gentle kiss, but she pushed it deeper. She opened for him, starting with her mouth, and deepening to her heart, her source. She welcomed him into her.

His tongue stroked hers as his magick enveloped her mind and cloaked her body.

She felt Jax's groan as she let her own magick intertwine with his. His hands slid down the tops of her thighs to the outsides. He pulled them up and shifted them, so he was stretched out on the chaise, her wrapped around and pressed against him, without breaking their kiss.

His fingers curled into her hair, tugging slightly, silently demanding more. So, she gave it to him.

———

JAX FELT IT THE MOMENT SHE SURRENDERED TO HIM FULLY. HE HAD TO fight hard against the desire to abandon the search into her memories and take her in that moment. He wanted to drown in her, the feel of her, the way she felt now that she'd finally caught up with him.

She was laid bare for him, and they were still fully clothed.

In Jax's mind's eye, he entered the chamber of Liv's memories, like a large room of crystalline green. Aisles spread out around him—it wasn't what her memories or mind really looked like, just what he had projected.

He summoned all his focus and pushed a little deeper, moving through her until he felt he might be close. *Bring me to that moment,* he whispered into her mind while his lips continued to move over hers. As if they were two separate planes, one where their bodies were connected, and one where their minds were.

Their kiss slowed slightly as things came into fuzzy focus. Jax descended deeper until he was standing beside Liv in her memory, looking over her shoulder.

She released a deep breath into him, laced with her power, and, as if the memory itself had been waiting for him, it began unfolding in front of him, picking up where it had left off.

This time when Liv turned from a young Ivy and opened the front door, instead of swirling darkness he saw the porch and the night sky.

In fractionated flashes, the memory moved, vestiges of anguish and other emotions trailing Liv as her body ran through the streets of Havenwood, her mind doing what it could to protect the current version of her and spare her from having to relive it all fully.

Then the memory stabilized, and he was there with her, feeling every second with her in a way he'd never experienced in any other memory walk he'd taken. If it were anyone else, he would have pulled out right then and there, but something told him this was her doing, her desire to open up and let him in, and he wouldn't turn away from that.

She didn't stop running even when she made it to his front door. He'd had a feeling she'd been coming to him that night, but seeing it released something inside him, knowing she'd followed through.

His mom's face appeared, but the memory flickered. He called it back to him as he coaxed her to relax into his hold, moving his hands down her back, around her hips, where he left one, the other rising to cradle the back of her neck.

The memory came back into focus and settled.

"Hi, honey." Sandra opened the screen door, inviting Liv inside.

Silently, Liv followed Jax's mom through the living room toward the kitchen while the older woman spoke. "Jax isn't home, but I'm sure he'll be back in no time. Why don't I make you some tea while you wait?"

Jax could see the weight in Liv's body, but his mom in the memory didn't notice as she moved around the kitchen prepping the tea.

"Oh, while you're here, what do you think?" Liv lifted the black envelope she was handed, and slipped the cream cardstock halfway out, exposing part of the Hawthorne family crest pressed in black wax in the center. Panic tried to crawl up her throat—she knew what this was: Jax's well-planned future closing in, while hers was in shambles.

"I think this is the one I'm going with. It's a bit more ostentatious than Jax would prefer, no doubt, but then again if it were up to him this party

wouldn't even be happening. I know it's formal, but what can I say, I'm just so excited for him and for me. Retirement here I come!"

The sparkle in his mom's eyes pulled at a familiar thread of guilt, one he could see reflected in Liv's stricken face, his mother still blissfully unaware, her eyes on her task.

"Jax officially taking over as Praefectus this fall is worth celebrating. I wasn't sure what he was going to decide with all these college acceptances and internship offers from far-off architecture firms. Spirit knows he made us wait long enough for his decision, but I suppose his love for this town, and a few other things, won out." Sandra smiled at her knowingly at that last part, and Liv averted her gaze, trying her hardest to hold back tears.

He's needed, and I need to go. What the hell are we going to do? Jax, where are you?

"I know working with his dad for a few years isn't exactly his idea of a dream job, but between you and me, I'm already laying the groundwork to lead Warren into retirement, as well. Soon enough Jax will be able to take over the business altogether. So many exciting things coming up."

So many exciting things… here. And I won't be.

Jax watched Liv give his mom a smile that would have been able to fool just about anyone, but he saw the way it didn't reach her eyes. And worse, he felt the way every speck of hope evaporated from her at that moment.

"Um, can you excuse me? I need to use the restroom." Liv made her way down the narrow hallway that led to the restroom, but instead of going in, she passed the bathroom, slipping into his bedroom instead.

She moved around Jax's room slowly, taking in every little detail and committing it to memory. She turned away from the picture of them snuggled up next to a bonfire at the beach he kept on his nightstand.

When she made it to his desk she lifted a small stack of creased papers, discarded off to the side. Pride rushed through her even as she felt the tears win out as she shuffled through them.

He already knew what the letter she was reading said. All the letters in that stack were variations of the same. She knew, too. He hadn't hidden them from her. Hadn't planned to go. He felt them hit her, though, as she read the words.

Dear Jaxon Hawthorne,

It is with great pleasure we wish to congratulate you on your acceptance to Superior d'Arquitectura, Barcelona.

The letters shook in her hand slightly as she returned them to where she'd found them. He saw the bit of blue peeking beneath papers and other clutter at the same time Liv did.

Their kiss slowed and then stopped as Jax's stomach dropped. Liv tucked her face into the crook of his neck, her hands landing on his chest, one clenching lightly in his shirt as they lived the rest together.

She pushed the rest of the papers and supplies aside, revealing a detailed set of plans. Plans for Havenhouse. Tentatively her fingers traced over the sketches and scaling, in awe. Of course he'd found a way to incorporate every little detail they'd dreamed up during the nights they'd spent on her small balcony under the stars, her tucked perfectly between his legs, wrapped in his arms, making wishes on dandelions together. No, she'd been making wishes. He'd been making plans. Plans that would never, could never, come to fruition.

Her throat clogged as it all became so clear. He had everything in front of him here. He'd already given up one future for his parents, for this town. He'd shaped himself to be who the town needed. He was necessary. He had plans and a future, and they were all here...and she knew without a doubt that he would give it all up to follow her into whatever mess her mother was dragging her and Ivy into next. He'd walk away from the life he'd chosen, he'd leave a family he loved and a town that needed him, for her. He loved her that much.

And she loved him enough to not let him.

Jax felt tears falling, watching her eyes nearly glowing as her tears streamed down her cheeks. Even if he hadn't been able to feel her every emotion, he could see the resolve that settled within her. She was right—he'd have gladly given it all up for her. He'd done it anyway, unable to stay in a town that was theirs without her in it. He watched her in his childhood bedroom, willing her to stay, even though he knew this wasn't a movie he could rewrite.

Liv turned from the desk toward the door, knowing it was time to go. Knowing she wouldn't have the strength to leave if she saw him. She paused near Jax's hamper where some of his clothes hadn't quite made it into the basket, lifting his favorite worn t-shirt and inhaling it deeply, nearly burying her entire face in it. Jax. She almost put it back in the hamper, but instead tucked the shirt into the pocket of her sweatshirt and left.

He couldn't tell whose emotions he was feeling now, hers from back then, or his own from right now as he watched her walk out of his room. He knew more or less what came next, for her and him, but he watched anyway. For her sake. For theirs, so she wouldn't carry it alone.

Liv passed the pictures in the hallway, so many with her in them, but she didn't let herself look. She let herself pause, though, for a quick moment to memorize the image of Sandra standing at the counter making her favorite tea.

He wondered if she realized what it meant that his mother still kept that special blend of tea in the house just for her. The same blend he'd kept on hand all these years—just in case. Because they all had been waiting for her, even after all this time.

Then she was running again. The faint sound of Sandra calling her name followed her down the street, but she didn't stop. She couldn't. Because if she stopped, if she even hesitated, she wouldn't be able to resist the selfish demand of her heart to stay.

He endured the pain of the choice she'd had to make that night and nearly buckled under the weight. How she'd managed to endure it alone all these years, he had no idea. He'd known she was selfless—to a fault, in his opinion. But seeing this, feeling it, and not being able to change it, to fix it... it filled him with a helplessness that made him want to tear the world down so he could build a new one. One where she never hurt again.

She found her mom outside, already loading the car. "I'll go, but we have to leave tonight."

Her mom looked at her for a moment and then nodded. "Better hurry up and pack, then."

Liv took little more than what could fit into a small duffle, leaving everything else—her entire life— behind as she turned the light off and closed the door without looking back.

Jax watched as Havenhouse shuddered and groaned as the last three

Terrabellas walked out the front door. He saw the emotion wrack through Liv, saw her push it back and leave anyway.

Rain sluiced down the windshield as Liv drove them toward the sign marking the edge of town. She peered into the review mirror as Haven-house—the place that was intrinsically tied to their very DNA—grew farther and farther away, then down at her little sister, asleep in the back seat. Though visceral pain raked its claws across her heart, she knew this was the right choice, the only choice that would allow her to protect the two people she loved most in life, Ivy and Jax. Even if that meant she'd have to leave one to go with the other.

As she crossed through the Umbra Aegis, Jax like a ghost in their car, he could feel Liv gather all her power as a cavern deep within her yawned open. Liv drove her magick inwards and down, down, down, until it met that cavern, where she let it consume the part of her that was no less integral than her blood, and let it close up around her essence, her being. *Her magick.*

CHAPTER THIRTY-THREE

*J*ax gasped as the memory winked out, and he was left standing there in the middle of all that crystalline green again, his own emotions a riot while a resigned calm emanated from Liv. Her hands traveled over his body in an attempt to comfort *him* from the pain that she'd had to live and then endure all on her own. It only made him angrier.

He summoned all his self-control and slowly receded from the deepest parts of her, withdrawing from her mind and back into his consciousness. There was a sense of loss inside him, for having to withdraw into his solo consciousness.

And for the boy who'd lost that girl.

He vibrated with the need to stand up, to move, as his frustration built. But she'd trusted him. And he knew if he exploded out of the seat and away from her, he could kiss every bit of the ground he'd gained goodbye. So he forced himself to stay right where he was, his hands fisted in the thin material of her dress.

Neither of them spoke for a minute, and then she tried to move back from him, but he only let her get far enough for him to see her face.

Was *this* what it had always been about? Did the last twelve years without her come down to a *fucking* miscommunication? To her simply not waiting around to even talk to him about it?

"I would have come with you. Gladly. I wouldn't have seen it as giving up anything." His voice was foreign even to his ears, coming from somewhere low in his throat.

Her smile was so sad. The entire thing was so confusing, and he hated the way he felt so young at that moment. As if the boy he'd been on that night in her memory was somehow merging with the man he was at this moment.

"I know." Her words were barely a breath and only served to confuse him more. "That's why I had to go. You'd have given it all up for me. For us. You'd have missed out on your future just to try to protect me from mine."

He rubbed his hands at his face, and this time when she moved to stand up, he let her.

"I know you don't get it, Jax. I'm sorry that I hurt you, but I didn't have a choice," she said, his eyes following her as she walked the tight perimeter of the room.

"That's the thing, Liv," he interrupted, "you did have a choice. You could have chosen to trust me."

"I did trust you, Jax." She stopped between the bookshelf and the desk. "But you were *nineteen*. I couldn't put all of that on you to figure out. The town needed you."

"I left anyway." The words came out louder than he wanted, with more emotion, and he tried to pull himself back. "I couldn't be here without you. I could have been *with* you."

"I wouldn't have been able to handle the guilt of it, Jax. Yes, you left, but to follow your future somewhere else. I barely handled throwing my future away to chase after my mom for Ivy's sake. But I did, and it was easier knowing you were out there, living the life you were meant to. I am okay carrying the weight of that decision. I am okay."

"I know you are, but it's so much to carry alone. It's too much."

She shrugged. "I'm fine."

He closed his eyes. "Stop saying *that word,*" he begged through clenched teeth. "You deserve more than that. When did fine become an acceptable standard for your life?"

She hesitated, almost like she was considering a way around the question, then relented. "The day I left Havenwood. I knew it was all I could hope for."

It was an unacceptable truth, but one he understood perfectly because he'd been living his version of 'fine' all this time too. He still felt it breaking inside him.

"Then why, *why* did you leave me at all?"

"I didn't leave you, I left for you! I couldn't lay my mess at your feet and ruin your future." Her brows were pulled tightly together, willing him to understand.

But it was she who didn't understand, and his control of his emotions finally broke.

"You were my future!" He stood up from the chaise, facing her. "And *we* had everything in front of us. *We* could have figured it out, together."

Jax walked toward her until the back of her legs hit the edge of the desk. He trapped her there with an arm on each side of her body and held the gaze of her tear-rimmed eyes that sparkled like the purest emeralds, needing her to hear him this time.

"It's not me who doesn't understand, Liv. It's you. It's the same damn thing I've been trying to tell you. There were so many things I didn't know back then, so many things I can't figure out right now, but the only thing I've ever wanted is you. Then and now. You don't need to do all of this on your own, not anymore. From now on, we do these things together. We figure it out together. That's it." His hands braced her hips, and he wasn't sure if he just needed to touch her, or if the memory left him with the need to hold her in place, to make sure she couldn't vanish like that again, couldn't leave him with their future slipping through his fingers like vapor.

"Let me take care of you. Not because you can't take care of yourself, but because you don't have to be the only one."

A tear slid down her face as she nodded. He kissed it away and then kept kissing down her neck. One of his hands braced the back of her neck and the other reached down between them, dragging up her thigh until he reached her core. "Will you let me take care of you, Dandy?"

Liv nodded again.

"Good, because I'd like to start right now."

"Okay." She'd barely gotten the word out before she was lifted into his arms. She held onto him, trailing her lips across his chin, finding his mouth. He navigated the stairs without issue, only pausing at the top to press her into the wall and grind his hard length into her. Then he pulled her back to him and started walking again. He groaned when she sucked his lip into her mouth. "Why is this hallway so damn long?"

At that moment something light hit him in the head, followed by another hit, and another. "What the hell?" They looked down at the ground to find condoms scattered all over the floor. Jax grinned, scooping one up. "Man, I love this house."

Finally, in her room, he dropped Liv onto the bed and took a moment to enjoy the sight of her from the end. Her dress was shoved up above her waist on one side, baring the thin band of a deep purple lacey thong. Her was hair falling out of its loose braid, and her mouth was swollen from his.

She lifted onto her elbows. "I'm sorry," she whispered, confusing his reverence for reticence. He hated how miserable she looked, but a selfish part of him was also soothed by the knowledge that she hadn't wanted to leave him. That he wasn't the only one carrying scars from her choices.

He was also done with those scars. Jax planned to erase them from their bodies, one kiss and one confession at a time.

He reached behind his head and pulled his shirt off in one swift movement. "I loved you the moment I met you, and every day since then," he said, followed by a slight flick of his wrist. The rest of their clothes vanished, eliciting a small, surprised gasp from Liv, and truly leaving nothing else between them.

Desire ripped through him, seeing her completely naked, physically and emotionally.

She tracked his movements as he knelt on the bed and crawled up and over her body. Her mouth parted just a little as he drew close, his hard cock pressing against her warm skin as he hovered over her, bracing his weight on his forearms.

"Jax—" she tried to speak, looking up at him, lust and vulnerability warring in her eyes.

"Every day that I was forced to remember you like you were right here, but I couldn't see you or touch you…" he trailed a feather-light finger over her smooth skin, from her collarbone down between her breasts to her navel, causing her skin to pebble and her nipples to harden. "For every moment of those twelve years, when you were alone and thought no one cared, I loved you." Liv folded under the intensity of their eye contact, trying to turn away from him. He stopped her, bracing her chin in a firm but gentle grip, forcing her to remain in this moment with him.

"And when you showed up in town again, I loved you still. And every minute since then. I love you, Liv. I don't need you to tell me you're sorry for leaving, I need you to tell me you'll never do it again." He released her chin and drove into her in a single thrust as if to punctuate his confessions and his demand.

"Jax!" She cried his name like a broken plea.

"Tell me," he growled through clenched teeth as he fought to maintain a slow pace. He knew what she needed, but he needed this first.

She nodded urgently, locking her legs around his hips and digging her heels into his ass, trying to force him deeper inside her.

"I need your words, baby." He didn't care if he sounded desperate—he was. Desperate to keep her. Forever.

"Yes, Jax." This time when she lifted her hips he slid a hand beneath her, gripping a handful of her generous ass. "I promise," she moaned, "I won't leave you again. I love you too, Jax. Only you. Only ever you."

Her words became a chant and his undoing.

With one hand pressed into the bed above her head and the other holding onto her ass, he thrust into her again, as deeply as he could go.

His name was a breathy cry falling from her lips over and over as he slid in and out of her in long, steady strokes. Her fingertips gripped at his back, her nails digging in, and he prayed she'd leave marks.

Jax rose onto his knees, lifting her legs over his shoulders. She whimpered at the change in position, and he nearly came at the sight of her. Tiny beads of sweat glittered between her perfect breasts. He leaned over and pulled one of her tawny nipples into his mouth, sucking and licking at it as he rocked into her.

Her moans turned into sobs when he reached between them and pressed gently on her clit. He released her nipple, needing to see the pleasure on her face. Pleasure he was putting there. Her eyes were shut tight, her mouth parted slightly in ecstasy.

Jax lowered her legs then, flipped over onto his back, taking her with him, and her eyes opened wide in shock and pleasure as the change in position forced Jax deep into her. Her hands braced on his chest roughly and he groaned in pleasure. She took a moment to adjust before she slowly started rocking and rolling her hips on him. Jax's hands roamed her body reverently. "That's it, baby, ride me."

"You're so deep," she whimpered, her head falling back in pleasure as Jax's hands and words rained down over her skin. He could feel the fluttering of her walls as her orgasm built within her.

He reached between them and ran his fingers over and around her clit. Her head snapped forward as her orgasm ripped through her, her muscles tightening around his dick, forcing his groans out through his teeth.

He caught her when she collapsed onto his chest, pulling her in close to him as he continued to thrust up into her limp, sated body. "Say it again," he ordered gruffly, his voice low in her ear.

"I won't leave you, Jax."

"Good, because I can't let you go again, Liv. I don't care what it means, what has to change—I'm keeping you now." He punctuated his demands, his proclamations with each thrust of his hips up into her warmth. "I don't care where, whose house, whose bed. I want to fall asleep with you every night and wake up to you every morning."

Liv wrapped her arms around his neck and began riding him again as he used a tight grip on her hips to work her up and down his shaft.

"Yes," she said again, her words turning into deep moans of pleasure. He wrapped his mouth around her breast, pulling her nipple between his teeth, and she cried out, clamping down around him again. "Now Liv, come on me again baby." His fingers clenched into her ass as her walls started to flutter around his cock. "That's my girl," he grunted, slamming deeply into her one more time, and then he followed her over the edge.

He caught her body against him as she fell forward, their skin sliding slowly against each other as they rode the last waves of their orgasms together, every clench of her pussy around him forcing another shot of his release into her.

He fell flat on the bed, holding her against his chest and inhaling the scent of her hair.

She shuddered slightly as he dragged a hand up and down her back slowly. They lay there, breathing heavily in the weight of their admissions and promises. "I love you," she said, lifting her chin to look up at him.

"Again, or still?" he asked, though he'd take either.

"Always."

CHAPTER THIRTY-FOUR

*T*he three women entered the small clearing that split the woods and the cliffs, far beyond Liv's property line and the protections of the house. The place where the residue of a foreign power still lingered.

The moon was nothing more than a tiny sliver sitting high in the sky, allowing the stars their moment to shine brilliantly above the dark ocean.

Liv pulled a few things out of a bag she'd brought with her. "I made these." She held up a tightly bound smudge stick. "I thought it might be helpful to use plants that grew with Terrabella magick in their roots."

Quinn took one of the bundles of cleansing herbs and inhaled deeply. "Mmm," she hummed, "these are amazing."

Jade took one as well, inspecting it before sniffing it herself. "They're perfect. The herbs you chose and everything you infused into them with your hands. I can feel the intent and magick in them. It'll make them even more powerful."

Liv smiled. It felt good to have her magick appreciated. The confidence she had in how she'd used her magick to amplify the natural properties of the plants felt even better. Each represented both sides of her. The herbs and plants that had grown with her power of life. Now dried out, technically dead, but not devoid of power or purpose.

"Oh, I almost forgot." Kneeling over a canvas bag, Jade pulled out a simple white garment box wrapped with a maroon ribbon. She handed it to a surprised Liv. "Jax wanted to be sure you had this for tonight."

She slipped the ribbon off and removed the lid. Her mouth fell open.

Folded neatly in the box was a gorgeous emerald green cloak. She trailed her fingers lightly over the soft velvety material.

A small white envelope was tucked inside the fold. She slipped a small white card out. Written in Jax's precise handwriting was a short note.

Good thing I had something to reference for the color.
I can't wait to see it on you…and then take it off.
Always, Jax

She bit her lip, noting that the color was almost identical to a certain piece of clothing Jax had recently refused to return to her.

"Well, let's see," Quinn demanded impatiently.

Liv lifted the cloak out of the box, holding it up for her friends. The deep green of the velvet outside was complemented by a similar green satin lining. A large hood hung at the back.

"Wow, it's beautiful. That color! It's perfect for you." Quinn beamed at the garment.

Jade nodded in approval. "Not bad, Jax."

They each pulled out their cloaks, Quinn's a lustrous silver, reminiscent of the moon, and Jade's black, the color chosen for Balancers, to signify the embodiment of all elements while not placing one above the others.

"Generally we do these kinds of rituals Digambara. It's not a requirement at all, but I will be, and Quinn definitely will be."

Quinn grinned with a little shrug, "Naked in the woods under the stars? Don't threaten me with a good time." She threw her hands over her head and danced in a small circle.

"Whether you decide to go sky-clad or not, you can wear that over top."

Liv nodded, remembering her grandmother telling her about her sky-clad rituals when she was younger. The nudity added a layer of freedom and wasn't—in this case—sexual. It removed barriers, something Liv knew she was still holding on to, the nude form being a physical representation of truth. Truth to the elements, truth to the Spirit, truth to Magick, and truth to oneself. The latter being something she knew was particularly important she embraced for this cleansing.

The dark magick had manipulated her with the lies she'd believed about herself, the lies she'd told herself for too long. If she stood a chance of ridding the land of its essence and protecting the people she loved by making sure she wasn't the weak link, she'd do whatever she needed to.

The three of them moved around the clearing, preparing the circle and themselves for the ritual.

Liv placed a small stone bowl at the North point of the circle. With a gentle wave of her wrist, the vial of *Earth* she'd brought from her garden tipped its contents into the bowl.

At the East point of the circle, Jade placed an intricately carved wooden disk that held a cone of smoldering incense in the center. The smoke trailed into the sky, twisting and turning, demonstrating the flow of the *Air* around them.

She then walked across the circle to the West point and placed a small chalice. With a graceful arc of her arm, Quinn filled the chalice with *Water* captured from the spray of ocean waves crashing into the cliffs. Liv placed a large candle to mark the southern point of the circle and then looked at Jade. With only her mind she summoned the *Fire* that lit the wick.

The circle formed, and the three women stood at the perimeter, facing the moon. "You ready?" Jade asked, looking to Quinn first then to Liv.

Liv's cloak lapped at her bare skin in the gentle wind. She drew in a deep breath, steadying the nervous excitement she felt inside her. She nodded. "Ready."

As one, the three crossed the perimeter.

The air within the circle warmed with energy as the invisible barrier they'd cast became a palpable force, separating them from the outside world.

They stood in the center of the circle close together, each bare beneath their cloaks.

Jade began while lighting one of the bundles of herbs Liv had made.

"In this place where our blood's magick is strong,

With reverence and respect, we call to those whom we belong."

Liv and Quinn's voices joined with Jade's creating one melodious sound.

> *"Ancestors ancient, spirits of the past,*
> *Guide our hearts as this cleansing is cast."*
> Their voices paused and then Liv continued alone.
> *"Ancestors dear, and by birthright,*
> *rid me of the dark that remains of that night.*
> *As I walk this path, guide me true,*
> *with wisdom of old and by the light of the moon."*

Liv's breathing seized as a heaviness moved through her, pulling down, trying to take her body with it. But then it began to rise. She felt it as it passed, icy through the center of her body, up her throat, and lifted from her entirely. It took with it a weight she'd been carrying with her for so long she'd grown accustomed to it, had stopped realizing it was there at all until the moment it was gone.

Her emotions followed the same path as the weight, changing inside her in a way she had no control over. Anger became anguish which gave way to elation, cycling so quickly she could hardly keep up. And then, as her physical body settled into this new state of freedom, so too did her emotions.

Her breaths evened out and, with a cursory glance from her friends, making sure she was okay, they moved on to the next step—one she knew wouldn't be as simple.

Moving their focus from Liv to the forest around them, the three moved out from each other, lifting their arms as they started together again.

> *"In this sacred space, our intentions align, we rid this place of dark design.*
> *Ancestors here lend us your sight, illuminate shadows, expel all blight!*
> *Terra elicitus, terra elicitus, terra elicitus!"*

Dark fog erupted from the ground and pressed in on the circle, twisting, separating, and reforming. Smoke from the incense swirled and the flame of the candle flickered. The chalice and stone bowl quaked, threatening to spill their contents. But all held within the circle.

Quinn moved her arms in a strong circle, and the fog lifted into one shifting mass.

Jade lifted her hands and focused on the mass, her magick filling the circle as she attempted to balance whatever dark magick had summoned it. But despite the way it shrieked, the mass didn't dissipate.

Purely on instinct, Liv grabbed Jade's hand, also taking the one Quinn wasn't using to hold the mass within the wind.

The three of them felt the weight of the darkness pushing in on them, but they didn't let it stop them. "We need to finish this and close the circle," Jade yelled above the howl of the fog that whipped around outside their sacred space. They moved to the middle of the circle again, hands still linked.

Their voices raised, still all but lost on the wind, they finished it.

"Elements of Earth, Air, Fire, and Sea,
We call upon your power to set this space free.
Terra restaura, terra restaura, terra restaura."

The three witches chanted three times, ensuring the earth there was restored to its natural state, before closing out the spell.

"As we will, so mote it be!"

As the last words left their lips, the tendrils of the dark fog dissipated with a sharp and angry hiss.

Liv, Jade, and Quinn stood in the still quiet of the forest. The only sound was the rustle of leaves, waves gently lapping at the cliffside, and their breathing as it slowly returned to normal.

"Holy crap." Liv blew the words out, pulling the edges of her cloak tightly around her.

For the first time, Quinn seemed frazzled. She blinked rapidly, opening and closing her mouth, at a loss.

Jade tossed her head, pushing her wild golden curls out of her face. "I need a drink. Immediately."

All Liv and Quinn could do was nod in agreement, more than ready to move on to the part of their girls' night that included more booze and junk food, and less…whatever the hell that had been.

CHAPTER THIRTY-FIVE

*B*ack in the old house and in their pajamas, the three women drifted into the sitting room where they found a fire already going in the large fireplace, accented by varying sizes of candles lit across the ornately carved mantelpiece.

A large table—that Liv had never seen before—draped in black material sat where the settee usually was. It was decorated with more candles in golden candlestick holders and rustic wooden platters set at varying heights. The platters overflowed with an exquisite spread of crackers, cheese, fruit, and sweets. Large cushions of varying rich jewel tones and throw blankets were scattered around the room.

"Damn, Liv." Jade and Quinn circled the table, "This is the perfect girls' night spread, but you didn't have to do all this," Quinn said around a bite of a chocolate-covered strawberry.

Liv stood half in shock, half not surprised at all. "Don't thank me. This was all the house." Her eyes roamed over everything it had done for them. "I have a feeling it thinks I need help making friends."

"Well then I need a magical house—maybe it could help me find a friend. A *special friend.*" Quinn popped another strawberry into her smirking mouth.

"But does it clean itself?" Jade's face lit with hope.

"Not so far." And Liv wondered for the first time why that might be.

Jade plopped down on one of the pillows, dropping her tote bag on the ground in front of her. The sound of glass knocking against glass and crinkling wrappers came from the bag as she shoved things around with both hands, her face halfway inside. She pulled out a granola bar and a half-clothed Barbie that had seen better days and tossed them aside.

"You're like a hot Mary Poppins."

"Liv," Jade paused her rummaging to give her a deadpan look, "Mary Poppins *was* hot. She was also clearly a witch," she added as she dove back into her bag.

Quinn and Liv blinked at each other in confusion.

Jade looked up again, probably at their lack of immediate agreement. "Endless supplies, the cure for literally everything, the ability to keep all those kids in line, flying. Do I really need to go on?"

"You do not," Quinn replied sarcastically.

"Ah ha!" Jade shouted in triumph, holding up a glass bottle with black and gold serpents weaving across the front. "Look what I brought." She waved the bottle in the air.

Quinn reached for the half-full bottle of whisky. "Did you steal that from Logan?"

"I plead the fifth," Jade said with a smug, self-satisfied smile, using Logan's own words even though he wasn't there, no doubt imagining the moment he realized it was missing. Liv hoped they'd be there to see it.

"Didn't he say this stuff was his favorite and he could only get it from home or something like that?"

"Yeah," Jade answered Liv, looking even more pleased with her theft. "They only make it on Orkney, the small island off Scotland where he's from. Something about special waters, harsh weather, and the peat moss they use makes it unique to the area." Jade shrugged. "Or something like that. So, who's taking the first shot?"

"I propose a toast!" Quinn held the bottle by the neck and lifted it high. "To Liv, for dusting off the cobwebs—of this house, of her magick, and of her vagina!" Quinn took a heavy swig straight from the bottle, Liv winced, and Jade laughed.

Quinn passed the bottle to Liv, who took a tentative sniff. "Oh, for the love of all things natural, there is no way anything from *this* earth made that!" She held the bottle away from her face.

"Yeaaahh. The people from Logan's island are descended from *both* Vikings *and* Highlanders," Jade said. "They do not fuck around with their whisky."

"That explains why he looks like a darker-haired descendant of Thor," Quinn noted.

Jade rolled her eyes. "Please never say that to his face."

"Oh, come on." Liv set the bottle down, hoping no one noticed she'd skipped her turn. "I remember how you looked at him when you were young, and he has only gotten better with age. You have to at least admit he's hot. He'll never know."

"Yeah right, the way that guy goes through women, he's probably summoned by even the mention of his name."

Liv rolled her eyes. "He's not Beetlejuice, Jade."

Quinn threw her head back in laughter.

"Well, maybe I'd like him better if he was. Stop stalling and take your shot."

Liv lifted the bottle slowly. "To friends, old and new," she looked from Jade to Quinn earnestly, "thank you for tonight, for welcoming me back, and for taking me in so easily when you didn't have to."

"Okay, okay. Now drink before you start crying." Jade pushed the bottle toward Liv's mouth. Liv scrunched her face but took a respectable pull from the bottle. She would have mentally patted herself on the back for the impressed look Quinn and Jade exchanged, but she was too busy dying from the inside.

"Oh shhhhhiiit!" she wheezed. "Why does it feel like there is a fire in my face?"

"That would be the peat moss."

"Oh, mother fuhh." The words came out in a breathless rasp. "I think I'm going to be tasting it for the rest of my life."

"That's what she said." Jade took the bottle from Liv and lifted it to her mouth.

"Wait!" Liv stopped her. "You have to make a toast."

"No thanks." Jade made to lift the bottle to her lips again.

This time Quinn stopped her. "Come on, give us something good. Unless you just don't have it in you like we do."

"I know you're manipulating me," she pointed the bottle at Quinn, "but damn you it's working."

Quinn smiled and gestured with her hand. "The floor is yours, oh tiny wise one."

Jade exhaled and eyed each of them, considering something, then started, "Here's to coming home, to finding your place, your people, your magick," she hesitated for a minute before continuing, "and yourself." Jade's voice wobbled at the last words, so she took a heavy swig to cover it up.

She knew Jade's toast was for Quinn and her, which would have meant enough, but she also knew those were all things Jade was facing or finding as well, as she navigated a divorce and began building a new life as a single mom.

"Don't start that. We aren't even drunk yet," Jade ordered noticing the emotion on Liv's face while fighting not to show the burn of the whisky or her own emotions.

AN HOUR LATER AND A FEW MORE SHOTS EACH, QUINN AND LIV HAD managed to work their way back around to their original line of questioning.

"Fine! Yes, he's hot! Anyone with eyes or ovaries can see that. Can we please move on?"

"I'd argue you don't need either of those things to see how hot he is." Quinn giggled at her own joke. Liv nodded in agreement, a little too emphatically for her inebriated state. She tipped sideways off her cushion into Quinn.

Liv winked at Quinn when she pushed her back upright. "Thanks."

"Did you guys ever... you know?" Liv hiccupped halfway through the question.

Jade's head fell back in annoyance.

"Just answer the question and we'll leave you alone," Quinn bargained.

Jade let her head fall forward again. She narrowed her eyes on both her and Quinn. "Oh, she's considering it." Liv nudged her acomplice.

"I don't even know how to answer that."

"Honey," Quinn leaned forward to pat Jade's leg, "you have a baby, you have to at least kind of know."

Jade ignored her. "He knows how I felt, uh, like my entire childhood."

"Everyone did," Liv said out of the side of her mouth to Quinn.

Jade also ignored *her.* "Something kind of happened once."

Liv's stomach flipped with giddiness. "Wha—" Quinn slapped a hand over her mouth.

"I thought it was going somewhere. He made it *very* clear it wasn't. I met Aaron shortly after, and that's that."

"Is that why you guys hate each other?"

"Does Jax know?"

Quinn and Liv asked at the same time.

"We don't hate each other, it's just... messy," Jade admitted.

"Of course Jax knows," Quinn answered for Jade. "You know how guys are. We get the bad wrap, but really it's men who are the real gossips."

Jade shrugged. "That's true as hell. And I do think Jax knows, but that's just because well...because he's Jax. He somehow manages to work everything out before anyone else."

Liv started nodding again, and she also started tipping again. This time Quinn caught her before she got too far.

"But no, Logan wouldn't have said anything. His sense of loyalty is too strong. Don't tell him I said that. That's it. No more questions."

Jade lifted the bottle to take a sip. "Damn." She closed one eye and squinted into the bottle. "I think it's gone."

"Wrong eye." Quinn flicked the glass.

"Oh." Jade switched eyes. "Well, it's still empty." She dropped the bottle onto the floor next to her. "Boooo. I'm still sober."

"Same," Quinn pouted.

Liv flopped back into a mound of pillows. "I'm definitely not sober."

"Me either," Quinn amended.

"I'm not sure, but I don't think that math adds up." Jade waved a hand. "Do you have anything, Liv?"

"Literally anything. I think Logan's hellfire singed off all my tastebuds anyway."

"No, I don't keep any alcohol in the house." Liv forgot to feel self-conscious. "Living with an addict and a sister with a pattern of question-able decision-making skills comes with more contingencies than most people realize."

"Speaking of sisters and questionable decisions," Jade started. "You ever plan on telling your sister you inherited your mom's toxic nightmares and, surprise, she might too?"

Liv groaned. "I'm going to need more alcohol if we're going to have this conversation."

"Fine." Jade stood up. "I know where we can get some, but you're going to need to put your bras back on."

Liv groaned again.

"I never had one," Quinn said proudly.

CHAPTER THIRTY-SIX

*M*ain street was quiet, all the businesses closed and the townspeople long in bed, except the three of them, who laughed and joked as they made their way through the Glen. Trees around them swayed and rustled trying to get her attention. When they extended their long branches out to drag across her skin, she could feel the reciprocity between her magick and their innate power radiating between them.

"Should we feel bad that we're technically stealing from Logan for the second time tonight?" Liv asked, scanning the street around Mac's to make sure there wasn't anyone around to catch them.

Jade searched for the hide-a-key they knew Logan kept buried in one of the flowerpots for the rare occasion Mac left the bar and neglected to take his keys with him. She could hear the Scotsman now, complaining about locks being an unnecessary thing "in his day" and listing the "trouble with youths".

"Well, now Logan will have a good argument for the alarm system he's been fighting Mac for. Think of it as us doing him a favor, if it makes you feel better," Jade reasoned.

Liv's mouth pulled sideways as she considered. "Yep, that works."

"Bingo baby!" Jade held the key up in triumph.

Quinn pulled them all into a small huddle, looping her arms over their backs. "Okay, Jade, you get the booze since you know where he keeps the good stuff. Liv, you grab some kind of chaser, and I'll raid the kitchen for something with a high carb count. Don't doddle, don't touch anything you don't need to. We get in, get out, we don't fuck about."

Jade and Liv stared at Quinn. "B and E much?" Jade asked.

"Like Liv said, booze before stories."

The three of them slipped through the heavy back door and split up to achieve their respective assignments.

They were back outside, contraband stuffed into Jade's Mary Poppins bag, within a matter of minutes.

"Wow, that was kind of exhilarating!" Liv beamed. "Oh shit, what does that say about me?"

"Relax, stealing tequila, limes, and cheesy bread from a friend who gives it to you for free anyway isn't likely to awaken some suppressed klepto-tendency buried deep within you."

Quinn gave her a mock-concerned look, her cat eyes blinking innocently. "If anything it's a little more indicative of the complicated relationship you have with fun."

Liv pushed Quinn lightly. "I have fun! I just had a good deal of it this morning actually, and I think I might be having more very soon." She smiled to herself just thinking of it. *Yes,* she thought, *most definitely having more of Jax very soon.*

Jade groaned. "Look I always wanted you to end up with my brother. But I swear to fuck if I end up with some ill-timed, intrusive thought of you and Jax going at it springing up at me, I'll end you."

"I welcome that intrusive thought, personally," Quinn said.

Liv pinned Jade's arms to her side in an aggressive hug. "Aw! You always wanted me to be with him? Really? That's so sweet."

"You're a mushy drunk, you know that?" Jade patted Liv before wiggling out of her arms.

They'd made it all of half a block when a disembodied voice cracked through the night. "Stop where you are."

The three of them spun around a little too quickly, swaying and bumping into each other and shielding their eyes against the glare of headlights. Jade clutched their bag of supplies to her chest.

The lights shut off, briefly revealing a Havenwood PD cruiser and someone stepping out of it before a bright flashlight replaced the headlights.

"Shit! Shit, shit, shit, shit." Liv whisper-yelled. Just her luck, her first real girls' night and she was about to get arrested. Ivy was never going to let her live this down.

"Lock it up, Terrabella," Jade snapped.

"Yeah, be cool, we're just three innocent women, out for a late-night walk. We're fine."

"No, we're fine because it's Havenwood. I've either babysat or made out with the entire police force," Jade corrected.

The tall broad form approached them, mostly hidden by the glare of the flashlight. "What are you girls doing out here so late?" The deep voice held no amusement.

"Uh, first of all, we're women, second of all, we weren't doing anything wrong, so we don't have to tell you crap. And third of all, can you please get your bright as hell light out of my face," Quinn demanded.

The flashlight clicked off, revealing a tall man dressed in dark jeans and a black V-neck t-shirt that showed a glimpse of a silver chain tucked beneath.

His short, dark beard matched dark hair on his slightly disheveled head, like he'd just rolled out of bed. He looked to be in his mid-to-late thirties, from what Liv could see in the limited amount of light.

Quinn swallowed audibly at the sight of him. "Is there some kind of law in this town that every man needs to be panty-meltingly good-looking?" she asked no one in particular.

"There is a law about being drunk in public. Also happens to be one about breaking into local businesses. Do you *women* have any ID?"

"Do *you* have ID? You're the stranger here," Jade shot back.

The man lifted the edge of his shirt, revealing a badge hooked to the waistband of his jeans, as well as a peek at some very toned tan skin. Liv averted her eyes. Eventually.

"Declan Stone. Now, your turn. IDs." His words were clipped, clearly not thrilled to be dealing with them.

"I've lived here my whole life, the sheriff is my godfather for shit's sake, why would we have ID. We're just out for a walk. Surely you have something better to do than question three upstanding citizens just out to enjoy the stars."

"Interesting. I don't recall becoming a godfather."

"Huh?" Liv was having a hard time following in her drunken state.

But Jade's buzz was wearing off, along with her patience. "He's saying he's the new sheriff."

"Ohhhh." Liv nodded catching up slowly. "Oh! Oh no." Liv's face drooped.

"I think I just discovered a new kink," Quinn whispered to the other two, not at all quietly.

The sheriff pinched the bridge of his nose. "If you don't have ID on you, I'm going to have to take you to the holding cell at the station until someone can bring it down for you."

"You can't be serious," Jade deadpanned. "This cannot possibly be the best—"

"Use of taxpayer's money," he finished for her. "No, I agree it is not. But we got an alert of a silent alarm triggered down at Mac's."

"Guess Logan already got that alarm," Quinn whispered.

"Guess so, and surprise, you three are the only other people out here. So, here I am. Chatting it up with three drunk women instead of in my bed. My lucky night."

"Well, that was kind of rude." Liv folded her arms across her chest.

"So is breaking into someone's place of business. What's in the bag?"

"You need a search warrant for that," Quinn interjected.

"No, I really don't. You need to watch less TV."

"I don't own a TV. So, jokes on you."

"If you say so. Bag. *Now.*" It was a demand this time, and he stuck his hand out, motioning for Jade to give the bag up.

"Damn. Why do I suddenly want to be a really good girl?" Quinn whispered out of the side of her mouth.

"You're a really bad whisperer," Jade said, still clutching the bag to her chest.

Liv stepped forward, confidence riding high on whisky and false bravado. "Look Sheriff, Stone, there's been a misunderstanding. I'm Liv."

She pointed to herself. "The one who looks like walking art is Quinn." Quinn dipped at the knee holding the edges of an invisible dress in mock curtsy. "And the pissed one is Jade. You see, our friend Logan, well he's her brother Jax's—well he's not *just* her brother, he's also my, um, I don't really know what we are. We were together when we were younger but then I had to leave—family drama, you get it. But now I'm back, and I said I wasn't going get involved with him again, but then there was like this thing that happened and then we kind of ya know," Liv wiggled her hips. "Yeah, you know. Annnyway," she released a deep sigh. "Wait…" she looked at Jade and then back to the sheriff, "what was I saying?"

Just as Jade was about to relent and give up the bag just to get Liv to shut the hell up, the worst happened.

"Good evening, ladies. Sheriff." Logan dipped his chin to Declan as he and Jax came to stand behind them, in a way that felt to Liv like it was meant to send some kind of message, but it only seemed to make Declan grumpier.

Liv smiled flirtatiously up at Jax. "Hi, Jax." She moved in closer. "Thank you for my gift by the way." Wrapping her hands around his biceps, she rose to her tippy toes to get close to his ear. "I wore it with nothing else under it." Thoroughly distracted, he turned a heated gaze on her and she bit the edge of her lip.

Jax rubbed a hand over his jaw to hide his smile, but his other found her hip, his fingers digging into her skin a little.

"Watch yourself. She's an affectionate drunk," Jade warned.

His eyes stayed on Liv. "I think I'll manage it." Liv liked the look of that wicked smile—it held promises she hoped he'd keep.

"Wow, you have a really nice smile. Like, really nice. Your lips are my favorite. Oh, and what you can do with—"

"Think we'll save that for later." Jax wound his arm around her, tucking her into the crook of his body, and covered her mouth with his finger. *Why did people keep doing that to her tonight?* "Then you can show me how you wore that cloak, and I'll show you what else I can do with my mouth." The smooth confidence in Jax's voice against her ear made her toes curl.

"Unless you two are bringing these women some identification I'm going to need you to go have a seat over there." Declan waved a dismissive hand in the direction of a bench.

"Yeah, what are you guys even doing here?" Jade turned to glare at Logan and Jax. "It's supposed to be girls' night. In other words, you're not invited."

"Oh, I'm sorry, are we intruding? I took the alert I just got on my phone of the back door of the bar opening as an invitation. My bad. I own Mac's." Logan added, turning back to Declan.

"Actually, his grandfather owns it, hence the name Mac's—MacIver. Unless, hmm, is that your name?" Jade feigned exaggerated confusion.

"Well, I can go get him if you'd prefer, Sunny, but I have a pretty good feeling he'd be a little less understanding, especially if he has to get out of bed at this hour."

"I feel like I've entered the fucking twilight zone," Declan said, exasperated, then turned to Logan. "As you're aware, the alarm was triggered at your bar tonight. I am about one hundred and ten percent positive whatever you might be missing will amount to whatever is in that bag." He pointed at the bag Jade still had tightly pressed to her body. "If you're interested in pressing charges, we'll need to take this shit show to the station and go from there."

Logan's eyes sparkled with amusement as he and Jade faced off, a challenge hanging between them, each waiting for the other to fold. It almost seemed like Jade wanted him to push it, while Logan just looked like he was reveling in having the upper hand on her for once.

Well, shit. Liv didn't feel like going to jail because those two couldn't play nice. Relief filled her as Logan's face softened, and his lips curved into a small smile.

"No," Logan finally said. "That won't be necessary, Sheriff. Sorry for the call out, but thanks for showing up."

Declan nodded once and turned back to his cruiser.

With their focus bouncing from Jade and Logan then to Declan, it wasn't until she was already across the street that anyone noticed Quinn had drifted away from the group.

"Oh, no, tell me she's not one of those wandering drunks," Logan said.

Declan changed directions as Quinn slowly moved toward a shadowy area between two buildings, walking around the back of his cruiser toward Quinn instead.

Liv stepped off the curb. "Quinn? What is it?"

"I'm not sure." Her voice held a hint of cautious curiosity.

"Quinn!" Liv took off running toward Quinn the moment she felt her friend's magick swell.

"Liv!" She faintly registered Jax calling after her but kept running.

A sudden blast of air whipped out of Quinn just as Liv reached her side, only to slam into what looked like an invisible wall. Liv tentatively reached out a tendril of her magick and then pulled it back at the first caress of thick, sludge-like power.

Meanwhile, in less than a heartbeat Quinn's magick seemed to have rebounded back on her, lifting her off her feet and throwing her backward.

Liv skidded back and fell to the ground as the edge of the small torrent of Quinn's magick whipped past her.

Before anyone else could react to the invisible threat, Declan jumped forward. A strange magick flowed from him, and the power of Quinn's magick vanished as if sucked in on itself. Quinn's body was suspended in midair before she could crash to the ground.

Another tether of magick flew from Declan, this one aimed in the same direction Quinn's had gone. The air seized, the breeze itself seeming to halt its momentum. Suddenly a whisp of shadow was ripped backward, sucking in on itself as if it was yanked into another dimension—but whatever had been using the cloaking magick had already vanished.

Liv's mouth fell open. "Whoa, nice catch!" She blinked up at Declan. Before she could stand up on her own Jax was there lifting her to her feet.

She attempted to avoid his gaze, but he lightly grasped her chin and brought her eyes up to his. "You weren't going to chase after her and whatever else was out there without me, were you? Because that would mean you were already planning to break a very important promise you recently made. One I take very seriously."

Oops-a-daisy. She was barely able to pull her lip between her teeth from the way he was grasping her jaw. "Of course not." She batted her eyes as her palms slid up his chest. "I'd never dream of it." He narrowed his eyes, the glow of the streetlamps casting light and shadows over him, highlighting the angles and planes of his beautiful face. She just smirked. "I knew you'd follow me."

He leaned in until his lips were nearly touching hers. "To the ends of the *fucking* earth."

Oh. Her brain went momentarily fuzzy.

Quinn giggled as her body tilted right side up and she hovered in the air for a moment longer. "I feel like a superhero." She placed her fists on her hips as her feet gently touched down to the ground.

Declan's hands fell to his sides and slowly everyone's eyes turned to him. His jaw tensed, and Liv could all but see the walls shutting down on his face like a metal door slamming closed on a panic room. "Someone want to tell me what the hell that was?"

"Not so fast, Sheriff. You've been holding out on us." Logan crossed his arms, verbalizing what they were all thinking. "I think it's your turn to do some explaining. Starting with what the hell kind of magick was that?"

"I think I'll pass," Declan said as he turned back to his car, apparently preferring to forgo any answers if it meant offering any of his own.

Jax stopped the man before he could get in his car, his hands held up in a placating gesture. "I know you probably don't trust us. But you felt what the rest of us did in those shadows, and I have a feeling the same base nature that drove you to take a job in this town will eventually override whatever is holding you back right now." Jax was doing some heavy hinting of knowing more about Declan Stone's past than the rest of them, Liv thought...but if it was meant to ruffle Declan's feathers it failed.

Liv glanced over toward the center of town, thinking of all the names on that fountain. *Stone.* She was starting to suspect Declan Stone being here was not at all coincidental.

"Take a few days to think it through. You can come find us when you're ready for more answers...and to give some of your own," Jax said, stepping out of Declan's path. "Or I'll come find you."

Then Jax took Liv's hand and led her back in the direction of Haven-house, Logan and Jade right behind them.

Liv pulled Jax to a stop a few steps away as Quinn lingered behind. "Hey, Sheriff..."

Declan froze halfway into the cruiser, looking back, and waited for her to speak. "Thanks for the helping hand. I'd love to return the favor some-time. I live above The Bookstore—blue door, you can't miss it."

"I'll keep that in mind." He let his response hang in the air for a moment, then he ducked into the cruiser and started the car.

"It's him. He's the sixth," Jade whispered to Jax as the five of them watched the sheriff pull away.

Before Jade could clarify, Liv made a confession of her own. "I-I think I've felt that magick before."

"We sure have," Jax confirmed, wrapping his arm back around her shoulders and leading the group toward home.

CHAPTER THIRTY-SEVEN

*J*ade was slumped over a laptop, her head resting heavily on her palm. Quinn didn't look much better, lying sideways across a large armchair near some bookshelves. Her legs draped over one arm, her head the other when Liv breezed into The Bookstore, a smile on her face, a heavy box in her hands, and feeling lighter than she had in ages.

"Morning ladies," she said with a smile as she walked behind the counter. Jade and Quinn both winced at the sound of the heavy box hitting the counter.

Jade scowled at Liv. "Where the hell is your hangover?"

"Did Jax orgasm it out of you? His hands can't possibly be *that* magickal. And if they are, can I rent him for an hour?"

"Uh, no." She pointed at Quinn. "Most definitely not. But I do have something better for you. Well, not better," she gave them a coy smile, "but something that will give you the desired effect, and that I am willing to share." Liv opened her box and pulled out two vials filled with a deep red liquid. She handed one to Jade and tossed the other to Quinn.

Jade eyed the vial warily. "What exactly is in this, your blood?"

"Whatever it is, tastes better than it looks," Quinn said, putting the stopper back into her empty vial.

Jade shook her head. "You didn't even wait to hear what was in it."

Quinn shrugged. "Sometimes you just gotta fuck the consequences."

"Sometimes I wonder how you're still alive."

Liv laughed, "It's actually a recipe Valeria came up with. I found it in one of her old journals, it's a mixture of *Pueraria lobata, Oenanthe Javanica—*"

Jade held up a hand. "In English, please. Some of us didn't read Latin for fun in high school."

"Oh sorry, Kuzu flower and root, Evodia fruit, Chlorella, a nice hit of Mint, Fenugreek, and…" Liv searched her mind as Jade pulled the stopper out and sniffed the liquid.

"Oh yeah and Water Dropwort," Liv added.

"What's Water Dropwort do?" Quinn asked as Jade tipped the vial into her mouth.

"It accelerates the metabolizing of the alcohol on its own, but I super-charged it. It's a type of algae."

Jade coughed around the liquid, but it was too late. "Algae? Seriously? I'd rather have the hangover."

"No way!" Quinn said standing up from the chair. "Just give it a sec, that stuff is a miracle. I don't care what it's made of. I feel amazing! Thanks, Liv." Quinn beamed at her.

Liv felt the flush work its way up her chest. "It's nothing, I just followed the recipe, not like I created it or anything." She started unpacking the rest of her box.

Quinn peeked over the counter trying to see into the box. "What else you got in there?"

Liv pulled out some dried cuttings and fine twine.

"Just some stuff to make a few more smudge sticks and a new batch of the candles Sandi asked me to make for her goat yoga class. She said she was going to come by for it all today." Liv paused to look at Jade, a line forming between her brows. "Your mom kind of has an absurd number of hobbies."

"Yeah, well, whatever keeps her busy. Imagine how much trouble she could cause if she had more time on her hands." Jade shuddered at the thought.

"Her meddling comes from love—she just wants you all to be happy. It's sweet."

"Easy for you to say, you've never been on the receiving end of it." One of Jade's brows rose and a conspiratorial smirk grew across her face. "Although, when she inevitably gets wind of what happened last night, you and Sheriff Gorgeous and Grumpy will absolutely be her next victims."

"I don't know what you're talking about." Quinn laughed Jade off, fiddling with a pen on the counter.

A slight blush crept into Quinn's cheeks, mostly hidden by her darker complexion, but it was there. Liv wouldn't have thought the woman was capable of anything resembling bashfulness. Despite his stoicism, she doubted the sheriff had disliked the attention. There probably wasn't a man on Earth who wouldn't give his left arm to be the target of Quinn's flirtations for even a moment.

"You basically torture every detail of my sex life out of me on a regular basis, there is no way we're just going to blow by the chemistry between you two." Liv eyed Quinn over her shoulder from where she was working some herbs into smudge sticks.

"Yeah, I think I got some third-degree burns from all the heat." Jade joked, the potion having wiped out her hangover.

"I'll keep that in mind," Liv said, impersonating Declan's deep voice. "Wow. Just...wow." She fanned herself. "And then his magick...now that was quite the surprise."

"You're telling me." Quinn jumped on the change of subject. "I thought for sure I was going to go splat."

"No one would have let that happen. But Declan was quickest to react, too quick to not at least be somewhat familiar with his magick."

"But," Liv interjected, "it was wild enough to suggest it's not a regular thing for him."

"You two put all that together just now, did you?" Quinn picked up one of Liv's candles and inhaled it deeply.

Liv sighed. "Hardly. Once Jax had *thoroughly* ensured I was...okay," her lips turned in as she fought a giddy smile at the memory of all the attention he'd lavished on her body—which kind of just made her want to provoke him more often, "I spent the next two hours playing sounding board to all of Jax's theories. I'm assuming you experienced a similar fate this morning?" Liv asked Jade.

"Yeah, via text…starting before seven, and caffeine." Jade grimaced.

"A regular energizer bunny our Jax. Or are you slipping something in his morning coffee to keep him…up?" Quinn waggled her brows.

"He doesn't need annnyyy help there." She didn't bother holding in the laugh this time. She didn't know when being so open with them had happened. But it felt good, knowing that nothing she did, said, or simply was, would drive them away.

"Annnyyy-way," Jade mimicked Liv, "he was keyed up about whatever you were chasing after, and the fact that he hadn't felt it first. Not to mention that Declan is definitely the other person I saw in my vision." Yeah, that little fact hadn't slipped past Jax either. But he'd told her he'd add it to a certain mental list he kept, whatever that meant, and shelve it until the new sheriff was more open to sharing with the group, as Jax had put it.

"So, once he works through the impending guilt spiral, prepare yourself for your own Jax-hole interrogation," Jade warned Quinn.

Liv felt a spark of defensiveness rise in her, knowing that he was doing so much to help the town, and the only feedback he ever seemed to get was that it wasn't enough. The entitlement of the townspeople as if he owed them his magick. As if he should know exactly what to do in any given situation, like he or any other witch in this town had ever had to deal with anything like sentient shadows, dead bodies, and a sudden housing crisis, let alone all at once.

It wasn't a guilt spiral. He just felt responsible for the safety of everyone in town, including the newcomers, and despite all of his work, he hadn't found any real answers.

He was protective by nature, but there was no denying the events over the last few weeks had amplified that trait. Last night had put him to a whole new level, especially when they had both confirmed for each other the familiarity of the magick from last night to what they'd felt from the guy who Ivy had been hanging around with.

But familiar didn't amount to proof of anything, something she'd had to remind Jax more than once last night. She'd barely been able to keep him from charging into Ivy's room in the wee hours of the morning to demand she stop seeing the Dark Douche, as he'd referred to him. But she knew that trying something like that with Ivy would only backfire.

At best, it would blow back on Liv and widen the divide they'd finally started to close. At worst…it might just push her away altogether. She needed to talk to Ivy, she wasn't arguing against that, but she was going to have to go about it very gently.

Before she could say as much, the bells dangling from the handle of the shop door chimed a moment before two women walked through.

"Hey, Reina," Jade greeted the first woman. "Let me know if you need any help looking for anything. Nina." Jade icily acknowledged the second woman. Then she sat down at her computer again. Liv didn't fail to notice that she never did answer Quinn's question.

Quinn stepped in close next to Liv. "Isn't that Bird Poop Lady?" she asked, indicating the one Jade had called Nina.

Nina's gaze drifted to them as if she knew they were talking about her. Liv shook her head. "I don't know," she lied. It was definitely her.

After a bit of browsing, Reina approached the counter, a book and a few other things in hand. Liv set the herbs aside to ring her up.

"What are those for?" she asked, looking at the smudge sticks. Liv had focused her attention on the work in her hands to avoid drawing Nina's attention. She hadn't realized she'd managed to turn out several in such a short period.

"Oh, uh…" She hesitated, searching for an answer, and coming up blank.

Jade turned from the endcap she was straightening and took a few steps toward Liv, eyes narrowing.

"They smell amazing." Reina inhaled the air between them.

She caught herself before she pulled her lip into her mouth. "You burn them to cleanse an area or person, to help remove negative energy or promote clarity," she said, fighting to keep any sign of insecurity from her voice.

"How much for three?"

"Oh, I'm sorry, they're not for—"

"Twenty-five," Jade interrupted, suddenly next to Liv.

She opened her mouth to protest but didn't get the chance. "Perfect, I'll take them." Jade nodded.

"What about those? What are those for?" Reina pointed to the candles she'd brought in for Sandra.

"Those are for relaxation and meditation. But they're already spoken for," Jade answered. Reina looked disappointed.

"Do you sell anything else in here?" She looked at Liv. "My mom used to rub this lotion on me when I was young and couldn't sleep. I think I heard her mention once that she used to get it from Valeria. Do you know what I'm talking about?"

She did. Liv remembered the balm well, but she'd never made it herself.

She nodded. "Yeah, I know what you're talking about, but I don't sell anything here," Liv answered, trying not to notice that Nina had drifted to the check-out counter as well.

"Anything like that, she means. But check back soon. Who knows what we might have," Jade added with a smile as she handed the woman her bag and receipt.

Nina stepped up and handed Jade her items to ring up. Feeling her stare, Liv met Nina's gaze, ready to face the woman head-on.

"Something else I can help you with?" Jade's tone was sharp, and she all but shoved Nina's bag in her face. Liv didn't blame Nina for recoiling—Jade had a way of making words feel like a physical assault when she wanted to.

"Um," Nina hesitated, "could I maybe get one of those? My daughter's been having a hard time sleeping. Do you think it would help with that?" she asked in a voice that showed no sign of the woman she'd seen screeching in the Glen a few weeks before.

"Sorry, we're out," Jade said, cocking her head with a smile that was far too sweet to be real. Nina looked down at the pile of smudge sticks that were still sitting there.

Nina just nodded and started to leave, but Liv remembered the little girl with the too-tight bun. "Wait." Liv walked around the counter and handed Nina one of the candles instead. "This will probably be better for that."

"Thank you," Nina said as she reached into her purse.

Liv reached out to stay her hand but caught herself before touching the woman. She drew her hand back slowly. "It's for your daughter, not you."

She walked back behind the counter without another word, her heart beating hard in her chest.

As soon as the bells on the door jingled letting her know the shop was empty, she turned on Jade. "Uhhh, what the hell did you just do?" Liv raised an arm toward the door the women had just left through.

"Whoa, I don't think I've ever felt that particular mixture of emotions on someone before," Quinn said, tilting her head to study Liv. "It's like irritation and insecurity had a baby with a top note of panic."

"Don't do that," Liv snapped.

Quinn lifted her hands. "My bad. But you're practically shooting it at me."

Jade didn't look sorry at all. "I'm not going to apologize for making you money. I know how much you make here, after all."

"You don't get to make that decision for me. Those smudge sticks were for us and your mom, that's it. And I don't even know how to make the balm that lady was talking about."

"Just because you haven't made it doesn't mean you don't know how." Jade crossed her arms and leaned a hip against the counter.

"If people find out I'm selling those things here, you know what will happen. It's not worth the trouble."

"Trouble? Those women were so excited about the idea of you sharing your gift."

Liv looked at Quinn. "You don't get it because you weren't here before. Some may like it, but if people find out I'm selling my magick it won't take long before I find myself accused of anything from a dead blade of grass to a dead husband."

"That's not true, Liv. And who even gives a shit about a couple closed minded idiots anyway? Valeria sold things out of your house for years."

"I'm not her!" Liv's voice cracked.

Jade's face softened. "I know that." She stepped closer to her. "But you are a Terrabella, and you are gifted. Sometimes I think everyone sees it but you. Including those bitches that made you think otherwise when we were younger…including your mom."

Liv's eyes flicked up to Jade's knowing face. Her mom. Her mom who pretended to hate magick, all the while resenting her for having the power she didn't. Who'd little by little chipped away at Liv's confidence and muddled her identity so thoroughly it had been a relief when they'd left town and given her an excuse to shut it away in the dark box inside her. Cutting herself off from her source.

Quinn stood silently, maybe not knowing exactly what they were talking about, but no doubt feeling every emotion passing between the two of them. Interpreting the story like an emotional translator.

Jade sighed. "Look, maybe I shouldn't have done that without asking you first. But the truth is, I've been meaning to talk to you about it since you agreed to work here in the first place. I got excited and I overstepped. I'm sorry. But you don't have to earn the right to use your power any more than the other Six families do."

"That's easy for you to say. You're a Hawthorne, that's always been the favored line."

"Everyone deals with their own shit, Liv," Quinn chimed in. "You know that."

Yeah, she knew that. The Hawthorne's may be favored, but she knew that came with a lot of pressure and expectations she didn't have to deal with and wouldn't trade for.

"Who gives a shit what anyone else thinks. But if you want people in this town to appreciate how incredible your gift is, the best way to do that is by letting them in. Even in this small way. Most people are too self-centered and blind to realize the judgments they pass on things they haven't even taken the time to understand. You don't need anyone's acceptance but your own. And I think that's what's holding you back from doing this. And as your friend, I want more than that for you. Whether you choose to sell your craft here or not." Jade shrugged. "But, then again you know my motto."

"Who gives a shit what anyone else thinks. Yeah, we got that." Quinn shoved her hands into the back pockets of her distressed and paint-flecked overalls.

Liv let out a harsh breath and mulled over Jade's words. She wanted to be mad, she wanted to reject everything her friend had said…because it was a lot more comfortable, a lot easier to do than admit the truth they held.

She wasn't her grandmother. But she wasn't her mother, either. And she didn't need to be either of them. She wasn't the culmination of her ancestry. The magick in her blood came from the Earth, and it was only *hers* while she was here. It was a gift. She wasn't ashamed of it, but that's how she'd been treating it for so long—hiding it.

"Okay." She didn't know what else to say.

Jade turned and met her eyes. "Okay."

Quinn moved to stand next to them behind the counter. "Well, that was fucking beautiful." Her golden eyes glowed. "And now look, there will be a small piece of each of us here! It's perfect! Can we hug?" She lifted her arms, reaching for them.

Jade leaned back slightly. "Fine, but this counts as your one hug for the month."

"Worth it!" Quinn wrapped her tattooed arms around them and yanked them into a tight embrace.

CHAPTER THIRTY-EIGHT

*E*ven from far back in the greenhouse, she could feel him the moment he crossed through the front gate. Anticipation built within her as he grew closer and closer. She hadn't turned when the front door opened, instead pretending to be busy finishing up tidying the workbench where she'd been making a salve for a few kids who'd found their way into a patch of poison oak.

His steps were light and nearly silent as he made his way down the long hall, but she felt every step he took. The rise and fall of her chest became more noticeable as he passed the sitting room, then the staircase and the kitchen, before he finally reached the threshold of the greenhouse.

It took a surprising amount of restraint not to respond to the feel of his eyes on her body as she bent at the waist to stow away the last few glass jars on the low shelf next to the workbench where they belonged, the temptation she hoped it provided a convenient coincidence—completely unintentional, of course.

She smirked at the sound of air being sucked between his teeth, which turned into a low rumble from somewhere deeper.

Though it had been exactly what she wanted, she gasped in surprise when he was suddenly on her. His chest was warm against her back as he brought as much of his body into contact with hers as he could. Too gently, his hands slid up the backs of her bare legs, up and over the denim shorts covering her ass. His weight leaned into her, forcing her to bend over the table slightly, her ass pressed against his groin.

"Well, hello to you, too. My day? It was great, thanks for asking, how was yours?" The slight shake in her voice probably weakened the false bravado she was attempting, but the feel of him already growing hard under his jeans was making it difficult to focus on anything except the places where he touched her.

His lips brushed against the shell of her ear, "I don't remember anything before the moment I walked in here and saw you bent over in these." His fingers danced under the edge of her cut-off shorts, barely touching the crease where her ass met her thighs. "But that was your plan, wasn't it Dandy?"

His ghost of a touch moved from her ass to her hips and up to the curve of her breasts. Her eyes fluttered as he turned the tables on her. "I-I don't know what you're talking about." *Dammit*. She cursed her libido. No one's hands should have this intense of an effect on a person.

"What did I tell you about games, little flower?"

"I'm pretty sure you said you love them, right?"

The light touch of his hands on her hips as his lips ghosted across the skin behind her ear and down her neck caused her to shiver, but she wanted —no, *needed*—more.

She pressed back into him firmly, grinding her ass over his hard length. His hands shot out and gripped on the edge of the table, caging her in.

"Liv." He growled her name but mimicked her move, the sensation, pressing himself against her roughly, arousing her to near ecstasy even though they were both still fully clothed.

A small sound left her lips—Spirit save her, just the way he said her name in that erotic voice made her core ache in response. He could read the dictionary with that voice and she was sure she'd come from the sound alone.

The anticipation was building quickly into something that needed release. She squirmed a little within the cage of his arms.

A light chuckle vibrated into her back. "Don't worry baby, I know exactly what you need." The feel of the calluses on his hands from all the hours he spent working only added to the sensation as he wrapped his large hands around her waist and slid them roughly up her sides, taking her shirt with them.

Instinctually, she lifted her arms above her head. But, just as Jax tossed her shirt aside the intrusive thought of Ivy coming home at any moment invaded her hazy mind.

The sound of the greenhouse doors snicking closed came before she could even voice the concern. A heartbeat later she was drowning in the feel of Jax's magick as it engulfed the room. The vines weaving around the room began to twist and writhe in response as if they enjoyed Jax's presence as much as she did.

"Be as loud as you want baby, no one can hear us now. No one but the flowers will even know we're in here." His tongue retraced the path his lips had taken down her neck and a light breeze trailed over her skin, leaving a cold sensation in the places where his warm tongue had just been. The quick shift of temperatures and sensations addled her mind and pulled her focus further from thoughts of anything but him and every place he touched her.

Then his touch was gone, and she had the sudden urge to groan in frustration. But when she turned to face him, the blazing gold in his eyes traveling down her body, lingering on her legs before returning to her own—which she had no doubt looked as wild as his—stole her breath.

Emboldened by the desire in those eyes, Liv matched the breeze of his magick still licking at her with some magick of her own.

She smirked at the small surprise on his face as a vine slithered around his waist and through a belt loop, pulling him back within her reach. The look quickly faded into a small smirk, her favorite one, the cocky one he got when he knew she wanted him. Good, because she did. She wanted him in a way that was making it hard to stand there and let him take his time rather than jumping on him.

Once he was close enough again, the vines slipped away and she lifted to her tiptoes and kissed him, feather-light, leaning away before he could deepen the kiss, instead pulling off his shirt, dropping it to the floor.

"Dandy," he growled as she kissed him too lightly again, creating a path of her own, starting at the dip in the base of his throat and down his chest, lowering herself so she could kiss him to the waistband of his jeans, then taking a page out of his book as she retraced the trail of kisses back up with her tongue.

"Fuck," Jax swore on a raspy exhale.

She smiled against his skin and rose. Even as she reached for the button of his jeans she was silently debating if her body could hold out any longer. She needed him *bad,* but she would also love to play this game with him all night. The way it felt to be his sole focus, the singular source of his desire, was intoxicating.

But before she could test his patience again, he scooped her up with an arm under her ass and sat her down firmly on the workbench in one smooth move that caused a surprised squeak to leave her mouth. He swallowed the sound, fusing his mouth over hers.

Liv locked her legs around his waist again, blindly working his pants open, reaching in and wrapping her hand around his hard shaft without hesitation. He bucked into her hand and their kiss turned aggressive, tongues plunging and circling each other as she began to work his cock in short, firm strokes.

He broke the kiss and wrapped an arm behind her lower back, pulling her closer to the edge of the bench. The sound of a metal button skittering across the ground somewhere was barely registered as she gripped his shoulders, lifting herself just enough for him to drag her shorts down her legs.

Jax's eyes flared as they landed between her legs, realizing she hadn't had any panties on. "*Dammit Dandy,*" he swore between gritted teeth.

"Couldn't risk losing another pair." Her giggle turned into a gasp when he tugged the strap of her bra down one shoulder, exposing her breast and sucking her nipple into his mouth, pulling it between his teeth and eliciting a cry that turned to a moan as the shock became a buzz that zipped through her body.

He released her nipple from the light bite of his teeth. The slip of his tongue across his lip was her only warning before Jax pulled her forward across the table, the rough wood on her bare cheeks burning deliciously.

Yes, she thought, preparing herself to be invaded by him, but before she could push down his jeans, Jax dropped into a crouch in front of her.

*"*Jax, I need you inside me.*"*

*"*How many times do I have to tell you, Dandelion? I know what you need.*"*

He spread her knees out wide and pressed his warm mouth over her clit.

Her body acknowledged the truth in his words as his tongue touched her center and her head dropped back between her shoulder blades.

His hands slid up her thighs until one of his long fingers came to her entrance, rotating around her opening, but never actually crossing into her. She lifted her hips, trying to force him in. "My, my, so impatient today," he chided against her mound before finally pressing a finger into her, curling it up to stroke the spot within her he seemed to be able to find without thought, like he had her body memorized.

She fought to keep her eyes open, to watch what he was doing to her body, but the smooth, repeating wave of his tongue and the pressure building inside her forced her head back and her eyes shut.

"Mmmm," Jax groaned onto her skin, sending little shock waves of pleasure from her clit to her belly button. "Did I get you this wet already, or have you been walking around here like this all day, just waiting for me?" he asked, lifting his mouth off of her and inserting a second finger.

Her mouth dropped open at the fullness rendering her unable to answer.

"Remember, no more secrets, Liv." The stroke of his fingers slowed just shy of halting.

"I-I've been waiting for you all day," she nearly cried.

And she had. It seemed like no matter what was going on around her, somewhere in the back of her mind she was always waiting, half ready for him.

"Well, I'm here now, aren't I?" Jax's wicked mouth dropped back to her mound, and his fingers began to move, giving her exactly what she needed to push her climax to soaring heights and then right over the edge, plunging into an ecstasy induced oblivion.

CHAPTER THIRTY-NINE

*J*ax rose, his fingers still inside her, moving slowly as he coaxed her back from euphoria. She faintly registered the shuffle of clothing and prayed it was him dropping his pants and boxer briefs. She *needed* it to be.

Her walls were still fluttering around his fingers when he replaced them with his cock in one quick movement.

They both moaned at the tight fit, the perfect way her core hugged him when he entered her, the way they fit together so perfectly, in every way.

With him inside her, it was all she could think about, the way he dominated all her senses. The scent of his magick in the air around them, the feel of his hands on her, like they were everywhere at once, the taste of him when his tongue worked against hers and their lips devoured each other, and the sight of him—she forced her eyes open, to watch as he breathed her name and began to move in and out of her in long, slow thrusts. Every bit of her awareness was consumed by him.

Jax's large hands gripped her hips, and she was grateful for the extra curve that gave him something to use for leverage.

"You feel so good," he moaned when she braced herself with her hands on the bench and lifted her hips, taking him even deeper.

"*Yes,* again," Liv panted, digging her heels into Jax's firm ass.

Was it always going to be like this? Needing him this badly all the time? How the hell was she supposed to get anything else done? How would she ever make a candle that wasn't tainted with their sexual chemistry and her intense desire *ever again*? At this rate, she was going to have to put a warning label on every candle in a ten-block radius.

He knew exactly what her body needed right before she did but gave her only enough to take her to the brink of orgasm, never over. Driving her up and then backing off again until the pressure had built inside her to a peak that felt higher and sharper than she ever thought possible. And yet, somehow, she knew there was more, more he needed to unleash, and she needed it too.

"Jax please, fuck me harder, please," she chanted the plea over and over, adamant on breaking his will.

Jax snapped his hips into her roughly, his arm a band of steel behind her, keeping her body from sliding away. Liv cried out, forgoing trying to brace herself on the table, moving her hands to grip his muscular shoulders instead, digging her nails into his skin.

He let out a low hiss. "That's fine, leave your mark, show everyone I'm yours." He gripped her long ponytail, wrapping it around his fist and pulling firmly, forcing her head back so he could lick up the column of her neck.

Their skin turned damp as the heat that built between them was trapped by the greenhouse. They slid against one another; the sensation unlocking something between them that they unleashed all over again, locking them into a near frenzied cycle.

Jax groaned against her hot skin as her walls began to pulse, and she held onto him tighter, the muscles of his shoulders and back coiling under her hands as he held her in place and moved inside her faster, faster.

She reached between her legs—the need to orgasm was driving her body to a place beyond anything she thought she was capable of handling.

Jax slid out of her, and she mourned the loss of his body, but before she could complain he had her on her feet with her back pressed into his front. With a hand between her shoulder blades, he folded her over the table and whispered into her ear, "Hang on to the table, baby."

She obeyed immediately. He grabbed her hips, pulling them up, and he slid into her again, the new position guiding him to that spot deep inside her with every single thrust.

Jax's pace picked up and all Liv could do was meet his strokes as best as she could and moan his name over and over. "Oh fuck, Liv." One of his hands left her hip, sliding back to grip her ass firmly.

She pushed back into him at his praise, canting her hip and working his dick on her g-spot. The shaky whimper of his name on her lips, the hot friction of his pelvis rubbing over the sensitive skin of her ass each time their bodies met, her entire body felt like little currents of electricity were humming, making her hyperaware of every place his skin touched her.

"Fuck Liv, yes." Jax slid his hand around, this time sliding his fingers through the wetness where they were connected and back up to circle her clit with just the right amount of pressure.

His other hand held tight to her waist, sure to leave his fingerprints deliciously marked on her skin. Liv screamed almost as soon as he touched her, her orgasm catching them both off guard. Jax didn't stop, fucking her through it, his pace remaining steady

"I'm going to... oh my—don't stop. *Please,* Jax, don't sttt..." she abandoned words as her head fell back onto his shoulder and her orgasm crested, and then crashed over her in a wave that seemed like it would never end. She held on as long as she could, but her body gave way to it, and her arms collapsed, bringing her down flat on the table, jacking her hips up even higher as Jax continued to drive into her.

The new position took what should have been the aftershocks of her orgasm and turned them into the beginning of another one.

"Jax..." Her body felt heavy and like she was floating all at once. Her thighs were shaking, her knees threatening to give out on her.

One of his hands slid down to her thigh, gripping it firmly, reinforcing her ability to stand. The other hand molded around her sex, applying warmth and lightly rubbing against her clit every time one of his deep thrusts pushed her body forward. She was so sensitive, even the light touch sent shock waves through her, "Jax, I don't think I can." He'd transformed her entire being into an erogenous zone—she was sure it was too much.

"Yes, you can. Just let go and trust me, let me give you what you need."

Jax brought the head of his cock to the entrance of her pussy and then slid back in, the pull as good as the push. Her exposed breast and nipple brushed against the workbench, sending shocks of pleasure down to her core.

"Be a good girl and touch your clit for me, so I can grip this fucking incredible ass."

Then his rhythm shifted, becoming slightly erratic. His hold on her ass and hip dug deeper.

"Now, baby, touch yourself. Now." Liv did as she was told and slipped a hand between her legs to her clit while she hung on to the far edge of the table with the other.

Jax's rhythm became erratic and punishing as he swelled inside her, driving her to the brink. The third orgasm rocked her body in a way that made it impossible not to cry out his name and Spirit only knew what other unintelligible, pleasure-induced nonsense.

Just as the aftershocks of her orgasm ebbed, Jax pulled out of her, and the warmth of his release hit her lower back and ass in several hot spurts. Her skin was so sensitive she could feel each rivulet as it slid over her skin between her cheeks.

A moment later Jax's body collapsed next to hers on the table, their satisfied eyes locking. A rush of dopamine flowed through her and moisture ran down her cheeks—she wasn't sure if it was sweat, tears, or a mix of both. His eyes softened and he kissed her forehead gently before pushing off the table and standing.

She couldn't hold in the laugh that bubbled out of her when the material of Jax's shirt slid across her hypersensitive skin as he cleaned her off.

Jax leaned over and kissed her roughly. "Stop making that noise or I'm going to have to fuck you again."

Liv smiled, and then she laughed again. "Dammit, Dandy." He launched at her, taking her mouth aggressively just as he snatched up her body and they crumbled to the floor together.

A bed of soft moss caught them before their bodies hit the rough ground. "You're certainly better with your Earth magick than you used to be," she said, relaxing into the moss he'd summoned.

"Someone needed to take care of this place while we waited for you."

"Hmm," Liv looked around the room with exaggerated skepticism on her face, "I don't know if I'd say this place looked very taken care of when I got here."

"Are you criticizing my work, Dandy?"

She laughed again as Jax kicked at his jeans and ungracefully climbed up her body at the same time. He kissed her again, long and slowly, not stopping until her lungs started to protest.

His eyes were so clear they looked like the summer sky on a cloudless day, framed by dark lashes that matched his messy hair. Thoughtlessly, she ran her fingers through his thick hair as he hovered over her, and she reveled in the casual caress and the fact that she could touch him however and whenever she wanted now.

"I don't know which sound I love more, my name on your lips while I'm inside you, or the sound of your laugh...but I need them both for the rest of my life."

"Well," Liv pulled her lip between her teeth, "I know one way you can get both." She reached between them, wrapping her hand around his cock, already hard again, and guiding him back to her entrance.

"Dammit, Dandy," he sighed into her ear. "You're going to be the death of me, and I can't seem to find it in me to care." Then he slid inside her again.

CHAPTER FORTY

*L*iv entered the kitchen to the mouth-watering sight of the broad, bare back of Jax. The muscles under his golden skin rippled and twitched lightly as he moved in front of the stove.

She crossed the space, drawn to him by the need to touch, to put her hands on his skin.

He stilled briefly as she wrapped her arms around his waist and ran her hands from the cuts of his obliques, over the ridges of his abs, and up to his defined pecks. A sound somewhere between a growl and a moan vibrated through his chest and straight to her core.

She rested her face into the curve of his back and let his warmth seep into her and leech away the last dregs of the anxiety brought on by all the thoughts she'd been assaulted by immediately upon waking. Her brain trying to sweep her into anxiety before she was even fully conscious.

Surprising her, Jax turned and lifted her by the waist and deposited her on the counter next to the stove where he was cooking. He pushed her knees apart so he could step between them. Then he kissed her. Hard and deep, his tongue diving into her mouth and his fingertips diving into her tangled hair. She moaned softly into his mouth and melted into his heat again. When he sucked her bottom lip into his mouth, she felt a mimic of the pull in her nipples. Then it was over.

He gently kissed her forehead and turned back to the food he was cooking. "Good morning, Dandy."

"Morning," she wheezed, attempting to pull herself from the lusty haze Jax had plunged her into.

"How did you sleep?" he asked as he handed her a cup of tea.

"So good." She hummed into her teacup. But as she sipped her tea, it occurred to her how true that was. Had been for several nights now. Collapsing into the post-orgasmic comfort of Jax's arms had become so natural so quickly that she hadn't even realized she hadn't had a nightmare since the night on the cliffs.

"Glad I could be of service," he replied like he knew what she'd been thinking. His lips tilted into a small smirk, the sexy one—she'd come to distinguish between it and the arrogant one—though she liked them both if she was being honest.

"Are you cooking for me?" She smiled hopefully and attempted to peek over his shoulder to see what he was cooking.

"I am." He glanced at her sidelong. "And if you want me to finish it, maybe you should take your perfect ass and go sit over there. Where I can't see you in my shirt." He jutted his chin over his shoulder toward the small table in the corner. "Otherwise, I'm likely to abandon our breakfast and eat you on this counter instead."

"Oh." She debated, curious to see if he'd do it. Wanting him to... but maybe not so much in a common area. "Jax!" She yelped his name as she jumped off the counter and slipped under his arm when he lunged toward her.

He laughed. A full, deep laugh. His beautiful smile lit up his face, his eyes crinkled at the corners. He was happy. Happy with her. She'd have fallen in love with him in that single moment, but that would have required her ever falling out in the first place.

Pulling herself from the second haze Jax had plunged her into, she sat down at the table and sipped her tea while she watched him move around her kitchen. He'd been here before obviously, many times, but this was the first time he'd ever done anything like this. He opened drawers and cupboards, finding what he needed on the first try every time. "How do you know where everything is?"

He lifted a shoulder casually. "I don't know, actually." It sounded like he hadn't even noticed until she'd pointed it out. "I guess everything is just where it makes sense to be, where I'd put it."

She nodded, even though he couldn't see her. Since neither she nor Ivy cooked much, she couldn't help but wonder if Havenhouse had arranged the kitchen for someone it hoped would. Someone who had taken care of it when they hadn't.

A few minutes later Jax set a steaming plate in front of her, and one to the side of her, before going back to the counter to make another. A moment later, Ivy appeared in the kitchen, "Why does it smell so good in here?" She rubbed the sleep from her eyes.

"Morning," Jax said cheerfully. "Have a seat. I hope you're hungry."

Ivy's eyes nearly bugged out of her head as they settled on Jax.

She nodded, slightly stupefied as she sat down in front of the plate of food he'd set next to Liv.

"Uh, Jax, maybe you should put a shirt on before my sister goes cata-tonic," she suggested.

Jax looked down at himself, a slight tinge of embarrassment flushing over his golden skin. "Sorry," he murmured as he headed out of the kitchen, "not used to being in a house with anyone else in it."

"Don't dress on my account," her sister murmured as she leaned forward to watch him down the hall.

Ivy shifted sideways in her seat. "Not a word," Liv said, avoiding her sister's eyes.

Ivy's lower lip rolled into her mouth as if it were taking all her effort not to speak. The two of them sat in tense silence, taking small bites of their food. "Ugh fine. Get it over with." Liv flicked her fork in the air and rolled her eyes.

"Thank god!" Ivy exhaled, shifting her whole body to face her sister. "Holy shitballs! Jaxon Hawthorne was just shirtless in our kitchen *making us breakfast, Olivia.*"

Liv gave her best attempt at nonchalance but couldn't fight the smile she tried to hide with her tea. Part of her wanted to give in and dance around the kitchen with Ivy, freaking out like she imagined teenage sisters did. They'd never had a moment like that, because Liv had always needed to be a mom more than a sister. But maybe they could start now.

"Oh sure, play it cool. But I know you're freaking out on the inside. Did you guys have *sex?*" Ivy whispered the burning question with enthusiasm. Liv opened her mouth but paused to peek down the hall for Jax. Satisfied he wouldn't overhear her this time, she leaned into her sister conspiratorially. "Yes." She bit into her bottom lip, fighting laughter.

"And it's as good as he freaking looks like it would be, isn't it?"

She nodded a little too enthusiastically, making their silverware chime against their plates. She brought her hands down into her lap. "Maybe even better. I can't put it into words."

"Because he broke your brains with soul-shattering orgasms and with all his muscles and sexy broodiness. Wow." Ivy flung herself back in her chair, sliding down a little like she was melting.

Liv laughed quietly. "You're arguably too excited about this. You don't think it's too fast?"

"I mean what's the right speed anyway?" Ivy shrugged, biting into a crispy piece of bacon. "Does the third date somehow unlock something magickal? Does a guy knowing my favorite color somehow alert my vagina that it's okay to be turned on now? It's all arbitrary." She waved her bacon in the air.

"Third date? I was going to say sixth at least. But then again, technically Jax and I haven't been on any dates." *He's just building you your dream porch, helped you embrace your magick, oh and saved your life, before giving you the best orgasm of said life.* "And part of me feels more like we're picking back up where we left off, rather than starting over or from the beginning."

Ivy nodded. "Makes sense to me. I'm glad you finally gave in, and not just because it will take some of your focus off me." Ivy winked at her.

The two of them leaned into each other, whispering back and forth until they heard—intentionally—the loud sound of Jax's bare feet coming down the stairs.

They quickly righted themselves in their chairs and pretended to be eating, trying not to look like two little girls who'd just been caught breaking the rules.

Jax eyed them suspiciously for a moment before walking over to the counter to get his food.

The moment his back was turned, Ivy leaned over to Liv again. "He even smells like he gives good orgasms." Liv pushed her upright just as Jax turned and came to join them.

"Thanks for cooking Jax, you *really hit the spot,*" Ivy emphasized the double entendre.

Liv coughed, trying to dislodge the bite of the egg she'd been chewing.

"No problem," Jax replied, eyeing Liv questioningly.

The three of them ate and laughed through their meal. The house was so thrilled to have Jax in it that when it dropped chocolate croissants on the table, it even gave Ivy one.

It was the closest thing to a perfect morning she hadn't dared wish for in over twelve years. She'd given up so much more than she realized sometimes. It wasn't the big obvious things she mourned, but the small moments. Moments like this, that they hadn't had because she'd been so busy trying to predict or prepare for the next moment that she couldn't be present and enjoy the small moments.

Because it was these little moments that stacked upon each other to equal a good life and carried a person, or a relationship, through the harder times. She knew she wasn't done facing hard things, and she wasn't trying to avoid that. She just didn't want to do it alone anymore.

Watching Ivy laugh over a meal made by the man of her dreams who ate across from her, she knew she'd delivered on her promise to her mom. No place was perfectly safe, but here in their ancestral home, in this town, where they had people who loved them and fought to protect these little moments, she knew their mom had gotten it wrong. This was the safest place for them. Not because of the lack of danger, but because of the people who surrounded them and would fight for and with them.

"What do you have planned for the day?" Jax asked Ivy.

"Oh, just work in a little bit."

"And your work, it's outside town right?" Jax asked. *Dammit.* Liv knew where this was heading. She opened her eyes widely trying to get his attention without alerting Ivy.

"Yeah, down by the pier."

"And after that? Planning on seeing that guy?" He pressed quickly, feigning nonchalance and failing miserably, while deliberately ignoring Liv's stare boring into him. She had no doubt he *thought* he could subtly coerce information out of her sister, and usually he could have employed that Hawthorne charm to get Ivy to comply with his requests. But he was too edgy to be smooth.

"Rett? I'm not sure, but whatever I do, I'm sure it won't be nearly as pleasurable as whatever the two of you will get up to." Ivy shoved a fork full of food in her mouth. "Or down to," she continued, mercifully oblivious to Jax's questioning.

"What's that?"

Oh for crying out loud, between Ivy's sexual innuendos and Jax's inquisition, they may as well have been speaking two different languages, and all it was doing was serving to stress her out. Jax had gotten a name out of Ivy, and that was going to have to be enough for now.

"Nothing," Liv rushed to answer for her sister. She stood up, grabbing her and Ivy's plates as she went. Ivy's face pulled into an offended grimace as she set both of their plates in the sink. "We do have a lot to do today, so I'm going to go get ready. You probably need to do the same, right Ivy?" Liv asked, nodding her head at her sister, casting what was supposed to be a scolding look over her shoulder at Jax. He just grinned and lifted one of his shoulders, as if to say, "Worth a shot."

Ivy smiled and thankfully complied. "Yep. Work. Gotta go. Byyyyeee Jax." Ivy lingered for a moment longer, looking at him like a smitten schoolgirl. Liv walked out of the kitchen, grabbing the sleeve of Ivy's shirt and pulling her with her as she went.

JAX SHOOK HIS HEAD WITH A KNOWING SMILE AND FINISHED EATING HIS breakfast alone, but not really. Content in the house that he'd known for so long, taken care of while they waited together for the girl they both loved to return. The kitchen lights flickered a couple of times then returned to normal. "Yeah, yeah. You were right, old friend." Jax looked up at the ceiling. "She was more than worth the wait."

CHAPTER FORTY-ONE

"*A*re you sure you're ready to do this?" Liv asked Ivy for what felt like the tenth time as they walked through the forest toward the old Weeping Willow tree.

"Yes, Liv," Ivy groaned, more like it was the hundredth time she'd had to answer. "She needs this to really be at peace or whatever, right?" she asked, walking barefoot next to Liv with their mother's clay urn in her hands.

Liv looked down at the plants that shifted just ahead, creating a path for them. Most of them, anyway. Some of the more brazen or needy plants reached out to caress and stroke them—well, mostly her. It felt like a sort of funeral procession, only instead of mourning family members and friends, they had plants. "Pretty much. We're of the Earth, just like our magick. We're both meant to return to it once we're done with it, our bodies merging with the life around us." She reached out, running her fingers over the soft blue petals of a particularly tall Starflower plant. "And our magick either goes back into the Earth to prepare for the next Terrabellas, or into a living one."

Ivy nodded absently as they approached the large Willow. Her eyes scanned the tree and their surroundings. "Now what?" she asked, looking up at Liv. She looked so young standing there, several inches shorter than her, clutching their mother's ashes to her chest. It tempted her to ask yet again if her sister was sure she was ready for this, but she refrained, because as young as Ivy might look in the moment, she wasn't. Something Liv needed to be better about remembering.

She tipped her head toward the tree and smiled when Ivy's eyes widened as the draping branches of the willow parted like a leafy curtain, inviting them into its depths.

Ivy followed Liv into the veil of the tree, turning slowly, taking it all in. The branches drifted closed, leaving them in shadows speckled with small beams of sunshine that found their way through the canopy.

"When you're ready you can place the ashes there." She directed Ivy to a hole between two smaller roots that split from one larger one.

"That's it? Just dump her on the dirt?" Ivy asked, mildly offended.

Liv shook her head. "No, but that's the start."

After a few moments and some hushed words, Ivy crouched over the hole and slowly poured Elena's ashes into its depths.

Liv knelt in the dirt beside her sister, taking a handful of dirt from the pile left next to the hole and dropping it over the ashes. Ivy followed her lead until the hole was filled again.

When they stood up, Liv took Ivy's hand. "I don't know if I remember the words," Ivy confessed.

"You will. They're in there." Liv tapped Ivy's heart with her free hand. "You're a Terrabella, after all. But I'll start." She'd taught Ivy the words of their ancestors after their Grammy had died so that they could say them together for her. But instead, she'd had to say them alone. She rejected the resentment toward their mother that reared its head and chose to focus instead on Ivy's hand in hers and the energy of the dirt caked to their palms humming between them.

Liv started, leading Ivy in the spell.

"From Earth, we're born, to Earth we're bound."

With a gentle squeeze of their interlocked hands, Ivy's voice joined hers.

"In her depths our power found. When at last, to ash we burn, to Earth our ashes, we return. In cycles of life, our power refined, and thus our endless journeys entwined. Revertere ad terram, revertere ad terram, revertere ad terram."

As the sisters' words melded together in a mournful chant, bright blue-white veining began to web from the freshly upturned dirt and moved outward as Elena's ashes returned to the Earth.

Ivy watched, her eyes shining brightly with unshed tears. "You don't have to hold it in. It's okay to miss her."

Ivy turned to her as a tear broke free. "How can I miss her when I never really had her? At least not that I can remember."

Her understanding smile was tinged with sadness, for Ivy and herself. "Maybe it's missing what we didn't have, mourning what could have been. I don't know. But I don't think we need to understand everything we feel. Sometimes we just need to allow ourselves to feel it," Liv said as she relented to her tears.

Ivy nodded, and her tears finally broke free and slipped down her cheeks, landing on the dirt near Liv's.

Once the bright veining faded away, a thin new root appeared in the dirt, breaking from another.

A moment later a small ember of light, no bigger than a marble, lifted into the air in front of them, hovering there for a moment, oscillating end over end. Neither of them moved, but she could feel the way her sister's body stiffened next to hers.

"What the fuck," Ivy said from the corner of her mouth in a sing-song voice.

"Just wait." Liv was guessing, not having had this exact experience before.

Ivy audibly swallowed and Liv sighed in relief when the small amount of magick split and settled evenly into each of them, relieved that the last moments with their mom weren't tainted by her doing something to drive a wedge between them.

"That was her magick, huh?" Ivy asked. Liv just nodded. "Did that happen to you with Valeria's magick?" She was looking at the dirt.

"No. I don't think that's happened in a long time." Liv walked over to the root that had appeared when she'd done this same ritual for Valeria.

"I'm sorry you had to do this alone for her," Ivy said from behind her. "I wish I could have been there with you, and I wish I'd known her like you did."

She ran a light finger over the thick root. "Me too." Her voice cracked. She stood and walked toward the curtain of branches as it opened, urging them out into the sun again. "But she loved you a lot." Liv draped her arm over Ivy's shoulders, leading her through the veil. "I remember when you were little, she used to take you out to the cherry trees with her. She'd climb up the ladder and pass the full baskets down to you, and by the time she came back down most of the cherries would be gone and you'd be stained red for days." They both let out watery laughs as they emerged into the sun.

"Sometimes I wonder if we hadn't left, maybe things would have been different."

Liv paused their walking and dropped her arm to face her sister, shielding her eyes as they adjusted to the bright light. She'd never heard Ivy say anything like that before.

"I used to wonder that too," she said, offering a truth of her own.

"I'm sorry you had to leave for me."

Liv was shaking her head before Ivy had even finished saying the words. "I'm not. I wish things could have been different of course, but not that."

"Thanks."

They walked toward the house in silence for a couple of minutes before Ivy spoke again. "By the way, when did you dig that hole?"

"Jax did it not too long after we got back so that it would be ready whenever we were."

Ivy tilted her head back and forth. "The fact that I find that wildly romantic probably means there's something broken in me, right?"

Liv laughed, "Probably, but if so, it's broken in me, too."

312

CHAPTER FORTY-TWO

*T*he same unsettling feeling of malevolence left behind at the first crime scene now hung in the air around Declan.

This death had been slower. This victim was secured to a tree, head drooping forward. Long, jagged lacerations ran vertically down the forearms.

Blood pooled on the ground below the victim's dangling arms, traveling in a near-impossible pattern, crisscrossing to connect the five swords that had been thrust into the ground at the victim's feet, creating a star.

The wounds weren't as gruesome as the first body, but the scene was no less disturbing. Or baffling.

Two bodies might not be serial, but it was the beginning of a pattern.

Fuck.

The sound of crunching leaves and snapping twigs reminded him he wasn't alone. "Dammit Grady, stick to the path we created walking in here."

"Whoops, sorry sir." Grady only walked far enough so they could see each other and speak at a normal level.

The man had been doing everything he could to ensure he didn't have to see the scene again, since accidentally stumbling upon it. Grady wasn't completely incompetent as a person, just as a cop, not unlike the few deputies under him. Considering not a single officer in town had been trained to deal with a crime scene, let alone a murder, he wouldn't have been much help.

But even for someone like Declan, who had extensive experience with murders, some even more grisly, this took him out of his depth.

Grady shifted on his feet, kicking dirt and other loose vegetation free with every nervous step he took.

"I need you to create a perimeter around the hot zone, but use subtle markers, not the yellow caution tape—we don't want to draw any attention."

"A hot zone is the crime scene," he ground out when Grady interrupted him to ask him what the term any cop should know meant. *For fuck's sake.*

"Then I want you to mark the way you entered the forest and scan the surrounding area for signs of foot traffic or any other potential evidence," he went on, hoping if he gave the guy a job to do it would calm him the hell down.

"Yes, sir." Grady turned to walk away, but stopped. "Do you want me to call Jax before or after I do that?"

"Tell me, Grady, what is the point of having a police force if every time there's a crime you call someone else, someone not even in law enforcement, before even *attempting* to do your job yourself?"

"Sorry sir, Harlan always—"

"What about me makes you think I give a shit what Harlan did?" Grady wisely understood that to be the rhetorical question it was. "Go scan the forest." He dismissed the guy to a job he knew was going to be like looking for a needle in a fuck ton of pine needles.

The last sheriff and the department—shit, the rest of the town for that matter—depended far too heavily on Jaxon Hawthorne and his family. It was off-putting and certainly not something he was used to.

But there was protecting the integrity of a case, and then there was refusing to accept help, and the difference between the two was pride. And pride had no place in his job.

Solving crime wasn't about ego, it was about the victim. When law enforcement, or any other civil servants for that matter, lost sight of that, they failed at their job—regardless of whether they eventually solved the case or not.

Even though it was painful, he had to admit that his experience solving homicide cases wasn't going to be enough here. He needed someone who could provide him with the information to fill the holes that magick put in this case.

"Grady!" he called out for the man he'd just sent away. "Give me your phone."

Fifteen minutes later, Declan watched Jax's truck pull off the road into the dirt from a decent distance inside the tree line. He still had plenty of apprehension about working with the man—hated the feeling of having to rely on someone else to help him do his job—but he couldn't deny the tiny ember of relief he felt as well.

He was a little surprised to see both Jax *and* one of the women from the other night—Liv, he thought, the drunk one—climb out of the truck. Apparently, they were a package deal. He did his best to ignore the annoyance of having to allow not one, but two civilians into his crime scene and watched impatiently as they made their way to Grady, who he'd had wait closer to the road.

"Hey guys," Grady greeted them. "Um, the sheriff wants anyone coming in and out to stick to this path." He indicated a discreet, narrow path marked by stones and branches.

"Hey Grady," Liv replied, and Declan saw her squeeze the younger man's arm, giving him a soft smile. Looked like she was trying to offer some kind of sympathy for the unfortunate situation. She must've made an impression, because Grady turned to watch as she made her way deeper into the forest, the fear that had been on his face all day turned to admiration. Declan scowled and moved forward to tell Grady to keep his mind on the damn case, but someone else beat him to it.

Jax cleared his throat from behind Grady, whose body went rigid as if the idiot had forgotten Jax was there. "I'd suggest keeping your eyes on less dangerous things, like the crime scene," Jax suggested as he walked past Grady, who nodded repeatedly.

For fuck's sake. Declan shook his head.

He watched Liv lean into Jax as they headed in his direction, glaring up

315

at her boyfriend. "He's harmless. You didn't need to freak him out even more."

"Some fear is healthy for a man." The cocky grin he directed toward Liv dropped away as they got closer. "You rang, Sheriff?"

Declan took a few more steps, meeting them before the crime scene came into view. "Yeah. But I want to warn you, this scene isn't any better than the last. You need to be sure it's something you want to see before getting any closer." His words were meant for Liv but directed to Jax. He'd seen the first body and had a better idea of what she would be walking into.

Something that looked very close to offense laced her expression, but Jax spoke before she could. "I didn't bring her here blindly. This is her forest, and she's capable of making that decision for herself."

"Which *she* clearly has." Liv looked pointedly between the two of them.

Declan nodded. "I haven't checked the body for ID yet. I didn't want to risk disturbing anything you might use to do…whatever it is you do," he began as he led them around the cropping of trees that had been shielding the ritual sight.

It took him a few more steps to realize they'd stopped just a few feet behind him. He took in their shocked faces and the way Jax looked at Liv like she might implode. Not good. "You knew him?" He asked aloud to be sure, but the look on Liv's face was all the answer he needed. He'd seen the same one every time someone positively ID'd a victim.

Jax stepped in front of her, blocking her view of the body, and took her chin between his forefinger and thumb. "We can turn around and leave right now if that's what you need. This is *not* your responsibility and not your fault, do you hear me? Not a single bit of this is on you. It's okay to have sympathy for him, but that's as far as it should go."

She nodded in Jax's grasp, but even Declan could tell it was clear she didn't believe him. "I want to stay. I want to help." The truth in her words was enough to erase the rising fear that maybe he'd made a mistake in allowing them into the crime scene.

"I didn't know him, not technically." Liv began explaining. "His wife, sort of. She showed up on our porch shortly after we came back to town."

Came back? He'd assumed she was from Havenwood. Declan tucked the small piece of information away for later. One thing at a time.

"She said he'd been missing for a week by the time she came to us for help finding him." Liv's gaze dropped back down to the body.

"Anything else?"

"She said he was 'like us' in a way, that he had a small ember of magick. She didn't seem to know much about magick, not that I gave her time to say much."

Her eyes found Declan's. "I could see the bruises she was trying to hide. Bruises he'd given her, and I just decided for her she was better off. If he was this close all along, I could have found him *easily*."

This woman was drowning in so much guilt he wasn't sure how she was still standing upright. But it wasn't the kind of guilt that lurked under lies. She hadn't lied once. This guilt was her truth, and something about that made Declan angry.

"Most people would have done the same. There was no reason for you to think something like this might happen. You have nothing to feel guilty for."

"He's right, Dandy," Jax said, pulling her attention. "You made the best choice you knew how to at that moment, with the information you had at the time. But that choice didn't cause this." Jax gestured behind him toward the body. "This is a result of someone else's choices. Period." She nodded, his words seeming to sink in this time.

"Is there anything else you can tell me?" Declan asked, trying to move the conversation along so he didn't have to pay attention to the way Jax's words hit him, or the pity on Liv's face for a man he wasn't sure deserved it. But that was why he didn't want to involve a civilian whenever possible. It wasn't incompetence he was worried about, not only that anyway. They didn't have the necessary skills to compartmentalize, especially when they had any type of connection to the victim.

He'd learned long ago how to maintain as much emotional distance from victims as he could. Distance equaled objectivity, while familiarity often led to oversight. It was better for both him and the victim if he kept things impersonal, no matter how callous it looked on the surface.

They took a few steps closer to the body, "I don't know what to make of all this." He gestured to the swords and the blood that connected all of them. "I understand the general connection to the first body. But even with the pictures and evidence from two scenes, I'm thinking it's not the kind of thing I can research on the internet."

Jax shook his head, eyes glazing over like he was having some kind of internal argument with himself. "I may have some ideas as to the symbolism here, but I'll have to do some research. These sigils are similar to the others as well, probably originating from the same source or index, but I haven't been able to figure out their origins yet." *Truth.* His frustration was evident in the small muscle that ticked along his tight jaw.

Declan rubbed his hands roughly over his face and muttered, "I never should have let Harlan trick me into taking this job."

Jax turned to him, eyes narrowing. "What do you mean, trick you into it?"

Declan shook his head dismissively, not intending to start a conversation. "Nothing. Just a year's worth of emails and phone calls, going on and on about how this was the perfect place to 'coast into retirement,' as he put it. Swearing Havenwood was practically crime-free, and that the job was more of a formality than a responsibility."

Jax's brows drew together, "So you didn't apply for the job here?"

Declan scoffed, "No."

Jax's expression flickered, something unreadable passing through his eyes, but before Declan could puzzle it out, both their gazes were drawn to Liv as she knelt on the ground beside the swords and blood.

She closed her eyes and began whispering something to herself. *What the hell was she doing?* He looked to Jax for answers, but the other man's eyes were solely fixed on Liv.

Declan's curiosity got the better of him and he stepped closer so he could hear the words she spoke. As if that would make anything about this make sense.

"*Terra Elicitus,*" she repeated in what sounded like Latin. This was all starting to get too strange, even for him. As if she'd heard his thought and wanted to raise the bar, Liv drove her fingers deep into the ground, until only a small patch of the backs of her hands were visible.

The words became a low chant, and though he couldn't see anything, his skin warmed. He looked up at Jax again, but of course, none of this would seem odd to him.

A moment later the forest around them seemed to shiver—that was the only way he could think to describe it—before coming to life in a way he'd never experienced. Though warmth engulfed him, goosebumps flared over his skin in response to whatever energy was moving around them. Energy he had a pretty good idea was either coming from Liv or responding to her.

Whatever magick Liv was using felt so controlled, gradually filling the air around him. It was nothing like the abrupt, disruptive force of his own. Liv's magick unfurled effortlessly, while the few times he'd been desperate enough to use his, it had taken every ounce of his will just to keep it in check. What he'd managed for Quinn the other night was the most precise he'd ever been, and it had drained him completely, leaving him barely able to make it back to his bed before collapsing from exhaustion.

The ground beneath the ritual site collapsed in, sinking away from the blood, leaving it suspended, motionless, hovering where the ground had just been.

"*Exsolvere*," Liv whispered, and suddenly the blood rose higher into the air above them. Liv stayed in the dirt, but Jax took a half-step closer to her, placing his palm on her shoulder.

"*Exsolvere*," she said again, but this time it was a command.

As Declan watched in awe, black tendrils that weren't quite liquid but not quite smoke separated from the blood, hissing and moving as if the shit were alive. He stepped away from it, his back colliding with a tree, unable to do anything but watch.

Jax lifted an arm, squeezing his hand into a fist, and air shot past Declan's face, glancing across his cheek like an arrow.

The black shit shrieked and slithered in the air, only able to get so far in any direction, caught in an invisible hold. Somehow Declan knew it was the remnants of something *wrong*. Something made of evil and wreaking of distortion of the truth. This was the physical manifestation of what he'd felt in the air when he'd first gotten to the scene.

The blood Liv had raised lowered back to the ground before slowly disappearing into the soil.

She rose to stand next to Jax. "*Dimittere!*" She threw a hand up and out toward the cliffs at the far edge of the forest. The blackness shot through the trees, slowly fading from sight the farther it got from its host until it faded altogether.

When Declan felt sure nothing else was going to happen, like that crap turning around and coming back at them, he released the breath that had seized in his chest. "What the hell was that?"

"*That* was the remnants of the evil that happened here. Of whatever magick they're using." Liv turned back to Declan. Her eyes, which had struck Declan as unnaturally green the first moment he saw her, were now electric—shit they were nearly neon.

He was never going to get used to this town, or these people.

Jax took Liv's hand in his. "The site is safe now. Nothing here will hurt anyone when you're ready to have it removed, but that's about all we can do for now. We can find his wife and let her know if you'd like."

"No," Declan was a little too quick to say. "That's my responsibility." Jax eyed him for a moment, then nodded, apparently having found whatever he was looking for.

He turned to leave the forest, Liv at his side, but she paused. "I know it's a lot to take in. But ignoring who you are doesn't give you more control over it. Quite the opposite. We won't tell you what to do," she looked up at Jax, who didn't look like he agreed, "but if there is one thing you should know about Havenwood, it's that secrets only stay hidden for so long. If you want this town to trust you, you have to start by trusting yourself first."

Jax stood silently, regarding her as if she had placed the rising moon in the sky with her own two hands. His gaze lingered on Liv for a moment longer before he tore his eyes away, turning them back to Declan.

"We came this time," Jax said, his tone measured but firm, "but we won't be relegated to being your on-call magick translators for free. I think we've shown you our value. Now it's time you show us yours. Tomorrow night at Mac's. Who knows, we may even have more answers for you. Maybe even some you didn't know to ask for." Jax added with a slight, knowing smirk.

Declan felt a flicker of uncertainty at the invitation—if you could call it that—and he wasn't sure what Jax expected from him, or what he was willing to give.

Jax took a few steps away but then stopped and looked back over his shoulder. "Oh, Sheriff, one more thing. How long ago did Harlan offer you this job?"

Declan paused, brow furrowing slightly, "The first time, maybe a little over a year ago."

"And the last?"

"Eight months," he replied, the memory of that day clear in his mind.

Jax and Liv exchanged a glance—a silent conversation passing between them—before they both turned and began walking back through the forest without another word.

Declan watched as they disappeared into the shadows of the forest, debating whether he should grab what little belongings he had and leave this town and its special brand of crazy behind him for good. But after watching what Liv had just done, he couldn't help but wonder what the rest of them could do. And maybe what *he* could do, if he were to embrace what he kept locked away inside him.

CHAPTER FORTY-THREE

The bar was empty except for Jax and Logan. And Mac, of course. He'd stayed glued to his stool in the far corner of the bar, muttering to himself about "shite business practices," and "numpties" ever since Logan had bellowed last call.

Jax nursed a beer while Logan finished clearing a few tables and peppering him with questions he didn't bother to answer.

Logan came back around the bar. "If you're not going to give me a sneak peek into this little meeting you've called, then at least tell me what's going on with you and Liv?"

He'd already told Logan his theory about the timing of Liv, Quinn, and Declan's arrival, but he was waiting on the rest, mostly to spare himself having to go over it twice and field multiple rounds of questions. Questions he didn't have many answers to.

Logan crossed his arms over his chest, leaned back against the narrow counter behind him, and waited.

Jax rolled his eyes. "I might tell you if I wasn't certain you're only asking to one-up the other old ladies in your yoga class. Besides, seems like you have enough to worry about with your own love life."

Logan gestured to himself. "Me?" His jaw dropped open in mock offense. "I'd never. And you already know the only important thing about *my* love life—I don't have one. Which is why I have so much free time to worry about yours, like a good bestie."

Jax shook his head. "Please never call me that again. And I know all kinds of things, if you really want to get into it."

"Like what? The last girl I—wait. Nice try, ass. Your mind games might work on the others, but I am *not* falling for that flip it and reverse it shit," Logan said, leaning against the bar with level eyes, but Jax was already turning away from him toward the entry expectantly.

A breath later the heavy oak door swung open to reveal Jade, Quinn, and then Liv. The last rays of the setting sun momentarily framed her figure in a warm, golden halo. The door drifted closed behind her, sending a breeze through her long hair, filling the air around him with her scent, and filling him with the need to touch her, to claim her, to keep her. For good.

A small smile curved her lips when her eyes found his across the bar, a million little unsaid things passing between them. Things that were just for them, and caused her eyes to twinkle and his chest to tighten, like he missed her even though she was standing right there.

"Well, I have my answer, don't I? She's home, you're back together for fifteen minutes, and you're already ready to propose," Logan's voice teased from behind the bar.

"If that was what she wanted," he responded absently as he slid off his chair. Not unlike the first time he'd seen her again, in this very place, she walked into his arms like it was the most natural thing in the world. He wrapped an arm around her waist and brought the other to her hair, gently sliding his fingers into it to tilt her head up to him.

She smiled up at him, letting him support her weight so she could lean back and see him. "Hi."

"Hello." He kissed her lips gently, then her forehead, before ushering her into the seat next to him at a round high-top table set for six.

"Let's make this quick. I had to get a babysitter and it's insane how much these teenagers are out here charging to sit on a couch watching TV while the kid is asleep in bed," Jade said, practically having to climb up into the chair on his other side.

"Need a boost, Sunny?" Logan asked, giving her a smug smile as he made a show of how easily he slid onto the seat next to Liv.

"Aw look, the beast is pretending to be civilized. It must have taken so many hours of training for you to learn how to sit in a chair. Someone get him a treat for being such a good boy."

Quinn eased into the chair on the other side of Jade. "Play nice children."

One seat at the table remained empty, but between Logan and Jade, he needed to get on with this if he wanted to make it out with his sanity intact. So, he decided to start with the new crime scene, knowing that if Declan decided to show, this would all be redundant to him anyway.

Jax rolled the paper out, holding one side down, Quinn placing a napkin holder on the other. At the center of the page were sketches that accurately depicted each of the crime scenes, simplistic line drawings denoting placement and positioning to scale.

Surrounding each sketch were neat blocks of handwritten notes, as well as recreations of the sigils he'd seen at each scene, separated in ways that he hoped didn't only make sense to him.

At the bottom were more notes on the very limited information he'd been able to find that he thought might be pertinent, though it amounted to frustratingly little.

Jade pulled her legs under her in the chair and leaned halfway across the table to look closer, covering half of his notes. "Jeez Jax, what is all this beautiful mind nonsense?"

He pressed his fingertips into his sister's forehead, sending her back into her seat so the others could see as well. "Surrounded by fucking children," he grumbled, not quite under his breath.

Liv suppressed a giggle, but her warm hand found his thigh under the table, her touch grounding and warm, calming as it glided up and down his leg, urging him on.

He took a deep breath and then dove in.

Thanks to about a hundred questions—mostly from Jade—it took about thirty minutes, twice as long as it should have, to get the others up to speed. He couldn't fault her, though—the recent changes in her life gave her very little extra time to focus on anything else, and while solving shit like this wasn't *technically* their responsibility, she still carried the same weight of duty as all Balancers.

Liv had just finished describing the familiarity of the feel of the magick she'd excised from the earth at the second crime scene to what the women had experienced the night of their cleansing ritual when the door opened and Declan walked through.

He didn't hesitate or balk as he approached the group, but Jax didn't miss the way his eyes scanned the room from corner to corner.

Just before Declan reached the table, Jade leaned into Quinn. "Keep it in your pants Wilder, we don't need you getting arrested for harassing an officer."

Quinn dismissed Jade with a smooth wave of her hand. "He's a big boy, I'm sure he can handle a little drunk flirting."

"A *little* flirting?" Jade's brows drew up toward her hairline. Quinn just tipped an unapologetic shoulder.

Jax cleared his throat. "Thanks for coming," he said in greeting, trying to get a read on the other man's body language.

Declan nodded silently and sat down in the empty seat directly across from Jax, placing a thin file folder on the table.

"Can I get you a drink, Sheriff Stone?" Logan asked as he started to stand.

"Declan is fine," he said, Jax wasn't sure if it was a desire to avoid addressing the recent revelation that the new sheriff not only possessed magick but, given the nature of it, was not just a descendant of the Stone line, but a very powerful one. Or possibly the cop's strong sense of right and wrong wouldn't allow his professional title to be brought into this. It would also explain the casual clothes—dark jeans and a flannel over a t-shirt—rather than his uniform, even though Jax knew he'd just come from work.

He hoped it was the latter. If Declan hoped to avoid the conversation of his heritage, he was about to be disappointed.

"And no, thanks. Let's just get to it," Declan went on, turning down Logan's offered drink, and leaning forward to rest his forearms over the folder he'd brought.

Declan looked over the sketch that was laid out across the table, his brows pulling together as he registered what it was. "That's the entire crime scene. In perfect detail. How could you possibly remember all that?"

"Let's just call it a gift. I have a very, *very* good memory," Jax said as he rolled the paper back up. It wasn't an answer, and it was clear Declan didn't appreciate the vague response. He stared, maybe waiting for Jax to clarify, and hoping the weighted silence would spur some kind of confession.

It wouldn't.

Declan's trust would make this easier, but all Jax needed was his cooperation. He didn't owe the man any type of deference. This wasn't some ordinary town where being sheriff automatically placed him above Jax. They were equals with different responsibilities. He'd hoped Declan showing up meant he was starting to realize that, but he also wasn't holding his breath.

The two of them let the awkward moment of silence pass stoically, ignoring the shifting eyes of everyone around them.

"I think I'm choking on testosterone," Quinn said, propping her elbow on the table and dropping her chin into her palm.

Jade snapped her fingers a couple of times between them. "Yeah, if you're both done with the silent dance for dominance, can we move this along? At this rate, I'm going to be paying the babysitter's college tuition."

The stalemate held.

Then Liv broke the ice with a soft smile, looking pointedly at the thin folder in front of Declan. "Something you want to share with the group?"

Declan glanced at the folder for a moment, then around the table at them, and sighed. "Look, I'm not exactly accustomed to sharing."

"Only child huh? Me too. But...I don't mind sharing. Sometimes I actually prefer it." Logan waggled his brows at Declan.

"Not. Helpful," Liv murmured.

Declan brushed Logan off with a slight shake of his head. "I'm only here because I want to find out who is doing this and stop them. It's become clear to me that, whether I want your help or not, you're going to be involved, and—" several of them made moves to speak but Declan held up a hand and continued before anyone could interrupt him, "it has also become clear that there's a lot about the nature of these murders that I don't have experience with. And your assistance might be, and already has been…valuable."

Logan leaned into Liv. "That looked painful," he said out of the side of his mouth.

"But let me be clear," Declan went on, speaking over Logan's jokes, "that it *is assistance*. This is *my* investigation. You maybe have been appointed to handle the magick or whatever the woo-woo shit is going on in this town, but I have been appointed to protect this town and its residents. *I* am the one with experience in that capacity. This investigation will not be turned into some kind of circus. We will do this my way, the *legal* way. I expect to be kept in the loop fully about anything you might discover along the way, not whenever it's convenient for your scheming— of which there will be none. You've had access to both crime scenes now, but I can ensure that is all you have. Any vigilante bullshit, any crossing of lines—no matter how minor—I am *out*, and I will make sure every detail is kept from you. Transparency and honesty. Period. Is that agreeable?" Declan looked around the table, evidently requiring a response.

"Wow, someone get this guy a soap box," Jade said, never one to respond well to being told what she could or couldn't do.

Jax spoke quickly and for all of them when he nodded and said, "Fine. We can *all* agree to that." And then he went on, "But that has to go both ways or *we're* out, and I think you'll find that you need us more than we need you."

He knew he probably shouldn't have added that last part but…baby steps.

Apparently satisfied, Declan leaned back in his chair and started to open his folder.

Jax stopped him with a gesture. "Before you start in on whatever is in that folder, and in light of that little speech, there's something I think I should share with you. All of you."

Jax recounted to the others what Declan had said about how he'd come to be the sheriff of their magickal little town. He could feel Liv stiffen as she no doubt recognized the similarities between her experience before coming back and Declan's.

"About eight months ago, Quinn turned up in town, apparently lost.

327

She'd never heard of Havenwood, had no knowledge of her family history here, or that she was a witch. But she quickly realized this was where she was meant to be all along and chose to stay."

Declan's eyes shifted to Quinn, who smiled at him and lifted her fingers, letting small sparks of electricity bounce between them. "I mean, I wouldn't say I was completely oblivious that I might be a little…different. And I wouldn't say I was *lost*, more like not heading anywhere in particular." She let out a husky laugh, and Jax was left to assume from her look that it was directed at whatever emotion she was picking up from their recalcitrant sheriff.

Jax waited until everyone's attention was back on him to continue. "Then, Liv came back." He looked over at her, the intensity of emotion he felt thinking back on the night of her return reflected to him from the depths of her sparkling eyes.

"Back?" Declan asked.

"Yeah, I left when I was nineteen," she answered simply, so Jax could continue.

"*Eventually,*" he pumped not-quite-false ire into the word, "she mentioned that she'd received the deed to Havenhouse about six months before she finally decided to do the right thing and relent to the inevitable." She rolled her eyes at his corny line, but he could also see the hint of color on her olive skin. He looked back to Declan, "That would have been—"

"Eight months ago." Declan finished for him.

After a few moments, he leaned forward again, resting his forearms back on the table. "If all of this is real and I didn't just become the sheriff of a town filled with delusional thirty-somethings who are hellbent on dragging me into their crazy—"

"I'm only twenty-seven," Jade cut in.

Quinn nudged her with her elbow.

"What? It's a crucial fact."

Declan ignored Jade's little tangent entirely and asked, "What does it all *mean*?"

And there it was, just one of the crucial questions Jax didn't have an answer to.

"I mean, I admit that's weird that we were all drawn here around the same time, but what makes you so sure it's not just kismet? I mean what else *could* it be?" Quinn reasoned.

"Maybe if it were just a few random people, but at least in Declan and Liv's case, they were both prompted to come here by random outside sources. Add in that all three of you end up being from founding family lines that have been absent from the town…" Logan shook his head. "I went through some of my grandpa's old books and notes the other night. From what I can tell, there haven't been this many descendants represented in town in nearly eighty years. If someone from the Vulcani line were to show up, that would be the first time all lines have been here in over a hundred years. No way that's a coincidence."

"So, what? I only ended up here because some magickal puppet master decided it for me?" Quinn looked between Jax and Jade, something passing over her face before Jax could get a handle on it.

Declan's eyes were fixed on Quinn, clearly trying to pick apart the emotions there too, or what they might mean.

"No, that's not what he's saying. Magick can't strip away free will. Your choices brought you here, and your choices are what have kept you here. Nothing else."

"Don't lie to her." Declan's voice was calm but sure, as if he were positive that Jade had been lying.

Jade's brows drew together. "Um, I'm not lying."

Declan didn't back off. "You're also not telling her the whole truth."

Liv shifted in the seat next to him, clearly not liking Jade being challenged, but Jax knew his sister could hold her own, and he was more curious to see where this was going. He slipped his arm around the back of Liv's chair, brushing her hair aside so he could place his palm on the back of her neck to reassure her.

Jade returned his challenge. "And how would you know that?"

How indeed? Jax scrutinized Declan.

"Let's just call it a gift." He used Jax's own words. *Touché, Sheriff. And also…noted.*

Jade sighed, relenting for Quinn's benefit. "Magick can't strip free will. It didn't force you to come here."

"But?" Quinn pushed.

"But...it could have played a role in the impetus or influenced certain aspects of the journey that made it possible for you to end up here. Let me be clear though, Quinn, you're here because you chose to be. It couldn't have forced you to stay once you were here. Period." Jade turned from Quinn to Declan. "Is that satisfactory, Sheriff?"

The explanation seemed to satisfy Quinn.

Declan didn't bother responding, but lifted his elbows back off his folder and slid it across the table toward Jax, apparently ready to move on to the next topic. The folder stopped just short of the edge of the table, a sheet of white paper slipping out to fall to the floor. Jax lifted a hand, catching the sheet with a wave of magick without even bothering to look away from Declan. The page lifted into the air, hovering above the table for a moment before smoothly coming down in front of him.

BFSC Labs was typed in a boring corporate font across the top. Below that was a table containing a list of chemical compounds as well as results and units.

"The stuff on top is related to the first scene, we were able to find out his name was Jeremiah Rouche. As for the second victim," Declan hesitated, "his name was Caleb Hendricks."

He could feel Liv's body stiffen, as she learned the man's name for the first time. He wished he could excise those last dregs of guilt from her, but all he could do was run a supportive hand up her back to remind her he saw her, and she wasn't alone in any of this.

"All we have are pictures for now" Declan went on, "which you don't need." he said, nodding to Jax's rolled-up sketches.

Liv leaned in close to him to look. "Maybe I should..." She gently slipped the report from Jax's fingers so she could get a better look.

"How were you able to get a Toxicology report when the closest thing we have to a lab is Liv's greenhouse?" Jade asked, shifting in her seat, no doubt antsy to see the report Liv held.

"I called in a favor. And before you bother, my contacts are discreet, and the sample was anonymous."

Liv scanned the ingredients listed, her brow furrowing deeper the farther down the list she got.

"It says belladonna—why do you seem confused by that?" Logan asked as he crowded Liv.

"No, it says belladonna alkaloid." She pushed Logan back upright in his seat—which he clearly let her do. "Which could be any number of deadly nightshades," she continued. "*Hyoscyamus* niger, henbane, for instance, would produce belladonna alkaloids. But the same genus that henbane comes from also includes nearly twenty other species, any one of which would also produce a similar alkaloid. The same goes for aconitine, could be wolfsbane or it could be about two hundred other plants. Neither tells us much."

Liv turned the document toward Declan and leaned over the table to point at one of the compounds listed toward the bottom, indicating a smaller amount had been found in Jeremiah's system. "But this one, ricinoleic acid? That could only come from ricin, an extract of the castor plant. I don't get why anyone would use that."

"Not everyone is as experienced in poisons as you Terrabellas." Liv quickly looked up at Quinn, who gave her an approving wink. "Allegedly."

"Keep going," Declan pushed. "Please," he tacked on, apparently trying to curb the demand in his voice.

Liv sat back in her seat, "It's just that assuming the goal of the ricin was death, poisoning someone with ricin would be slow, and…messy, if it worked at all. And if they had these other poisons, I don't know why they would even bother."

"Maybe they gave it all at the same time, like some kind of super poison?" Logan suggested.

"Maybe, but doubtful. This number here," she pointed at the third column that listed the levels in the blood volume, her brows pinching in contemplation as she worked through it all, "considering the half-life for each of these other poisons, versus the amount of ricinoleic detected, it had to have been taken before the other two poisons. I'd say probably by a day at least. The other two could have been much closer together though. I'm a little rusty, but…"

Liv looked up, realizing the table had gone quiet. She pulled the corner of her lip between her teeth in embarrassment.

There's my girl, he thought, loving the way these little parts of *her* kept emerging, as she merged the woman she was now with who she was at a soul level, embracing her truest self a little more every day.

"Sorry." She smiled bashfully. "That's probably not useful for anyone not interested in phytotoxicology." She handed the paper back to Jax.

"That's fairly helpful," Declan said, quickly relaying his train of thought. "Tells me whoever was doing the poisoning most likely didn't know what they were doing. They probably used the ricin because it was more easily accessible but when it didn't work fast enough, they used the other poisons to speed up the process. Meaning they were on a time crunch."

"How does that help us catch the killer?" Quinn asked.

"Well, it doesn't. Not directly anyway, but this is how you build a case. We know now that they didn't know what they were doing, and if they were in a rush, as the evidence suggests, those things lead to mistakes. And mistakes are how you catch killers."

Jax opened the folder, removing a picture of some sort of altar or ritual space set up in an otherwise empty room.

"My deputies found that in the bedroom of the first victim," Declan explained. "The symbols are similar to what we saw in the cave where his body was found."

Jax nodded, handing the picture over to Jade so she would stop crowding his space trying to see. "I can tell you that these runes are of the same origin or context as the ones at each crime scene. I've been searching through some of the older books in both the Hawthorne and Terrabella private libraries and haven't been able to find anything that looks like these. It's almost like they're some kind of hybrid, or maybe a code." Jax fought to ignore the burning building in his chest that followed having to share yet another failure on his part.

Quinn took the folder from in front of Jax, but before she could open it Declan's hand came down on top of it. "The rest of the pictures are of the actual crime scenes. You saw Jax's sketch. I don't think you want to see these."

"I appreciate your consideration for my delicate feminine sensibilities," Quinn said playfully, mimicking Declan's subtle southern drawl, laying her hand on top of Declan's, "but I assure you, Sheriff, I'll be just fine." She made to brush Declan's hand off the folder. He resisted for a moment, searching her face before finally relenting.

Quinn opened the folder and scanned the pictures—to her credit, she didn't wince.

"What did the second victim's wife say when you went to talk to her? Did they have anything like that set up in their place?" Jade asked, handing the picture of the altar set up at Jeremiah's to Quinn. She studied it for a moment, looking between it and the pictures of the crime scene before returning it to the folder and offering it to Logan.

Logan lifted his hands. "Nuh-uh. I was at the first one. Unlike Quinn, my feminine sensibilities are delicate. I'll stick with Jax's doodles."

"She didn't say anything," Declan said. They all turned to look at him. "When I went over there to talk to her, the place had been cleared out—in a hurry from the looks of what was left behind."

Liv's lip pulled between her teeth, and he knew she was silently battling her guilt and hoping Emma had chosen to leave on her own.

"We gathered the few things that were left behind, just in case. It's all locked up in evidence. I can arrange for you to have a look at it, but I doubt it will be much help."

Jax gave Jade a pointed look. "Actually Sheriff, I have some *Gifts* of my own. I'd like to come down and have a poke around those things. If you don't mind," she added belatedly.

Declan nodded, looking down at his hands in contemplation.

"Whatcha thinking, Sheriff?" Logan smiled widely and Declan's raised brow. "Sharing, remember?" It was hard to tell if he was teasing the sheriff or attempting to charm him. Either could be true. Neither was working.

Declan ran his hand roughly over the beard on the side of his jaw and around to the back of his neck and sighed heavily. The influx of information and lack of answers were getting to all of them.

"The night I caught you guys breaking into this place—"

"Allegedly," Jade added this time.

Declan looked at her blankly for a moment. "Sure." Then he turned his attention to Quinn. "Is there anything you can tell me about that? What caught your attention?"

"I could feel a presence, but I couldn't see anything. When I got close I was even more sure, but I still couldn't see anything. I only intended to use my magick to see if a gust of wind might...stir something up. I don't know, I wasn't exactly firing on all cylinders that night. But my magick rebounded off of whatever was there."

"Did you recognize the magick or whatever presence you felt?" Logan asked.

Liv looked up at Jax, questioning if they should share their theory. The shake of his head was so subtle no one else would even notice. Despite his misgivings about Rett, he wasn't ready to share them yet, no matter what he agreed to about total transparency.

"No. It almost felt more like an absence in a weird way. But I wouldn't say it felt evil or anything. Just different than anything like our magicks. Including yours."

Declan kept going, showing zero acknowledgment of his magick being mentioned. "Assuming there was an actual human behind whatever magick that was, seems like a pretty handy skill for someone who wants to be able to commit murder and not be seen."

"Except that's not possible because of the Umbra Aegis." Logan pointed out.

At Declan's what the fuck look, Quinn piped in. "Umbra Aegis... Umbra, usually translated to mean hidden can also mean shadow. Aegis translates to shield or protection," she recited, showing off some of what Jade has been teaching her. "It's the invisible magick encompassing Havenwood that weighs the intentions of those attempting to cross into town...along with some other cool stuff," she finished proudly.

"Well done, young Padawan," Jade praised.

"Thank you, Miyagi-san." Quinn dipped her chin in a slight bow.

Declan blinked a few times, "Those aren't—you know what? Never mind." He didn't bother correcting Quinn. "So as long as people stay on this side of the town line, they're safe, right?"

"I mean it's not like no one's ever stubbed their toe, but compared to what goes on the outside, yeah."

"And, assuming the town is the safe haven it was meant to be, I don't suppose forcing everyone to stay in town until further notice is an option?" Declan asked.

Jade shook her head. "Even if we could find a loophole to the whole free will thing, too many people work or have family outside town. We'd end up with a whole host of other issues on our hands."

Declan nodded subtly as he looked away from the others for a moment. "It can't be a coincidence," he said, turning back to them, "that these murder scenes were both staged just outside the town line and the Umbra whatever. It has to mean something."

"Like?" Logan asked.

Declan pushed a breath through his nose. "I have a feeling that is going to be our million-dollar question."

Yes, Jax thought, the million-dollar question and his greatest fear—that this might not be about the specific victims, but the town as a whole.

The conversation stalled, the weight of those unanswered questions reflecting on everyone's faces. Jax consoled himself that at least Declan was less guarded than he'd been when he'd first walked in. Knowing that going forward they'd be able to work with the sheriff didn't eradicate the pressure Jax felt pressing in on him, but it would be a hell of a lot easier than having to find ways to work around him. For now, he'd take the wins where he could get them—and that was a win.

Because for everything that remained shrouded in secret or hidden in the dark, there was one thing that had become clear to him. Whatever came next, they were meant to face it together.

But not tonight.

Jax caught Logan's eye, giving him a barely detectable dip of his chin, knowing his friend would understand the request for him to shift the mood and bring this to an end.

"Well, on that note...*now* who needs a drink?" Logan pushed himself back from the table and made a beeline for the bar, the rest of them not far behind.

CHAPTER FORTY-FOUR

*T*he air cracked with an unfamiliar energy when Liv walked through the front door.

"Ivy?" she called, but the only response she received was a slight sputtering of lights from the house.

She traced the flow of energy and the soft glow of flickering light toward its source.

So much of the house had been renewed simply by their presence, and the greenhouse was no exception. Where once she wouldn't have been able to see through the foggy panes in the French doors, she now had a clear view. On the other side of the crystalline glass sat Ivy, facing away from her and encircled by flaming candles.

This close she could just make out the low hum of Ivy's voice. Suddenly the plants on the shelves and the different species of viny plants growing along the walls surrounding Ivy awoke to her sister's presence. The Wisteria that hung in heavy clusters from the roof swayed, and the butterfly-like petals quivered in recognition of her magick. Long tendrils of *Hedera* helix and jasmine began coasting against each other as they slowly made their way down the walls and flowed toward Ivy, rising and falling like tiny little waves heading to shore.

Within the circle, her sister continued to chant, causing a brusque shift in energy. Black wisps emerged from her, uncoiling into the air around her.

Immediately the green vines halted, retreating from her as the serpentine magick filled the air around Ivy and slithered across the invisible walls of her circle.

Her sister's hands reached out for the shoots of the magick, allowing the black wisps to wrap around her arms and coast over her skin. They reacted to her sister the way plant life reacted to her.

Liv stood there, frozen, watching her sister play with the unfamiliar magick, the essence of it making her chest tighten painfully. Or maybe it was her heart. Either way, it prompted her into action. But when she tried to open the door, she was met with the resistance of an invisible barrier pushing back on her.

It had to be from the circle Ivy had created. The vines that had recoiled from Ivy's magick still danced anxiously a safe distance from the circle. Liv focused her energy on a thicker shoot, urging it to do her bidding.

Through their earthen bond, she could feel its apprehension to get close to her sister's magick, but it didn't hesitate to follow her directions. The vine struck out like a whip, wrapping around one of the candles establishing Ivy's circle and yanking it out of place, extinguishing the flame and effectively forcing Ivy's circle closed.

It was a dangerous move, not unlike removing a plug from a socket by yanking the cord, but it was effective.

Ivy spun on her as the barrier evaporated, and she fell into the room. "Did you see that?" Ivy asked, her breath coming in little pants, her mismatched eyes wide. Proud, Liv realized. She was proud of the strange, dark magick she'd conjured. Liv's fear slowly mutated into anger, for her sister's naivety, for whoever had taught her to mess with that, and for herself, for being so wrapped up in her own life that she'd allowed this to happen.

"What the hell are you doing?" Liv snapped, as her eyes quickly roamed Ivy's set up, including the runes drawn on the floor in chalk. She rushed over and smudged them away with her shoe.

Liv faced her sister. "What was that magick?"

Ivy's brows drew together. "It was my magick."

"That was not your magick, nothing about that was natural. It certainly wasn't anything that comes from us, let alone something you should be messing around with."

Ivy scoffed. "Of course you'd think that." She shook her head in disbelief. "How stupid of me to hope that maybe this would be something I could share with you. That maybe you'd finally be proud of me." She flung a hand out, extinguishing the remaining candles and shouldering past Liv as she left the greenhouse and stormed up the stairs.

Liv ascended the stairs after her. "Where did you even learn how to do that?"

Ivy ignored her, blowing into her room. "Ivy, this isn't a fucking joke. You're messing with magick you don't understand. You could have hurt yourself, or someone else for that matter, using unfamiliar magick when you don't even know what the hell you're doing."

"And whose fault is that?" Ivy yelled as she yanked on the brass handles of her bureau drawers, tossing clothes around and slamming them closed again. "You were given every opportunity to learn your magick, and you were supposed to teach me. That was your job," she accused. "But instead, all you've ever done is force me to hide myself, and I'm sick of it!"

"I've tried to teach you, Ivy. Your magick is different, but it's not whatever the hell that was. Where did you learn that magick?" Liv demanded again. "Rett?" She blocked Ivy's path as she moved around the room.

Ivy laughed angrily. "You're nuts if you think I'm sharing anything with you anymore. I'm not going to risk you putting an end to the only opportunity I have to learn, and I don't owe you an explanation." She stepped around her.

"I'm sorry your plan to be the only one with magick is ruined. You had your chance to teach me, to include me in *my birthright*. But instead, you kept everything for yourself and forced me to hide who I am." She threw a duffle bag on to her bed and started furiously shoving things into it.

"Well, I'm done hiding. You can live this way if you want. Stuffing all your power down, afraid of what anyone might think, but I'm not. I can't do it anymore. And if I can't be free to be who I am here, I'll go to where I can be." Liv watched her sister storming around her room like a tiny tornado, trapped at the center, being sliced bit by bit by Ivy's verbal shrapnel.

She tried to keep up, tried to keep calm as her mind spun, littered with explanations—or were they excuses—and questions of her own. "Maybe I should have done things differently, but you don't remember how things were when you were younger. Yes, I had Grammy to teach me, but it was at a huge cost. Mom—she hated it, they fought about it until the day Valeria died. And then she resented me for it until *she* died. I just wanted—"

"Control! You just wanted control over me!" Ivy looked down at her phone and then yanked her bag off her bed and hooked it over her shoulder, pushing Liv out of the way as she stormed for the stairs.

"That's not true," Liv said chasing after Ivy again. "You're twisting everything. I know I'm not perfect, but I just wanted to give you more and better than what I had. I didn't know how to help mom without my magick. I just wanted to take care of you. I was trying, I *am* trying, that's why we came back here." The explanations felt weak and ineffective even to her ears.

"No!" Ivy rounded on her at the bottom of the stairs. "Don't you dare! Everything you've done has been for you! For you to have control. What *you* decide. If I'm happy enough for *you*. If my behavior was as good as *you* decided it should be. If *my* life was what you decided it should be. You didn't even ask me if I wanted to move here. Live in this house where *you* had so many memories and felt so at home."

Ivy's free arm swung around wildly as she gestured to the house and everything in it. "Meanwhile I'm surrounded by the ghost of every good thing you had to walk away from for me. You think I don't see it when you look at me? You were so worried about mom resenting me the way she did you, but all you've done is replace her, anyway. I see it every time I do something you don't approve of. Every time I make a mistake you have to clean up. With every one of my failures. I'm done. You're not my mom, and since I can't just be your sister, I won't be your burden anymore, either." Ivy turned and headed for the front door.

"Ivy, no. You've never been a burden to me. Please, at least tell me where you're going." When she didn't stop, Liv acted without thinking, switching the locks on the front door with her magick.

Ivy stopped in her tracks and glanced over her shoulder at her sister, the air snapping with their charged energy as their eyes locked, her Terrabella green eyes pleading with Ivy's mismatched ones.

They stood like that, suspended in a moment that felt just long enough that she dared think maybe...but the fragile hope she'd been building around her sister the last few weeks shattered like an explosion of glass as Ivy turned for the door.

Blackness yawned open where the door should've been, rippling like some kind of inky portal to nowhere, just ahead of Ivy.

The old house groaned in response, shaking in protest from foundation to roof shingles. The chandelier hanging in the entry way swayed on its long chain as Ivy walked under it and right through the front door, the portal crackling and snapping closed behind her.

Liv shook herself from her shock, unlocked and swung open the door, and flew outside. A desperate panic flooded her as Ivy reached the curb, where a motorcycle was already waiting. The driver looked like he was dressed in actual darkness, the wings of a crow peeking from the collar of his leather jacket. A blacked-out helmet obscured his identity, but she knew who it was. Rett took Ivy's bag from her and strapped it to his motorcycle as she climbed on behind him.

"Ivy please!" She tried one more time. Her voice broke on the realization that she was losing her sister. "Please." Tears began to slide down her face. "Please don't do this."

"Sorry Liv, I'm going to be with people who aren't trying to manage me, people who trust me and see me as more than a to-do list of things to fix. I'm going to figure this out by myself, for myself. So don't try to find me."

Rett leaned back, asking Ivy something she couldn't hear over the idling engine. A moment passed between them before Ivy nodded once and then they were pulling away from the curb.

Liv considered a million things she could do to stop the bike, but instead wrapped her arms around herself and fought hard to keep the tears at bay until she watched her sister disappear down the street.

JAX PULLED UP JUST IN TIME TO HEAR IVY'S PARTING SHOT AND TO SEE HER ride off. He considered chasing after the bike, but the cut of Liv's pain was so visceral—it may as well have been his own. He was out of his truck and to her just in time to catch her in his arms as she crumpled in on herself.

She curled into him, tucking her face into his neck. Her body shook gently from the weeping she fought to contain, but the hot tears that dropped from her cheeks and seeped into his skin flowed steadily as he carried her up the porch steps and back into her empty house.

CHAPTER FORTY-FIVE

*P*hysically, Liv hadn't moved from where Jax had laid her on the settee for the last hour, but mentally it felt like she'd run a marathon in that time.

Between the house and Jax, she hadn't needed to move. The house had lit the fireplace and had been cycling through all her favorite snacks delivered to her on silver trays. Between bringing her cups of tea, Jax had alternated between holding her through her silent contemplation and gently coaxing answers from her.

Now she was watching a pissed-off Jade, in a pair of sweats and an oversized t-shirt, with a sleeping Cori draped over her shoulder, as she paced a hole into the floor in front of the fireplace. Jade was doing her best to curtail her protective streak and be supportive, but it didn't take an empath to see what was going on inside her. She should appreciate her friend showing up for her hard moments, but she couldn't quite wade through the uncomfortable feeling of being a burden to get there.

"You didn't need to wake her up and come this late, you know?" She looked at a sleeping Cori slung over Jade's shoulder again.

"I told her that," Jax grumbled, returning from the kitchen with a third cup of tea she was sure her bladder couldn't handle. She also wasn't convinced he wouldn't try to follow her if she got up to use the restroom.

"Of course I did." Jade shifted Cori in her arms to get a better grip on her.

Did that mean she felt like she *had* to come? Liv picked apart Jade's words, even though it wasn't like Jade ever did anything she didn't want to do.

Jax handed Liv her tea and then walked over to his sister, crouching to smoothly transition Cori's little body from Jade into his arms. Cori roused only enough to bury her little face in her uncle's neck.

"I know you don't feel like talking right now." Jade sat down on the small couch next to her, scooting close enough to share Liv's blanket. "But I have to ask, did anything about the magick Ivy was using feel familiar?" Both her words and her expression were softer than usual.

"Jade," Jax snapped quietly from in front of the fireplace, "this shit can wait." The harsh look on his face was a contradiction to the way he was absently swaying with Cori in his arms.

"I don't like the idea any more than you." Jade spoke to Jax rather than her. "But come on, you have to admit, it makes sense. At least enough to explore the idea."

Jax glared at his sister as he shook his head at her so slightly it was barely more than a twitch.

"Well, I think you're letting your emotions cloud your judgment, and if you're not going to ask the hard questions, I will."

It felt like they were communicating in code to intentionally exclude her, and she was too tired to try to piece it together.

Liv cut Jade off before she could respond to whatever silent threat Jax had just made.

"Stop talking like I'm not here!" Her eyes flew to Cori and then closed once she was sure her outburst hadn't woken her. She let out a heavy sigh and fought to control herself. "I don't have the energy to decode your weird secret sibling language right now." She looked between them. "He's not my keeper," she was speaking to Jade, but she was reminding both of them. "This isn't the time to practice honing your subtlety skills Jade, just say whatever you need to say." Liv drooped back onto the couch, ignoring what she was pretty sure was the sound of Jax's back molars shattering.

"Fine." Jade muttered something under her breath that sounded a lot like *snippy when you're emotional,* but she gave Liv what she asked for. "The way you described the magick that you and Jax fought the night you were lured out to the cliffs sounds pretty similar to what you saw your sister using before she left, and the wards wouldn't have kept her out."

"No." Liv didn't hesitate. "We've had our issues, but my sister wouldn't try to take my power, let alone...I could have died."

"I'm not saying she wanted to do any of that, or even that she knew what would happen, just that, knowingly or unknowingly, maybe whoever did used her to get to you.

"She doesn't even know what happened that night. I never told her, and she never said anything either."

"And you don't find that a little odd? *Everyone in town felt the effects of your Tempeste Venefuror,* even if they didn't know what it was. You don't know where she goes when she leaves, or who she's with besides tall, dark, and dubious. Did you ever find out who that guy is?" Jade asked Jax.

"No. Not beyond a first name, Rett. I gave his name to Declan earlier. He said he'll look into him." Jax's displeasure was palpable.

Jade nodded, turning back to her. "I know you don't want to hear it, but it's something we have to consider. Not tonight, but soon." She stood up from the couch and reached to take Cori from Jax. "Not just for your sake, but for everyone in town."

She knew Ivy wasn't perfect, but reckless as she may have been as a teenager, it was a huge leap from that to what Jade was suggesting, and the ramifications of it...

The conversation alone felt wrong, and to consider it at all, a betrayal. Especially when they were finally getting to a place she'd been hoping for, for years. Every sacrifice was finally starting to pay off with the life they were just beginning to settle into and finally feeling like sisters... even if Ivy had just blown that to shreds. Liv had to believe she'd come back. She wouldn't give up on her sister, not after all they'd been through. Ivy would come home once she blew off some steam.

She followed Jade to the front door. "I hope I'm wrong, I really do," she said as she expertly balanced Cori in one arm and opened the door with the other before Liv could open it for her. "But people don't change," she added as if every one of her thoughts had been displayed on her face. She understood why Jade thought that—hell, she'd spent years believing it herself. But she'd learned better since they'd come home, and not just because of what she'd begun to build with Ivy, but also what she started to build in herself.

Liv placed a hand on Jade's arm, stopping her before she could walk out. "Thank you for wanting to take care of me. Maybe I'll have to eat my words. But," she stroked Cori's silky red hair from her face, "people can change, and when they're people we love, they deserve the benefit of the doubt." She looked into her friend's ocean-blue eyes, "They at least deserve the opportunity to try."

A long moment stretched between them as Jade considered her. "You're going to keep sacrificing pieces of yourself until there is nothing left." Her words were slow and deliberate, not angry, but adamant. "Some people only know how to take, and I don't want to stand idly by and watch that happen to you. But I also can't make you see it."

She angled her head to the side to look at her daughter's sleeping face, resting on her shoulder. "Some of us don't have the luxury of giving away any more pieces. I don't." The last two words were a whisper, as if they were meant more for herself than Liv. "I don't know how you possibly can either." Jade kissed her cheek and disappeared through the door.

CHAPTER FORTY-SIX

She stared into the swirling, warm liquid as she poured it into the amber glass jar, secured the wick, and set the candle in line with all the others. She'd been doing the same thing absentmindedly for the last few hours. Trying to keep herself from wondering where her sister was, who she was with, and if she was okay, for the hundredth time since she woke up.

"Liv, honey." A warm hand settled on her shoulder. She had to blink a few times before Quinn's face came fully into focus. "Maybe we should just take a little break from the candle-making for now." Quinn gently removed an empty jar from her hand.

"I'm—"

"Fine. We know." Jade glowered down at her from the other side of the greenhouse where she was flipping through an old book Jax had found in Havenhouse.

"Mhhmm," Liv hummed, her disbelief evident—and founded. "I'm just saying, you guys don't have to keep interrupting your lives to check on me."

They'd been doing this for the last week, finding excuses to drop by when Jax was at work, and they weren't the only ones.

Yesterday not even twenty minutes after Jax had left for work, Lynn and Warren had appeared in the back gardens where she was drinking her tea —and had yet to put on a bra— to take their turn on the pity train. Logan had come by to bring her tacos twice—which she'd minded a lot less.

But even Mac had shown up once, pretending to need to borrow some pruning shears. He'd brought her a bottle of that firewater he called whisky, and then left—without the shears.

Maybe it sounded ungrateful, and she knew how lucky she was to have people who cared enough about her to want to check in. There had been a lot of time she hadn't had that in her life. But this was starting to feel like pity, and like they didn't think Ivy was coming back.

"We know you're okay," Quinn started.

"No, we know you're going to say you're okay," Jade corrected her. "Also, if it makes you feel better, we really do need those candles. We're out again. We're almost out of everything, actually. People have been going a little feral, and I'm afraid of what they'll do to the store if we don't get something in stock soon. But I need you to be careful how much sad girl energy you're pumping into those things. Those crazy horny candles you accidentally made a few weeks back were one thing, I mean you should see some of the names we have on the waitlist for those." Jade silently mouthed words that looked a lot like *Mrs. Dottie,* but Liv chose to forgo clarification. "But inadvertently depressing a whole town via aromatherapy would be a business death sentence."

"What she means is that we care about you, and that it isn't going out of our way to check on you when you're going through it."

"Yeah, that's what I said...more or less."

"Less, much *much* less. How are we even friends?" Quinn lifted her hands and let them drop down to her sides again.

"Because I gave you a job, your first one at least, and shelter, *and* I don't charge you pet rent even though I know you've got a borderline zoo up there."

"I would never!" Quinn clutched at her chest in mock offense. "I don't believe in cages," she whispered to Liv behind her hand.

"Whatever, I'm never going to get the smell of incense and owl out of there anyway. I'm already calling it a total loss."

"Owl?" Liv latched onto that little detail.

"Yeah, this chick has a pet freaking owl! No wonder you were living in your car, I'm the only idiot that would rent to you," Jade said as she walked from shelf to shelf, taking lids off jars and inspecting their contents.

"It was a van. It had a bed! Kind of. And Striga isn't a pet, he just likes finding me on a regular basis and sleeping where I happen to live."

"Semantics. What ever happened to that van?"

"I lent it to a cousin, or maybe it was a friend of a cousin?" Quinn cocked her head in thought and then shrugged it off.

"How do you not know who has your car, how will you get it back when you want it? Or when I evict you?" Jade asked.

"Meh, usually it just shows up when I need it, and the few times it didn't, all it took was a little scrying."

"Oh. Well then. Sounds like a fool-proof system to me. Lo-Jack for witches." Jade shook her head as she took the lid off another jar and lifted it to her face.

"I wouldn't," Liv raised a hand to Jade in warning, "do that," she finished, even though she was too late.

"Oh, burning ball sack, what the hell is that?" Jade slammed the lid back down on the jar. "Why would you keep it?"

"Valerian root." Liv winced. "It's good for anxiety and sleep. It's just not ready yet."

"Ready? Ready for what? Permanently eliminating a person's desire to ever smell anything again? Because it's ready. I'd say it passed ready and entered the toxic stage."

"You know there is a theory that if you don't like the scent of an herb or oil, then it's a potential indicator that it's exactly what your body needs."

"Oh, now *you're* a plant expert, too?" Jade rolled her eyes at Quinn. "Well, what stinky thing do you have in here to turn off a person's libido? Let's get some of that in bulk for this one."

Liv couldn't fight the laugh that bubbled up her throat, listening to her friends' banter. The ease with which they moved around her house so comfortably, like it was theirs too. How Quinn had taken her shoes off at some point, and Jade had found snacks somewhere. The familiarity of it soothed her, made her feel like they were settling in, like they weren't going to leave. She was grateful for the distraction…and for the idea Quinn had just given her.

AN HOUR LATER AND ALONE AGAIN, THE ONLY SOUND IN THE HOUSE WAS the sound of books hitting the ground as Liv yanked them from their shelves, shook them out by their covers, and dropped them to the floor when she didn't find what she was looking for. She tore open drawers she'd already opened twice, shuffling things around chaotically. "Come on, I know it's here somewhere."

Spinning away from one set of shelves to another, she shoved her arm deep inside a line of small drawers, feeling around blindly until she reached the last one.

Finally. Tucked all the way against a corner, her fingers grazed rough wood. She withdrew the small box and flipped the lid open. "Ah ha!" she shouted, pulling out a small pillar of smoky quartz that hung from a silver chain.

Liv shoved the crystal into her pocket and dragged the heavy chaise from the middle of the room and closer to the tallest set of shelves. Balancing on the curving headrest, she stretched to reach the top shelf and slid the tips of her fingers along the edge as far as she could reach without losing her balance and crashing to her death, or at least having a lot of explaining to do. Something she realized she would probably have either way.

She nicked the corner of a thin piece of paper and the map fluttered down in front of her, landing on the chaise.

Doing her best to avoid crushing any of the old books she'd already treated so badly, she hopped down. "Sorry." She wasn't sure if she was apologizing to the books or if they were considered part of the house by default. She really needed to invest some more time in understanding the house's magick.

But that would have to wait.

Liv snagged the map and raced around the house, grabbing the last few things she needed before heading out into the garden.

It had been years since her Grammy had taught her to scry, but she trusted herself to figure it out. Plus, finding Ivy should be even easier since they shared blood, not just with each other, but also with the magick flowing all around her.

She could have kicked herself for not thinking of it sooner, but when Quinn had mentioned scrying, she'd known it was her next step.

Liv had already argued with herself about it being intrusive, considering her sister had been pretty clear about wanting space. Then she'd reasoned that just knowing where Ivy was staying would be harmless. Only meant to give her peace of mind.

Even she didn't really buy that lie, and neither would Jax or any of the others. Which was why she'd waited for a rare moment alone. As much as Liv appreciated having her friends there, having Jax there, she knew there were still some things a person needed to deal with on their own—and for her, Ivy would always be one of those things.

She spread the map out on the ground where the light from the nearly full moon could shine across it. Her hands shook slightly as she set a candle on the map then uncorked a small glass bottle of dried Yarrow. The gold kernels fell into an uneven circle around the candle.

After lighting the candle, she took the pendulum and a needle from her pocket and pricked her finger, letting her blood build and then drip onto the map. The droplets hit the parchment haphazardly before soaking in.

Holding the end of the pendulum chain lightly in her fingers, she let the rest of the chain drop to its full length, the weight of the crystal dangling above the map. The shard of smoky quartz swayed gently in the moonlight. Rich tendrils of gray and brown were mesmerizing as they appeared to spin within the opaque stone. Liv let the movement lull her as she took a few deep, calming breaths. Once she felt her heartbeat begin to slow, she let her attention drift to her mind's eye.

"Blood of mine, the tie that binds,"

Liv reached for Ivy and willed her location to come to her.

"Ostende soror, my path unwinds,
by crystals gleam, guide my gaze true,

Ostende soror, her location I view."

She held the image of her sister in the center-point of her consciousness and let the old words of her ancestors become a chant.

"Ostende soror, ostende soror, ostende soror."

Vaguely aware of the weight of the crystal swaying at the end of the chain, Liv watched as it slowly increased in speed before pulling downward and going still. Her vision focused on where the crystal indicated Ivy was.

How close she was, maybe had been this whole time. Not within Havenwood, but still.

She reminded herself that she was just scrying to see where her sister was for peace of mind but that lasted about thirty seconds before fear for Ivy's wellbeing took over and she grabbed her keys, typed the address into her phone GPS and was heading for the front door. The lock flipped over just ahead of her.

"Unless you want me to start mopping with bleach, I suggest you rethink playing games with me right now, you obtrusive old nag." She didn't love having to threaten the house, but it did the trick.

She threw open the door, prepared to run to the car, and then stopped at the sight of her freshly rebuilt porch. Jax…she looked back into the house, caught on the precipice of her old life and her new one. And she made a decision.

JAX GLANCED UP FROM HIS BLUEPRINTS TOWARD THE SUN AS IT DROPPED off the cliffs at the edge of town, painting the sky with bright oranges and pinks that faded into soft blues and purples. He loved the way every Southern California sunset was like a new watercolor, all painted by the same artist. Each one was different, but unmistakably belonged only here.

He didn't want to be stuck at work seeing it, though. He wanted to be wrapped around Liv, watching it with her.

He spent most of his days in some state of wanting to be near her. Anxious to get back to her when he was on a job site. Desperate to be inside her immediately after finishing. Wanting to cook every meal for her and take care of any need she might have before she had it.

On any given day he had to fight pretty hard to rein in those desires as it was, but it had been harder this last week. If she wasn't distracted by worry, she was lost in thought, replaying her sister's harsh words. She'd accidentally projected some of them into him a couple nights ago when she was sleeping in his arms, and the pain he'd felt through those memories had been enough that he'd wanted to break something in helplessness.

He also knew it was probably time to call off the rotation of check-ins and visitors before it pushed her too far.

"Hey!" he called up to Logan. His friend's head peeked up over the ridge of the Dade's roof, where he was replacing tiles that had broken during that "freak storm they had recently," as Mrs. Dade had put it. But before he could tell Logan he was calling it a day, his cell phone rang. The screen lit up with Declan's name.

Jax hesitated for just a moment, pleading with the Spirit that it wasn't another body. "Hello?" He did his best to use his polite voice.

"Um," Declan paused, "I think you might want to get over to your place."

"My place? Why? Something wrong with my house?" Jax's brows drew together as he ticked through possibilities in his mind.

"Well, it's not your house, it's Liv's, and I don't really know how to describe what's happening."

What the fuck did that mean? "Well, where's Liv? Is she okay?" He felt the beat of his heart accelerating all the way in his throat.

"I'm thinking she's not here, and that maybe that's at least part of the issue, I don't kn—"

Jax hung up before Declan could finish talking and started running.

CHAPTER FORTY-SEVEN

ifteen minutes later, Liv's car was steadily climbing the winding roads on the opposite cliffside from Havenhouse. She didn't know what she'd expected the neighborhood harboring her sister to look like, but it most definitely hadn't included opulent mansions with ocean views.

That wasn't true, she did know what she'd expected—something like the shady neighborhoods she'd pulled Ivy out of in the past.

And what did that say about her, that she still expected the worst from her sister?

Liv shook her head. Thoughts like that would have to wait. She gripped the steering wheel tighter. Before she could try to heal their past, she'd need to find her. That was all that mattered—she just needed to find Ivy.

The car continued to climb, turning up yet another steep and narrow road, finally ending at a set of iron gates. They sat wide open, as if they'd been expecting company.

She didn't give herself time to think, just accelerated across the threshold. Tall Italian cypress trees interspersed with in-ground lighting guided her down a private gravel road that turned into an arching driveway made of some sort of expensive stone, all ending in front of a modern mansion.

Several other cars were parked in front of the grand house, most of them of the expensive variety. Quickly, she exited her car and headed for the front walk, trying to outrun the nerves that were creeping up on her.

The lanky man leaning against one of the columns that lined the large front steps didn't bother to acknowledge her until she was standing in front of him on the marble landing in front of the enormous set of doors. His relaxed posture didn't change, but a smile crept across his thin lips as his eye rose to meet hers. She wasn't sure if it was meant to be welcoming, but if so, he was seriously missing the mark with the major "Creepy Thin Man" vibe he was giving off.

Liv lifted her chin, ready to blow through the man, if need be. "I'm here to see my sister."

Creepy Thin Man looked back down at the coin he was spinning between his fingers. "Yeah, Ivy should be on the grounds at the back of the house."

It took her a second to process that he'd known who her sister was, who she was, without her telling him, but she moved past, partly not wanting to risk him changing his mind before she got inside, and partly wanting to get away from him as fast as possible.

The doors creaked open before she could open them herself, welcoming her into an opulent and notably empty sitting and dining room. "You're just in time, Liv," Creepy Thin Man called after her as she walked in, and the heavy doors slammed shut behind her.

In front of her, shiny marble floors reflected the light from an obnoxious crystal chandelier, ending at a wall of glass that had been pushed aside, opening up to a terrace. A terrace that no doubt overlooked a pristine patio and the back gardens where she'd been told she could find Ivy.

Liv's steps echoed on the marble as she descended a few small steps into the large living area, passing ostentatious pillars and furnishings, heading for the terrace.

Sticking close to the walls, Liv used the shadows to peer over the railing and down into the gardens. The grass gave way to stone pavers that created a circular space positioned close to the cliff's edge, a space that the builders had probably intended for al fresco dining, and not what she was looking at right now.

Unlit torches created a semi-circle around a large altar draped in deep velvet and littered with objects she couldn't make out through the dim light. *What in the Spirit?* She leaned forward trying to get a better look, her fingers wrapped tightly around the wrought iron spindles that dropped from the balcony railing,

Drumbeats began beating from somewhere below, joined by the faint sound of chanting that grew louder as figures wrapped in white robes slowly filed out onto the grass surrounding the altar. Her pulse pounded so loudly in her ears that it drowned out the drums as she scanned the crowd in earnest for the familiar form of Ivy, torn between wanting to find her and desperately hoping she didn't, that her sister hadn't gotten caught up with whatever this was.

Plumes of smoke rose from the crowd, carrying the scent of incense up to her as a man cloaked in black approached the helm of the group, stopping next to the altar.

The drumbeats increased in intensity. Torches surged to life, their flames reaching high above his head, sending embers snapping into the inky night sky. Liv's eyes widened, her muscles tensing as if ready to flee, but she remained rooted to the spot, despite the growing dread coursing through her veins.

Slowly, the mass of at least sixty spread into a large circle, encompassing the altar and taking up the majority of the yard. The one in the black cloak, the apparent leader, invoked the elements one by one, beginning with Air. But rather than an object being placed to represent the element, a man stepped forward, pushing the hood of his cloak back from his head, and moved to the Eastern point in the circle.

The leader of the group turned toward the altar, placing a large chalice at the center. Thanks to the light from the brightly flaming torches, Liv could see the jeweled athame the man lifted off the altar, and she suddenly wished she couldn't see what was coming. Her breath quickened, and she pressed a hand to her chest, feeling the frantic beat of her heart beneath her ribs.

The black-cloaked man carried the athame and chalice to the man—Air—and she watched as he took the athame from the leader, the sharp blade glinting in the torchlight. She flinched when Air slid the blade in one swift stroke across his palm.

The process was repeated three more times. A dark-haired man took the place of Water at the western point, followed by a red-haired woman who sliced her palm while standing at the southern spot for Fire.

Liv felt a moment of relief when Earth was invoked and a tall man stepped forward to claim the northern point—relief that quickly vanished as the leader invoked Spirit.

Her heart sank as the unmistakable form of her sister stepped into the center, marking the fifth and final element.

The chanting continued, seeming to grow in intensity, ringing through Liv's entire being and freezing her in place as her sister accepted the athame. Disbelief coursed through her veins as she watched Ivy slit her palm and let her blood—a gift of the Earth and the essence of all the Terrabella's before her— flow into the chalice. And though it was her sister's blood, she felt every drop that Ivy so carelessly gave away.

As the crimson lifeforce trickled into the chalice, mixing with the others, a shiver of recognition ran through her. The dark magick she had excised from the Earth, not once but twice now, surged back to her memory, its noxious energy now unmistakable in the air.

Liv's whole body shuddered, an involuntary response, as overwhelming helplessness and sudden understanding crashed over her like a tidal wave.

A potent mixture of emotions flowed through Liv and consumed her thoughts as she struggled to reconcile the sight before her with a stubborn denial, a refusal to accept that her sister would knowingly take part in the kind of dark magick that had led to the death of at least two people, and could have led to her own.

She had no choice but to cling to the hope that there must be some mistake, some misunderstanding, anything to explain Ivy's actions, while deep inside her, a growing sense of dread whispered about betrayal.

And that she should not have come here alone.

The leader returned to the altar when all five had given their blood, where he dipped the athame into the chalice and then cut into his palm.

Magick filled the air, engulfing Liv, drowning her in an invisible mire that no one else reacted to. It smelled of death—not recent death, but the depths of a long-forgotten crypt. It was something beyond decay, the complete absence of life altogether.

Wrong.

It was so wrong. But familiar, if significantly more potent.

Then Liv was choking. It dropped her to her knees before she thought to react. The vile magick permeated her nose, her mouth, her very skin, sinking in and filling her insides until she was cold, so cold.

Desperate, she reached for her power. For that source of life, that vitality, that living force within her. It bloomed in answer to her call, branching out from within, forcing the wrongness from her body.

Light and heat flared from below and then suddenly everything ceased. The torches extinguished, the chanting voices cut off and the dark magick was gone. Not with a slow withdrawal, but just *gone.*

Liv pulled herself up to stand again, drinking in the cool night air and allowing her magick to warm her from the inside out.

Once she'd caught her breath, she peeked over the terrace railing. All the robes had been discarded, leaving beautifully dressed people milling about below. The scene had completely transformed in a matter of moments. The torches that had blazed one moment and extinguished the next were lit again, now offering a subtle warmth to the ambiance. Wait-staff emerged with trays of champagne and hors d'oeuvres. Light music began, and suddenly the scene was nothing more than a cocktail party at a cliffside mansion.

What the hell was this? Where was her sister?

No sooner had she asked herself the question than a peel of laughter drew her attention to the corner of the garden. Liv's eyes landed on her sister, standing amongst a group of strangers, champagne in her hand and laughter on her lips.

"I ASSUME THIS ISN'T NORMAL EVEN BY THIS TOWN'S STANDARDS?" Declan asked as Jax jogged past him and into the house.

Every light in Havenhouse flashed on and off, joined by the cacophony of all the windows and doors repeatedly opening and slamming shut. Even the roof tiles were chattering from above, joining the chaotic rhythm. It was clear Liv wasn't there, but that was the only thing he could figure out through the house's meltdown.

"Enough!" Jax yelled at the house.

Everything stopped.

"Why didn't you try that?" Logan—who'd followed him from the site —asked Declan.

"I need you to tell me what happened. Where did she go?" Jax asked.

Declan peeked into the house from the safety of the newly finished porch before tentatively entering. "I wish I had more to tell you. I was just patrolling and saw whatever the hell *that* was going on." He and Logan followed Jax as he walked through the house.

"Give me something," Jax demanded hoarsely, fighting to remain calm.

His stomach dropped when he saw the mess in the library, but the flash of the hall light stole his attention. It flicked on and off again, the signal echoed by the light farther down the hall.

"I don't have any more to tell you. I didn't come in until you got here. This shit can't be normal, right?"

"He's not talking to you, man. He talking to the house."

"Oh. Of course," Declan muttered as they followed the path of flickering lights until they stopped in the greenhouse.

The doors that led out to the garden opened in front of them. Jax scanned the small patio, looking for what the house was trying to show him. A subtle movement under the old oak tree just off the patio caught his eye. "Fucking stubborn witch!" he swore as he took in the supplies she'd left out. He ripped the fluttering map off the ground, not caring when everything on top of it scattered. A white piece of paper was whisked into the air, pausing briefly in front of him before it started to drift back down toward the ground. Jax snatched it out of the air before it could.

Jax,
I have to talk to Ivy.
She's my sister, and this is something I need to do on my own. I'm
sorry.
Don't worry...I'll be home soon, and you can show me how mad
you are then.

I love you,

~L

Jax had known what she'd done the moment he'd seen the map. He could even understand why. What he didn't understand was why she needed to do it *alone.*

But he was damn sure about to find out.

IVY LOOKED BEAUTIFUL IN A GLITTERING SAPPHIRE GOWN THAT SWISHED around her body as she chatted carelessly with those around her. These were the people her sister had been talking about when she'd left. The people who trusted her. Who didn't try to manage her. Ivy had no clue what this group was involved in, because there was no mistaking that the magick she'd just felt was what had lured her out to the cliffs that night.

Despite any issues between them, she knew Ivy wouldn't have knowingly put her in that kind of danger.

The only thing that was clear to her in this mess was that this time Ivy had gotten herself into something not just over her head, but above Liv's as well. What Jade had said to her the night Ivy left came back to her. She knew her friend was right—Ivy was taking little pieces of her. But even knowing that, she just wasn't able to give up on her little sister.

Liv had never hesitated to go headfirst into the fire for the sake of her sister before, and she wasn't going to start now— not when it mattered most.

She turned toward the staircase at the far edge of the terrace and made her way down into the throngs of people below.

She slipped through the crowd slowly, braced for a confrontation but making her way to her sister without incident. Her sense of discomfort grew with each vaguely familiar face she spotted within the groups of strangers.

Ivy's eyes caught hers over the shoulder of the person she was talking to. They flared with recognition and then narrowed. Liv slipped back out of the way and waited as Ivy politely excused herself from whoever the hell she'd been talking to. She could hardly recognize her sister, from the clothes down to her mannerisms.

"What the hell are you doing here? How did you even find me?" Ivy hissed as she slipped her arm through Liv's and led her to a more deserted corner of the garden.

"What am *I* doing? Ivy, what the hell *is* this? What have you gotten yourself mixed up in? Never mind, tell me on the way. We need to get out of here."

Ivy yanked her arm out of Liv's grasp, her champagne splashing with the force. Her face twisted up into a sneer. "I'm not going anywhere. Especially not with you."

"Ivy, you don't understand. These people—"

"These people accept me for who I am! They don't force me to hide myself or my power. They aren't threatened by me or what I'm capable of."

"I'm not afraid of you, Ivy. And I never wanted you to hide yourself! These people don't value you. Do you even know what you just took part in? You gave away a part of yourself and you don't even know what for. I've seen what these people are doing—it's much worse than a little slit in the palm, and it certainly wasn't willing."

"You don't know what you're talking about. Just because I'm not dancing in the forest with my friends doesn't mean what I'm doing is wrong. Maybe if you weren't so judgmental you could see there are more ways to do magick than the one way you think is best."

"Ivy, do you remember the woman who came to see us when we first got here? The one with the missing husband? I think he was part of this group. And do you know what they did to him?"

Ivy's brows drew together slightly, and she opened her mouth to answer, but Liv never got the chance to find out what she would've said.

"Ah, Ivy, there you are! I've been looking for you." A man in an expensive tux approached them, placing a hand on the middle of Ivy's back.

CHAPTER FORTY-EIGHT

*T*he man directed a gracious smile at Liv. "And who is this lovely companion you've brought to our little gathering?"

Ivy looked up at the man and then back to her sister. "This is Liv, my sister."

"Of course you are. I'm delighted to have you join us, Liv. Ivy has mentioned you a time or two." His blonde hair was slicked back with so much product the distorted light from nearby torches reflected in it. Despite the well-tailored suit and the fine lines that creased around his brown eyes when he smiled at her, the attempt to charm and disarm her fell very short.

How did everyone here not see right through his too-perfect mask when it so poorly hid the darkness that hovered just below the surface? His appearance, like this party, was nothing but a mask to cover up the dark magick she'd witnessed. Why couldn't Ivy see that?

The man extended a manicured hand toward her. "I am Ash."

She didn't take his hand.

"So, Liv." Ash tucked his unshaken hand into the pocket of his trousers in a smooth movement. "What brings you to our little party?" he continued with a smile, blowing right past her slight.

"Actually, Ash," Liv returned the saccharine smile, "I need to speak with Ivy alone if you don't mind."

Ivy's posture tightened. "We don't have anything left to discuss, Liv. You should go."

Ash lifted his hands in front of him, "Now, that's no way to treat our guest, let alone your sister. Liv, you are more than welcome to stay and enjoy the evening. Ivy has plenty of selections in her closet if you'd like to change into something more appropriate for the occasion."

Her closet? Ash's brow ticked up ever so slightly, letting her know he knew exactly what he'd said. She did not doubt that every word out of his mouth was carefully considered and intentional. For now, she'd do her best to play along.

"Considering her closet is back home in Havenwood, I'm not sure how that would help me," Liv said, her small fake laugh underlining the obviousness of her retort. "No, I'll stick with my clothes, if it's all the same to you. I'm not here for the party, just to speak with *my* sister. I wouldn't want anyone getting the wrong idea."

"And what idea would that be?" Ivy asked through gritted teeth.

"That I'm hiding behind something as flimsy as fancy clothes, using it as a façade to cover up who I really am or what my true intentions are," Liv answered, not taking her eyes off Ash.

Ash blew passed her obvious insinuation. "Whatever makes you most comfortable." The arrogance was astounding, almost as if he believed his own farce. "You mentioned Havenhouse," he went on, and she could have sworn his pupils dilated at just the mention of the house. "I've heard it's quite the *unique* place. I hope to see it for myself someday soon."

Over my dead body, Liv thought. Though she was sure the house would make good use of the free rein she would give it to fuck with Ash. The image of him being swallowed up by the earth, or having a trip and fall face-first "accident" into the Blackthorne tree, was the true source of the wicked little grin that curved her lips.

"Yes, the gardens and forests around the house are also quite special, especially out near the cliffs. Are you familiar with them as well?" She alluded to the night she'd been drawn out there by magick she was sure was related to whatever the hell was going on here, and they both knew it.

"I can't say that I am," Ash lied smoothly, turning to grab two glasses of champagne off the tray of a passing server. "Anyway," he continued, handing one glass to Ivy, "feel free to enjoy the festivities, explore, mingle. I think you'll be pleasantly surprised by what you find. From what your sister has told me, you have great power of your own. Who knows, you might even want to join us." He placed a hand on Ivy's lower back, making like he was going to lead her away with him before Liv had even gotten a chance to talk with her.

Her admittedly poor attempt at playing the game with Ash wasn't working. The man wasn't going to give her an opportunity to be alone with Ivy, but she couldn't let him lead her sister away. Not now that she'd seen what she had and knew what she did.

Simply talking to Ivy like she'd planned wasn't going to be enough. She needed to get Ivy out of there. But if just talking was this difficult, getting Ivy to leave—possibly against her will—seemed impossible. But maybe...if she could hold on long enough, Jax would find her note after work and come looking for them. All she had to do was keep Ivy here until then, which meant she needed to hold onto Ash's attention.

She cursed herself inwardly for not just texting him. For insisting on doing this by herself.

"And does this open-door policy extend beyond the sisters of your newest... initiates," Liv rushed to say before they could walk away, "or to anyone who stumbles across your path? Like maybe Jeremiah Rouche? Or Caleb Hendricks?"

Ash's synthetic smile faltered. "I'm afraid I don't know those names."

"That's odd. Both of them were recently found murdered, not far from here actually. Their bodies were left mutilated in ritual sites that looked strikingly similar to the circle you led tonight." Her words were light, not carrying the weight of the accusation they so clearly implied.

Ivy's face paled, "Liv!" she snarled under her breath and stepped toward her.

Ash laughed loudly this time, the sound practiced and rigid, as he pulled Ivy back closer to him. "That's alright, Ivy. No need to feel defensive of me. Olivia is just being the best *half*-sister she knows how to be."

His attempt to weaponize their relationship didn't go unnoticed.

"Olivia, my dear, such an overactive imagination. This is simply a coven of like-minded individuals who were given some small amount of magick, but who were never as fortunate as you were to be taught what they truly are. People who were never shown how to harness what the Spirit saw fit to bestow upon them, and who were never given the privilege of living somewhere as special as Havenwood."

This was pointless and she was done with Ash's spinning of the facts.

Fuck it.

"Cut the act, Ash." Liv stepped closer to them. "I can see everything you're trying so hard to hide. All of this," she gestured toward the party and then to him, "is nothing more than a pretty guise used to hide the truth of what you really are and what you've been doing here from the people you lure and con. But I'm not going to let my sister be tricked by your pretty words and deadly lies."

Ash leaned into her sister. "Ivy, my dear, I think I am beginning to see what you were dealing with."

Liv ignored his words and looked at her sister. "Ivy, please. I will explain everything once we're home. But I need to get you out of this place. And I especially need to get you away from this man. Please."

Ivy let Ash guide her in taking a step back from Liv. "Her lack of confidence in your ability to make your own decisions is becoming clearer by the moment."

"Don't listen to him, Ivy." Liv's voice broke on the plea. She could see her sister withdrawing from her, physically and emotionally. "He's manipulating you. You're nothing more than a means to an end for him."

"And what am I to you? Besides just another burden, another person to clean up after."

"That's not true, you know it's not. I'm your sister. We're the only family either of us has left."

Ivy opened her mouth to speak but Ash beat her to it. "Well, *that's* not exactly true, is it Ivy?" Again, he didn't give her sister the chance to answer. "You know, I think you were right, dear," he pulled her still more tightly into his side. "Olivia seems a bit on edge tonight. Or maybe she's simply too closed-minded to be part of what we have here. Either way, I think it's best if you go now." The edge to his words gave away the frustration he was trying to suppress.

Good.

"I'm not leaving here without you." Liv took a couple of steps forward to close the space Ash was gradually putting between her and her sister.

Ivy looked around her as a few people hovering nearby began to take notice of the tension building between them. "Just go, Liv."

Ash noticed the growing crowd, too. He looked over Liv's shoulder, nodding to someone behind her, but she was too afraid to look away from Ivy to see who he had signaled.

Rough hands wrapped around Liv's arms and started to pull her away. "Let's not cause a scene now, beautiful," the voice of Creepy Thin Man whispered near her ear.

Ivy just stood there watching as another man moved toward Liv. She turned from the indifference in her sister's eyes and summoned the heavy limb of a nearby tree. It slashed through the air, knocking the wind from her would-be captor before dragging his body back and trapping him against its trunk.

A quick burst of oppressive magick crashed against her, knocking her to the ground. Liv looked up to see Ivy step toward her. "I want you to leave." She enunciated each word as she moved closer and closer. Ivy's magick snapped out again, the chaotic energy missing its mark, but she still held Liv's dumbfounded stare with unapologetic defiance radiating from her body. She'd been practicing with someone. Still, Liv could see the hint of uncertainty in Ivy's eyes, she could feel it in the frenetic energy clinging to the magick her sister was wielding.

"That's enough." Ash recalled Ivy, who went to him with hardly any hesitation.

Creepy Thin Man yanked Liv to her feet, and a second asshole grabbed her other arm a moment later. She jerked, trying to break free. "Ivy!" Liv called out to her sister as Ash began leading her away. Ivy glanced back, and Liv thought she caught a flicker of regret in her sister's eyes. But before she could be sure, a red-haired man stepped between them.

Panicking as she lost sight of her sister, Liv released a wild shot of magick that jolted the ground beneath them and sent the men holding her arms tumbling away from her.

A few shocked cries came from people nearby. But the red-haired man wasn't fazed. He sent a sharp hot blast of magick that flew right past her head. A warning, she realized, as he followed it up with a quick succession of three small balls of fire. Liv batted away the man's weaker magick, but it was still driving her back little by little. *Shit, shit, shit.*

Creepy Thin Man and his friend recovered and were closing in as Liv focused on deflecting the fire magick. The tree swung out to assist her again, but in a flash, the red-haired man had the tree engulfed in flames.

Liv gasped in surprise which quickly turned to anger. She tunneled into herself and the earth around her and directed the force at the red-haired man. Her magick barreled into him, rocking him with the force of a small earthquake. He crumpled to the ground between the other two men, but the use of force had cost her, too.

This had been a mistake, coming here alone. And now when Jax found her note, there was a good chance it would be too late.

The fire drew the attention of more partygoers, and suddenly she felt like she was being circled by sharks. Then, like the choice to throw the first stone, someone in the crowd decided to test their abilities against her. The small shock of power did little more than sting, but it was followed by another, and then another from somewhere else.

Suddenly it was all she could do to fend off the barrage of magicks that rained down on and around her. Each small strike chipped away at her defenses, zapping her strength and resolve a little at a time. The ground rippled at her command, knocking some of the coven members off their feet. She hardly had a moment to breathe when the men from before were there again, grabbing her and shoving her roughly toward the ground. Then her head snapped up at a sound that took her breath away.

"You shouldn't touch what isn't yours." The gravel of Jax's voice reached her a moment before a warm shot of air blew past her, and Creepy Thin Man spun sideways, landing roughly in some gravel twenty feet away.

"Jax!" she gasped his name in relief. And it wasn't just him, but all of them. Even Declan had come.

They'd come for her. To help her bring her sister home. Her heart swelled with gratitude, and then all hell broke loose.

CHAPTER FORTY-NINE

"*D*idn't you hear the man?" Liv turned just as Logan appeared behind the other asshole who was still trying to push her down. "Hands off," he growled. One moment the man was there, pressing into her back, the next he was flying into the crowd of people surrounding them like a bowling ball, sending them scattering like pins.

Logan pulled her up to stand. "You okay?"

"I'm fine, just a little drained," Liv answered as she took in a deep breath.

"I'm glad to hear it, but may I suggest a different choice of words when Jax asks?" Liv stared at Logan—only he could make jokes at a time like this. He shrugged. "Just a suggestion."

Spotting Jax taking on a group of people in cocktail attire, she took off across the grass, Logan beside her.

A ring of fire drew their attention—Jade stood in the center, surrounded by several coven members, using the flames to keep them at bay. "Keep going," Logan ordered, making a beeline for the fire and the witch within.

Liv kept running, only slowing to look back when a thunderous roar echoed behind her. Logan's body surged with magick, muscles swelling as raw power radiated from him—no longer just a witch, but a force of nature, more beast than man. Liv almost felt sorry for whoever was on the receiving end of his wrath. *Almost.*

"Nice of you to join us," Quinn said with a smirk as a bolt of lightning lit up the sky, but Liv's eyes were locked on one person.

Jax's hand wrapped around the back of her neck as he pulled her into him possessively. She smiled up at him. "You came for me."

"I told you I always would." He kissed her hard and fast before shoving her out of the way of a small ball of magick.

"But I'm very unhappy with you right now, Dandy," he said as he slapped away more magick. "We said together, remember?"

"I know. But it's not like all of this was part of my plan when I went to talk to my sister." She waved one arm at the chaos all around them while she called to the vines that climbed over the side of the house with the other. "And in case you forgot, I left you a note!"

The vines she called shot out, reaching for two men and a woman who were running toward Quinn. They recoiled, trapping the coven members against the wall, but one of the men broke free and charged. Declan appeared just in time to shove a heavy boot into the chest of the man running wildly toward her, sending him backward several feet, gasping and clawing at his chest.

"For the record, Dandelion, a *note* is *not* an acceptable form of communication."

"He's not wrong," Declan said, adding his two cents from a few feet away, where he was sticking to using his fists rather than his magick.

"And what exactly was the plan? Because I'm having a hard time wrapping my mind around any scenario where you leaving town *alone* would seem like a good fucking idea." Jax's pale blue eyes were wild and his hair slightly disheveled, like he'd been running his hands through it in frustration—or fear.

"Maybe you two can talk about this later?" Quinn offered sarcastically.

"Maybe somebody needs to teach you how to multi-task, Wilder," Liv faintly registered Declan saying to Quinn as he stuck close to her side. Was he flirting? Liv shook off the wholly ill-timed thought.

Quinn was right, they needed to focus and figure out where Ivy was so they could get out of there. She turned to tell Jax as much when a weak shot of magick fizzled out on Jax's shirt. He looked down at the small singe marks the magick had left behind and then up at the man who'd sent it. "That was really embarrassing for you," Jax said, and then the man was tumbling ass over end across grass and stone pavers.

"Let's try not to kill anyone, please. It's hard to justify bodies flying around as self-defense." Declan said, and from his tone, she couldn't tell if he was being sarcastic or genuine in his request.

A surge of magick much more powerful than any before sliced through the air, narrowly missing her. Liv turned, searching for the source of that now familiar magick.

Ivy stood with her hands raised on the other side of the garden, Rett, who Liv hadn't seen at the gathering before now, at her side, and Ash just a few steps behind her, looking on like a proud...

"Is this what it takes for you to hear me?" Ivy yelled at Liv. "How delusional do you have to be to think this was going to convince me that you care about me? Or that I should trust you?" The other members of the coven began to slink back, but not leave, wanting a front-row seat to whatever came next as Ivy got closer.

"Your sister keeps such rude company," Ash commented as he followed Ivy. "No manners at all."

"Fuck your manners," Jax spat. "As far as I'm concerned, you're lucky I haven't brought this whole house down on you."

Rett smiled arrogantly beside Ivy. "You could try." The black tattoos covering him seemed to move as his strange magick hummed in the air around him and then expanded to embrace Ivy, like some kind of shield. It was clear to Liv now that as different as his magick might be, and despite how he was involved in all this, Rett's magick wasn't the darkness they'd felt at any of the crime scenes.

Liv ignored them all, knowing her window was closing quickly. "You can believe what you want, but don't you dare tell me I didn't care about you." She took a step away from Jax toward her sister. "Maybe I didn't always do it the way you wanted me to. You were a child, and you shouldn't have been stuck with only me as a mother. But you were, and dammit, I tried." Liv glanced down at her hands, noticing the small crescent-shaped indents in her palms where she'd been clenching her fists as if squeezing tightly enough could somehow keep hold of her sister. She looked back up at Ivy.

"All I wanted was to be your sister. We never had that luxury, but we do now. Don't let this manipulative snake take that away from us." She pointed at Ash, who only smiled.

Liv batted away Ivy's next burst of magick, sending it into some bushes that withered immediately upon contact. She held out a hand, not wanting her friends to get involved.

"You're always blaming someone else for everything you did or didn't do," Ivy said, her power flying at Liv again. "You blamed Rett for teaching me magick when you wouldn't." Another blast of power. "You blame Ash for ruining our relationship, but you did that. No one else." Ivy unleashed yet another tendril of magick, this one as erratic as her behavior, her control waning the more she used it.

"Do you see that?" Liv gestured to the bush. "That is not your magick! You've allowed him to twist and pollute your mind, and now it's affecting your magick. Magick that was given to you by our ancestors, a gift from the Earth, and look at what it's becoming."

"Ah, but that is where you're wrong." Ash stepped up next to Ivy.

Jax matched Ash's move, stepping up beside her, his hand brushing hers.

"Do you see how little she knows you? She calls me the great manipulator, but the truth is, she wants you to return to that town, that house, where you and your power will be limited by her envy. She will stifle you just like your mother and your grandmother did. Ivy, you're standing on the precipice of true greatness. Don't let Liv's fear hold you back. It's time to embrace your potential."

Liv watched as Ash's words charmed her sister. Became her truth.

She saw the moment her sister made her choice, and something inside of Liv realized, finally, that no matter how much she wanted to protect her little sister from the repercussions of her actions again, she couldn't. Not this time.

Jax must have seen it too, the look on her sister's face. She felt his power gathering as he stepped around her, ready to go for Ivy, to take her by force.

"No." The word was gentle, but it was certain and utterly resigned.

Liv stepped forward when he stepped aside, looking her sister straight in the eyes. "You're not a child anymore. I'm sorry it took all of this for me to see that. I know I was your only family for years, and I know I wasn't perfect. I want you to know I did try."

Her voice started to break, but she willed herself to keep speaking. To give her sister the words she needed, the freedom to choose her path. "I love you, Ivy. If this is what you want, if this is what you think family looks like, I won't stop you. I hope they're everything you didn't find with me. And if they're not—"

"What? Too bad for me?" Ivy sneered.

"No." She smiled sadly at her sister. "If they're not, you know where to find me."

"Yes, she does," Rett said in an odd voice as he gently tugged on Ivy's hand.

"Don't come back here, Liv," Ivy said, and then she turned away, letting Rett lead her through the crowd of people and into the house.

Once they were out of sight, Ash looked at Liv. "And then there was one last Terrabella." His eyes narrowed meanly. "By the way, did you receive my condolences?"

Her body stiffened as Ash continued. "It took quite a while to lure Elena out from under Valeria's watchful eye. Imagine my disappointment when I finally had her, only to learn how little magick she had." He signed dramatically. "But I never would have cast her aside had I known what she was hiding inside her. What belonged to me," he nearly snarled, as he stabbed himself in the chest with a stiff finger.

"Every attempt I made to get to you through your mother, and by other means," he smiled then, regaining his composure, "was thwarted by that damn Terrabella magick. But Ivy... she came right to me. All on her own. Well, not exactly on her own. You played a hand in that, didn't you? Elena would be so disappointed in you." Ash tsked, and Jax let out a low, livid sound from beside her. "But I guess you'd be used to that, wouldn't you?"

His words slowly sunk in. It had been him all along. Haunting their mother, hunting them all, driving them from town to town. He was what her mom had been fleeing all these years. What drove her mad, drove them from Havenwood, from their home. The realization ripped through the last dregs of restraint she had left in her body.

The rage swelling inside her wasn't all her own, it was pumping off Jax as well, as he slowly lost his grip on his control, trying to allow her to do this on her own.

"I have to admit it wasn't something I saw coming," Ash continued, but she was done listening.

"Enough!" Liv yelled, triggering Jax, who gathered his magick as he made for Ash. But Liv was faster. She thrust her hands forward, fingers spread wide. Magick surged through her, a force that she channeled into the Earth beneath her. The Earth trembled with raw power as it ripped through the ground, quaking violently in response to her command.

With a forceful downward motion, Liv drove her hands toward the ground, palms down. The terrain responded instantly, splitting open in a jagged line as a deep chasm tore open between them and Ash. Cracks radiating outward, forcing him to leap aside as the ground beneath him crumbled, barely avoiding the gaping crevice that yawned before him.

A disgusting smile slid across Ash's face as he recovered. "Such great power," he yelled across the space. "A pity it's wasted on descendants of cowards. Don't worry, with what I've got planned, I'll make sure Ivy's power doesn't go to waste."

Liv lashed out with a vine across the chasm, slicing it across Ash's face, then snapping it back where it hovered like a snake waiting to strike again. He hissed, raising his hands to his face and the slash marks the thorny vine had left behind. "I said shut the hell up," Liv nearly growled. The energy coursing through her vibrated with its intensity as the chasm reached the side of the house, shaking the foundation, and sending chunks of stone and wood tumbling into the abyss she had summoned. The ground was now a chaotic landscape of upheaval, with Ash stranded on one side and Liv, panting and drained, on the other, with her friends.

"You've deluded yourself into thinking you've won... you haven't. "The Spirit will never tolerate the unforgiveable crimes you've committed against fellow witches. You'll never be one of hers. So it doesn't matter what your plan is, because you'll fail. Just like you've failed with every other ploy you've tried over the years. You've coveted my magick all this time, you've tried to drive it out of me, trick me into giving it to you, and you've failed every time. You can try to steal it from me, but you will fail at that, too. And you may have Ivy for now, but that was her choice, not your victory."

She stepped up close to the edge of the ravine she'd created, her friends standing behind her, close, but allowing her to have this moment.

"And if you hurt Ivy in any way..." she shook her head slightly and looked into Ash's dark eyes, ignoring the few acolytes that gathered behind him, "you don't know what true power is—but you will." She felt her friends' magick touch her, felt them lend her strength and support.

"You will feel my power as it courses through you, obliterating every cell in your entire being, turning them to ash one by one. You'll feel it, the magnitude of the entire Terrabella line, as you wither, slowly, from the inside out. And once I've drained you of whatever pathetic bit of life lives inside of you, I'll have Jax take your putrid husk of a body into my green-house, where I'll grind your remnants into dust and feed you to the worms in my garden, if they'll even have you."

Her chest was heaving, and her muscles ached, but she refused to waver as she stared down the man who'd been a plague on her life.

Ash didn't bother with a cunning retort this time. He stared at her for a long moment, then, lightning quick, reached into his tux jacket and with-drew the athame from the ceremony, gripping it in his hand and pushing a blast of its collected magick out through it. The shot of amplified magick barreled toward her, but just as Ash released his retribution, Declan stepped forward.

The air above the chasm stilled completely, halting the magick in place for one long moment before it dissipated into nothingness. It was as if the space between them had opened and sucked all that power into it.

Ash's eyes went wide and locked on Declan, and he clapped in amused delight. "I haven't felt Aether Magick that powerful in ages! You must be a Stone. How interesting." An insidious grin slipped over his face. "What other gifts do you possess, I wonder?" His tongue slid over his teeth like Declan was some sort of dessert he wanted to sink them into.

Jax's magick blew past her, knocking Ash off-kilter, and one of his henchmen barely caught him before he fell into the gaping chasm below.

Ash pushed the man off him as he righted himself, his fallacy of poise dropping away completely as fury engulfed him. The acolytes tugged at Ash, pulling them with him as they fled. He resisted weakly, his over-whelming fury evident even as he took a few backward steps. "You were right about one thing, I'm not one of you, but do not delude yourself into thinking the Spirit will save you from what is coming."

Lightning broke across the sky, and traces of Quinn's magick lingered in the air. It was time to go before this devolved any further.

Liv let the full potency of her magick rise to the surface of her skin. She embraced it, letting every single bit of the life and death the Spirit had gifted her crack in the air around her, seeing fear as she locked eyes with Ash, and then…she smiled. "See you soon, Ash," she called as he finally gave in and ran, he and the few others disappearing into the night.

"Wow. I know this may not be the appropriate time, but that was fucking hot, Liv." Quinn looked at her with wide eyes. "I have a major girl crush on you now."

Logan gave her a giant smile. "I second that."

"Time to go," Jax said, turning to catch Liv just as her knees began to buckle. Without hesitation, he scooped her up into his arms, holding her close.

"I can walk," she insisted, though her voice was weak.

Jax kept moving, ignoring her protest. Exhaustion finally took hold, so she didn't argue again. She relented to the safety of his arms wrapped around her and released the last of the adrenaline she'd been running on.

Jax looked down at her, concern in his eyes. "This is *one* time I really need you to say it."

Liv smiled softly. "I'm fine."

CHAPTER FIFTY

*B*right.

Beyond her shut eyelids it was so bright. The rising sun warmed her skin. It felt good.

It should've felt wrong, she supposed. A bright sun shining after all that had happened last night.

But the warmth surrounding her, the rise and fall of the warm bare chest beneath her, and the weight of the arm draped around her countered the rise of anxiety that threatened to pull her under. Her legs were still tucked between his, the way they'd settled into bed the night before—after he'd carried her in from the garden.

When they'd come home from the mansion on the hill, Liv had wordlessly wandered out into her gardens. She'd once again unintentionally found herself at the old Willow tree. Settling at the foot of it, she'd laid herself bare to the roots, to her Grammy and her ancestors. She'd confessed to everything she felt and what she hadn't. Then she'd cried, for her sister, for their mother, for the mistakes she'd made. For all the times she hadn't allowed herself to cry, and for the parts of herself she'd hidden away for too long. She'd cried for everything she'd lost, and then for everything she'd gained since she'd come home. She'd cried herself empty.

She must have fallen asleep in the dirt and moss, because the next thing she knew Jax was scooping her from the ground, cradling her in his warm arms, and carrying her through the quiet forest, into the house, and to her bed. Where she was now.

Instinctually, she lifted an arm to rub at the rock in her solar plexus where she usually stored all her anxiety and pain, but it was gone.

Left in the dirt with her tears, no doubt. She shifted slightly to look up at the face of the man she was wrapped around.

"Hi." Jax didn't open his eyes immediately. He stiffened his arm when she attempted to move. "Not yet." His hands ran up and down her body in soothing strokes. She wasn't sure who they were meant to soothe though, her or himself. "Let's at least wait until the house can make us some coffee and tea."

She was about to argue that it didn't do that, but Jax moved and suddenly she found herself tucked beneath him and caged within his arms. The press of his body against hers was a pleasant weight on muscles that ached from the expenditure of magick and emotion.

He didn't say anything, just loomed over her, his eyes so bright in the morning light they looked like crystals. Jax wove his fingers into her hair, tugging it slightly, keeping her from looking anywhere but at him. "You smart, beautiful, brave, stupid, stupid woman. Never again." His voice was raspy from sleep and emotion. That muscle in the side of his jaw tensed. "*Never again.*" There was an edge in the timbre of his words, but the slight crack in them and the way his breath fanned over her face in a small pant spoke of fear, not anger.

"I won't apologize for going after her. I needed to do that." The gold rim around his iris almost seemed to pulse, but she didn't waver under his scrutiny.

"But I won't do it, or anything else, without you by my side again." Her eyes bore into his, telling him more than what she was saying with her words. She may have regretted trying to get to her sister alone, but she didn't regret her reasons for going. Her promise must have eased some of his fear because she felt the tension retreat from his muscles, his body softening against hers.

His forehead met hers and rolled back and forth like he was having some kind of internal conversation with himself.

Liv buried her face in the smooth spot where his shoulder met the column of his neck and inhaled the strong scent of sunshine on pine trees that mixed with the musk of his skin. She didn't try to hide the deep inhale of him, she just breathed him in, using his scent to ground and drown out the remaining dregs of unease.

***

JAX LET HER TAKE HER FILL, REVELING IN THE WAY SHE USED HIM FOR HER comfort. He held her there until he felt her breathing even out and her body relax under his. Leaning back slightly, he finally acknowledged what she'd said.

"Then we're going to need to get a bigger bed." The corner of his mouth kicked up despite his attempt to keep a serious face. Liv rose and covered his smirk with her kiss.

"Are you okay?" she asked.

He sat up and ran a hand through his hair roughly. "The last thing you should be worrying about is if *I'm* okay. But because you're a stubborn witch, I'll answer you." He sighed heavily, his breath fanning across her loose hair that was spread out around her wildly. "No. I'm not okay. I'm not okay with anything that happened last night. But I will be. Are you okay?"

He was relieved when she answered, "Yes. No. Both." Because it was the truth. "I don't know if I'll ever be okay knowing my sister chose him over me, or knowing the role I played in driving her to that." Jax opened his mouth to defend her, to remind her Ivy was an adult, and that just because they'd had to leave her last night didn't mean they were giving up on her for good. Not by a long shot. But she cut him off before he got a word out.

"I played a role, no matter what my intentions. I know it was her choice to make—I know that, Jax. But there is still a lot of regret and pain, things that I'll need time to work through."

Of course there would be pain, and of course it would take time. It was still hard to hear. It was hard to fight the desperate drive inside him that wanted to find a way to relieve her of that pain, and to make things right, to give her the perfect life she deserved. But all the magick in the world couldn't do that. So, he'd do the only thing he could and walk through it with her, however long it took, and through whatever lay ahead of them.

"But," she laid a hand on his bare chest, looking serious, "I've never been happier than I was a moment ago when I woke up intertwined with you. To get this second chance at building a life here, with you, and the rest of the family I've made here. Not that long ago, I wouldn't have felt entitled to my happiness. I would have pushed it away out of guilt. But I understand now—it's not one or the other. I'm heartbroken over my sister and I'm excited for this life with you. That I get to love you. So, it's both. I'm not okay, and I'm so much better than just okay."

The truth of her words loosened the tension in his body he had been carrying around for…well, too long. He kissed her forehead. "I love you."

"Again, or still?"

"Always." He paused, then smiled. "Until we're nothing but ashes in the ground fertilizing all your pretty flowers."

She sat up and draped her arms around his neck. "We'll see if the Earth will even take you. You're not a Terrabella, after all." Her lips curved up.

"The house likes me more than anyone else, I like my chances of winning the gardens over too."

"The house does not…" He smirked when he felt the small thud on the nightstand behind him. He loved this house's timing.

Liv peeked around him, "Wow, okay maybe it does like you better, I've never gotten room service before." She pouted as he shifted to hand her the steaming cup of tea.

Jax waited for that sweet little moan that always followed her first sip of morning tea, then regretfully slipped out of her bed. Snagging a shirt off the floor, he pulled it over his head and sipped his coffee before heading toward her door. "When you're ready I'll have some food for you downstairs."

She sat up with round eyes. "Breakfast?"

He nodded. "But I highly suggest you take a shower first. With that

378

much dirt in your hair, the vines may start getting ideas. I could get into a lot of things with you, but I think I'm going to have to draw the line at foliage play." Jax pulled the door closed behind him just before the thud of a book hit the other side, and he laughed.

Downstairs, he found their friends spread throughout the house. "Is she up?" Logan called from the chaise in the library before he even made it down.

Jade, who'd gone straight home to check on Cori last night, emerged from the kitchen, eyes red-rimmed, though he had no doubt she'd assure him it was not from crying if he asked. Quinn and Declan stood from the settee in the sitting room. They all waited for him to answer.

"She is."

"Is she okay?" Jade demanded.

"She is."

"Like emotionally? And I swear if you say, 'she is,'" Jade did her best impression of Jax's voice, "one more time I'm going to freak the fuck out!"

"As opposed to whatever this is, you mean?"

Declan shook his head at Logan. "I really can't tell if you're brave or stupid."

"Brave."

"Stupid." Jade and Logan spoke at the same time and then smiled despite themselves.

Quinn took a few steps toward Jax, "Did she say what she wants to do? About Ivy?" Jax could see the unease and exhaustion in Quinn's eyes—it was impossible to miss. As natural as magick seemed to come to Quinn, learning how to navigate her Empathic powers was especially tricky. Even for an experienced witch, being able to balance a stressful situation and keep control of an ever-present gift like hers would be difficult. She'd no doubt been bombarded by intense emotions from everyone since last night. Especially what Liv had felt when her sister had made her choice, and she had to finally let her go…

Quinn had been sitting with those whirlwind emotions all night. She was either even stronger than he'd initially realized or especially skilled at hiding her own emotions.

Maybe both.

Before Jax could answer anyone, Declan spoke up. "If we're planning to go back in for Ivy, we'll need a better plan, and ideally more people this time. I'd suggest using the cliffs to gain access to the property. It's risky, but if we managed to pull it off undetected it would give us the advantage of surprise, something that would work in our favor since numbers aren't. But if we were caught in the ascent, we'd be sitting ducks, and then we'd be the ones needing rescuing." Declan rubbed his hand over his beard and looked down as if he were considering holes in his plan.

"It's only considered a rescue if she wants to leave. That's not what I saw."

"Who knows what Ash has done to her. It's clear he's manipulating her. Maybe he's even using a spell on her," Quinn said, playing devil's advocate with Jade.

Jax turned to look up the stairs as the others began arguing about Ivy and plans. Liv stood a few steps up, leaning a hip against the banister and looking down over the friends who hadn't yet noticed her.

⁂

LIV WAS OVERWHELMED BY THE MIXTURE OF VOICES THAT CARRIED UP THE stairs to her where she lingered just out of sight, listening. These people who owed her nothing were already planning the ways they were going to risk themselves for her, for her sister—the sister who'd chosen the group that was actively threatening their town and way of life over them. It was one thing for her to be unable to give up on Ivy, but they weren't giving up on her either, despite not knowing what role she'd played or the damage she'd caused.

She closed her eyes as gratitude and sorrow mixed within her, coexisting in a single tear as it slid down her face. The duality of the moment threatened to crack her in half.

She gave herself a moment to bask in the beauty of that kind of friendship and love before continuing down the stairs to stand next to Jax.

"Liv!" Quinn wrapped in her a tight hug.

"You okay?" Jade said as she walked closer.

"Yeah, I'm..." Jax looked down at her with a raised eyebrow as if daring her to say the word. She couldn't help but laugh a little. "I'm a lot of things, the sum of which mostly amount to, okay."

"Well, good because if you ever—"

"Yeah yeah, your brother already gave me the threatening speech." She wrapped Jade in a hug. "I'm sorry I scared you," she whispered into her friend's ear, squeezing a little tighter when she felt the subtle way Jade nodded her head against her.

Logan was right there scooping her up off her feet into a bear hug the second Jade had ended their brief embrace. "Glad you're okay *mo piuthar.*"

Declan remained on the outskirts but gave her a gentle nod from where he stood with his hands in his pockets. It was clear he wasn't sure of his place within the group, or the house for that matter, but he'd come.

"It means a lot that you guys were worried about me, but you didn't have to stay."

"Oh, for Spirit's sake. Is she still trying to act like she doesn't need us? *Already?*" Jade groaned at the ceiling, walking back toward the sitting room and dropping onto the settee.

"No, you all just look like you could use some sleep and showers."

Logan lifted one of his broad shoulders, sniffing at his armpit, and shrugged. "She's not wrong."

Shaking her head, she joined Jade on the settee. The others followed her over. "I've been thinking though, and I do need your help with something."

"If it's about Ivy and how to get her back, we've been going through ideas about that too," Quinn said as she looked at Declan.

"I do have some ideas, but I think Liv has something else in mind." Declan read her easily as he leaned a shoulder against the wall near the fireplace and waited for her to speak her mind.

She didn't bother easing into it. "I don't want to go back."

Quinn's face pinched. "Look I know you're mad, but maybe you should give it a few days before we decide anything."

"I'm not mad. I'm hurt, disappointed, and scared. Along with a whole slew of other emotions I couldn't even hope to identify right now, but I'm not mad. At least not at Ivy." Liv took a deep breath. "I know that it sounds harsh, but she made her choice, and trust me I wish I could have changed her mind. I understand wanting to force her into something better, but that's what got us here in the first place." She looked around at her friends. "I haven't given up on her. But this time she needs to figure it out on her own, and if we want to be the ones she turns to when that happens, then we have to let her go. For now." Quinn squeezed Liv's hand and then nodded, clearly reading that she meant it, and sitting back in her seat.

"What if she doesn't figure it out?" Jade asked the hard questions as usual.

"We have to believe she will. Despite everything, I don't believe she knows about Ash's involvement with the rituals. He'll only be able to hide who he is for so long. Especially from Ivy."

Declan sat forward, clearly homing in on what she wasn't saying. "What do you mean by that?"

"I mean that while there's still a lot we don't know about Ash or his powers, I do think we were on the right track with how he's been able to work around the wards on the house. I thought the magick I saw Ivy doing the night she left was something she'd learned from Rett or someone else. That someone had warped her magic somehow. I wanted to believe it was some manipulated effect Ash had caused, but I was wrong—it's her. How she's channeling it is different, but I could feel it last night, and it's similar to Ash's."

"Like he's sharing it with her?" Quinn's eyes widened, "Is that even possible?"

"It's possible. Just like stealing magick is, but I don't think that's what she means." Jax leaned onto the side of the settee next to her.

"He's her father," Declan said. It wasn't a question.

Jade shook her head in disbelief. "What? No fucking way."

"Do you think they know?" Logan asked.

"Ash does. Did you hear him before we left? He didn't know about Ivy, but he was delighted to find out about her. And she's how the essence of his magick was able to get on the land—because of the blood he shares with Ivy, and now the blood she's given him. And while I don't think she knows everything, she knows he's her father."

Everyone was quiet for a moment as the revelation and its implications settled.

"Well shit, I didn't see that one coming." Logan ran a hand over his hair. "So, what is it exactly that you want to do? If Ash can piggyback off of Ivy's magick, how can we keep him from getting to you or anyone else on the grounds?"

"We'd have to remove her from the wards." Jade looked almost as miserable as she felt.

"Not just the wards. We have to remove her from Havenhouse altogether. We have to unroot her."

Quinn blanched at the idea. "But what will that do to her magick?"

"I don't think there's any way to know for sure, but we do know her magick comes from more than one source now. It won't leave her defenseless. But I'm sure she'll feel it."

The others shared looks, and Liv understood why. There were consequences to what she was saying. It would make it much harder for Ivy if she changed her mind and came home. But they couldn't afford to operate on what-ifs. She wouldn't risk the rest of them, her family, this town, her home, on just the hope that her sister might come to her senses.

Jax's large hands slid over her shoulders from where he stood behind her, his silent support of what she was asking, and her decision.

Jade surprised her the most when she asked, "Are you sure Liv? We wouldn't be able to do something like that until the full moon, which isn't for another two days. You could take some time to think about it."

"I won't lose any more pieces to him."

Jade nodded knowingly. "It will take all of us." It was a fact, but also a question, one that hung in the air between them all.

"You know I'll do whatever to keep you and this old place safe." Logan patted a hand against a wall. The house lights flickered, and Logan barely reacted in time to catch what looked like some kind of candy to him.

Logan looked down at what he'd caught and then up toward the ceiling. "Ooh, peanut butter cups, my favorite. Thanks, bud." He patted the wall again.

"If you're sure, then of course I'll help," Quinn said.

Everyone's eyes lifted to Declan. "Well, Sheriff? What's it going to be?" Quinn tilted her head in question.

He looked at them, considering, then shook his head in resignation. "Fine."

Logan clapped loudly as he shot out of his chair, breaking the pensive moment. "Full moon it is."

CHAPTER FIFTY-ONE

*M*aybe she should've felt anxious being in that spot again, facing the reminder of how far the fall from the cliff's edge to the sliver of beach and waters below. No one would blame her, considering the last time she was there she'd nearly experienced that fall firsthand.

But she wasn't anxious.

Jax wound his fingers with hers as they stood side by side looking out over the water. He'd been right there that night, too. But she'd saved herself when it came down to it. He wouldn't have let her fall, she knew that. But rather than rush to save her, he'd reminded Liv what lived inside her and showed his unwavering confidence in her by trusting her. He'd given her the gift of knowing she could save herself, and the comfort of knowing she didn't have to do it alone.

There would be darkness to deal with tomorrow. Tonight, she just wanted to celebrate the love she'd found again, and that she knew would never leave.

He sat there with her until the very last rays of the sun faded into the ocean, until it was too dark for her to see the opposing cliff faces anymore.

Then he led her away from the cliffs and back into the forest. "Where are you going?" he asked when she didn't take the path back toward her house.

She batted her lashes at him playfully. "Didn't you say you'd follow me anywhere?"

He took her chin lightly in his fingers and dropped his mouth close to hers. "To the ends of fucking earth," he whispered across her lips.

She stepped back just as he intended to take her mouth. She hooked a finger in the waistband of his jeans, his body obeying as she pulled him in, kissing him feather light again, then stepping away before he could deepen the kiss. "Liv," he said with a growl as her finger slid free of his pants.

"Prove it." She took one tentative step back. Then another. Her eyes sparkled like she'd trapped starlight in them.

They called for him to move toward her. Dared him to take a step. "Be sure you know what game you're playing, Dandelion."

She smirked. And then she ran.

He gave her just enough time to vanish into the forest before he took off after her.

Her footfalls were silent, soft moss rising in small inhales to meet her steps. Even a slight crunching of leaves was like the beat of drums in the quiet of the forest. She darted away from him, holding in a nervous giggle. The rush of anxiety from being chased matched with the anticipation of what he'd do to her once he caught her, heightening every sense. She kept running, weaving between trees, using a soft breeze of magick to cover her steps and leave a breadcrumb trail of magick.

Branches and curls of vines brushed over her sensitive skin, sighing at the feel of her magick dancing all around her. She paused just long enough to duck into the darkness of a large tree. Laying her palm on the ground, she searched for the feel of him on the forest floor. Nothing.

SHE'D BEEN LEAVING HIM A TRAIL, WANTING HIM TO FOLLOW HER, BUT HE didn't need it. He'd meant it when he said he wouldn't lose her again—in any sense of the word.

Jax dropped from a high branch of the tree, landing silently a few steps in front of her.

Liv's eyes went wide before narrowing, excitement dancing in them, that sultry smirk curving up one side of her lush lips.

They stood there, little more than arm's length away. Watching each other's chests rise and fall—not from the chase, but from the anticipation of what they both knew came next.

It was impossible to know who moved first, but they collided mid-step, their lips finding each other's easily. Jax's tongue stroked into her mouth, tangling with hers. He groaned, and Liv jumped into his arms. He caught her, of course, like he always had. Always would.

Her legs wrapped tightly around him, squeezing and lifting, his hard cock pressed against the zipper of his jeans as she rubbed against him.

"F-fuck." Jax pressed her back into the tree, keeping himself between her thighs.

Her breathy words and erotic whimpers caressed his skin, as the hand he wasn't using to hold her up roamed over her body, and up to massage her breast. He rocked between her thighs and loved the, "Please," she moaned into his mouth.

"Mmm, maybe I do need you to beg after all," he said against her lips.

"I will. Jax. I need you inside me. Please." Her back arched off the tree as she tried to find more friction against his hard length behind his jeans. "It's not enough." Suddenly their clothes were gone, and he was pressed against her skin-to-skin.

"Shit. I love when you do that."

He growled, sliding his cock through the wetness between her thighs and over her clit. Once. Twice.

A thin sheen of sweat covered them as their movements grew more fevered. Jax leaned down, skimming his tongue from the center of her breasts, up the column of her neck, and back to her mouth.

Impatient, Liv reached down between them and wrapped her hand firmly around his cock, stroking it twice in return, before lining it up with her entrance. At the same time he thrust into her he kissed her, swallowing her scream and pressing her flush against the tree. Jax hummed his pleasure at the feel of her. The walls of her pussy tightened around him as he settled deep inside her.

Ecstasy. That was the only word he could think of to describe what it felt like each time they came together this way. He was consumed with the need to touch her everywhere, to relish every delicious curve of her body.

Slowly he withdrew and slid back in. Thrust by perfect fucking thrust she met him as he worked them into a rhythmic pace. Her hips rose to meet his with every withdrawal and plunge back into her. It took all his self-control not to thrust hard. Fast. But her ragged moans of, "Yes" and, "Jax!" chanting through her lips, into the night air around them, into his mouth, made him want to make this last forever.

He dipped his head to her dark nipple, licking it and then pulling it deep into his mouth. He sucked on her, matching his pace to the flutters of her pussy around his dick.

"More," she whimpered, "please."

Her eyes slammed shut and her mouth dropped open as he lifted her hips, driving deeper, increasing the force but not his pace.

He dropped a hand between them, pressing lightly against her clit. Then lower to where they were joined, bringing the wetness back to her clit, circling, circling, circling.

HER NERVES WERE FRAYING AS HER BODY SOARED HIGHER THAN SHE'D ever been before. The warmth of him all over her, the scent of their skin, their sweat, their magick engulfed her. She'd never felt closer to another person in her life, like they were merging into one. Closer, she needed to be closer, to climb inside him and erase any space between them.

Wrapping her arms around his shoulders, she pulled herself up flush with him. His hands came around to her ass, gripping her cheeks in his hands and spreading. Knowing exactly what she needed, he lifted her, dragging her clit over his pelvis and bringing her down hard on his cock. He repeated the move, grinding her against him, up and down. Their breaths came heavier, and his cock got harder with each thrust.

"Twelve years of not being able to touch you." His fingers dug into the flesh of her ass, "of not being able to taste you." He licked and sucked her neck, dragging his teeth up to her ear. "Not being able to be *inside you.*" The pace grew faster, more erratic. "Never again." It wasn't just a demand this time. It was a promise. "Eyes Liv. Give me your eyes and give me the words." Glassy green emeralds blazed brightly with embers of gold and locked on his.

"Never again." It was half promise, half cry of ecstasy.

"Tell me you won't spend a single night away from me, ever again."

"That seems a little unrealistic," she panted as she used her legs to gain more leverage so she could work herself up and down his shaft over and over.

He looked down at where he moved in and out of her and groaned. "I know. I also don't care. It's so damn consuming, the way you make me feel. The need to touch every part of you all at once."

HE COULDN'T TAKE IT ANYMORE. HE DROPPED THEM DOWN ONTO THE SOFT, moss-covered ground so she could straddle him. She leaned flush against him, using his tight grip on her ass and hers on his shoulders to slide up and down his body. Her breasts rubbed against his chest. He turned his face into the sleek, damp skin of her neck, inhaling her scent into his soul. He rained promises like a sacred chant into her skin, into her heart.

Inevitable.

This was the only thing in this life, in this world, that had ever been, *always* been, inevitable. Them. Woven together, tangled into one being. He wanted to erase every bad memory she carried, wanted to take back every day, every moment, every fucking breath they'd spent apart.

But since he couldn't, couldn't keep her from whatever lay ahead of them, he'd make sure to engulf her in so much good, in everything she deserved. It would eclipse all the bad.

Her thighs began to quiver around him. "Yes, baby. Now. Come on my cock right fucking now. I'm right there with you. Always right there with you. Together."

Her body stiffened, her thighs squeezed against him. He moved beneath her, thrusting up into her as her orgasm rocked through her, and her walls closed more tightly around him with each pull of his cock in and out of her.

"Jax" She cried.

He came. His orgasm drove hers even higher. He couldn't take his eyes off her as she writhed above him, riding out the last dregs of her orgasm, taking every bit of pleasure he offered as they came apart together. Spirit save him, she was beautiful when she came. Her dark hair cascaded around her wildly, naked in her forest, free in her element.

"I love you so damn much, Dandelion."

"Still and always." The words were an exhausted whisper as her legs skated down his sides to rest on the ground.

She collapsed against his chest, draping herself across him. Their damp skin adhered them together as their breaths returned to normal.

He stroked a hand over her hair, smoothing the long strands, brushing them away from her face, and tucking them over one shoulder.

Liv's breathing slowed as he slid his hand up and down her smooth back.

Stars twinkled over them, peeking between the branches.

"Jax." The way she said his name when she was breathless and satiated was almost as satisfying as getting her that way.

THE MOMENT LIV HAD BEEN WAITING FOR WAS FINALLY HERE. AS JAX gently lowered them into the large bathtub, the hot water enveloped their thoroughly spent bodies, pulling a shared groan of bliss from their lips.

The scent of lavender and cedarwood wafted up with the steam that rose from the tub. Above them, the soft glow from the stained-glass window bathed the room in hues of gold and green, the dandelions depicted there casting a delicate pattern over the water. *Dandelions.*

Jax's hands moved tenderly through her hair, gathering the damp strands and sweeping them over her shoulder with such care that it sent a shiver down her spine. Liv leaned back into him, her body molding perfectly against his as his fingers trailed over her skin. Each caress soothed her in a way she'd never known, drawing her into a state of deep, contented relaxation as she stared up at the glass.

"I bought this place sight unseen when I decided to come back. That," Jax had followed her eyes to the beautiful window, "that was already here when I moved in, if you can believe it. I stared at it on and off for days, trying to figure out what it meant."

"I'm surprised you didn't throw a rock through it." Liv laughed sleepily.

"It crossed my mind, but I couldn't do it."

"Because you love old things too much."

Their bodies shifted with Jax's laughter, causing the bathwater to lap at the edges of the tub. "No, Dandelion, because I loved you too much."

She lost herself in the feel of him, in the warmth of the water, in the quiet intimacy of the moment.

Sometime later the sensation of floating, weightless and free, took hold of her and then landed gently against soft blankets. The rich and comforting scent of Jax engulfed her, Jax's magick, the familiar scent easing her into a deep, dreamless sleep.

CHAPTER FIFTY-TWO

*T*he Fifth Wind whipped up the cliff face, across the Earth, and through the draping branches of the old Willow tree. The strands of her hair whipped wildly around her as she listened to the sea far below her, surging as it pounded relentlessly against the cliffs, just beyond the garden, mimicking the way Liv's heart slammed up against her rib cage. The clarity and resolve she felt in what they were about to do did nothing to assuage the pain of having to do it.

But she *would* do it. For the people standing next to her, but also for herself and the plans she had for Havenhouse, to return it to what it was always meant to be. If Havenhouse was going to live up to its name, she needed to do everything she could to make sure it was safe first.

Liv closed her eyes for a moment, welcoming the cool, salty sea air on her skin. A warm hand slipped into hers—long, deft fingers wrapped around her hand and squeezed gently, telling her it was time.

Fragrant smoke from piles of smoldering herbs billowed into the night sky, drifting toward each other, creating a smoky dome that swirled and curled above them, writhing on a wind controlled by Quinn. The fires built beneath each pile flickered but never caught or extinguished, balanced expertly by Jax.

The ocean grew restless, the tides pushing and pulling in unnatural directions. Heavy waves converged into one large wave that rolled toward them, building like an oceanic avalanche. The impact of the sea reverberated through her entire body as it collided with rock. But the enormous wave that should have crashed down on them stood frozen in a beautiful arc above them by Logan.

The ground beneath their feet rumbled and shifted lightly, revealing narrow channels through the ground, weaving, and crossing through the Terrabella lands, creating an elaborate earthen tapestry.

Logan directed the salty seawater, slowly easing into the channels she'd created.

She looked out beyond the tree, and the gardens, to the full moon that hung so low she was sure if she reached out she'd be able to hold it in her hand.

"Are you ready?" Jax asked, his voice muffled by thrashing waters and the crackling bonfire Jade had created just outside their ritual site. Her eyes drifted around the circle to Jade and then to Logan who stood to her right. On her left, Quinn gave her a small, sad smile. Next to Quinn, Declan stood ramrod straight, eyes fixed on her—he gave a small nod, letting her know he was with her.

> *"Mother Moon we call on thee,*
> *hear us, three plus three, and grant us this plea..."*

One by one they each slid the small dagger across their palm, releasing a small amount of their blood and their magick, dripping into the Earth where it joined with hers. Then they called on their ancestors—the ones who had first created this Haven in the wildwood, to protect it once again.

IVY SAT ON A LARGE FOUR-POSTER BED IN THE GRANDEST ROOM SHE'D EVER stayed in. My bed, my room, she reminded herself. Her eyes drifted to the French doors that led out to a small Juliette balcony overlooking the cliffs. Cliffs that she'd only recently realized were directly across the cove from the cliffs that edged the house she'd left behind.

She figured it wasn't an accident, but didn't know what to make of it. Didn't know what to make of anything. Ivy opened her palm, calling a small ball of black fire, and let it roll between her fingers, distracting her from so many still unanswered questions, when the French doors blew open and a heavy pressure hit Ivy as if some invisible force was pushing her back...no, *away*.

"Ash!" she screamed as she fought to rise from the bed. The feeling was crushing, while somehow remaining painless. The sound of approaching footsteps was drowned out by a heavy wind that swept in through the open doors and ripped at the gossamer material that hung from the bed, sending small items scattering around the room.

Ivy was able to stand just as Ash appeared next to her. He scanned the room, ran to the balcony, and then back to her. He grabbed her by the shoulders and shook her slightly, "It's your sister." His voice sounded farther away than it should. *What was happening?* Ash snarled, gripped her arms roughly, and forced her out onto the small balcony. She couldn't see it, but she could feel the heavy press of magick in the air, whipping through the dark night. "You have to fight her!" Ash yelled over the gale, "She's forcing you out."

"What?" Ivy rasped.

"Banishing you. Your sister is locking you out of your home! *Fucking Bitch!*" he snarled.

Something inside her recoiled at the slur he felt so comfortable slinging at her sister in her presence. She pushed it aside like she had so many other feelings lately, scrambling to understand what he was saying. Liv was locking her out? It shouldn't matter, didn't—this was exactly what she wanted, wasn't it?

She'd finally done it then, she realized. Finally pushed her sister too far. Forced her to give up on her.

Or maybe it was just easier for her now that she had her new family. *Good.*

"You have to fight back, like I showed you," Ash said.

"I don't care. Let her." Ivy turned her back on the opposing magick even as she felt it tearing at something deep inside her. He'd shown her how to harness her power more effectively than she'd ever been able to before because he understood it, but that didn't mean he understood her.

Ash's eyes flared with something Ivy hadn't seen before. "Fight," he commanded. "Or are you going to let her decide yet another thing for you? Let her take the house and the town that are just as much your birthright as hers—more so! Are you going to just give up like that?" He didn't bother hiding his disappointment. "No child of mine could ever be so weak."

Ivy winced. Weak? She'd been a lot of things in her life, but weak wasn't one she was willing to concede to. Was that what Liv thought, too? Did she just assume she wouldn't fight back?

Of course she did. Liv had always expected so little of her. Found her incapable of taking care of herself, found her unworthy of her magick, her heritage, now her *home*. Ivy stepped up to the edge of the balcony and, after the briefest moment of hesitation, rose to her sister's challenge.

A MILLION TINY KNIVES CUT AT HER MAGICK. SHE RECOGNIZED IT AS HER sister's immediately this time. "She's pushing back," Jade yelled around Jax.

Liv didn't flinch. Didn't back off. She closed her eyes and let the magick flow through her freely. She felt it as Jax opened his power to her, and then Quinn took her other hand. Then Jade's and Logan's magicks joined in, and after a moment, Declan's, slightly different than the others, but powerful. Each of them linked to the other, their magicks merging with hers.

Woven together, she could recognize them individually, the imprints of each uniquely distinct.

The long branches of the Willow swayed and then parted, revealing roots of all sizes that twined across the ground and then plunged deep into the Earth. The channels Liv and Logan had created began to illuminate, the water within churned and redirected from its intricate patterns to flow directly into the roots of the ancient tree. The roots that represented every Terrabella that had come before them, held their power, and then returned it to the earth with their ashes, forever imbuing themselves with this sacred place.

Ivy's magick receded steadily as they repeated their chant, their voices melding with the wind until they spoke the final line. It was punctuated by the deep groaning of the land around them as it responded to their will. The bonfire surged as the wind kicked up again, and a crack of lightning lit up the sky before crashing into the side of the cliff face at the opposite end of the cove.

Somewhere in the recesses of Liv's mind, she thought she heard a faint scream of frustration before the night went silent. The wind abruptly stopped, and even the crashing of ocean waves quieted, giving her a single moment of complete silence, before returning to its natural rhythms. As if the natural world itself was acknowledging her sacrifice.

CHAPTER FIFTY-THREE

"*I* can't believe you guys are making us move all of this over here when you're just going to be moving out soon anyway."

"We are not moving out." Liv slapped Logan's arm. "We are *not* moving out!" she repeated loudly, reassuring the already volatile house. "We are making room for even more people to enjoy Havenhouse. We're giving it some well-earned TLC, to ensure it's at its best for when guests start arriving. Which requires some shuffling around and reallocating of belongings." She smiled widely.

"I know you're going for convincing cheer, but maybe use less teeth. You're giving crazy witch vibes. Ach!" Logan rubbed the back of his head where Jax had had smacked him as he walked by with a heavy box under one arm and Cori clinging to his back.

"You're doing wimpy otter vibes," Cori taunted Logan. "Did I say it right, Uncle Jax?" Liv heard the little girl whisper as they vanished up the stairs.

She picked up a couple boxes full of things they were planning to temporarily store at Jax's and made her way toward the open front gate. At the last second the gate snapped closed, forcing her to halt abruptly and her boxes to go flying.

They froze just before hitting the ground on the other side of the gate.

Declan stepped up onto the curb, grabbing them out of the air, and opened the gate for her. "It's a pull not a push." His lip twitched.

"I'm not sure what I'm more surprised by, the magick or the joke." Declan shifted the boxes away from her when she moved to take them back, nodding for her to lead the way. He'd found reasons to be around quite often since the night they'd done the ritual two weeks before. Liv thought it might partly be out of curiosity about the source of his magick, wanting to understand.

She also knew just how impossible it was not to be sucked into this group. No matter how hard one tried to remain solitary, once they'd decided to adopt you into the family they'd created, it was all but impossible to escape. Which was perfect for people like Liv and Declan, who found it hard to accept even the things they wanted most in life.

Quinn winked at Declan as she headed back toward Havenhouse. "Neat trick, Sheriff." Liv held back a laugh as she watched Declan's eyes follow her friend the whole way across the street.

He cleared his throat, "Um, I needed to talk to Jade and figured maybe you guys could use some help."

She tried to hide her smile. "Thanks. She's around here somewhere."

He lifted the boxes a little. "Where should I put these?"

"Just in there is fine." She directed him toward the foyer of Jax's house and then crossed the street back to hers with a couple boxes of Jax's things. It really was like a game of merry-go-round home edition. It would be worth it, she reassured herself.

This time she waited for the gate to close in front of her before opening it herself. She threw Jax under the bus to the house as she dropped into her new porch swing on her new porch of her old house. "It was his idea, you know." The air was cool, and leaves were starting to fall off some of the trees, while the apple tree in the yard was just beginning to produce its fruit.

Liv took the moment to watch the scene in front of her. Logan and Jax stacked boxes in the yard of the craftsman across the street from her. Cori was squealing as she clung to Logan's back this time, her little arms wrapped so tightly around his neck that Liv was sure she was choking him. Jax plucked her off and set her on top of a large box he handed off to

Logan, who walked across the street, giving Liv a wink as he passed her going into the house with his precious cargo.

The old house practically vibrated with excited energy. It understood what they were doing, and she knew it couldn't wait to be filled with so many people again. Even if it was acting like it was upset with her.

When the town had first been established, Havenhouse had served as a sort of inn, giving people a temporary safe haven while they figured out something more permanent.

The idea to turn Havenhouse into a bed and breakfast had occurred to her weeks ago when she'd learned about the struggles facing those trying to settle into town. But at the time she'd been so unsure—about a lot of things, but mostly whether she was going to be able to stay in Havenwood or not—that she'd dismissed the idea.

But as she'd reclaimed her roots here, she'd realized her purpose was intrinsically tied to this town, and the same went for Havenhouse. She wanted to share the safety of her home with others who might need it. So, returning Havenhouse to the refuge it had once been felt like the right step.

It was going to take some work to get it ready for guests, but luckily, she knew a guy. And she had a pretty good feeling the house would pitch in, too.

"Do you think when we're done building the new cottage out back it will have the same spirit as Havenhouse?" Logan asked, propping a foot on the lower porch step.

Quinn paused as she walked out of Havenhouse with a lamp. "Yeah! I was wondering the same thing. Like, is it one spirit that would pop over for a visit to say hi, or is an omnipresent kind of thing? It's just everywhere all at once?"

Liv weighed their questions. When she and Jax had decided to build a separate cottage on the Terrabella land, their main focus had been coming up with a solution that would give them some privacy from the guests in the main house, while allowing her to stay on the land. She'd kind of just assumed "the house" or whatever consciousness dwelled within it would be there, too.

"I actually don't know," she confessed, unnerved.

"What are you doing with that lamp?" Jade asked, having followed Quinn out.

She shrugged with a smile. "Oh, Havenhouse said I could have it."

"Nope, that's definitely not how this works." Liv pointed for her friend to put the lamp back. Quinn pouted, but went back into the house.

Liv stood on the last porch step and took a moment to appreciate the sight of Jaxon Hawthorne walking across the street carrying a large box that had his biceps bulging from under his white t-shirt. His lips tilted into a crooked smirk as the front gate swung open for him enthusiastically, welcoming him home.

He stopped in front of her, lifting his box slightly. "Where should I put this?"

"I guess that depends. What is it?"

"My collection of taxidermy. Didn't I mention that particular hobby? I hope you don't mind the smell of formaldehyde, because it's too late to change your mind now."

Liv smiled, the step almost allowing them to be eye-to-eye, and leaned over the box toward him. "I don't think I could change my mind now even if I wanted to." Her tone was seductive, though she hadn't meant it to be.

"Oh, is that so?" Jax matched her tone as he set the box down next to her feet. "Too thoroughly in love with me, hmm?"

Liv did her best to feign seriousness. "Not at all. But I'm pretty sure the house would choose you in the break-up, and I finally got the kitchen organized the way I like. It would just be such a pain to have to start all over again."

"Mhm," he hummed. "That particular excuse would be a lot more believable if the house would let you anywhere near the kitchen." Jax stepped onto the same step as Liv, forcing her to step up again.

"Speaking of organization...I've been meaning to talk to you about the closet space."

Jax followed her up again, grabbed her by the hips, and placed her on the new porch railing. "Yes."

"Yes to what?" she asked as he pushed her knees apart with his hips.

"Yes to whatever crazy idea you were about to propose. Yes to everything." Then he kissed her.

Jade walked out the front door and down the path toward Jax's house. "Ugh. Aren't you guys a little old for all the PDA?"

"Not everyone hates feelings as much as you, ice princess," Logan shot back, following her down the path. Jade stopped abruptly, rounding on him. He jerked to a stop a second before crashing into her and threw his hands up as if she were holding a gun on him. "Queen, I meant queen! You're far too old to be a princess." Jade's face scrunched up in offense. "Mature? Not old. You're not old." Logan gestured at her body. "Obviously you're not old. You know that."

Jade just slapped his hand to the side and pushed him out of her way, something he clearly allowed since she was about half his size. "Move ogre." She took a step closer to Jax and Liv. "Hey Jaxy, my most favorite brother."

Jax narrowed his eyes on his sister suspiciously. "Yes, Jade?"

"Whatcha planning on doing with that house?"

"What's it to you?"

Jade leaned down and whispered into Cori's ear.

"Uncle Jaxy, it would mean the whole entire world to me if you would let Mommy and me live in your gorgeous house."

"Playing dirty with the kid," Declan murmured under his breath.

Cori and Jade both gave Declan matching glares, and Liv didn't bother trying to fight the laughter that bubbled out of her.

"What happened to your house?" Jax asked.

"It's time for a fresh start." That seemed to be all Jade was willing to give at the moment, but it was enough.

Logan batted his lashes at Jax. "So, what's it going to be, Uncle Jaxy?"

"I spent the majority of my life living across the hall from my sister. Living across the street couldn't be any worse."

"And at least across the street I won't have to hear the two of you doing it every night."

Cori looked up at her mom. "What's doing it?"

"Nothing!" everyone said in unison.

"It's definitely something," Cori mumbled suspiciously.

"Anyway. Hope you're all free to do this whole moving thing again next weekend," Jade said as she walked down the path.

"I just have to ask…if you're all witches, can't you just use magick to do all this?" Declan asked, indicating the box in his hand.

"Sure could, buddy. Sure could. Also, *we're* all witches." Logan clapped a hand on Declan's shoulder as he followed Jade and Cori down the path.

"So why aren't we?"

"What's wrong, gramps? Too much wear and tear on your tired old muscles?" Quinn teased as she walked past him again and into Havenhouse.

Declan abandoned his questions and followed after Quinn as Jax and Liv looked on, amused. "I'm only six years older than you."

"So, you looked me up, huh?" Quinn laughed as their voices drifted away.

Alone again, Jax lifted Liv down off the rail, took her hand and pulled her behind him, into the house and toward the staircase. "What are we doing?" she asked as she followed him up the stairs and then down the hall to her bedroom.

"I have something for you." He guided her through her window and out on to the small balcony.

Jax sat down and then pulled her down between his bent knees, just like he had a hundred times before.

He reached to his side and then handed her a slim, square package wrapped in brown paper that was already waiting up there for them. She recognized it immediately as the package he'd picked up from Quinn not long after she'd first come back to town. It felt like a lifetime ago that she'd been dying to know what was inside.

She didn't waste any time slipping her fingers under the tape and chucking the paper away.

Her mouth dropped open in a silent gasp. It was a beautiful painting of Havenhouse, except, not exactly…

"Is this the same package you picked up from Quinn that first day I was in The Bookstore? She made this then?"

"Same one."

Liv looked back down at the painting of Havenhouse, looking exactly as it did right now. Lush green vines with heavy bushels of purple Wisteria hanging from them crawled over the house and up the trellis, thick enough to support the weight of a teenage boy. An apple tree, full of shining fruit, surrounded by a lush thriving garden, speckled with bright yellow and fluffy white Dandelions—and at the center of it all, the house, with the beautiful new porch Jax, Logan, and Cori had just put the finishing touches on a couple days before.

"How? That was before you, and before we..." she stuttered as her eyes began to sting.

"I remembered what it had been. And I always knew what it could be, what we dreamed it would be. I showed her the blueprints, told her my memories, and then she brought it to life."

"But you made it come true," she whispered as she stared down at the painting.

Jax gathered all her hair and swept it around to one side so he could lean in close to her. "*We* made it come true," he corrected.

He was right. Even after all the years they'd spent apart, all those dandelion dreams whispered between them and the stars, made in this very spot so many years ago—they'd found a way to make them come true.

She didn't know what lay ahead. Ash was still out there, his hold on Ivy unbroken, and so many questions left unanswered. This was far from over. But she knew now she didn't need to hide from hope—for her sister, for this town, for their future and whatever it held.

Because for the first time in a long time, she knew, no matter what came next, she wouldn't face it alone.

"Thank you," she breathed, her voice cracking.

He kissed the top of her head as she leaned into him. "I love you, Dandelion," he whispered into her hair.

She turned to look up into his crystal blue eyes. "Again, or still?"

A smirk—her favorite, maddeningly cocky one—lifted his lips. "Always."

EPILOGUE

" *lue door. Can't miss it."*

That's what she'd said, along with a few other things. But if he was going to survive this, he couldn't think about the other part. As if he'd be able to do anything else facing that damn door every time he came or went.

Declan stood at the bottom of a wrought iron staircase that led to a concrete landing. Old case files, random paperwork, and a single picture were all jammed into a single cardboard box tucked under his arm. One duffle hung from his shoulder and a guitar case was gripped in his hand. That was it. The entirety of his belongings. The sum of his thirty-seven years of life, and he had an entirely free hand.

He pushed a hard exhale through his nose and climbed the, one, two, three—sixteen steps, dropping his belongings at the foot of the door. His door now, he guessed. That would take some time. If he stayed. Somewhere deep down, he wanted to want to. Or maybe he just felt like he should…it was getting harder to tell.

"Shit," he swore under his breath. What was that, maybe ten feet *max* that separated the blue door from the black one just across the landing?

A "wipe your paws" doormat was centered in front of the blue door flanked by several plants in deep-colored pots. A wooden sign that read,

"100% that witch," hung in the center of the door. *Covering the peephole.*

The black door he stood in front of compared to all the color of hers wasn't intentional, but didn't it make sense? All that bright and life suited her. Reminded him of the colors that decorated her body.

How much of her body?

He'd never find out.

He argued with the part of his brain that had no self-control. That was a new condition he hadn't dealt with before, one which only seemed to spark when it came to her.

A distraction, when that was the last thing he needed. A complication, when that was the last thing he had time for. A possible attachment, when that was the last thing he wanted.

That last one was a stretch.

Simple. Stable. Secluded. That had been the goal when he'd taken this job. That promise had already been shattered to shit. He wasn't about to add to it. Not that someone like her would ever really be looking for someone like him. Despite her drunken flirting.

It was like their respective doors. Someone like him would only be a shadow on someone so bright.

The sound of muffled voices came from behind the blue door. A deep baritone and then the sound of a sultry laugh. Just the sound threatened to gouge out a piece of the hard cold casing he'd laid brick by earned brick around anything soft inside him. Anything vulnerable.

He dropped the thought and the rest of his things, patting his legs and chest for the key Jade had given him last week. Damn, his uniform for having so many fucking pockets.

Before he could hurtle himself and his stuff into the dark apartment, the blue door opened. The large back of a man filled the space. He was pulling on a flannel, shrugging it on over his shoulders. "Thanks, Q. Will I see you tomorrow?"

"Of course. If you're lucky. Who knows what the day will bring." Then, from somewhere hidden, that laugh again.

Logan turned around, stopping briefly when he saw him. "Oh, hey. Finally making this place home, huh?" He took inventory of Declan's things on the ground. "I'd offer to help you move in but uh, from the looks of it, not much to move." He stepped out of Quinn's doorway and headed for the stairs, finally revealing the amber-eyed witch. He couldn't help but look into those eyes. They tilted up at the edges, matching the crooked lift of pouty, pink lips.

She leaned gracefully against the frame of her door. Warm lighting and rich aromas emitted from inside, encasing her, and made the idea of following her back into it far too enticing.

A scoff and then fast, heavy footsteps descended the stairs. "Goodnight and good luck, Dec." A bark of laughter followed Logan into the night.

It was too late by the time Declan realized he'd barely acknowledged Logan. He wasn't even sure he'd blinked.

His eyes trailed up long, toned, brown legs in cotton shorts. A t-shirt splattered in paint and cut short enough to reveal the skin from her belly button, where a gold ring glinted, to the waistband of her shorts, where black ink peeked up. He was *fuuucked.*

An open flannel hung loose, far too large on her, the sleeves rolled and pushed up above her elbows.

It had to be a man's. Was it Logan's? Had his instinct been wrong? He'd assumed Logan had something for Jade, something complicated. But he'd been here, and what other reason would there be for a man to be leaving a woman's apartment this late?

Any sliver of warmth that had slipped through the mortar securing the bricks around his insides evaporated. And it pissed him off that he missed it.

"Well, I guess this means you're staying after all." His insides groaned at the sound of that smoky voice. It was hypnotic.

"Guess so." It was curt, and only a step from being a grunt.

She tilted her head and gave him a slow once-over before moving to his stuff on the ground. He wanted to step in front of the guitar, not because he was self-conscious, just private, he told himself.

Her eyebrow ticked in curiosity, the light tilt in her lips spreading into a knowing close-lipped smile. But she didn't push. "That all you got with you?"

"I've got a few things coming, but yeah, this is mostly it." At least until he made the time to borrow Grady's truck to pick up the few other necessities he'd had to go outside town to order.

"I hope a mattress is one of those things. We need our sheriff well rested."

"I'm sure I've slept in worse conditions." He ran a hand up the side of his jaw, finding comfort in the abrasive burn of his beard chafing against his palm.

Her smile faded slightly. I can relate to that. Truth. So much truth all over her. He hated lies, but it had become comfortable. People lie all the time, even in casual conversation. He should hate that more, but it meant that they remained strangers. No matter how much time he spent with them.

"So," he cleared his throat, "you have a lot of late-night visitors?"

"Are you jealous, Sheriff?"

"Declan," he corrected her. "And that's not an answer."

"Neither is that." She lifted a shoulder and the flannel slipped down, revealing more ink there. He fisted his hand at his side, against the instant desire to reach out and pull it back into place.

"Just wondering how frequently I'll be responding to my own noise complaints."

Quinn nodded slowly. "You know, for someone who has such an extraordinary gift for perceiving lies, you're pretty bad at telling them. I have an idea."

Four words never sounded so dangerous, and he was very familiar with danger.

"How about a truth for a truth?" she offered.

Their gazes met and held. Alarm bells sounded in his mind. But the reckless passenger within won out. He lifted his chin, asking for her truth.

"Yes, I do tend to have late-night visitors. We'll try not to disturb you. But I can't make any promises." She grinned.

Visitors. With an 'S' and a little sparkle in her eyes...that he hadn't put there.

And it was the truth. But there was something more there. She wore her emotions so clearly, but they wove like her tattoos in a way that made her as hard to read as the way she played with the meaning of her words.

He hated this game.

"Your turn. Give me your truth." The words lapped at his skin, making sand of the mortar between those well-earned bricks. Was that what had just landed in the pit of his stomach?

He stood silently in front of her. Debating what harmless fact he could give her.

"I can't tell if I relish or dread the prospect of sleeping this close to you every night." He hadn't meant to say it. Hadn't even known it was his truth until the words were hanging between them.

Her eyes flared, her throat worked, and then that bravado slammed back down over her face. He held in the groan that wanted to join the words hanging between them. He loved the way it'd felt the few times he'd been able to momentarily see beneath that cool confidence.

That feline grin returned, and she unfurled from her perch against the doorway, slipping halfway behind the blue door. Putting a very smart, and miserable, barrier between them.

"Well then, Sheriff. Sweet dreams." The feather-light breeze of the blue door closing felt like a gale-force wind.

He waited, then stepped close to her door. "Declan. And lock your damn door." The soft snick of the lock catching and a retreating, velvet-smooth laugh was her only response.

And a little more light broke through in the depths of his darkness. He tapped his forehead against her door. "Goodnight, *Twila*," he whispered, the name pulled from the depths of his memory. *Light in dark places.*

FOR READERS

Dear reader, thank you for taking a chance on a baby author, I hope you enjoyed this story and that you'll come back to Havenwood soon, Declan and Quinn can't wait to share their story with you in 2025! Well, Quinn can't wait, Declan's not a big fan of public speaking-can't imagine why.

If you did enjoy An Inevitable Magick and your visit to Havenwood, please consider leaving a review on Amazon, Goodreads, or social media. Reviews mean the world to all authors but are especially helpful and all-around encouraging to us baby authors.

ACKNOWLEDGMENTS

This is my debut novel. the actualization of this life-long dream. While I wrote the words, they may never have amounted to a book without the contributions of so many others. It truly took a village to raise this book-baby.

My husband and best friend, it's because of you I can write romance, that I understand second chances and happily ever afters. Thank you for celebrating every little win, bragging about me, for drawing me baths, buying me snacks, and sneaking me love letters, those little acts were the biggest gifts of support through this process. Thank you for being a true partner, for coming home after exhausting workdays and making dinner, coaching the kid's teams, doing bedtimes, and so much more, so I could work. Thank you for believing in me so vehemently, it was impossible for me not to, even on the hardest days. I'll never take for granted how lucky I am that you're mine and I'm yours. *Always*.

My beautiful babies, thank you for all your supportive notes, drawings, "visits" to my office, and most of all for aways being so proud of me. My deep desire for you to pursue your dreams, unencumbered by what's realistic, was a huge motivating factor in why I finally decided to do it myself and write this book. That being said, I hope you never read it—or at least wait until my ashes are in the lake.

Cassie, my sister-soul mate, thank you for the unconditional support you've given me through this process, it's been more than I could have ever hoped for from a friend. From the moment I shared the first ideas of this book, (can you even remember what they were because I can't lol), and every step it took to get here, you have been there with and for me.

Kearstie, my editor, my friend. I had an idea of what I hoped to find when I set out looking for an editor and I knew you were the one for me from the first meeting. But the word "editor" will never be able to encompass all I found in you. This book would simply not exist without you and the way you went above and beyond for me. Thank you for keeping me in your pocket, for loving my book-baby so much, and thank you for loving me as I am, your squirken.

To my friends and fellow authors, Halle Jane, and Rachel, thank you for being in the weeds with me. Thank you for giving me the staying power it took to finish this book. You're all stuck with me for life now, so buckle up.

Marie Maravilla, our rambling voice notes and all your advice and patience is how I know you love me—that and that one time you said it— it's also how I was able to stay sane and something resembling confident through this whole process.

Rikki, I never have to explain, hide, or filter myself with you, I'd say you don't know what that means to me, but you know exactly how rare and special that is to find in another person. Thank you for always being mine.

Reegis, thank you for loving my son like your own encouraging me toward my goals. You alleviated from me what could have been crushing mom guilt.

Morgan, our walks and talks kept me sane. Thank you for getting me out of the house and out of my head.

Krystal, look at us, all these years later—thank you for always cheering me on and for being my first trusted beta reader.

Babs, we make the rules. Love, Tootsie.

Mom and dad, thank you for always believing in me no matter what crazy idea I'm pursing on any given day. Writing this book took two things I know I got directly from watching you both as I grew up, hard work and creativity.

To the best little brother in the world, you're the most special person I know. I love you.

To the rest of my family, so many authors in this genre understandably have to hide what they write from their families. I don't. Thank you for your support and your acceptance. (Grandma Sandi, for the record, I warned you.)

A few other creatives—who are each masters of their crafts— thank you for contributing to the overall experience of this book, and bringing it to life for me and the readers. Viki (@forensicsandflowers), for designing such a beautiful cover and turning my book into shelf candy. Taylor (@full_mooncreations) for perfectly encapsulating the scent of Havenhouse in a beautiful candle. Mario, (@tiredbeartea) for your generosity, and expertly crafting Liv's magickal blend of tea. Jax can swear it's not a love potion all he wants but we know the truth.

To my bookstagram family- thank you for cheering me on and journeying with me through every step of this process. Your excitement kept me going.

AUTHOR'S NOTE

When my husband and I would talk about dreams I would say, "I don't really have a dream. I'm a dream enabler." Meaning I'm just here to support him and the kids in chasing their dreams. Which is both true and a lie, and we both knew it.

"But you said being an author was a life-long dream!" I hear you all yelling at me, and you're right. It was a life-long dream. One I never expected to achieve, or even bothered to pursue because I "knew" becoming an author was out of my league. I "knew" I wasn't smart enough, creative enough, or educated enough. I simply was not *enough* for my own dream. I would watch people achieve their dreams, listen to them, encourage others toward their dreams, and agree that yes, anyone can achieve their dreams. All the while, that inner critic whispered, "Just not me."

If you have one of these dreams, and you're thinking, "Just not me," let me tell you something: I am pushing forty, I have sometimes crippling ADHD, I didn't graduate college, I never got an easy A in English, and was constantly told, "You write like you talk," whatever that means—it was intended as a criticism (hopefully you enjoyed the dialogue/banter in this book, giving me the ultimate vindication).

I have kids who participate in what feels like every activity on earth, a very hot and incredibly distracting husband with a demanding and important job, as well as countless other responsibilities.

All excuses I used for years.

Luckily for me, dreams don't really care if you find them realistic. When they're imprinted in your heart, it becomes painful on a soul-level after you ignore them long enough.

So, I stopped making excuses, and started believing maybe it IS me.

The publication of this book means I am now a recovering, "Just not me," girl (though it's an ongoing mental battle). And the only thing I had to do was start...and then I kept going.

So many people passed me by on this journey. Some published multiple times while I worked on this one book.

People have, and will, write better books than this. Some people won't like what I created, and that will suck, I'm sure.

But I still did it.

While the fears you and I have are valid, they're not more painful than stifling that dream written on your heart. Whatever those doubts are...if you can feel them, and do the work anyway, you won't regret it.

I'll leave you with my best advice, comprised of four profound words that helped me while I fought to overcome everything I listed above: Who gives a shit?

Any time that inner critic pops up whispering about how ill equipped you are, it takes longer than you expected, others pass you by, someone doesn't understand your art or your dreams, remember—Who. Gives. A. Shit? Because you shouldn't. Not about that stuff. So start.

And then keep going. No matter how long it takes.

P.S. I showed this letter to my editor, and she pointed out something...they say your characters carry different parts of you in them. Well, I gave that doubt, that, "Just not me," to Liv, without even realizing it. I wrote my own doubts, my own tendency to put the dreams and lives of others before my own, into my main character. And then we conquered it together. Pretty cool, past me!

ABOUT THE AUTHOR

Lex Kelly's love for writing started shortly after receiving her first Lisa Frank diary when she was a little girl. She filled hundreds of those glittery pink and blue pages with poetry, stories and secrets, before graduating to her parent's giant word processor. (Those two sentences alone should give you a solid indicator of how old she is.)

Lex's stories reflect her love for relatable characters, banter and a well-placed f-bomb. Her childhood fantasies of being able to speak to her pets and control the weather are brought to life through the whimsical use of magick woven throughout her books.

She lives in southern California with her husband, two kids, two dogs, and one black cat. When not writing she enjoys spending time in nature, spontaneous adventures with her family and of course, reading.

Email: Lex@authorLexKelly
Socials: AuthorLexKelly
Website: AuthorLexKelly.com